ALSO BY DARCY COATES

WHERE HE CAN'T FIND YOU

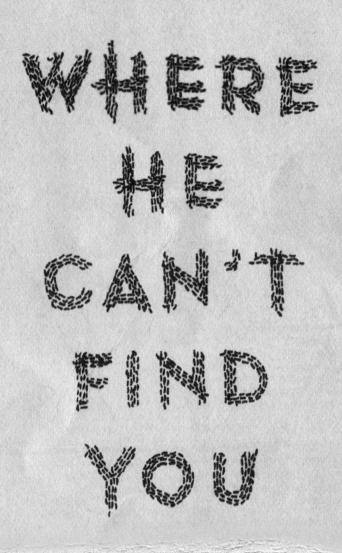

WHERE HE CAN'T FIND YOU

DARCY COATES

sourcebooks
fire

Copyright © 2023 by Darcy Coates
Cover and internal design © 2023 by Sourcebooks
Cover lettering by Katie Klimowicz
Cover images © Andriy Bezuglov/Stocksy
Internal design by Brittany Vibbert and Tara Jaggers/Sourcebooks
Internal art © Skylar Patridge
Internal images © tomograf/GettyImages

Published by Sourceooks Fire, an imprint of Sourcebooks
P.O. Box 4410, Naperville, Illinois 60567–4410
(630) 961-3900
sourcebooks.com

Cataloging-in-Publication Data is on file with the Library of Congress.

Printed and bound in the United States of America.
VP 10 9 8 7 6 5 4 3 2 1

PART ONE

OMENS

BEFORE

THE AIR WAS ROTTING. BITING COLD AND HEAVY WITH MOISTURE, it filled January's throat with every inhale, so dense that it felt as though it was suffocating her.

She crawled through the dark. Sharp rocks scraped her palms, her knees, her shoulder blades. She flinched and dropped lower, hunching to fit through the narrow tunnel, her hands feeling to find a path forward.

How long had she been down here, in the dark and the cold and the damp?

Days?

Weeks?

She couldn't stop moving. The thing in the dark would come back for her soon. And she didn't think she could survive the next time.

Her fingers touched something delicate and disgusting. Threads, criss-crossing the darkness ahead of her. They were as fine as spiderweb and slimy from the damp. When she tried to swipe them away, they refused to break.

She couldn't see them, but she knew what color they were. Red. It was always red threads. They trailed through the maze, gathering drops of moisture from the air, tangling over the rocks and one another. They bit into January's flesh when she tried to force her way past them. Cutting into her throat, into her face, into her numb fingers.

A distant sound broke through the background noise of dripping water and her own uneven, echoing breaths. January's heart pitched, jittering in her chest. She clamped a hand over her mouth, fighting to muffle her breathing.

It couldn't see well in the dark. The maze held no light; January had been staring into the nothingness for so long that she'd started to hallucinate things moving around her. Unnatural shapes danced, taunting her, only to vanish when she looked at them directly.

The sound repeated: hands grasping at rocks as it pulled itself closer. The shift of flesh against flesh. A dry, hollow exhale.

It couldn't see well, but it could hear and smell.

It knew where she was.

Terror overwhelmed common sense. January threw herself forward. She didn't feel the rocks cutting into her palms or the drop of blood trailing down her cheek. But she felt the threads as they snagged around her, tightening.

She'd rushed right into them. January fought, thrashing like an insect in a spiderweb as she tried to break free. Some of the threads snapped. They gave her just enough room to drag herself forward another inch, then another foot, until she was nearly on the other side of the web of red threads—

A cold hand fastened around her leg. January had just enough breath left to scream. Then the thing in the dark dragged her back to join it, and her voice cut out into nothing.

ONE

$\bigwedge\!\bigwedge\!\bigwedge$

"DO YOU WANT TO SEE SOMETHING BAD?"

Abby woke with icy sweat plastering her clothes to her skin. Her breathing came in rough gasps as she stared into the darkness flooding her room.

The nightmares were always the first warning. They came before any of the other signs—before the birds that plunged out of the sky, before the streetlights all died, before the sickness.

Before the disappearances.

She reached for her nightstand and turned the clock to face her. Four-fifteen. She watched the second hand tick forward, making sure it was still keeping time. Technology always broke when things were getting bad.

She'd been having nightmares for nearly two weeks. This one was the worst, though—a memory from that night at Jessica's house. It was supposed to be a girls' sleepover, but Abby had been the only one who arrived. She and Jessica had sat at an empty dinner table for half an hour, no parents in sight, before Jessica had asked the damning question.

"Do you want to see something bad?"

It was Abby's first time facing a dead body.

Not her last, though.

Now, her mouth was parchment dry. Sweat stuck her hair to the back of her neck as she slid out of bed. The wooden floorboards creaked as she left her room and crossed the hall to reach her sister's.

Hope lay on her stomach, one arm thrown above her head, her blankets tangled.

The window over her bed was open an inch. Hope liked to feel the cold air at night, but they weren't supposed to keep any part of the house—doors, windows, anything—unlocked after dark. Moving silently so she didn't disturb her, Abby slid the pane closed and fastened the latch.

At the opposite wall, near the door, was Hope's desk. It was covered with equipment including a webcam, a ring light, and a computer that could handle the editing software she needed to piece together her videos. Even with technology becoming so unreliable, Hope was serious about making this a career. And Abby thought she might just have a chance.

When Hope first started posting videos, it had felt like she was yelling into the void. She'd get a handful of views but no likes. No comments. She later admitted that she was on the edge of giving up when her first fans found her. Just five accounts to begin with—but those five accounts watched every video and always commented, asking for more. So she kept filming. Kept posting.

Now, she had nearly two thousand subscribers. She'd started to get small sponsorship deals. But those five original followers were still there, still cheering her on with each new video, and she always replied to thank them.

Abby hadn't told Hope that the accounts were hers. She probably never would.

She left on silent feet. At the end of the hallway was their mother's room, its door opened a crack. Abby wrapped her arms around herself as she approached and leaned forward.

Moonlight came through the thin, torn curtains. It trailed over the edge of their mother's silhouette. She sat on the end of her bed, staring at the wall.

There was just enough light to make out her long, unwashed hair. The sharp angles of her thin lips. Her long, delicate nose.

Abby hadn't made a sound. Hadn't even so much as breathed. But her mother seemed to sense her presence. She turned, suddenly, her eye flashing in the cold light. Abby backed away, her tongue pressed between her teeth.

She didn't let herself breathe again until she was back in her own room. Then she curled up on her bed, her knees drawn to her chest.

There wouldn't be any more sleep that night. She reached for her phone and was grateful when the display came up after only a brief flicker.

She opened the group chat titled *Jackrabbits* and typed: Anyone awake?

A reply came from Rhys. I'm here. And then, almost immediately after, u ok?

He always asked. Every single time. Abby could imagine his shoulders hunching and his eyes darkening, the way they did when he sensed the chance of danger. He was more attuned to threats than any of their group, and *no one* in their group took threats lightly. It left him always on guard, always cautious.

Abby couldn't blame him.

Not after what the Stitcher did to his parents.

All good, she texted, and she knew him well enough to visualize the tightness draining out of him again. She hesitated, then added, I had a nightmare.

Me too, he replied. Bad night.

Yeah. Abby rolled over, bunching the blankets over herself. She might be physically alone in her room, but the group chat stopped her from feeling completely untethered. She needed them, just as much as they needed her.

A new text appeared, this time from Riya. Hey guys. Followed by, Rhys?

He responded with a single question mark.

There was a long pause. Riya had to be taking care with what she wrote next. Abby felt a sense of unease creep into her stomach as she waited. A flicker of static cut over the lower half of her phone's screen, then vanished again.

Then, Riya posted: Can you handle bad news right now?

His response was fast, decisive. Yes. What happened?

Abby's unease redoubled.

I think they found a body. She could picture Riya's face, pinched and tight and frightened. Police just went by my house. Headed toward Breaker Street.

There was a pause as they absorbed the news.

Rhys was the first to reply.

Ok. Let's meet.

TWO

ABBY STAYED ONLY LONG ENOUGH TO SLIDE A NOTE UNDER Hope's door, saying where she was going.

That was one of their rules: don't leave without telling someone.

Her silver bike waited for her against the house's side. She jogged with it to the street, then climbed on and turned toward the main road.

When people wanted to say something nice about Doubtful, Illinois, they called it a bike-friendly town. What that really meant was that cars were too unreliable. Most of the time they'd work as intended. But sometimes, with no warning, they would stall. Or grind to a halt. Or simply refuse to start.

The town's mechanics would look at a car and say, *It's got the jitters*. That was slang for when they couldn't find anything technically wrong, but it simply refused to work.

And it wasn't just cars. Phones were unreliable. Streetlights went out. Televisions would play static or display a mangled version of two channels spliced together, audio and graphics merging into one.

Things in Doubtful just broke easily.

Not bikes, though. The rubber and spokes and brakes didn't rely on electricity, and so the town's decaying effects left them alone. If you wanted to be certain of getting somewhere in Doubtful, you rode a bike.

Abby's breath came hot and fast, spiraling out behind her like smoke. She moved quickly, air funneling around her body, her legs heating from the exertion, and at that moment she felt as though she could outrun the darkness itself. A streetlight behind her blinked and then vanished, extinguished like a candle being snuffed out. She rode faster.

It was still well before dawn. The houses around her were dark. With the lights out, it was sometimes hard to tell which houses held sleeping forms, and which had been abandoned for years.

A shadow raced toward her, emerging from one of the side streets like a phantom. It skimmed closer until it ran alongside her, matching her pace. In the intermittent streetlight, she could make out dark hair and wild, intent eyes. Rhys.

They shared a look, then turned back to the road ahead.

Don't travel alone. That was another Jackrabbit rule. Rhys could have taken a more direct route to Breaker Street, but he'd taken the longer path to join up with Abby instead.

The road vanished under them. Rhys matched her furious pace perfectly, and they stayed abreast, each turn anticipated, until the rusted sign for Breaker Street rose out of the gloom.

Abby's lungs burned from the exertion, but it was a good kind of ache. The kind that told her she was alive and moving. That her body was strong. She let her bike roll to a halt and put one foot down as she stared along the road.

Red and blue lights flashed, lighting up the asphalt and the washed-out houses. She counted three police cars and an ambulance, all parked askew on a lawn that was long dead and choked with dry, rattling weeds.

Breaker Street was residential but right next to a strip of industrial stores: cube-like buildings with bars over their windows and flat roofs. The area had all been built around the same time—decades before Abby had even been born—and then left to slowly be consumed by neglect.

Rhys gently tapped her arm to draw her notice, then nodded toward the shops across the road. Two figures stood in their shadows. Riya, small and tense and with her dark hair tightly braided, had one arm raised to hail them. Just behind her was Connor, his curly flaxen hair mussed from sleep, his large teeth working at his lower lip as he tried to control his nerves. Abby and Rhys silently crossed the road to meet up with them.

"There's a ladder," Riya whispered as they drew near. Even her warm complexion looked washed out and strange in the frantic, undulating red and blue lights. She nodded to the store behind them, which had once printed commercial signs but had been out of business for more than a decade. It still held advertisements in its fogged windows, promising forty percent off everything. "We might be able to see better up high."

Rhys gazed up the metal ladder bolted to the building's back wall. "Good find," he said.

They left their bikes at the store's back, where they were less likely to be seen. The shops along that stretch of road, right on the outskirts of town, had been left to neglect. Rust flaked off the ladder as Abby climbed, and the wall was full of cracks, zigzagging along the lines of the bricks hidden beneath the concrete, like a map of a hidden city. She reached the ladder's top and swung her legs over the half wall.

The flat concrete roof was barren except for piles of rotting leaf litter gathered in the corners and a stack of old boxes and abandoned furniture clearly intended to be thrown out but then forgotten. The half wall ran around the roof's edges, like a battlement, and Abby held her breath as she crossed the space to get a better view of the streets.

On the other side of the main road, Breaker Street was alive with activity. Abby lowered herself, her arms braced on the half wall, as her three friends took up their places next to her.

Every house along the street looked like it was built from the same mold. They were all Midwesterns with sagging porches and shutters over their windows, and picket fences that sliced the lawns into portions.

They could have looked beautiful once, but Breaker Street had succumbed to time and apathy. The fences leaned and the lawns had lost their color. Children's toys had been abandoned in a nearby yard: tricycles and a small plastic slide now overgrown with weeds.

The police cars had all parked outside one of the worst houses. Pots were spaced about its porch, but none of them held any plants. The shutters were cracked, boards coming loose, and the painted siding was peeled and discolored.

Riya leaned close to the wall, her small hands gripping the cracked concrete, her expression tight. "I pass that house every day," she said. "I've never seen anyone in it."

Abandoned houses weren't uncommon in Doubtful. Properties were cheap, but there were few jobs to attract new residents. Forgotten *For Sale* signs dotted the town, weathered or tipping over like loose teeth, abandoned where they stood.

Abby remembered how, when she was young and eager to have adventures, she'd wanted to explore some of those empty buildings. She'd quickly learned why that was a bad idea. It wasn't unheard of to *find* things in them.

Figures moved in and out of the house, flashlights in hand. The ambulance's back doors were open, but Abby couldn't tell if anyone was inside. Most of the activity seemed to come from the police. Their uniforms and badges caught the red and blue lights, but their caps were pulled too far down for her to recognize any of their faces.

Rhys had one forearm resting on the wall as his dark eyes took in the scene. "Do you think the new transfer's there?"

One of the deputies had left town nearly six weeks before, bundling his family into his car and tearing out without even putting in his resignation. The town had been forced to hire an outsider. The new transfer and his daughter had apparently moved in just days before, but Abby had yet to see either of them.

"I can't imagine what sort of *welcome to town* this would be." Connor poked around the pile of abandoned items before pulling something free. He'd found a folded metal chair, red with rust. He shook it out to open it.

"You'll get tetanus," Riya said at the sound of whining metal, without even taking her eyes off the road.

Connor made a faint noise in agreement, but still positioned the chair near the half wall and sat. His pale, densely curly hair absorbed the undulating lights, turning a different shade with each flash.

"There," Riya hissed, rising up another inch. "Look!"

The activity inside the house seemed to have condensed into one room. Flashlight beams cut over one another, bursting out of gaps in the tattered curtains and broken shutters.

Abby craned forward, breath held. She knew what was coming. A part of her didn't want to see it, but a larger, stronger part of her *had to*.

This was how you survived in Doubtful.

You watched. You learned.

And you figured out the rules that would keep you safe.

Figures appeared in the doorway, carrying something on a stretcher. They wore thick gloves. Large masks covered the lower half of their faces. Their heads were tilted to one side, watching first the lopsided porch, and then the steps, and then the desiccated grass as they traced their path to the ambulance. Abby was struck by the impression that they weren't just watching where they walked, but that they were desperately trying to avoid looking at their burden.

The shape on the stretcher was covered by a white sheet. It wasn't large enough to be a whole human.

But it was undeniably part of one.

The first stretcher was closely followed by a second. Just like the first, its contents were covered. It was a larger burden this time. But still not the size of a full body.

Abby couldn't read the officer's faces except for a glimpse of their eyes: narrowed in revulsion.

"Who do you think it was?" Connor asked.

Abby couldn't bring herself to answer. It felt too grim, too sour, to be betting on whose family would be receiving a call later that morning. Whose lives would be irrevocably changed.

A third stretcher came through the door, and the sheet covered something smaller than either of the first two.

Riya took a quick breath. "There's more than one."

Abby sent her a look. Riya's eyes were almost fever bright.

"I counted three feet. They found more than one body this time."

Abby leaned forward, her heart running fast. Chips of broken concrete shifted under her hands. The first stretcher had already been moved into the ambulance, but she thought Riya was right. Each bundle alone was less than a full body. But, together, they amounted to something more.

The officer on the final stretcher slipped as he stepped off the porch. Even with the distance between them, Abby heard him yelp in shock. The stretcher tilted. The sheet slid down. Another officer moved forward, grabbing the cloth and dragging it back over, but not quickly enough.

She saw a glimpse of the burden underneath.

Flesh. Red thread woven through it, stitching it back together.

"Was that..." Connor's voice lost its joviality. His words were hushed, uncomfortable. "A hand?"

Yes and no. Part of a hand. And other things.

She watched, sickened and transfixed, as the final stretcher was lifted into the ambulance.

Then Rhys's hand shot out, grasping her upper arm. "Vickers," he whispered. The four of them reacted in unison, dropping down below the half wall.

Rhys didn't need to explain what he'd meant.

Charles Vickers was here.

Of course he was.

He was at every crime scene, every discovery. Often before the police themselves arrived.

The store's roof was dark. It would make them hard to see. Slowly, breath held, Abby raised herself in increments until she could see over the wall.

Charles Vickers sat on the porch across from the crime scene. He was in a rocking chair, his hands folded in his lap. His pale hair, balding on top, was neatly combed, and he wore one of his navy sweaters, an intricate knit pattern running across his torso. He gave the impression of just having stepped outside to relax.

Only, it wasn't his house. Charles Vickers lived across town, on Stokes Lane.

He didn't seem uneasy that he was sitting in someone else's chair, on a porch that didn't belong to him, watching a crime scene be established across the street.

"How long has he been there?" Abby asked, knowing none of them had an answer.

The porch was shadowed and his clothing was dark. He was barely visible, except for the small, rhythmic motion: the chair rocking back and then forward again in lazy arcs.

For all she knew, he'd been there when she and Rhys biked past. Sitting in the dark, watching them.

"They've seen him," Riya whispered.

Two police officers crossed the street in slow, measured strides, backlit by the flashing lights. One officer stopped in the middle of the road, hands on his hips, legs planted. The other continued on for another few paces before also halting. She was speaking to Vickers.

"I bet he called it in," Riya murmured.

"Huh?" Connor asked.

Riya's voice was wound tight. "How else would they know the bodies were there? Who's exploring abandoned houses at four in the morning? Vickers set it up and then called it in and sat down to watch them process his crime scene."

It made too much sense. *He's growing bolder.*

The conversation was inaudible, but it seemed to stretch out. Vickers, calm as always, rocked the chair as he spoke. Then, at last, he stood.

Charles Vickers wasn't an intimidating figure. He wasn't tall, and he didn't try to seem threatening. Most of his clothing—even in summer—were knit sweaters or windbreakers. His shoulders were curved. His demeanor, unassuming and calm. He looked like he could be a high school teacher, or a counselor, or a coach.

Until you saw his smile. It was small, chilling, and full of quiet knowledge. As though he was a part of a joke you didn't understand. As though he was laughing at you behind his teeth.

He wore that smile as he climbed down from the porch. Both police officers took a step back. He said something, raised a hand in farewell, then turned away.

"They must have told him to move on," Connor said, his voice raspy. "Look, he's going."

Charles walked to the end of Breaker Street, following the cracked sidewalk, then turned down the main road. He was almost past the store when he paused.

Abby's heart squeezed painfully. Charles Vickers stood almost directly below their hiding place. He tilted his head, angling his gaze up toward them. And sent them one of those small, knowing smirks.

They all drew back. Abby's shoulder pressed against the concrete half wall. Riya's breath was hot and shallow on the back of her neck.

Charles Vickers's smile widened a fraction, showing just a sliver of small, immaculate teeth. Then he turned and continued walking along the sidewalk, disappearing deeper into the town.

Abby's blood pumped too fast. Her throat ached. Even with Vickers gone, she couldn't relax.

Riya groaned as she leaned back against the wall. She didn't seem to care that she was sitting in decaying leaves and forgotten trash. Connor gingerly raised himself back into the rusty chair and spread out there, legs askew, one hand pressed to his chest to signal his own racing heart.

"Stitcher." Riya spat the word like it was a curse. "More bodies, and the police just let him go. Again."

Abby looked back toward the house where the remains had been found. The two officers who had spoken to Charles Vickers had returned to their companions. A different officer was unrolling police tape around the building. It would probably stay there, knots coming loose and plastic decaying, until strands broke free and were lost in the mud and bushes. Just like all the others.

A broken spiderweb of forgotten police tape across the town.

The ambulance started up, its engine a deep growl, as it prepared to take the bodies away.

"At least we were here for this one," Connor said. He hesitated, his eyebrows pulling together incredulously. "That was the plan, right? Remind me again why this was something we *wanted* to see?"

"Knowledge will keep you safe," Riya said, reciting from their rules. She closed her eyes, grimacing. She'd been watching the scene intently, and Abby knew she was reliving the images of red-threaded flesh underneath the sheet.

"Yeah, I get that." Connor leaned back and his chair groaned. An apologetic smile twisted his broad lips. "But also there was that whole thing about *don't go out after dark*. And look where we are now."

Riya flicked a hand, her grimace deepening. "You're right, but this is *morning* night."

"It's…what?"

"Haven't you noticed how they're different?" She squinted one eye open to see him. "Late night, and early morning? You can go jogging at four a.m. and people will think you're just a little too healthy for your own good. But go jogging at midnight and…well. It's *weird*, right? It's just not normal."

They sat for a moment, letting the silence flow around them.

Then Connor said, "I've gotta be honest. I don't think this town is built for *normal.*"

The tension from the previous hour broke, like a snapping rubber band. Abby keeled forward and chuckled, even as her chest continued to ache.

Even Rhys, at her side, let a ghost of a smile tease the edges of his lips before it vanished again.

She didn't get to see that often, but she treasured it when she did. Rhys almost never smiled anymore.

"You know what I'm saying," Riya said, eyebrows lifted pointedly. "No one should be out after dark. But there's a difference between dusk and dawn. And, if we have to leave our homes, I'd rather it be on this side."

Abby knew what Riya meant. On the distant horizon, morning was gasping its first breaths. There was safety in light. As much safety as you could hope for in Doubtful, anyway.

And it was always better to be on the *approaching* side of daylight, not the receding.

Their levity had been brief and almost desperate. Then Abby asked, almost against her better judgment: "Is anyone else having nightmares?"

"Oh, yeah," Connor said. "Three in the last week."

"My TV won't turn on," Riya said. "And my radio sounds strange. Things are getting bad again."

There was a second-long whoop of a police siren before the driver turned it off. One of the patrol cars was leaving, following the ambulance.

Things are getting bad again. If Doubtful's cycle had followed any kind of logical pattern, the discovery of a body should be a culmination, a final blow. It never was. *Things getting bad* meant more disappearances. And soon.

"Remember the rules," Rhys said. His voice was soft, but they all turned toward him. "And keep your distance from Vickers."

Abby remembered the way Vickers had gazed up at them, his secretive little smile lit up in the red and blue lights. He'd seemed… *delighted.* Chills moved through Abby, and she pulled her jacket tighter around her chest.

Rhys continued. "If you find yourself somewhere alone with Vickers, call me. If you feel unsafe, call me. No matter where, no matter when, I'll come."

It was a promise he'd made before, and Abby knew it was meant for all of them. But Rhys looked directly at her when he said it.

Her heart gave the strange, uncomfortable shift it sometimes did around him. Like misjudging how many stairs were ahead and having your foot land in thin air. A drop of the stomach, a catch of breath. The slightly giddy, slightly shocked sensations as your body regained its balance.

She looked away, focusing her eyes on the rapidly fading stars above. She didn't like to think about those sensations, or what they might mean, or where they might lead her if she listened to them.

There was no point thinking about normal things like that anyway: there were no happy endings to be found in Doubtful.

THREE

MISSING

The word was huge, all caps, bold and black. It was positioned beneath the photo of a woman, her blond hair pulled into a high ponytail. She looked young, only nineteen or twenty, with a huge smile that seemed too white in the black-and-white print's high contrast.

Jen stared at the flier, her hands gripping the straps of her backpack too tightly.

It was surreal to see that image on her locker. Even more surreal following the updates she'd caught on the radio on the way to school.

This is the dead girl they found last night.

Isn't it?

Jen turned. This was supposed to be her first day at Doubtful High. The name alone didn't do much to inspire confidence. She'd arrived early so that she could figure out her classes, but the hallways were already busy, full of shuffling footsteps and tired, brief conversations.

No one seemed to pay any attention to the poster.

Hadn't they heard yet? Didn't they know about the crime scene just fifteen minutes from the school? Jen's father hadn't said much, but she'd been able to tell from the set of his jaw during that morning's drive that it was a bad one. His third day on the job and he'd been summoned to attend the scene.

The dead girl's photo smiled at Jen from a half dozen surfaces. She'd probably graduated from the school not long before, and now the fliers were stuck to lockers, notice boards, and bare patches of walls.

MISSING
JANUARY SPALLING
ANYONE WITH INFORMATION IS
ENCOURAGED TO CONTACT DOUBTFUL PD

Hers wasn't the only missing person poster. Jen had seen two others while walking into the school, and a third further down the hallway. They all had different photos, different blocky font choices, different names, but otherwise followed the same format.

And no one seemed to care.

Bodies jostled past her. Students opened their lockers without even glancing at the posters taped to their fronts.

As though this was *fine*.

As though this was *normal*.

Jen's blood crawled through her veins. On the surface, the high school didn't seem much different from the one she'd left behind in New York. A little older. A little drabber. Two of the hallway's lights were out. None of that should have been enough to make her uneasy, but something about the town just felt deeply, thoroughly *wrong*.

She tore the paper off her locker's face and folded it before shoving it into her backpack.

"You can use the one-dollar budget white bread loaf, if you insist, but I find superior results are achieved with the more upmarket one-dollar-fifty variety instead," Connor said.

They sat under the spreading oak near the chain-link fence. The grim school building still dominated their view, but they were as far from it as they could get without leaving the grounds.

Abby loved the tree. It had been their lunchtime meeting place for years. Even during biting winter, she preferred it over the dingy, flickering lights and stale smells of the cafeteria, or the cold concrete of the stairwells where some of the other students ate.

She sat with her back to the trunk, Rhys at her side, and Riya and Connor beside him. Riya's carefully plaited black hair draped across her lacrosse uniform. Abby knew, from experience, that the silky plait would be mussed and sweaty and frazzled by the end of practice. Riya gave the impression of being impeccably contained in most areas of her life, but she threw herself into sports with the kind of vicious intensity few could match.

Connor, his wildly curly hair swaying above his head, had opened what looked like a tradesman's toolbox and was slowly, painstakingly constructing his lunch out of an assortment of ingredients inside. He'd draped a napkin over one forearm like a sommelier as he laid two slices of white bread onto the paper plate sitting precariously on one of the tree's roots.

"Now, the secret to a good ham and cheese sandwich is to locate the finest quality highly processed meat-based product your local budget grocery store supplies." Connor held a finger up pointedly. "I like mine to be at minimum thirty percent real pork."

"Can't you just bring a packed lunch?" Riya asked. She was already eating her lunch, a smear of sauce on the corner of her lips.

Connor's whole face scrunched up in horror. "It would spend hours sweating in my lunch box, and then the mustard would soak into the bread and make it damp."

"Of course." Riya sighed.

Abby's own lunch box sat at her side. It was old and built out of stiff metal. The embossed front held a print of a watercolor forest scene, with small woodland animals peeking out from behind trees. The box was bordering on childish. She'd tried to buy a new one two years before, using part of her precious savings, but when it had come time to pack her food she'd balked at trading out the old tin box.

It was the last present she'd gotten from her father. One of the last nice memories she'd had of him, before he'd tried to challenge Charles Vickers.

Just like too many things in her life, it had become a bittersweet staple. Each day she saw the box, it hurt something inside her. But giving it up would have hurt more.

She let her fingers linger on the faded watercolor print for a second before opening it. Inside were two sandwiches, one stacked on top of the other, and two apples. She took the top sandwich, then glanced toward Rhys.

He hadn't brought any lunch. Mornings were difficult for him. Sometimes it was all he could do to just step out of the house. Very often he neglected everything else. Including food.

She slid the box toward him. "I accidentally made too much. Help me out."

He glanced at the sandwich, then at her. "We both know you didn't."

She leaned toward him, her shoulder bumping his, and for a second she was transported back to the first time they'd sat like that. During first-grade recess, back when they were both five and had been exhausted and giddy from racing back and forward across the jungle gym together. Back when Rhys still remembered how to laugh.

"Eat the sandwich. Things are going to get ugly if you refuse."

"Oh?" One of his eyebrows twitched up a fraction, intrigued. "Are you threatening me?"

She couldn't stop herself from smiling. "This is a reverse bully situation. You have to take my lunch or else I'll beat you up."

"So violent," he said, but there was a hint of warmth in his voice.

She gave the box two insistent nudges toward him—tap, tap—and he finally picked up the sandwich.

"And the apple," she said, and refused to relax the intensity of her stare until he took that, as well.

"Thank you," he murmured, and those two simple words felt like hot coals in her chest.

Connor ignored them as he continued his plating ritual. He laid slices of cheese over his ham, carefully adjusting them to get maximum coverage. "The goal is to arrive at a balanced palate. Today, I will be pairing my meal with an exquisite bottle of reconstituted orange juice, which you might notice is quite a bold flavor pairing—"

"You're not going to have time to eat if you don't hurry," Riya said. She'd already finished her food and used a paper napkin to clean her fingers.

"Please." He held one hand up for silence. "The artist is at work."

His fingers curved too far back as he held them up, each joint bending beyond what Abby's could handle.

He'd been diagnosed with EDS when he was twelve. That meant his tendons didn't hold his bones together the way they should. It left him hyperflexible, but also extra vulnerable to injuries. His PE coach had been the first to suggest his parents see a specialist after Connor's list of sprained ankles and dislocated joints and inexplicable bruises grew too long to ignore.

Connor could stretch his arms out straight, and then keep stretching them, until his elbow bent backward twenty degrees past anyone else's. It was his favorite party trick to deploy when he wanted to make someone squirm.

He wasn't supposed to do that. With the tendons failing to hold his joints together, most of the pressure was taken up by his muscles. And they weren't designed to be pulled that far. He'd once admitted to Abby that, after showing off his flexibility, his arm would ache for the rest of the day.

"Hey," Riya said, sitting forward abruptly. "Hey, hey, that's her."

"Hm?" Abby looked up from her partially eaten sandwich.

"The new girl."

"Huh." Connor craned, shielding his squinted eyes. "She looks cool."

Riya's gaze was intent. "She is. She really, really is. I met her briefly," she explained. "Earlier. Well, I saw her. We didn't exactly meet. Or talk. Or…yeah."

It wasn't hard to find her, even with groups of students milling across the grassy field. Her jacket, pants, and boots were all black, but she wore a vivid orange shirt that contrasted against her surroundings strikingly.

Colors didn't seem to endure in Doubtful. The orange top was the brightest thing in any direction. But, if the new girl realized just how much she stood out, it didn't seem to bother her. There was a quiet intensity in the way she carried herself. She stood, one hand in her pocket, scanning the straggling groups spaced around the school's outside. As though hunting for something. And her eyes landed on the Jackrabbits, hidden in the shade cast by the tree.

"She didn't hear me, did she?" Riya dropped her voice to be quieter. "Oh, no, no, no."

She was walking toward them. Her head tilted, her hair bouncing a fraction with each step, she strode with purpose, as though they were exactly what she'd been searching for. She came to a halt with her hands in her pockets, her legs planted, her head tilted slightly to the side. She blinked down at them, then said, "Hey. I'm Jen."

"Abby," Abby said, raising a hand in greeting, then indicated her friends. "Rhys. Connor. And Riya."

"I love your everything," Riya blurted.

There was a second of painful silence. Then Jen said, her eyes narrowed and her tone dubious, "Thanks."

Deeply mortified color spread over Riya's face. She couldn't meet any of their eyes. Abby gave her shoulder a brief, reassuring squeeze before turning back to Jen. "You can eat lunch with us," she offered.

It wasn't one of their official rules, but more of an unspoken agreement. It was dangerous to be isolated in Doubtful. If you saw someone on their own, you were supposed to try to invite them in.

"I can make you a sandwich," Connor added, indicating his own. "It contains succulent alfalfa freshly harvested from the jar on my kitchen counter just this morning."

"Thanks," Jen said, no less dubious. "But I'm only stopping by."

Jen's eyes passed over them. Abby could picture the group from her perspective. Connor, as spindly as an insect, but with a smile so big and loud that it was impossible to feel threatened. Riya, color flooding her face, tiny and wound tight and impeccably put together in her lacrosse outfit. And Abby herself, too pale, too intense, too often told that her gaze was unsettling.

Finally, Jen's gaze lingered on Rhys. Trying to read him.

Not much about Rhys was easy to gather at a glance. Not his mood and not his thoughts. People tended to avoid him. They thought he looked threatening. Which was laughable to anyone who really knew him. Rhys wasn't dangerous.

No—Abby had to correct herself. He was *rarely* dangerous.

He wasn't quick to anger. He'd taken taunts and insults without reaction. The boys in school had tried throwing baseballs at him once, and he'd barely flinched.

She'd only seen him lash out once: when Sam Gunner had hit her across the face with a hockey stick, splitting her lip. There'd been blood. Not just on Abby's mouth, but on Sam's face and Rhys's hands, as well.

No one in school had tried to give the group any trouble since then.

Rhys met Jen's querying gaze. Just like he was being assessed, he was assessing her in return. He rarely spoke in social groups. But he was always on watch. Always on guard.

Always prepared to defend.

Then Jen broke eye contact and drew a deep breath. "Can I ask you all a question? Do you know who January Spalling is?"

"Oh yeah," Connor said, with more relish than Abby would have liked. "Missing girl. Well, dead girl now. She used to work at the post office."

They'd learned her identity from Riya earlier that morning. Riya's mother ran Doubtful's small post office and had received a call saying that her employee would not be returning to work. January Spalling had been missing for nearly three months by that point.

Jen raised her eyebrows. She didn't speak, but her silence was expectant, asking for elaboration.

"They found her body last night." Connor, always happy to talk, laid the final slice of bread onto his sandwich and examined the result with a critical eye. "Her, and part of someone else."

"What?" Jen took half a step forward. She didn't seem eager to actually sit with them, but she lowered herself into a crouch, forearms braced on her black jeans. "There was a second body?"

"Oh, yeah, absolutely. Not an entire body, though. About half of one. They still don't know who it is." Connor delicately rotated the plate to view his lunch from different angles. "The whole thing's kind of messed up."

Jen's eyes were narrowed, uncertain. She worked her jaw.

Abby leaned forward. She tried to keep her voice soft. "Have you heard about the Stitcher yet?"

"No."

"Okay." Abby ran her tongue over her dry lips. "Doubtful isn't a safe place. People…go missing here, sometimes. People…die."

Jen remained on guard. "You don't need to sugarcoat your words."

"Someone's killing people in Doubtful," Abby said. "And he's been doing it for a long time."

Connor nodded. "The Stitcher."

"Your father works with the police, so he'll probably be able to tell you more," Abby said. "But there are things you need to do to keep yourself safe. Lock your doors and windows, and don't go out after dark."

"Try not to travel alone." Riya, still not able to meet any of their eyes, had managed to regain some of her voice. She joined Abby in reciting their rules. "Tell someone before you leave your home."

"Stay in areas with lots of people," Connor continued. "Don't rely on technology. It breaks. And most importantly…"

Rhys finished: "Stay away from Charles Vickers."

Jen seemed frozen. Her eyebrows were low, but her eyes were wide, intent. "Who's Charles Vickers?"

"He's the Stitcher," Connor said. "He's the last thing you'll ever see before you die."

For a second, the school grounds seemed perfectly silent. The leaves above their head rattled, and they sounded like a thousand fingertips tapping at a window, asking to be let in.

Then Jen leaned back, rocking on her heels, her teeth bared in a grim smile. "I get it. This is what you do to the new people, huh?"

Abby shared a glance with Rhys.

"It's some kind of hazing thing, right? Trying to scare me?" Jen stood, her jaw set. "I don't appreciate it."

"We're not trying to scare you," Connor called as Jen turned away. "We're trying to warn you!"

She ignored them as she strode across the sparse grass and toward the school building.

Connor sighed and slumped back. Even his hair seemed fractionally deflated. "We messed that one up, huh?"

Abby watched her go. "Someone else will try to warn her. Someone she'll believe. And in the meantime…let's keep an eye on her. Just in case."

Riya groaned, both hands pressed over her face. "Why did I say that to her? Learning to speak was a mistake."

"Honestly? I'm impressed." Connor finally picked up his sandwich and ate half of it in one massive bite. He spoke around it, cheeks bulging as he chewed. "*I love your everything* might just be the boldest pickup line I've ever heard."

Riya groaned louder and flopped over, burying her face in the fallen leaves.

FOUR

JANUARY SPALLING WAS NINETEEN WHEN SHE DIED. SHE'D HAD respectable grades right through middle and high school, though she'd always shone brightest in classes with a social side and truly excelled at singing.

She'd gotten a job at the post office not long after graduation, restocking shelves and taking payments. She was saving to rent a room in California. She'd wanted to escape her hometown. She thought she might be able to make it as a singer.

Most people in Doubtful had a dream of one day leaving.

Not many ever did.

January Spalling was reported missing when she failed to show up for work one morning. Her mother saw her leave their shared house at eight forty, purse over her shoulder.

Work was a ten-minute walk from her home. A delivery driver saw her at the end of her street. Both her mother and the driver agreed that she seemed to be behaving normally.

That was her last-known sighting.

Five days later, her purse was found near the edge of the forest, a twenty-minute walk from her home, and in the opposite direction of her work. It appeared to have been dumped there some time in the previous days and had suffered water damage. The contents—credit cards, phone, cash—hadn't been touched. The only sign of tampering was six inches of thin red thread tied into a knot and placed inside.

Three months later, the majority of January Spalling's body was recovered from the abandoned home on Breaker Street after an anonymous tip directed the police to it. She'd been cut up and spliced back together with a second victim, identity unknown. The red thread stitching pieces of her skin into place matched the material left inside her purse.

Those facts jumbled through Abby's head. They didn't tell her much. Most of the disappearances were like that—there were the facts you could establish, things you knew for certain, but so many holes left that you never felt as though you truly *understood* it. January Spalling knew about Charles Vickers. Everyone in town did. So how had he managed to take her with no one seeing or hearing even a whisper?

"Hey," Abby called as she entered the house.

"Up here," Hope shouted from the upstairs floor.

Checking that Hope was there was always the first thing Abby did when she got home. She was terrified of the day when her greeting might go unanswered.

Thudding noises came from the second floor: the sounds of Hope moving about her room. "Abs," she called. "I'm making a video. Can I borrow your blue top?"

Abby slung her backpack onto the living room chair and stretched. "The one with the lace? Sure."

"Thank you!" Hope appeared at the top of the stairs, beaming. She was already wearing the lacy blue top, and Abby had to laugh.

"Made much progress?" she asked.

"The equipment's being a nightmare. I had to rerecord one section three times just to get it to save." Hope's hair, dyed with streaks of rose pink and lilac purple, was jaw length, but she'd knotted part of it up behind her head. "But I really want to get this uploaded tonight."

Hope was an anomaly in Doubtful. In a town that drained dreams and sapped color, Hope stood in defiance of it all. She struggled with erratic technology far past what Abby could have endured, and forced colors into her naturally flaxen hair, and lived life with a pure vivaciousness that might have exhausted any other person.

A lot of people dreamed of leaving Doubtful.

Few did.

Her sister might be one of those rare exceptions.

Abby had been saving up for years. A dollar here, a day's lunch money there, hidden in a wooden box in the back of her drawers. She hadn't tried to count it in a long time. But she thought it might be enough for at least a month's rent somewhere else. To at least give Hope a chance.

She just had to keep them safe—keep them together—long enough for Hope to become a legal adult.

Her younger sister spun at the top of the stairs, her skirt flaring. She'd clearly put time into her appearance that day. Even the failing technology hadn't been able to dampen her spirits.

Abby hesitated. The house was very quiet. "Have you seen Momma yet?"

Hope stumbled to a halt. "She was in the back garden when I got home, digging. I haven't seen her since."

"Sure."

Hope disappeared back into her room, and Abby crossed to the kitchen. The window over the sink looked out over their rear garden, a tangle of unregulated bushes and sprawling roses, their thorny tendrils waving in the wind.

Her mother was no longer there. But the mounds of fresh dirt were. Heaps onto either side of the hole she'd been digging.

Abby could picture her there, crouched, bones showing through her thin nightdress, her hands smeared with dirt past the elbows as she clawed and clawed deeper into the earth, trying desperately to reach something below. It was just one of eight holes she'd been working at for weeks.

Abby turned aside. They had leftovers in the fridge—tuna bake Abby had re-created from an old recipe book with discolored edges—and she spooned some onto a plate before putting it in the microwave.

The holes were another bad sign. Her mother started expanding them when things began to turn bad. The erratic technology. The nightmares. Now the holes. They all pointed to one thing.

Someone was going to be taken soon.

The microwave beeped. Abby took the plate out and laid a spoon on its edge, then carried it up the stairs.

Hope's bedroom was to the left. She could hear her sister's voice through the thin wood, bubbling and excited as she talked to her webcam. Abby's own door was to the right.

At the end of the hallway was the master bedroom. It was still open a crack, the way it had been earlier that morning. The curtains were drawn. Inside was dark.

"Momma?"

Abby hesitated, waiting, but there were no sounds of acknowledgment.

Their mother's moods ebbed and flowed like a tide. Mostly they were slow and steady and predictable. But sometimes, if you weren't paying enough attention, they could turn and catch you by surprise.

When her mother was good, she'd eat any food she was given. Abby could help her bathe. Brush out her thinning hair and plait it to keep it neat.

When she turned bad…

The holes in the back garden were a bad sign. But there should still be enough time to get her some food, to fend off the horrible thinness of her frame for a little more.

Abby nudged the door open with her elbow and leaned forward. The main bedroom was dark and dusty and smelled stale. Abby held the plate of food out, a peace offering. She couldn't see her mother. "Momma? Do you want to eat?"

Still no response.

Abby took a step deeper into the room.

Beside the door was a tray of food. Porridge, cold, and a bowl of sliced apple and orange segments. She'd left it there that morning before leaving for school with Hope.

Flies crawled over the food. The apple had turned brown, the skin peeling back at the edges. Something squirmed in the porridge. Abby frowned, straining against the dim light. Maggots? The food hadn't been there long enough to get maggots—

She had a sudden mental image of her mother hunched over the bowl, picking at scabs in her skin. Pulling maggots out, one at a time, and letting them drop into the food. And then using one long, dexterous finger to stir them in.

A rattling noise pulled Abby's eyes up.

There was a narrow gap between the wardrobe and the wall. No more than a foot. But in that cramped space, one wide staring eye glittered.

"Momma," Abby whispered, her mouth dry. She held the bowl out. It shook in her hands. "Food, Momma."

The eye was fixed on her. Round, unblinking, intense.

Abby edged forward. She began to crouch, one hand reaching for the tray and its rotting food to pull it away and leave the fresh meal in its place.

Her mother lunged forward.

Limp arms swung at her side, still caked with dirt from the back garden. Her hair trailed across her face. Her jaws were open, showing long, narrow teeth.

Abby dropped the bowl and darted back. Her mother crossed the space between them in long, loping paces, her bony knees flashing out from under the nightdress, her arms swinging. Abby grasped for the edge of the bedroom door and pulled on it, shutting it hard.

Her mother slammed into the closed door. The wood shuddered. Abby clenched her teeth, gripping the handle, holding it closed.

Bang. Bang. Her mother wasn't just beating at the wood, she was hurling her body into it. *Bang. Bang. BANG.*

The sounds abruptly fell silent. In their place was just low, rattling breathing: air sucked in and out through bared teeth.

Abby's hands shook as she slowly, carefully let go of her hold on the doorknob. She stepped back, and then turned.

Hope was at the other end of the hallway, her face white, her eyes frightened.

Abby forced herself to smile, fighting to keep the trembles out of her voice. "Momma… Momma's not feeling well right now." She swallowed a lump in her throat. "How about we head out for a bit? Give her some space?"

Hope nodded once, a small, frightened smile flashing up and then vanishing again. Abby held her hand out. Her sister took it and didn't let go as they went down the stairs to escape into the late afternoon daylight.

"I'm home," Jen called, using her shoulder to push through the front door.

The hallway was still lined with packing boxes. Neither she nor her father had brought many possessions when they moved, but even with their minimalism, she'd underestimated how long it would take to unpack into a new home.

The real estate agent had told them this was one of the nicest houses in Doubtful. That boded very badly for the rest of the town. The wooden floors were scuffed and somehow always dusty, the kitchen desperately needed a renovation, and Jen kept discovering cracks running through the walls.

The new house was a lot bigger than their apartment in New York, though. The rooms weren't much larger, but there were more of them, and they had both a seemingly endless back garden and a front yard too. Jen was still getting used to the sheer quantity of plant life outside every window.

"Hey," her father called. "How was school?"

She was still getting used to the home's layout and had to follow his voice to find him. Thompson sat at the kitchen island, his reading glasses low on his nose, a mug of coffee at one side, and a stack of paperwork spread out on the table ahead of him.

Thompson was their surname, but, growing up, it seemed to be the only thing anyone called her father. His supervisors, his coworkers, even his neighbors. Jen had started calling him Thompson as a joke, but, over the span of years, it had stuck.

"School's fine." Jen dropped her bag at her side and then pulled one of the stools up to sit opposite her father.

He was getting older. It was only something she'd started to notice in the last year, but now she couldn't stop seeing the gradual changes. The gray flecks speckled through his short dark hair. The creases on either side of his eyes.

Sometimes she wondered how many of those budding gray hairs she was responsible for.

Those new wrinkles were a big part of the reason for their transfer to Doubtful. Not that Thompson would admit it. New York was a vibrantly alive city, and the police dispatchers never saw a quiet moment. Her father had kept up with the pace for twenty-five years, but now, he was ready for a break.

Doubtful was a quiet, rural town, with a population of no more than twenty thousand. There would still be crimes—where were there not?—but they wouldn't be anywhere near the scale of a major city's.

At least, that was what she'd thought.

Jen pulled the zipper back on her bag and took the missing person poster out from inside. She slapped it onto the kitchen island, facing her father. "What's happening in this town?"

"Oh." His eyes fluttered closed momentarily, then opened again. "Sweetheart. Yes. This young woman was found last night. I'm so sorry. That must have been an awful first day at school."

Jen leaned forward. "That's the weird thing. It wasn't. It was…just like any other day. This group I encountered tried to scare me with a story about a serial killer called the Stitcher, but other than that, no one said a thing."

"Huh." His eyes narrowed a fraction. She knew that look; he was being bothered by a mystery of his own, and she'd just added another piece to the puzzle.

"Tell me," she demanded.

He slowly took his reading glasses off and stared at a smudge on one of the panes. "It's nothing important."

She directed a sharp, unforgiving finger at him. "Thompson, tell me."

He chuckled. Jen knew he found it funny when she acted like his superior, and she used that to her advantage. "All right," he said. "You asked me what was happening in this town. And I can honestly say that I don't know."

"But it's weird, right?" Jen leaned forward. She needed someone to agree with her, to acknowledge just how bad everything felt. "There's something really...*off* about this place."

"You could say that," he agreed. "That body we retrieved this morning? That was worse than just about anything I've had to deal with before. It was...it was like something out of a nightmare. And, once we got back to the station, no one wanted to talk about it."

Just like how no one at school seemed to want to look at the missing posters. Jen hunched forward.

Thompson tapped the corner of his glasses against the papers he'd been examining when she arrived. "I even brought it up a couple of times. They just switched the conversation to something else. And this isn't the only thing I haven't been able to get clear answers on."

Jen tilted her head forward, her eyebrows raised. "What do you mean?"

He sighed, looking tired. "People just aren't talking to me. At first I thought it was because I was the new guy, or maybe I was replacing someone they liked, or maybe because I was transferring from the city. No one likes change, or even the threat of change. I get that."

"Yeah?"

"But then today an officer who sits opposite me made a comment about how they were *grateful* I'd transferred. That they'd been trying to fill my desk for months, and they were glad someone had finally taken it. And yet…conversations end when I enter the room."

Jen frowned.

Thompson released a small, weary chuckle. "And here I was thinking small towns had a reputation for being friendly. Well. That aside. I've been able to glean *one* thing. The people here seem to keep a curfew. Indoors after sundown. I'm thinking we should follow their example, at least until we're more settled in."

He very badly wanted to fit into his new community, she knew. He'd already bought new clothes for his off-duty days to better fit into the rural atmosphere and even had a generator taking up half of their garage because "that's how people live here."

Jen knew better than to argue. If she tried to fight it, her father would never let up. He'd worry, and nag, and watch her every move. It was easier for everyone involved if she agreed, then left later once he'd gotten so absorbed in his endless stacks of work that he'd forgotten his own decree. "Sure. Sounds good."

"Okay." He gently pushed the missing person poster, and January Spalling, aside. "Back to you. How's the homework situation looking? Any difficult teachers?"

"It's…" the word *fine* died before even reaching Jen's tongue. She stared through the kitchen window at the grassy stretch running down the side of their house, her heart leaping unpleasantly.

Something long and lanky moved there, its body undulating as it walked past their home.

FIVE

THE SIDEWALKS RUNNING THROUGH THE TOWN CENTER WERE broad and nearly deserted. Abby and Hope had room to spread out, but they instinctively walked close together.

Abby couldn't stop herself from pulling her phone out of the brown leather satchel she wore. The screen flickered before coming on, showing the time. Four-eighteen. They had another hour and a quarter until dusk.

She knew when sundown arrived each day, to the minute. Each day, she ran the new calculations: adding and subtracting seconds as the seasons waxed and waned.

It wasn't as though getting indoors before dusk was enough to keep someone safe. People were still taken during daylight, including January Spalling. But Abby's friend group had gone through the archives the previous year, jotting down the dates and times each victim was taken, and there was a clear bias. Nearly two-thirds of all victims were taken between nightfall and dawn.

Add in other factors—including how drastically fewer people were outdoors at night, and the way darkness made it impossible to see danger until it was nearly upon you—and it was enough to make that one of their rules: Get indoors before dark.

But home wasn't a good place to be that day. Abby was willing to push the limits of the ticking clock simply to get them both some space to breathe.

"We've got some time," she said to Hope. "Is there anything you wanted to get while we're in town?"

"Yeah." Hope still seemed unnerved, even though she smiled. "I… I was going to put together a witch's hat for a video next week. I have cardboard at home, but I just need black felt."

"Then let's get some."

They passed by a store with dark windows. A sign hung on the door, written in swirling cursive: *Back in Five Minutes*. The sign had been there for nearly eight months. Its owner, Pat Chandler, had stepped out one day and simply vanished. Unlike January Spalling, her body had not yet been found.

Spray paint had been left on a broad brick wall next to that store. **HIDE SOMEWHERE HE CAN'T FIND YOU**, it said. The color had been bright red once, but years had faded it to a rust brown. The words had been there for as long as Abby could remember.

Missing person posters rustled. There were a lot of them along that stretch of the walk. Dozens of faces stared out at Abby from the brick walls, from the bulletin board outside the butcher's, and from every pole they passed.

A lot of those pages were water damaged, the paper stiff and crinkly and warped. Many were sun bleached too; it washed the smiling faces out until they were barely recognizable. Any edges that weren't fixed in place with rusty pins or yellowing tape fluttered in the wind, sounding very much like dead leaves in autumn.

Abby met the gazes as she passed them. It felt wrong, the way so many of them were smiling, so unaware of what had happened to them.

Doubtful's general store was owned by the Bridges, an older couple and their adult son. They only had a small selection of fresh foods—the grocer's two blocks down was better for that—but their shelves were filled with the sorts of odd materials and supplies that could be hard to find elsewhere in town. The high, cramped aisles held everything from party hats to shovels, from sewing patterns to patio ornaments. It was a treasure trove for someone like Hope, who kept her wardrobe full of odds and ends for her videos.

The door creaked as Abby pushed through. The store only had one large window overlooking the street, and the light from it was partially blocked by piles of display items. It left the space dim, especially deeper between the shelves, where the old tube lights struggled to reach.

Hope was picking up energy now that they were in the store. She darted along the aisles, her steps light as she searched the contents. Abby stopped long enough to raise a hand to Mr. and Mrs. Bridge behind the counter. They were in their sixties and both beginning to stoop, but they were always friendly. They'd told her she could use their given names, but she couldn't bring herself to do that.

"Anything I can help you with?" Mrs. Bridge asked.

"Felt?" Abby asked. "Black felt?"

"This aisle here, near the back."

Hope made it there first, and followed the rows of baskets and section dividers down to where stacks of fabric were bundled into the shelves. Abby followed.

There were a handful of other shoppers already in the store. Abby recognized a few of them. None paid any attention to her. She knew she had a tendency to slide into the background, invisible to almost everyone, but she didn't mind. It made it easier to appreciate the people who *did* notice her. Hope. Her friends. Especially Rhys. She picked up a porcelain sheep statue from the shelf to keep her hands busy while Hope sifted through the fabrics.

The door rattled as someone entered. Slow, measured steps echoed as they moved into the store.

The space had been quietly busy before, in a way Abby was familiar with. The wiring in the walls hummed faintly. Shoes scuffed across the floor. People inhaled and sighed and placed items into their baskets with soft thuds.

Now, abruptly, the shop seemed to grow deathly silent. Abby lifted her head. In the porcelain sheep's glossy veneer, she could see a dull reflection of the counter, and a figure standing before it.

"Good afternoon," a voice said, velvety and smiling.

Abby clenched her teeth. At her side, Hope had gone very still. Her hands were clasped around a roll of fabric and her eyes were huge as she stared down at it, unseeing. She didn't move, not even to glance up at Abby.

Good girl. Stay still. Stay quiet.

"Afternoon," Mr. Bridge said after a second's pause. It wasn't the warm and mellow welcome every other shopper received. His voice was restrained. Tense.

"It's a surprisingly warm day outside," Charles Vickers said. She could imagine him surveying the store, the artificial lights glinting off of his thick glasses. "Summer doesn't want to give up, does it?"

One of the other shoppers moved, dropping their half-filled basket by the door and stepping outside without a word to the owners.

Mr. Bridge's voice was low and clipped. "Can I help you with anything?"

Charles Vickers chuckled, and let his own voice drop in volume and tenor to match Mr. Bridge's. "I placed a special order last week."

Mrs. Bridge pulled something out from the shelves beneath the counter and wordlessly pushed it toward Charles Vickers.

Hope remained still. But Abby tilted her head, just a little.

Knowledge is safety. That was one of their rules. But at the same time another, more urgent rule rang through her mind: *Stay away from Charles Vickers.*

But Abby was in the dim part of the store, and she easily blended into the background. She let her long hair cover part of her face as she leaned back slightly, trying to see around the shelf's corner.

A wooden box—about the size of a large textbook—sat on the counter. Charles Vickers rested his fingertips on its top, then reached down to unfasten a latch. The lid had a glass pane in it, but he still lifted it as he leaned forward to examine the box's contents.

Abby thought she could glimpse a trace of something red inside. She didn't dare breathe as she stretched her neck, gaining a few precious centimeters as she tried to see—

Charles Vickers's head snapped toward her. Their eyes met. An icy smile stretched over his pale, round face.

Abby turned away, her heart racing, her fingers growing numb around the porcelain figurine she clutched.

"That's all in order," Charles Vickers said, gently closing the box's lid. His voice was velvety again. He seemed pleased. "How much do I owe you?"

"We don't want your money," Mrs. Bridge whispered.

"Well, that won't do." A soft chuckle. Then there was the rustle of paper bills and the clatter of coins as Vickers dropped them onto the counter. "I like to pay my debts."

His shoes squeaked as he turned. Abby stared blindly ahead, listening to the footsteps retreat. Only…they weren't growing fainter. They were approaching.

He was moving toward her.

Fear cut through her like fizzling electricity as she turned.

Charles Vickers stopped directly ahead of her. A moss-green knit sweater covered his gently sloping shoulders. His hair was combed immaculately, thinning strands covering the top of his head. He held the wooden box under one arm. A faint, unpleasant smell clung to him, like mildew and old water.

"Hello, Abby Ward," he said. His gaze flicked to her sister. "And little Hope. Though, you're not so little now. You children grow up so fast."

Abby's mouth was dust dry. She shifted, reflexively putting herself between Vickers and Hope. She couldn't stand the thought of his eyes lingering on her sister.

"How's your mother?" Vickers asked. His thin, pale lips curled up at the corner, as though relishing a private joke. "I haven't seen her around town in *years*. Not since your father left. I hope she's not unwell."

Abby didn't speak. She felt Hope's hand on her back, clutching at the fabric of her dress, as though terrified that Abby would be snatched away if she didn't hold on to her. Charles Vickers's pale blue eyes moved languidly, tracing over Abby's face, as though relishing her voiceless reaction.

"Stay safe, children," he murmured, and then finally turned away. "Not everyone in this town is your friend."

As he turned, she caught a flash of the box he held under one arm.

Inside were dozens upon dozens of spools of vivid red thread.

The door creaked as Charles Vickers stepped through. It rattled closed behind him, and the awful, suffocating silence seemed to melt. Hope's grip slackened on Abby's dress.

Mr. Bridge muttered under his breath and wiped a cloth across his forehead. His wife patted his upper arm. She stared at the money on the counter—smooth folded notes and a handful of coins—with revulsion.

"Abby," Hope whispered. Her voice was so quiet that Abby had to strain to hear. "Abby, I don't want the felt anymore."

"Okay." She swallowed. The store, which had been comforting before, now seemed stifling and claustrophobic. As though it was a trap—the kind that closed in around you before you even knew there was any danger. "Okay. Let's go."

They moved to the front of the store to leave. Mrs. Bridge watched them with sadness in her eyes. "Are you okay, girls?"

Abby didn't trust herself to speak, but forced a tight smile and nodded.

"Wait a moment." Mrs. Bridge reached for her husband. "Bob, you go with them. It's…not safe outdoors. Walk them home. Make sure they get there safely."

He mutely dipped his head in agreement, then began to move around the counter.

"We're fine," Abby managed. Her voice sounded strained. "We'll be on our bikes."

That was a lie, but the older couple let them leave without another word.

It was common knowledge that Charles Vickers placed special orders at the store for cases of red thread that matched the shade and thickness of the stitches in the bodies. He'd order a new box two or three times a year, she'd been told. It was the first time Abby had seen the purchase with her own eyes, though.

She didn't blame the Bridges for selling Charles Vickers the delicate thread. They were only trying to keep themselves safe. She knew, all too well, what happened when you tried to stand against the Stitcher.

Her father had made an attempt, years before, when Abby was only eleven. A group of five men had fueled themselves on liquid courage at the bar, then approached Charles Vickers's house, armed with baseball bats and shovels.

That night happened shortly after the fourth victim of that year had been discovered, their reworked body bloated and floating in the river. The police were doing nothing, the men had all agreed. There was very little doubt about who the killer was. If the police weren't going to arrest him, then the town itself needed to rise up to protect itself.

Five men went up to Charles Vickers's house. Abby's father had been the leader, though. And Abby's father was the only one who didn't return home the following morning.

The police investigated, the way they always did. Missing person posters were taped to the streetlights and pinned about town, the way they always were.

He'd never been found.

Some people tried to tell Abby that was a good sign. That maybe, instead of being a victim of the Stitcher, he'd simply fled town.

It was possible. Like so many, he'd dreamed of a life outside Doubtful. Maybe an encounter with the killer had been enough to galvanize him to vanish into the wider world, leaving his wife and two daughters behind. Maybe, at that moment, he'd realized they would be deadweight in his attempts to escape the town.

The thought would consume Abby some nights. She'd lie awake in bed, picking over the idea, alternately picturing him in some faraway city, maybe with a new wife and new children, and other times picturing him as one of the Stitcher's victims, red thread running through his sagging, lifeless body.

Sometimes, she didn't know what would hurt more.

Then she reminded herself about what Rhys had gone through. Not having answers was a mercy compared to that.

So she didn't blame the Bridges for selling red thread to the Stitcher when he asked for it. They were kind people otherwise. But Abby still didn't want to get close to them. Not to call them by their given names, or to let them walk her home.

She and Hope stopped on the sidewalk outside the store. Abby's heart was running hard. Hope had seemed to shrink into herself, a hard angle to her jaw and dampness around her eyes. She'd been nine when their father had left and their mother had started to crumble. It had hit her far harder.

Abby pulled her phone out of her satchel with unsteady hands. They had just forty minutes until dusk. They needed to go home.

Home. To Momma. To another sleep filled with nightmares.

She glanced at Hope, whose eyes were fixed on the pavement.

Abby began texting furiously. The screen flickered before stabilizing, and for a second she thought her message might not have gone through, but then it popped up in the Jackrabbit group chat.

Hope and I need to get away from the house. Does anyone want to go to the lake?

Rhys's reply was first. Of course.

Followed by Riya: I can bring snacks!

And Connor: Meet you at the usual place. I'll have the radio.

Abby smiled, then turned the phone so that Hope could read the messages. It was like watching a veil being lifted from her sister's face. The horrible slackness retreated. Color returned to her cheeks. It was almost enough to quash the uneasiness running through Abby's chest.

"Yeah," Hope said, breathing deeply. "Let's go to the lake."

SIX

〜〜〜

"DEER," JEN GASPED. "THOMPSON. IT'S A DEER!"

She felt as though the air had been sucked out of her lungs. She'd seen deer once before, during a zoo trip, but seeing one in the wild was *different*. When you took away the fences and feed bins, it stopped being just a novelty and became something special. A flash of pure wildness. Something bordering on magical.

"Wow." Her father rose out of his seat and approached, adjusting his glasses. "Look at that."

Jen leaned close to the kitchen window. Her breath clouded the glass for a second before fading. The deer walked in the passageway between their house and the split rail fence separating their property from their neighbor's. The grass was long and half obscured the creature. Its body undulated gently as it paced. It was a buck, with small antlers raised above its head. Jen blinked, then felt her smile fade.

No…

Something wasn't right.

The deer paused, as though it could feel her staring. Its head turned toward the window. Jen's blood ran ice cold.

Tumorous growths sprouted across the deer's body and face. There were at least sixty of them, growing in bunches, some as large as a tennis ball. They interrupted the beautiful rich brown fur, bulging outward, an ugly, tar-colored shade tinged with red.

They were worst around the deer's face. Clusters burst out around its nose, its jaw, and its eyes. There were so many of them. It was hard to believe the deer could even see anymore.

It can't, Jen realized. Where its eyes belonged were empty sockets, crowded around by the horrible tumors. A trickle of blood ran down to its muzzle.

"Oh," Thompson whispered. He placed a hand on Jen's shoulder and gently pressed, then turned away. "I'll call animal control. They'll probably want to have it put down."

Her heart sank, full of grief for the animal, and for the magic that had been poisoned.

The deer flicked its delicate ears, then turned back to its path. There was no way for it to see where to go, but it seemed to have an idea of where to walk, even though it stumbled every few paces.

She turned from the window. Her father stood at the kitchen island, his phone held to his ear. He took it down, frowning at the screen, before tapping buttons and lifting it up again. "Call keeps cutting out," he muttered. "Cell reception was supposed to be good here too."

The deer was nearly past their house. Their back garden—just as weedy and overgrown as the side—stretched on for nearly the length of a football field before ending, not in fences, but in the wild forest. That seemed to be where the deer was headed.

Thompson saw her watching it. He raised dark eyebrows that were growing flecked through with gray. "Try not to think about it too much. Maybe you can focus on something else for a while, yeah? Do you have homework?"

"Sure," she said, without feeling.

Thompson muttered and lowered his phone again, frowning at the screen. Jen turned away, plucking up her backpack as she left the kitchen.

The hallway branched: stairs led to a second floor where Jen's own room overlooked the forest. Straight ahead, though, was a rear door into the backyard. Jen tucked her phone into her jeans' pocket, dropped the backpack by the stairs, and stepped outside. Her father was too distracted to even hear the door close.

The deer had nearly vanished into the trees. She broke into a jog as she followed. If animal control was going to help the creature, they'd first need to know where it was.

Long grass whisked across her legs and left little burrs on her boots as she ran to close the gap between them. She didn't slow down until she'd reached the trees.

Leaves crackled ahead and slightly to the right. Jen followed. She tried to tread carefully, but it was impossible to keep silent in the forest. Branches snapped and leaves crunched with every small movement. Dead twigs snagged in her hair and scraped at her hands.

The light grew dimmer as she followed the deer deeper into the trees.

Occasionally she glimpsed it: a flicker of rolling tan fur. Sometimes she thought she could hear its labored breathing.

The ground tended downhill into something like a hollow. Jen stopped. There was something in the indent that didn't match the unyielding grays and browns around her. Something bright and vividly red.

Blood? No. That looks like…

Thread. Coils and coils of it, so strikingly red that it looked almost unreal against the dead leaves and dry branches.

Jen hesitated. The deer was just out of sight, its slow footsteps leading away. But there was something captivating about the thread. Something that made it hard to turn away.

She swallowed as she approached the arrangement. The thread was delicate—the kind you'd use for cross-stitching or maybe to mend smaller pieces of clothes—but there was a lot of it. Yards, probably. It stretched out like some kind of spiderweb, looped around branches, across the ground, and threaded around an old, rotting stump. The structure was nearly as tall as Jen and twice as wide.

A person must have done this. Right?

It was hard to imagine how nature could have pulled those loops up to tie them around tree branches. But there was also a kind of chaos in the way the threads had fallen. Organic. Wild.

And the lines didn't end at the forest floor, she realized. Some of them seemed to disappear *into* the earth. There was no sign of the ground being disturbed, though; the dirt was pale and compact and covered in leaf litter. It was as though a needle had been run through the space, piercing air and dirt and leaving a trail of red in its wake.

Jen reached a hand toward a thread that ran between two trunks. Her fingertips hovered over the delicate, vivid line.

Don't touch it.

Hairs rose across the back of her neck. She pulled her hand back.

The threads no longer seemed like a minor mystery. They seemed dangerous, even disturbing. As though the very air around them was poisoned.

Jen staggered backward, away from the threads, then drew a sharp, shaking breath. It seemed too loud—because it was.

The forest was perfectly silent. She couldn't hear any insects. No birds. And, most importantly, no crackling leaves under cloven hooves. She'd lost the deer. She tried to orient herself, to remember which direction it had been walking, and rushed forward.

She didn't try to keep her footsteps quiet this time. As irrational as it was, she didn't want to be anywhere near those threads. And, slightly more rationally, she didn't want to lose the deer. Even as she stumbled between the trees, arms outstretched to keep the branches from slicing across her face, she couldn't tear her thoughts away from it.

Red thread. In the middle of the forest.

Who put it there?

And why?

Leaves crackled ahead. Jen squinted and moved toward it, breathing heavily. The trees were thinning. More natural light began to filter through. She ducked under a branch and saw the deer.

Its beautiful brown fur rippled as it walked. It paused, golden light falling across its form, and its awful, swollen head turned toward her. A drop of blood fell from the space where its eyes belonged.

There was the deafening crack of a gunshot.

Jen flinched, ducking down, her eyes squeezed closed. She waited to feel pain. There was none. Which was a small miracle. The gunshot had sounded close.

She opened her eyes, her teeth clenched. The deer was gone. "Hey!" she yelled, so that whoever had fired the gun would know there was a human in the woods as well. There was no answer. Jen moved forward, toward where the deer had stood, and found herself at the end of the trees.

A dirt road—not much more than a lane—ran ahead of Jen, separating her from a field of ripe sorghum opposite. And, in front of that field of sorghum, stood a man with a rifle.

He was old, at least sixty, with heavy creases marking the loose skin drooping over his face. Muddy boots came up past his knees, nearly meeting the hem of an old, stained flannel shirt. He didn't seem surprised to see Jen there.

She couldn't keep her eyes off the rifle. Guns were practical in the country, she told herself. Animals, both wild and farm, would need to be shot.

Still, she didn't like how casually it was being carried. Like it was an extension of the farmer's own body. Her whole life, Thompson had drilled the importance of gun safety into her; when he wasn't on the job, he kept his own issued pistol in a hidden safe. He never, ever would have fired his gun blindly into a forest where people might be walking.

The farmer sighed, staring at the place where the deer had been, his jaw working. Jen couldn't stop herself from asking, "Did you kill it?"

"Naw." He lowered his gun to point the barrels at the ground. "Got away. It's not gonna live for long, though."

Jen glanced toward the forest. She could no longer see or hear any trace of the animal. There would be no chance of finding it now that it was spooked. "What's wrong with it?"

"Tumors." The farmer inhaled deeply, his heavy-lidded eyes watching Jen. "Those won't kill it, though."

"They won't?" Jen turned back to him, frowning. "Then…what?"

He stared at her for a very long time. Jen felt her skin crawl. There was an entire road separating them, but that still felt too close. She took half a step back.

"It's close to dusk," the farmer said at last, and swung the rifle to indicate toward the fading sun. "You'd best get back inside. And stay there until morning, y'hear?"

This was uncomfortably close to what the group at school had said. "Why?"

"The Stitcher's getting hungry again." The farmer began to turn. "You're still new here. You don't know about our town yet. But take my word for it; you don't want to be outdoors while the creature's roaming."

"But—" Frustration bubbled in Jen. She needed answers. She needed *honesty*. This was the second time that name, Stitcher, had been mentioned, but the farmer was already shuffling away, toward a distant house half hidden behind his field. "Hey, wait!"

"Your home's that way," he called over his shoulder, and gestured along the path Jen stood beside. "Turn right at the crossroads."

Jen grit her teeth as he disappeared into one of the rows spaced through the field.

No one seemed to want to answer any of her questions. And, apparently, it wasn't much better for Thompson at the station.

Do they hate outsiders? Is this whole town trying to frighten us away? Jen glanced between the forest she'd emerged from, and the dirt road the farmer had pointed her toward. She wasn't sure she could find her way back through the trees. At least, not without ending up in someone else's yard.

Which meant she'd just have to hope the farmer actually knew where she lived, and wasn't just pointing her in a random direction for the fun of it.

As she walked, she let her thoughts swirl. A murder victim had been found on the other side of town. That was irrefutable fact—not a gimmick, and not a scare tactic. If people in the town were trying to frighten her and her father away, they could be leaning on that, not on foreboding warnings about *creatures* and *Stitchers*. Which meant…what, exactly?

The town actually harbored an active serial killer?

There was good reason for her to stay indoors after dark?

Jen quickened her pace. Small clouds of dust plumed away with every scrape of her shoe. The farmland ended and was replaced with small crumbling houses surrounded by large overgrown yards.

The buildings radiated neglect. Paint peeled. A wind chime, half rusted, rattled in the distance.

Properties in Doubtful were cheap. Their new house was easily three times the size of the New York apartment, but there had still been significant money left over from the purchase.

She'd heard that, even though houses in rural areas were cheaper, other things were more expensive. Fuel, for example. Which might help explain why there were so few cars on the roads.

There were cars *about*. Plenty of them. In driveways. On blocks by the side of a house, slowly turning into scrap metal. One old sedan was abandoned on the side of the road, half tilted into the ditch. Jen couldn't resist her curiosity; she crossed to look through the dusty windows.

The car was old. It was the kind of car her grandmother had driven, back before she'd been taken by breast cancer. There wasn't much inside; a few crumpled receipts on the floor, a spiderweb over the steering wheel.

And a coat and wallet draped over the passenger seat.

Jen stepped back, her curiosity vanishing into unease. This wasn't a recently abandoned car. Leaves and dead insects had collected across its roof and hood. Dirt, washed across the road by some long-past storm, had built up around the stationary wheels.

If Jen was right, no one had touched this car in months.

Who leaves their wallet and coat in a car they don't want?

There had to be an explanation. Maybe the wallet was empty and the coat was torn. Maybe they genuinely weren't wanted anymore. And maybe no one in Doubtful was ever tempted to steal from a clearly abandoned car.

Maybe.

She didn't want to be close to the sedan anymore.

Ahead was the crossroads the farmer had told her to turn right at; she paused, staring along its length. The houses were denser in that direction. She was pretty sure she recognized the cluster of trees and signs at the road's end, which meant the farmer hadn't been lying and, somehow, did actually know where she lived.

A sound from behind made Jen turn. Five figures crossed the road, moving toward the forest. They carried bundles of objects in their arms. Their heads were close together as they spoke; they hadn't noticed Jen yet.

But she'd seen them. More than that, she knew them.

A flutter of a faded sundress and the flick of a glossy black braid were the last things Jen saw before they vanished between the trees.

She sent one final glance toward her street and home, then turned to follow the strange band she'd met at school.

She was going to get her answers.

SEVEN

ᏇᏇᏇᏇ

"MY NEIGHBOR'S DOG HAD PUPPIES THIS MORNING." CONNOR'S long, narrow face was covered in leaping shadows from the fire. "Three of them were missing limbs. One was missing a head. They were all stillborn."

Abby held her hands clasped between her knees. They were at the lakeside meeting spot. Old logs were arranged in a circle around a firepit in the clear patch of land between the forest and the lake. Behind them, the water was lit up with red: the last traces of fading dusk.

If you're going to break a rule, have a good reason.

If the group ever stayed out past dark, it was to visit the lakeside. It was one of the few places in town that felt *safe*, which was ironic since they were so far from any habitation that they could scream until their throats turned hoarse and still not be heard.

But, somehow, the remoteness was what helped. It felt freeing.

When they met at the lakeside, they talked about things they didn't dare speak about in town. It was at the lakeside where they'd first started calling themselves the Jackrabbits. *Because a jackrabbit never drops its guard*, Rhys had said. *A jackrabbit runs, and it runs fast, and it survives.*

It was at the lakeside where they'd traded stories about the strange house on Cawley Avenue, and the man who lived there. The building was surrounded by thick hedges on all sides, built so tall that it was impossible to see the home they shielded, except for just one part: the attic and its round window. Supposedly, if you visited in the evening, you would see a man standing at that window, staring outward for hours on end.

And it was at the lakeside that they'd first agreed that they needed to learn about the Stitcher if they were going to be able to effectively protect themselves.

They'd built up the fire, not just for its warmth, but for its light. Rhys had brought blankets and five lanterns. The latter were spaced around them, creating a second ring of light outside the bonfire. An extended field of view. Extra protection.

Between two of the lanterns was their radio. It was an old, dusty, battery-powered box, and they'd set it to the dead space between stations. Soft static, barely more than white noise, hissed from it.

It was the closest they could get to an early warning alarm.

"It's getting so bad," Riya murmured. She leaned forward, her thumb rubbing at her forehead. "We found another two dead birds outside our house today. My mom doesn't want me going to work."

Abby inhaled deeply. The fire left the tang of ash across her tongue. Hope, who was calmer now that she'd eaten some of the coconut ladoo Riya had brought, leaned against her left shoulder. She used a marker to draw inscrutable designs on her palm, a habit she'd taken up to relieve stress. Rhys was on her other side, his face unreadable as he watched the flames. Riya and Connor were opposite, a mass of writhing shadows at their backs.

Hope had been staring into the flames, but abruptly lifted her head. "What scares you?"

Connor chuckled and raised his drink in a *cheers* motion. "No points for guessing the answer to that."

"No, no, I mean, other than the Stitcher." Hope smiled tentatively. "No one's ever scared of just one thing."

"I'm not sure I follow," Riya said.

Hope took a short, sharp breath. "I want to know the things you're scared of, that are unique to you. The things that *define* you."

Abby thought she knew what her sister meant. It was the sort of question that could only be asked at the lake edge.

"I'll go first," Hope said, and the small, nervous smile reappeared. "That's only fair, right? So, for me, I'm scared I'll be forgotten."

Riya cupped her head in her palms, her elbows braced on her knees. "Do you mean…like going to the store with someone and having them leave without you?"

"Kind of?" She fidgeted, adding lines to the drawing on her palm. "But not really. More…in a bigger sense. It's why I like having color in my hair. And it's why I love my video channel. I want people to *see* me and *know* me. I want them to ask what happened to me if I don't upload a video on time. I…"

There was a horrible gap as Hope fought to find her words. The fire popped, then hissed. Hope almost looked like she was going to cry, as though giving voice to her deepest fear was choking her.

"I don't want to be forgotten like we forgot Dad," she managed, finally. She looked ashamed the moment the words left her.

That small admission hurt Abby more than she'd thought it could. She opened her mouth, then closed it again.

Is she right? Did we forget Dad?

It had been years since the night he went out drinking with his friends and they decided to confront Charles Vickers. Years since she last saw him. His face had started to grow smudged in her mind, the shadowy stubble on his jaw and his smiling eyes never quite the same each time she tried to picture them.

Did we give up on him?

There was nothing they could have done when he went missing. Both Abby and Hope were just children. And their mother… The grief had hit her in unending waves. She'd been different ever since. It had put her into this spiral, where she slowly slipped further from them, day after day.

But Hope was right, in a way. They never talked about their missing father. Never acknowledged his birthday, or their parents' wedding anniversary, or Father's Day.

Abby couldn't. It hurt too much to talk about him, or to even think about him. The pain stung her every time she opened the lunch box he'd given her. And she'd thought she was shielding her family by keeping that small, constant ache locked inside.

But she hadn't realized that her silence might be hurting her sister in a completely different way.

We didn't forget him. But we pretended we did.

She didn't know what to say, so she lowered her head instead, unable to meet Hope's quietly yearning eyes.

"I'm scared of being left behind," Connor said, breaking the silence. He was smiling, but his lips were pale. "You're all going to graduate next May. But I've got one more year to go…and I'm scared I'm on the edge of the Jackrabbits already, and I'm scared that next year I'm going to slip out of it completely and there's nothing I can do to stop it."

"Connor, no." Riya reached toward him. "We're not going to let that happen. We'll…meet up with you after school each day, we'll…"

He smiled, but it was watery. "You won't be able to. You'll have jobs. Or you'll have moved away. And that's fine, you know? That's how your life is supposed to go. That's why it's a deep, dark fear, yeah? Because you can't stop it. Not completely."

Riya swallowed thickly. She drew her hand back.

"Your turn," Connor said, and his smile was a little bit more genuine. "Soul-baring time, Ri."

She chuckled, then grimaced. "Okay. Oh, this hurts. I'm afraid that all of my work will be for nothing. I spend weekends working at the pizzeria to earn as much as I can. Because I want to get out. *Away.* I want to live in another town, and I want to have a family, and I want… I want to be happy. And I know that can't ever happen as long as I stay in Doubtful, so I work hard to make sure that's not my future. And… I'm still scared that it won't be enough."

We're all scared of that.

Doubtful, Illinois, was a glue trap. People sometimes came in, but they very rarely left.

There was something about it that stuck with you. That stole away your will to fight, your desire for a future. The longer you spent in the town, the more you felt trapped there. As though there wasn't any space for you in the outside world.

Abby's mother had tried to leave, once. The neighbors had told Abby about it in hushed whispers. Apparently, she'd been gone for four months before coming back, quietly, in the middle of the night, to take up residence in her old home and pick up her job as a teacher again. She'd been pregnant with Abby at the time.

Abby just hoped she'd been the motivation behind her mother's desire to leave, and not the deadweight that had dragged her back in.

It was just another aspect of the town that Abby couldn't explain. There was nothing special about Doubtful to keep its occupants haunting its crumbling dwellings. But it was a pattern that had repeated again, and again, and again. People arrived. They rarely left.

The friend group all had plans to move one day, Abby included. And none of them would know how successful those plans were until they actually had a chance to try and see if they could carve a place for themselves in the outside world.

"What about you, Rhys?" Riya asked. Her bangs hung close to her eyes, throwing shadows over them. "What's your deepest, darkest fear?"

He glanced toward Abby then looked away again. It was so quick that she would have missed it if she hadn't been watching him.

"Loss," he said, simply. "I fear…losing the things I care for."

They'd all tasted loss. But he knew it better than anyone else there. Like Abby, he rarely spoke about his parents. But she knew he thought about them, just as often as she thought about her father. Perhaps even more.

"Abby," Riya said. "Your turn."

She ran her tongue across her lips, wetting them. "I fear...being lost in the dark."

Rhys shifted to watch her.

"I didn't peg you as someone who was scared of the dark, Abs," Connor said.

"I'm not. Normally." She shuffled her feet across the sandy ground. "It's a recurring nightmare I have. Being lost somewhere very dark, and I'm all alone, and no matter how loudly I yell no one answers me."

She wasn't telling the entire truth. The nightmares were real, and they were worse than what she'd described. In her dreams, she was lost somewhere dark, but she wasn't alone. Her calls for help were never answered, but she could feel the other entity shuffling closer, dragging dry skin across rocks, its fingers inching toward her.

In the dreams, it felt inevitable. As though it was a moment her whole life had been leading toward.

She thought Connor had been very right. A deep, dark fear was so much worse when there was very little you could do to prevent it.

The radio behind them had been playing soft static until that point. Abruptly, it began to hiss. Strains of an old song—a love ballad from her grandparents' generation—began to play. It was so distorted that they could barely make out the lilting notes as they slurred into one another.

As one, they turned to stare at the old radio. The dial didn't move, but new sounds began to blend over the music. An angry voice, muttering so quickly that none of the words could be heard.

"Okay," Riya whispered, and her voice almost faded under the radio. "Okay, we're okay. We're safest here out in the open, where we can see."

A branch snapped. They all flinched. Abby darted her eyes from the radio to the forest's edge. Their outer ring of lanterns barely touched it; she could see the rough texture of the nearest trees, but nothing beyond.

There was something *inside*, though. Something moving toward them. Leaves crackled, then fell silent again.

Rhys didn't take his eyes off the darkness, but he reached behind the log he sat on and brought out a baseball bat he'd stored there.

Dead branches crackled as something stepped over them. Abby's eyes moved almost faster than her mind could keep up with, searching the darkness, hunting for any sliver of motion between the tree trunks. Hope found her hand and gripped it painfully tight.

"Hello?" Connor called, half rising from his seat. His voice cracked. He swallowed. "Is anyone there?"

The radio's tune distorted again. The achingly slow melody still played, but now, instead of the rapid voice, the sound of breathing was layered over top. Inhale, exhale, inhale, exhale, coming in ragged gasps. Louder, and louder, and louder.

An arm reached out from between the trees.

EIGHT

⋁⋀⋀⋀⋀

JEN WAS BREATHING TOO FAST.

She'd thought there would be a trail through the forest. It had taken her less than two minutes to catch up to the place where she'd seen the group enter the trees. In that time, they'd not only vanished from sight but from hearing as well. A ghost of a path led between the trees, so she'd taken a chance and followed it.

This was different from the woods behind her house. The trees were denser, darker, and taller. They felt like giants as they tilted above her. Their massive roots pushed through the uneven ground, making every step unsteady.

She'd always had a strong sense of direction. But there was something disorienting about the forest. It was impossible to follow a straight line, and it robbed her of her sense of space, her sense of time, and her sense of how to retrace her steps.

Jen paused to glance behind herself. Everything looked the same. Ragged, rattling branches twining around heavy, leaning trunks. She couldn't tell which gaps she'd just walked through. Or how to find the road again.

Jen's mouth was dry.

She'd heard stories of people becoming stranded in forests, spending days walking in circles without realizing it. Slowly dying of dehydration and hypothermia while search parties scoured the wrong areas.

Don't panic. You're fine. You have your phone.

The trees couldn't continue forever. Doubtful was spotted through with patches of forest, but eventually they would be interrupted by roads or farmland or houses, and she could find her bearings again.

Surely.

Jen paused, her tongue between her teeth, as she listened. She couldn't hear any trace of the group she was following.

Except…

Behind her, a heavy, stuttering breath was drawn in.

Jen swung toward the noise. All she could see were endless trees, crowding in around her from every direction. The last traces of dusk were fading. She could barely make out anything beyond ragged lines of bark.

The sound repeated. A breath being sucked through a dry, tacky throat. It sounded sickly. Painful.

"Hello?" Jen called. Her voice stayed strong, something she was grateful for.

There was no answer, but the breathing came faster and wetter. It was joined by another sound. The scraping of dry skin rubbing against skin.

Nope. No. We're not doing this today.

Jen pulled her phone out of her pocket. The screen was black. She tapped it, then tapped it again. It couldn't be dead; she'd charged it just that morning.

Leaves crackled as the unseen presence took a step closer. The natural light was fading shockingly fast. Jen's eyes were fighting to adjust to the near-perfect gloom. And, still, her phone wouldn't come on.

Is that someone between the trees?

It almost looked like a person was standing there, no more than fifteen feet from Jen, buried in shadows. They would have to be tall, though. Taller than her. Taller than her father. Taller than anyone she'd ever met before…

She desperately pressed her phone's power button, trying to reboot it to get some light.

The shape between the trees seemed to move a fraction. Quivering. The sound of breathing came again, only, this time, it was less like breathing and more like dead words falling from a torn throat.

"Hhhh…hhhh…ahhh…"

Jen turned. Her blood rushed through her ears as she ran, nearly blind, through the forest. *Just nature*, she told herself, the words sounding increasingly desperate as the trees grazed her shoulders and left bruises on her shins. *Just a wild animal. An owl. Or a coyote. Or, or…*

She stumbled over upraised roots and fell, heavily, onto the forest floor. The scent of damp earth and decaying leaves stung her nose. She lifted her head, panting, and listened.

There was no ragged breathing. No crash of footsteps chasing her.

It had to be a wild animal. Right? She hated the way she felt like she was trying to convince herself.

Jen pulled herself to her knees. A different kind of noise faded in and out at the edges of her hearing. Music, she thought, though it didn't sound like any kind of song she could identify.

She didn't want to be in the forest any longer. More than that, she didn't want to be *alone*. Jen forced her way forward, close to blind in the stifling trees. The music was growing louder. It sounded like a badly tuned radio; static and something like a voice bled over it.

A shimmer of moonlight cut through the darkness. She stretched her arm out, reaching for it, and abruptly passed through the final row of trees and onto clear ground.

Jen froze at the edge of the forest. A bonfire had been built on a strip of sandy ground. Behind in, she thought she could see a lake, though it was so huge and dark that it could have been an ink stain across the landscape. The four people she'd met at lunch, plus one she didn't recognize, sat around the bonfire, staring at her, half risen from their seats.

The quieter one—Rhys, she thought his name had been—was holding a baseball bat. Jen stared at it. Slowly, he lowered it back to the ground.

"You startled us," the one with the curly hair, Connor, said. He laughed, exposing large teeth, and patted his chest to show how fast his heart was running. Jen doubted it was galloping nearly as bad as hers was.

"I thought people in this town didn't like to stay out after dark" was all she could manage.

"We made an exception." That was the flax-haired girl, the one with the unsettling eyes. She tilted her head a fraction. "Come and sit with us."

This is what I wanted, isn't it? Jen glanced back toward the trees. Then, hoping the perspiration wouldn't show on her skin, she crossed the space, passing between two of the lanterns. Connor and the fidgeting girl, Riya, shuffled to make a gap for her on one of the logs. She sat. "Your radio's not working."

"We know. We like it that way," Connor said, passing her a can of soda. It was lukewarm, but Jen still took it, grateful to have something to wet her throat. He grinned at her. "Hey. We were talking about our darkest fears. Want to play?"

The kids at her old school had told scary stories late at night during sleepovers. Jen shouldn't have been surprised that a group of friends gathered around a bonfire would want to do the same. She shrugged. "Okay. Do you want a story, or…?"

Connor just said, "Your deepest, darkest fear."

"Hmm." She pursed her lips, casting around for something fun. "Okay. Zombies. The maggoty kind that won't die when you shoot them."

A few eyebrows rose, and Jen had the distinct impression that she'd missed the point of the assignment.

"I mean, zombies would beat my own existential dread any day," Riya said. She chuckled, her knuckles white around the can she held. "So I'd say that works."

"Sure," Connor said, at the same time as Abby and the girl next to her nodded. "It works."

Jen found herself staring at the girl next to Abby. She also seemed younger than the others there by at least a few years, and her hair was dyed with bright colors. That was something Jen had noticed was missing from Doubtful's high school: everything and everyone seemed so colorless, as if they were afraid of being noticed. "I haven't met you yet," Jen said, to break the silence.

"I'm Hope," she said, leaning forward, her smile huge and warm. "But don't try to make my name into a pun. I've heard them all before. I'm Abby's sister, by the way."

"Oh." Now that she knew to look for it, she could see the resemblance: pale hair, slight frames. That was where the shared genes ended, though. The older sister's gaze was steely and intense. Hope's heart-shaped face radiated something much more bubbly and welcoming. She looked like the kind of girl who could go to a comic convention and make a hundred new friends over the course of the weekend.

"You're Jen," Hope continued. "Abs told me about you earlier. How do you like your new home? No one's died there. In case that matters to you. Riya was worried about that, so we checked."

"Oh," Jen said for the second time, and glanced toward Riya, who looked like she was sinking into a pit of embarrassment, her eyes huge and her cheeks flaming red. "Thanks, I guess."

"How are you finding the town?" Connor asked, possibly to make small talk, and possibly to save Riya from Jen's scrutiny.

She cast around for something that wouldn't sound like an insult. "It's…different." That still wasn't as friendly as she'd wanted, so she added: "I'm not used to empty streets."

"Yeah, not many people use cars here," Connor said, smiling mildly. "The roads don't get much use."

"I noticed that." She nodded toward the forest she'd just come out from. "The only car I've seen this afternoon is one that was abandoned one on the side of the road—"

"Old sedan?" Riya asked, seeming to abruptly break out of her fugue. "Tan coat and wallet in the passenger seat?"

Jen's eyebrows rose. "That's the one."

"Mm." Riya nodded. "That was Jonas Caulk's car. It's been nearly eighteen months."

"Since…?"

"Since he was taken," Riya said. Her eyelashes were very long, Jen noticed; they fanned out over her eyes, shadowing them. "His body hasn't been found yet. That's why his car is still there. There's this kind of rule in Doubtful… When someone goes missing, you leave their stuff where it is."

Jen found herself staring. That story was, somehow, even stranger than believing the car had just been abandoned. If the owner was one of the missing persons whose posters seemed to litter the town, wouldn't the police want to search his car and wallet for leads?

"It's more superstition than anything," Abby said. She sipped from her drink. "Some people believe that touching another person's belongings before their body is returned will attract the Stitcher. Like putting a mark on yourself."

This was exactly the topic Jen had been hoping to shift the conversation around to, but the small scraps she was getting were only making her more uncomfortable. "Hold up. *Before the body is returned*? What's that mean?"

"Well, people get taken," Connor said. He had very long fingers, which he used to gesture to help make his point. "But their bodies aren't ever found straight away. This isn't like a spontaneous murder where a body's left on the road. The Stitcher takes his time with them. Sometimes days, sometimes weeks, sometimes longer, depending on how complex the sewing is. When he's done, he returns them. He'll put them somewhere they'll eventually be found."

"I met a farmer today who wanted to talk about the Stitcher," Jen said. "Only, he didn't call the Stitcher a *he*. He called it a *creature*."

"Yeah," Connor sighed. "Some people will do that."

Jen spread her hands, exasperated. "I've had enough cryptic answers to last me to next summer, thanks. You wanted to tell me about the Stitcher earlier, at school. Well, I'm ready to hear it. Who, or what, exactly is a *Stitcher*?"

The mood seemed to shift. It was as though the casual part of the evening had ended, and now they were focusing in on a job. A *mission*. They all straightened a fraction, shifting forward, the nervous smiles fading from their faces.

"Abs?" Riya said. "You're good at explaining it. Did you want to field this one?"

"Sure." Abby was directly opposite Jen. The fire flicked between them, sending strange light and shadows over her face. "For as long as anyone can remember, Doubtful has been home to a serial killer."

Jen scratched at the nape of her neck. She'd watched her father work cases long enough to pick up some knowledge. "This is a small town. There's not much room for a serial killer to hide."

"Yes," Abby said, and there was something heavy and unhappy about that single word.

"So…"

"Every time a body is found, a small list of suspects are interviewed. Every time, those suspects are let go."

"How long's the list?"

"Now? One name," Abby said. She drew a deep breath and let it out in a sigh. "Charles Vickers."

That was the name they'd brought up at school. The man they'd warned Jen to stay away from.

"The Stitcher doesn't just kill his victims," Abby said. "He keeps their bodies. Sometimes for a long time. He'll dissect them and sew them back together in unnatural ways. Hands connected to the face, arms and legs stitched end to end into a long line. Organs placed into stretched skin that's sewn back into a parcel. And worse."

The fire hissed as sap leaked from one of the split pieces of wood. Just past the lamplight, the radio murmured, static and voices competing.

"Let me guess, this is the scary story part of the evening," Jen said. She forced a laugh that she didn't quite feel.

"No one here's trying to scare you." Riya folded her arms around her chest to hug herself. "You asked us about January Spalling earlier. She was one of the victims. Found combined with sections of an unknown man."

Jen remembered the look that had passed over her father's face when she'd brought up the dead girl's name. He'd seen a lot during his decades in the force. But something about January's death had shaken him.

Jen wanted to argue, to force them to admit that it was just a big joke they were playing on her, that they were making up the details to get a reaction. But there were no barely hidden smirks around the campfire. No eagerness or raised eyebrows. Just grim, unhappy honesty.

And that was when Jen noticed something else. The thing they all had in common.

They were wildly different people—different body builds, different facial shapes, different personalities. But, with the exception of Hope, they all had the same look around their eyes.

Haunted. Tense.

Like prey animals that had spent their entire lives trying to outrun a tireless predator.

"You can keep talking," Jen said, her palms sweating.

"The Stitcher strikes erratically," Abby said. "But there are usually signs leading up to an attack. Technology will stop working. Animals grow sick or die. People…get worse. You'll have nightmares. When you notice the signs, it means the Stitcher will take a victim—or victims, plural—soon."

Every time she tried to trust them, even a little, the story became more fantastical. Jen tilted forward, eyebrows high. "You're telling me a serial killer can give the entire town synchronized nightmares?"

Abby's eyes didn't leave Jen. "There are some things we don't completely understand. It's a big part of what sparked the urban legend. And why some people call the Stitcher *it* instead of *him*."

The farmer had told Jen to stay indoors because *the creature* was prowling. And he'd seemed completely serious when he'd said it. "Tell me about that."

Abby indicated Connor, who leaned forward, a grin stretching his cheeks. "Okay, so, the Stitcher urban legend is really more of my area. Basically, a couple hundred years ago, Doubtful was founded as a mining town. There were a lot of them through Illinois. Still are. Doubtful was an early one, though, and safety precautions weren't exactly enforced back then." He shrugged. "People died. A lot."

"Yeah." Jen had heard about some of those mining disasters. Men and sometimes boys being trapped after a cave collapsed, knowing that rescue would be impossible. In some cases, they survived down there long enough to write goodbye messages to their loved ones, and those notes were found clutched in their hands when they were finally exhumed.

"The legend says that the Stitcher came from the mines. That the men dug further than they were supposed to and unlocked something ancient and evil. The theory says that a monster existed in a little pocket miles deep, and now, it stalks the abandoned mines beneath our town, snatching people when it grows too desperately hungry. Or, it would be, if the mines hadn't been collapsed and flooded a long time ago."

Jen let those words linger in the cooling night air, before a thin, coughing laugh escaped her. "Sure."

"Yeah, that's what we think." Connor shrugged. "It doesn't even make sense within its own logic. If the Stitcher is hungry, why does it return the bodies? What's making it sew them up? Where's it even getting the thread from?"

Jen tried not to let too much of her doubt show on her face. "Are you saying you'd believe in the monster if its story made more sense?"

"Eh…" Connor's hand flopped limply as he gestured toward the town. "It's just that plenty of other people believe it. Including my mom. We have a rule not to talk about the Stitcher in our house because it just leads to arguments."

That seemed impossible to believe. Even the most open-minded people Jen had met—a neighbor who lived his life by the horoscopes, a barista who was constantly adjusting crystals over her body to balance her energies—would have balked at the story of a monster.

But the farmer's voice echoed in her mind. *The creature*, he'd called it.

"There are reasons they believe it's supernatural." Riya spoke quickly. "Apparently, the killings started around the time the mines were shut down. The tunnels had been the town's livelihood for decades, and then they were sealed off overnight. And, well… That was in 1930. People have been going missing in Doubtful ever since."

This time, Jen couldn't keep her face neutral, and let it scrunch up into a grimace. "People have been dying here for *a hundred years?*"

"Well, yes, but there are possible explanations that can account for all of that," Riya said, and Jen was amazed she could get so many words out without pausing for breath. "It's reasonable to believe the killings *were* related to the mine's closing. The town *survived* on the mining jobs. It was almost everyone's livelihood, and it was snatched away with no warning. It might have been enough to cause someone with a volatile temperament to, well, snap. The killings might have originally been in revenge. And then, after a while, a copycat or multiple copycats could have taken over."

"For *a hundred years?*" Jen pressed.

"We don't actually know how consistent the murders have been through history," Connor said. "There was a major fire about twenty years ago. Lots of records were lost. Including details on all the past murders."

"We've been able to glean some information from the library's newspaper archive," Abby said, "But they're not as complete as we'd want either. We know, for certain, that there have been murders scattered through the town's history. And we know, for certain, that the killings have been happening regularly since we were children, at least. And we believe we know who's responsible for this current generation's deaths."

"Charles Vickers," Jen supplied.

"The police tell us that he's been cleared," Riya said. She looked like she wanted to apologize for it. "Of all the deaths. They say he's not responsible at all. But he's also their only suspect in nearly every case."

"A portion of the town believes the Stitcher is a monster," Abby said. "Something evil and ancient that was woken inside the mines. Another portion believes the Stitcher is a man, and that he lives inside our town. A final portion—the larger portion—tries not to think about it at all. You ask them about the Stitcher, and they'll change the subject as quickly as they can."

"Really?" Jen asked.

"When I was little, a woman on the street slapped me for asking too many questions," Abby said. "Yes. Some people will do anything not to think about the evil that lives next door."

"I get the sense that you've made up your minds, though," Jen said. "You're convinced it's this Vickers man. Why?"

"Because of me," Rhys said.

It was the first time he'd spoken since Jen arrived. He'd been so quiet that she'd almost lost him in the shadows at the opposite side of the fire.

Abby reached toward Rhys, her fingertips lightly resting on his forearm. She must have been able to communicate with him with just a look, because he murmured, "It's fine. She should know."

"Know *what*?" Jen pushed.

"His parents were taken by the Stitcher." Riya was close enough that Jen could feel the trembles through the dirt as Riya tapped her foot, nervous. She kept her voice low. "Years ago. It was…bad."

Jen stared at Rhys, challenging him. The glare didn't get any kind of reaction, but he gently placed his drink on the ground before clasping his hands together.

"Most people in town know the story," he said, his voice low and measured. "It's been a long time since I've had to tell it."

"Rhys," Abby murmured. Her fingers were still on his forearm. He gave her a very small nod, and she took a deep, slow breath, before nodding in return.

"I was eight," Rhys began, his eyes on the bonfire. "And it was storming."

NINE

RHYS'S STORY

MY PARENTS' NAMES WERE ANGIE AND HUGH.

Hugh was an assistant regional manager for a tin distributor that used to have a shipping depot in this area. Angie was a dental hygienist. She worked in Doubtful three days a week, but the town's dentistry couldn't support a full-time wage, so twice a week she drove an hour to the sister office in Whitestone.

A year before their deaths, the depot servicing this area shut down, and my father lost his job. He tried to pick up work in town, but the only jobs available were part-time. They always acted as though everything was fine around me, but the lost income created a gap they couldn't fill. They started arguing about Mom's student loan debts, and about Dad's inability to get a job, and when the stress turned bad enough, they'd argue about things that didn't matter, like the way the front door creaked and how they'd forgotten to buy milk.

They sold their second car to tide them over. That meant, twice a week, Dad would need to drive an hour to drop Mom off at Whitestone, come back to take me to school, and then drive another hour to pick Mom up after her workday ended.

They knew about the Stitcher. They knew people were being taken and killed. But they also believed that the people who had been taken must have done something reckless, like stepping into a stranger's car or leaving their doors unlocked.

I've met a lot of other people who thought the same way. They treat the Stitcher as a horrible concept, but not something that would ever happen to *them*. It's human nature. We want to feel that we have control over our destiny, that we wouldn't ever make the same mistakes that cost someone else everything.

Most of the victims probably believed that, too, right up until they were taken.

Although my mother and father weren't afraid for themselves, they were still careful with me. They watched me whenever we went out in public. And they never let me stay home alone. That meant, twice a week, I would join Dad as we drove to pick Mom up.

The trips there were good. We sang to the music, and he'd tell me jokes that he'd looked up on his computer that morning and try to make me laugh. But once Mom got into the car, the mood would always be a bit quieter and a bit tenser. We'd still play music, but we'd no longer try to sing.

The day it happened was bad. The sky was so overcast, it felt like dusk. And even on the drive to pick Mom up, Dad had been edgy. He'd gained a notable smell over the previous months, and it was strong that afternoon. I didn't know what the smell came from until years later, when someone tried to give me a drink made with brandy at a party.

Other things had been going wrong. A deer had died in our garden, and Dad had to find a way to drag it off our property. The car's radio kept fading to static, so eventually we turned it off and drove in silence.

We picked Mom up and things became worse. Because I was in the back seat, Mom tried to keep her voice light, but she was asking my father a lot of questions: about what he'd been doing all day, about whether he'd applied to any new jobs. Dad said he'd had other things to deal with. Mom said new bills had arrived.

Then the storm clouds finally broke, and it started raining so heavily that we could barely see the road. Mom said we should pull over and wait it out. Dad said he knew how to drive through rain. I think he just wanted to get home, to get out of the car.

There was lightning. We passed the sign welcoming us back to Doubtful, and it had collected a pool of water around its base. We were still twenty minutes from home when the car stalled, and refused to restart.

My dad managed to steer off into a dirt patch at the side of the road. Mom said, "We can't afford car repairs too," and she sounded like she was close to crying. Dad snapped that he was going to fix it, and got out. Instead of looking under the car's hood, though, he walked away.

Mom must have seen I was scared. She stroked the side of my face and told me everything would be all right. She told me to stay where I was. And she got out to run after Dad.

The downpour was heavy. Within seconds, she'd vanished from sight, as well. And that's when I noticed the man.

He stood off the side of the road, between the trees. He would have been less than thirty feet away but I could barely see him through the rain. But I could see the outline of his face every time the lightning flashed. He wore dark clothes and his hair washed over his forehead. He was staring directly at me.

I was afraid. I wanted to run to my parents. But I was trying to prove that they could trust me, that they could rely on me, so I stayed where they'd told me to stay. Instead of looking at the man, I put my head down and covered it with my jacket so that he couldn't watch me.

Minutes passed. Then I heard him circle the car. His hands picked at the doors and windows, trying to get in. He scratched at the glass. He didn't speak, but I could hear him breathing. And then the noises stopped.

When I lifted my head again, the man was gone. But something red ran down the windows. Streaks of blood being washed away by the rain.

The storm slowly ended over the next two hours. I could see further down the road but my mom and dad were nowhere in sight. Vehicles occasionally drove by but none stopped.

I was convinced that, if I got out of my car, the man in the trees would catch me. And so I stayed where I was. I stayed there all night. Morning came and my parents still hadn't returned.

Police officers found me later that day, dehydrated and terrified. They'd been alerted when my mother failed to show up to work. It wasn't hard for them to link the disappearance to the abandoned car on the side of the road.

For the first few days, people tried to feed me pleasant stories about how they were going to find my parents and bring them back to me. My grandmother—my father's mother—moved into our home to look after me. The police asked me a lot of questions over multiple days, but even though they didn't try to contradict me, I'm still not sure how much of my story they believed.

Between the calming lies—that my parents would come back, that everything would be all right—I heard whispers. That I'd been spared. That I was one of the few who had survived the Stitcher. A miracle amid a tragedy.

I didn't feel like a miracle.

During those weeks, I had constant nightmares. One woke me close to dawn, and as I lay in bed, I heard cars in the distance.

Not many people drive through Doubtful, and almost no one leaves their home after dusk. If you hear multiple cars at night, it's almost certain that it's the police.

All of my encounters with the police until then had been related to Hugh and Angie. It just made sense to me that, if the police were driving somewhere, it meant my parents had to be there too.

My grandmother was still asleep. I slipped out the back door and walked in the direction of the cars. They weren't far away. I found them parked outside the eastern forest. I was still afraid, but more than the fear, I was desperate to see my parents again. I followed the trail leading into the forest.

I'd been right. The police had found my parents.

Their remains had been left in a small clearing. Their skin had been removed from their bodies in pieces and stitched together like a patchwork. Everything else—bones, organs, hair, and teeth—had been piled inside the cloth made of their skin, and then sewn up into a bulging, wet parcel. It was suspended about fifteen feet above the ground. Yards of red thread looped around it and held it in place, tying it to the surrounding trees.

Disassembled and sewn back together like that, they no longer looked like my father and my mother. They just looked like a swollen bag with splitting seams, dripping old blood onto the forest floor. But I still knew it was them.

Almost the entire police station was gathered there. Two of the officers who had questioned me before rushed to push me away. *This isn't something you need to see*, they told me. Even as they led me back down the path, I could still *hear* it. Drip, drip, drip, and then a slow creak as the dozens of loops of threads strained under the weight.

Years later, I found out that forensics had examined the remains. They said my father died first, by about ten hours. I want to believe he was protecting my mother.

There were coffins at the funeral, but I didn't get to see what was inside. Nothing that would have looked like my family, I suppose.

It took me a long time to realize that the repeated questions from the police weren't to try to find Hugh and Angie. They already believed they were dead. The questions were because of the figure I'd seen in the trees.

It's very rare for someone to be nearby when a person is taken by the Stitcher. And it's unheard of to have an eyewitness. I answered their questions the best I could, but there wasn't much I could tell them, even when the memory was fresh.

Over the years, I've tried to recall that face again and again, trying to make out details that were blurred and faded and distorted by fear. But he was just too far away, and the shadows were too heavy, and the rain too thick.

I wish I could be certain. I wish I'd kept my head up to see him get nearer to the car.

But I believe the man I saw was Charles Vickers.

Not many people in town wear sweater-vests.

TEN

^^^^^

THE BONFIRE WAS GROWING LOWER. GLOWING SPARKS spiraled toward the sky before burning out above their heads.

Jen didn't know what to make of the story. Or of the boy sitting opposite her. Speaking for so long seemed to have cost him; he looked tired, worn down. He wouldn't meet her eyes.

But there was one part of his story that echoed Jen's own experience earlier that day. Before she could stop herself, she said, "Earlier, I was following a sick deer. It had…some kind of tumors all over its body. It looked like it was dying. And I followed it through the forest past this web of string…"

She was on the edge of telling them about the way the string had made her feel—sick and horrified and vulnerable—but pulled it back. They didn't need to know. "Anyway. A farmer shot at the deer but missed. He said it would die soon, though. And not from the tumors."

"That string you passed." Riya spoke slowly. Her eyes were very intense. "Was it red? Red *thread*?"

"Yeah." Jen, abruptly uncomfortable, stared at her. "Why?"

There was a prolonged silence. The five friends shared looks that Jen couldn't quite parse. Then Riya, her fingertips nervously tapping together, said, "You might want to mention that to your father. And, uh, ask him to tell the other officers at the police station."

The fire should have been enough to keep her warm, but Jen found her skin prickling into gooseflesh. "Why?"

Riya grimaced. "It's just…"

"Why?" Jen pressed.

Abby spoke instead. Her voice was cool and unflinching. "If you see gathered red thread, there's almost certainly a body nearby."

She couldn't doubt it any longer; they were trying to scare her. Jen, unwilling to let them see how much they'd succeeded in getting under her skin, kept her face as hard and expressionless as a wall.

"I'm sorry," Riya said. "It might be nothing. You should tell your father about the thread, though, and stay away from those trees until the police have searched them."

"It's not always a body," Connor said. "Sometimes it's just…a part of a body. A foot or something."

"And it could be old," Abby added. "Sometimes there's not much more than bones left when they're discovered. But a lot of people have gone missing in Doubtful, and a lot of them were never found."

"Okay." Jen clapped her hands together, a fierce grin on her face. "Okay, great, thanks for all of this."

It was too much. She'd tried to trust them. She'd tried to leave her mind open, but it seemed like the more open she was, the more they tried to cram into the gap. And she'd passed her breaking point.

A single word echoed through her mind: *gullible*. That was something she'd never called herself before. Back home, with her old friends, she'd usually been the first to sense when a situation felt unsafe, or to guess that a part-time job posting was bait for a pyramid scheme, or to notice when someone was trying to manipulate her.

It was different in Doubtful. She felt unsteady, like she didn't know where to place her feet. And she needed friends. So she'd tried to trust the five teens around the bonfire, and all they wanted to do was play games with her. And the town had been so foreign and so unsettling that for a painfully long moment, she'd believed their stories. Now she just felt gullible. And she hated it.

"Jen?" Riya reached a tentative hand toward her. "Is something wrong?"

"Nope, I'm done." Jen stood, and hoped the clipped note to her voice would hide how humiliated she actually felt.

"Are you leaving?" Connor asked.

"Yeah. Enjoy your…whatever this is."

They shared a look, then they all rose as one, gathering up their bags and belongings. Rhys pushed his baseball bat into a backpack, then crossed to collect the radio. Abby grabbed up armfuls of blankets while Connor and Riya poured water over the fire.

She hated the way they compelled her to ask: "What are you doing?"

"Coming with you," Abby said, shoving the final blanket into her bag.

"Please, don't let me spoil your night here," she muttered, already turning toward the forest's edge.

"It's not safe to be alone after dark." Abby swung her backpack over her shoulder and took one of the five lanterns Rhys was passing out. "If you're going to leave, we'll walk with you."

"What, so you can play more of your games?" Jen set up a fast pace as she entered the forest, hoping to leave them behind, and was frustrated when they crowded in behind her. "I'm tired of it. Find someone else to torment."

"No games," Abby said bluntly. "We won't even talk if you don't want. But we've got to stay with you until you get home. It's one of our rules."

The trees pressed in overhead. The lanterns cut through the darkness, revealing rows upon rows of ancient, crumbling trunks.

Jen hated to admit it, but she wasn't sure she could find her way out of the forest without some kind of light. She pulled her phone out of her pocket and pressed the power button again, just in case.

"Phones become erratic when the Stitcher's active," Abby said. "It'll start working again on its own. It just needs time."

"I thought you promised not to talk."

Abby shrugged and faced forward again, her lantern extended to light the path.

Jen was hyperaware of how close they were. Their footsteps were heavy on the fallen leaves. The lantern lights overlapped, sending far too many shadows over the trees.

It was possible this whole evening had been staged. Maybe they'd made sure she would see them entering the forest. Maybe they'd brought something that would disrupt her phone. Maybe one of them had stood in the shadows, making strange, gasping noises.

Her skin prickled again, the hairs rising. She didn't want to think about it. She just wanted to get home.

The forest ended. They were back on one of the main roads. But not any street Jen recognized.

"This way," Abby said, turning left.

If they're trying to get me lost—if this is another game—

But then Riya sent her a small, reassuring smile, and Jen found herself tamping down on the doubt one final time.

Streets branched away as they entered the town. It was at least easier to see; streetlights rose high above them, though at least half of them were dead, and still more were flickering. Jen wanted to ask about them, but she knew that would only invite more taunting.

Even though it was easy to see the path, the others still kept their lights running. They were gas lamps, Jen realized. Small fuel reservoirs wicked up to a steady flame, protected from the wind by glass sides. It seemed bizarre when battery-powered was so much simpler.

As they passed by a side street, a strange rattling noise caught Jen's notice. The others turned their heads to stare along the road. The movements were so synchronized, they felt rehearsed.

It was a small cul-de-sac with no more than fifteen houses. They were all badly neglected, with grass grown high and dark holes in their roofs marking where tiles were missing.

All except the last house. At the very back of the cul-de-sac, facing toward them, was a two-story home. Its lawn was mown. Its white painted facade seemed fresh.

That wasn't the strangest thing, though.

Objects had been tied to the fences leading down the street. They were scattered down the whole road, but grew denser near the final house's boundary.

She could make out some of the nearer items. Dolls. Baskets filled with either fruit or flowers that had long ago rotted and gone putrid. Bundles of fabric and pieces of tarnished metal and the kind of stuffed bears people buy in hospital gift shops.

They all looked unearthly and nightmarish in the pale moonlight.

"I'll give you permission to speak again if you tell me about that," Jen said.

"It's Charles Vickers's house," Riya whispered.

"You're kidding." Jen frowned toward the final building, the one where most of the items were condensed. "So what's with the stuff?"

Connor chuckled, but it sounded thin and stressed. "Sometimes people leave…offerings. Gifts to gain favor with the Stitcher. They think if they can, I dunno, *appease* him, he'll leave them alone."

"It's superstition," Abby said. "It won't keep you safe. He never takes the gifts, and he wouldn't know who left them. But people still try it. Fear will make you do strange things."

Jen found herself watching them again. The haunted eyes. The intense, almost feral desperation around their features.

"Except for this, almost everyone in town avoids him," Connor said. "They hide in their homes if they see him coming. The movie theatre empties when he buys a ticket. You'd think anyone would hate that. But he doesn't. He seems kinda…weirdly *pleased* every time someone crosses the road to get away from him."

Jen stared along the street. The houses there weren't just neglected, she realized; they were abandoned. Several of the lawns had for-sale signs on them, though they looked ancient. The plywood was peeling and weeds had grown high around them.

Vickers wasn't just mistrusted. He was feared. And feared so badly that the people living nearest him had left, and no one wanted to take up the empty homes.

"What if you're wrong?" Jen asked, and her voice sounded low and strained in her own ears. "What if you made a mistake, and Vickers is just some guy who gets off on being the local boogeyman? What if he's playing up his involvement to get more of a reaction?"

"If we're wrong?" Abby's gaze turned so suddenly that Jen's breath caught in her throat. The girl's eyes glinted strangely in the moonlight, like disks of pure reflection. "There are no other suspects. If we're wrong, it can only mean the Stitcher isn't human at all. That the legend is true. That the Stitcher is some monster. And if that's true… I don't think that's a world I know how to live in."

Jen's eyes were drawn back to the final house, perfectly maintained despite the dereliction around it. The lights were on. She thought she saw a figure moving in one of the upstairs rooms. It paused, and one of the long curtains parted an inch.

He was watching them.

ELEVEN

THEY LED JEN BACK TO HER HOUSE, JUST LIKE THEY'D PROMISED. And, like the world's most unnerving spectators, they stood at the end of her driveway and watched her until she'd opened the front door and stepped inside.

She found Thompson in the kitchen.

"Hey, honey," he said as she stopped in front of him. He was still leaning over the stacks of paperwork, his glasses pressed high on his nose as he struggled to read some handwriting. "Finished with your homework yet?"

He didn't even know I was gone. That probably should have hurt, but only came as a relief. She hadn't been able to call him. She'd been prepared for him to be frantic by the time she got back. Her absence being unnoticed wasn't exactly comforting, but it *was* easier. "Nearly."

"I couldn't get through to animal control after all," Thompson said, still without looking up. "I'll try again later if that deer comes back."

"Don't worry about it." Jen couldn't stop her mouth from twisting. "Apparently it's going to be dead soon, anyway."

"Hm." Her father, his pen lightly tracing across the papers as he read, failed to pick up on the ominous undertones. Which meant she was unlikely to spark any kind of deeper conversation that night.

That was fine with her. She wasn't sure she wanted to tell him about the things she'd heard around the bonfire. Or the things she'd *thought* she'd heard, earlier, in the forest.

Jen moved toward the stairs. In a twist of ugly irony, she actually did have homework, and she didn't like the idea of falling behind on her first week.

She hesitated at the base of the stairs, her eyes trailing toward the back door. Through the hazy pane, she could barely make out the trees where she'd found the loose thread.

Things are getting bad.

Jen, her mouth dry, crossed to the door. She locked it, pulled the dead bolt, and then stared through the narrow window toward the thin, shivering forest.

The group broke up one house at a time. They trailed through the town, dropping Connor off at his home, then Riya at hers, and finally passing by Rhys's house.

"Let me walk you home," he'd said, but Abby just gave him a tight-lipped smile.

"Stick to the rules," she'd said, and after a second he'd reluctantly nodded.

Abby had Hope at her side. Which meant they would be safer as a pair than as a lone soul wandering through the dark streets. Their house needed to be the last stop.

He'd still stood in his doorway, watching as they left.

The night had stretched out longer than Abby had planned. It was after ten by the time their house came into view, faintly illuminated by one of the few surviving streetlamps.

They'd been silent through most of the walk. It wasn't a rule, but more like common sense. It was easier to sense if someone was following you if you kept your mouth closed and your ears open. But, as they entered their yard, Hope seemed to feel it was finally safe to speak again. She swung her lantern and skipped lightly as they approached the front step. "So. Rhys seems awfully fond of you."

She was in a teasing mood, which meant nothing Abby could say would dissuade her. She still tried, though, as she slotted her key into the front door. "I'd hope so. He wouldn't be much of a friend if he hated me."

"Abs, if *my* friends looked at me the way he looks at you—"

Hope's voice trailed off as the door opened. Inside their home was almost perfectly dark. They still carried the two lanterns Rhys had given them, but the flickering flames didn't reach far past the entryway.

In the distance, Abby heard a slow *scrape, scrape, thump*.

Her mouth turned dry. She reached out, her fingertips grazing the old wallpaper as she searched for the light switch.

A slow, muttered word echoed through the cold house. It didn't sound like any language Abby knew. The noise repeated. *Scrape, scrape, thump,* reverberating through the old rooms.

Her hand found the plastic switch and turned it. The hallway light fizzed as it came on. One out of the three bulbs flickered and then, with a sharp high-pitched pop, burst.

Bad, bad, bad.

The voice came again, low and muttering and furious.

To their left was the archway into the kitchen and dining room. To their right, the living room. Straight ahead the hallway cut through the house and led to the back door. The stairwell ran along its left wall, its shadows growing heavy near the second floor.

A ghostly white figure stood at the top of the stairs, facing the wall. Long emaciated arms clawed at the wallpaper. Shreds of it came free under the scrabbling, chipped fingernails. The figure raised one fist and beat it into the plaster.

Scrape, scrape, thump.

Abby ran her tongue across her lips as she stared up at her mother. Hope hunched close at her side, the bubbly girl from outside vanishing into a quiet, withdrawn shell of her normal self.

Normally she'd tell Hope to wait in her room, but their mother was blocking the stairs. Abby kept her voice lighter and calmer than she felt as she said, "I'm going to talk to Momma. Why don't you watch some TV? You can have the volume nice and loud. I'll tell you when it's time for bed."

"Okay." It came out as a whisper. Hope sent her a nervous glance and then slipped away, through the open doorway into the living room.

Abby took a step toward the stairs. On the higher landing, her mother swayed. The old, discolored nightgown grazed her bare feet. Her hair hung in knots down her back. She raised her arms again, and her hands contracted into claws as she scraped at the wall.

There was a click from the living room. The TV came on. Static played, loud and unstable, with bursts of overlapping voices. It wasn't working right. It wouldn't; not now that technology was getting the jitters.

"Momma?" Abby whispered as she reached the base of the stairs.

Scrape, scrape, thump.

Above, the lights flickered. The strobing effect sliced across the old walls, showing jagged lines where the pale, graying wallpaper had started to form cracks and peel back.

Abby climbed a step. The crackling static from the TV was cut through by a laugh track, loud and unnaturally vicious. Her mother's lips were moving, too, and Abby thought she could hear an echo of that same laugh rattling out of her throat.

Scrape, scrape, thump.

Her fingernails were cracking and bleeding. Each time she raised her hands to scrape them across the wall, she left little lines of red on the exposed plaster. Abby's skin crawled.

She moved carefully as she climbed. As she drew nearer, she realized her mother was speaking. The words were mumbled and unintelligible, but Abby was certain it was the same phrase being repeated over and over again.

The light flickered, seeming to rattle in their holders. A sharp, hissing pop announced the second bulb's death. With just one bulb left, the hallway and stairwell were dropped into heavy gloom. Bars of harsh, artificial light from the TV cut across Abby's form.

"Momma, are you ready for bed?" She kept climbing, even though her knees were going weak and no air seemed able to reach her lungs. She was nearly at the stair's top now. The faint tang of blood saturated the air.

Her mother's eyes were wide and unblinking as she stared at the walls. Her damaged fingers stabbed into the plaster again and raked down it, sending small flecks of dust trailing toward the floor. As she clawed, she continued muttering, and Abby finally began to make sense of the words.

"Somewhere…somewhere he can't find you…hide you somewhere…"

The phrase from the wall in town. The paint had been there for as long as Abby could remember; her mother must have seen it every time she walked to get groceries, back before things turned bad. And it had become embedded in her. She repeated it over and over, the words slurring into one another.

"Somewhere…can't find you…"

"Momma."

The laugh track coming from the TV seemed to grow louder, fiercer. It wasn't fading out. Through the static, the cackling laughs echoed longer than any human's lungs could sustain them.

The final lightbulb burst. Abby and her mother were plunged into heavy shadows, lit only by the flickering, prismatic light from the downstairs TV.

"Can't find you…you…you…"

Abby reached out. Her shaking fingers were distorted by the artificial light coming from below. That same light played over her mother's face. She was turning in slow, stuttering movements, her hair quivering around her pale, stretched face.

Her unblinking eyes were fever bright as they landed on Abby.

"Can't find you…" she whispered, and then lurched forward.

Her damaged fingers hit Abby's shoulder. Abby skidded backward. The heel of her left shoe slipped over the edge of the stairs. She pictured herself tipping over, being swallowed down the long passage down, the sharp wooden steps biting into her skin. Terror ran through her and it tasted like steel and bitters.

She grasped for her mother. Her fingers bunched in the nightdress. But instead of anchoring her, her mother leaned forward, into the momentum, and they both tipped over the edge.

Abby gasped, then clamped her mouth closed. There was movement everywhere: a flurry of limbs, of tangled hair, of her mother's hot breath on her skin as teeth grazed her flesh. Pain shot through her shoulders and back as they fell.

Then the movement stopped. The flickering, unnatural lights from the television bathed them. They'd become wedged halfway down the stairs. One of Abby's hands gripped the railing. The other palm pressed flat into the wall.

Her mother's body crushed into her, leaning on her, and Abby felt her breath catch as she slid an inch.

She could feel the texture of the wallpaper under her hands: the same wallpaper her mother had torn through. Felt sweat bead on her palm.

Her mother lifted her head. Heavy eyes, just inches from Abby's own, stared into her.

"He's coming," she whispered, and her voice sounded like the rattle of dry insect wings. "He's coming. We need to hide you where he can't find you."

And suddenly, the pressure vanished. Her mother crept under Abby's outstretched arm and descended the stairs in slow, lithe motions.

Abby sagged, her breathing ragged. A slow ache radiated through her shoulders and back where she'd hit the wall. Her muscles burned from how tightly she'd been holding them. And there was a low stinging pain across her upper chest. Abby touched her fingers there, just above her clavicle. The fingers came away tinged with blood. Where her mother had bitten her.

Sarah Ward staggered as she reached the ground floor. She hunched as she disappeared along the hallway.

Abby coaxed her shaking legs to carry her down too. She stopped in the hallway. The television's volume was muted now, the awful laugh track no longer ringing through the house. Hope stood in the archway. The television played behind her, its harsh light framing her and making it hard to see her features. All Abby could make out were her wide, frightened eyes.

"Did she hurt you?"

Even her voice sounded tiny.

Abby tried to smile. She hoped the smear of blood wouldn't be obvious under the harsh light. "No. We slipped. That's all."

The door at the end of the hallway closed, and Abby felt her heart squeeze. She tried not to let it show on her face.

"I'm going to stay up for a bit more," she said. "But you get some sleep, okay? I'll see you tomorrow."

"Okay."

Hope climbed the stairs quickly. She only paused when she neared the stretch of wall that had its paper torn away. She stared at the bloody streaks for a second, then darted past them and into her room.

Abby breathed deeply and slowly, and then followed the hallway to their back door.

Her mother was outside, crouched in the soft ground as she dug at one of the holes she'd been widening. Abby pulled her cardigan tightly around herself as she sat at the edge of the back porch.

Things were bad. It wasn't safe for her mother to be outside after dark. But she wouldn't come in willingly either. Not when she was like this.

Her mother sucked in deep, huffing breaths as she dug. Her back rocked, the muscles straining as she clawed fistful after fistful out of the ground. As though, if she could only make a hole big enough and deep enough, she could save herself.

People were almost always alone when they were taken. Abby hunched over to protect against the cold but kept her eyes wide open, scanning the dense, moon-drenched plants and the indistinct shapes that shifted beyond their high fences.

She'd stay there until her mother returned to the house...or until dawn ghosted over the horizon.

Whatever it took.

PART TWO

THE

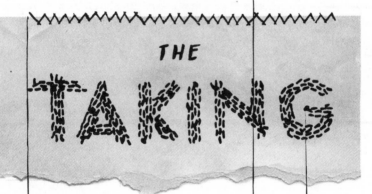

TAKING

TWELVE

〜〜〜〜

"HEY," CONNOR YELLED UP THE STAIRS, HIS BACKPACK HELD IN one hand. "Hey, which of you shrimps took my workbook?"

Footsteps thundered overhead. There was a sound that might have been someone launching themselves at a wall.

Seven siblings was too many. Way, way too many.

Doors slammed. Someone screamed at a perceived injustice. The washing machine churned through what was probably the third load of the day.

"Workbook!" Connor yelled to be heard over the chaos. "If it's not in my hand in thirty seconds, I'm going to start strangling my loved ones!"

Cackling laughter came from some distant corner of the house.

Sometimes he wondered what it would be like to be an only child, like Riya, or to just have one sibling, like Abby. To live in a house that was always quiet, where people took turns to speak at the dinner table and you didn't have to yell to make yourself heard. He thought he'd probably hate it.

"There you are." His mother swept down the hallway, a washing basket full of towels under one arm, and grappled him into a side hug. He endured both that and a forceful kiss on his forehead, which she had to strain to reach. "Dinner's in twenty. And you have to be more careful. You left the door unlocked."

"I *didn't* though," Connor protested.

"Everyone else was upstairs. I know it was you."

"I didn't!"

His mother was already moving away, the washing in the basket bouncing with every step, and he wasn't sure she even heard him under the earsplitting scream from upstairs.

Life in his house was chaotic, but they had a few concrete rules that no one—not even the youngest—dared break. Their house had four doors leading outside, and all of them had to stay locked at all times.

They each had a key ring, each with their own key, and unlocking and relocking doors every time they stepped out was so common that it had become second nature.

No one in their house could agree on what the Stitcher was or where it came from. But they could all agree on one thing: none of them wanted to let it into the house.

A cold gust of air touched the back of Connor's neck like a ghostly finger grazing his skin. He crossed to the hallway and looked down its length.

The front door stood wide open. Outside light and air flowed in, and they formed swirling dust motes in the hallway. Connor stared at it, incredulous. "If you see it's open, at least take a second to close it!"

Footsteps thundered overhead. "Take it easy up there!" his mother yelled from the laundry room, and once again he doubted she'd even heard him.

"Ridiculous," Connor muttered, crossing to the door. They were all careful with it, but his mother was the most paranoid. He couldn't believe she'd seen the door was open and had not done anything about it.

No.

His hand was still outstretched toward the handle. Cold air raised gooseflesh across his arms. Their house was crammed full of people, but suddenly felt very empty.

She wouldn't.

The first thing she'd have done was lock the door. No question about it. And yet, it was open again.

Against his better judgment, Connor stepped through it.

Branches scraped together as a warm evening breeze moved through them. They sounded almost like fingernails against the house's cladding.

Connor's house was set back from the road, with a chaotic mess of overgrown plants and tilting trees crammed in around the curved driveway, blocking his view of the main road. If you wanted to be charitable, you'd say it was secluded. Uncharitably, it was isolated. The sun hadn't quite set, but it was close, with the clouds diffusing streaks of reds and purples across the blue sky. People always said sunsets were beautiful. To Connor, it looked more like a massive bruise swelling out across the horizon.

I know I locked the door. He slowly turned to see the keyhole. *Mom would have locked it when she saw it too. So that means...*

There was no sign of damage around the keyhole. But then his gaze drifted higher.

The door was painted a teal blue, matching at least a few of the shutters. But now a dozen long lines scored through the color, showing the natural wood beneath.

Like someone dragging a knife across the door.

A knife, or broken fingernails.

Connor, half in shock, reached up to touch the space where the lines began. They started nearly at the door's top. Higher than an animal could reach.

There was a soft rush of sound behind him. Connor swung, his back to the door. The yard was empty.

It could have been the wind in the trees. Or a distant car. But it had sounded almost exactly like someone releasing a held breath.

There was a tree near their house that was so old and massive that its lowest branches had drooped to rest on the ground. It left one half of their house in perpetual shade, but the younger kids loved playing in it.

The space around its huge, gnarled trunk was in deep shadow as the last of the light faded. Connor squinted. He thought he could see something there. A dark shape between the leaves. Something tall. Something with limbs that branched out from its sides, almost as long and as heavy as the tree's own branches.

Something staring directly at him.

A hand pressed into the small of his back.

Connor would have screamed if he'd had the breath. He swung, his heart in his throat, and saw Brynn, dark haired and dark eyed, standing in the doorway.

"I'm here to tattle," she said with gravity that only a six-year-old could muster, and held out Connor's missing workbook. "It was Miles. You should punish him."

"Oh," he managed, and took the book. When he turned back to the tree, he could no longer see the dark patch. Or hear the breathing.

He pushed Brynn back into the house ahead of himself, then slammed the door. This time, he didn't just lock it, but pulled the dead bolt as well.

<hr />

Jen stood by the window of her half-unpacked room. It was growing dark. She could barely see the police tape fluttering in the breeze.

Men and women, all wearing replicas of her father's uniform, moved in and out of the trees. They'd been there for hours. They still looked like they were far from being done.

She'd mentioned the thread to her father. Not because she *believed* their story, but…simply to prove them wrong. She hadn't told her father about the supposed implications, only that she'd stumbled on a whole pile of red thread in the trees behind their house and suspected someone lost their craft project back there.

He must have told someone at the station.

And now those woods were crawling with officers.

Huge lights had been rigged up. Half hidden behind the trees, they looked like distant spotlights, focused on a stage she couldn't see. She *could* see the officers, though. They traveled in pairs or sometimes in groups of three, their movements sharp and tense.

She'd already seen three body bags carried out, and they still weren't done.

Be careful tonight.

Riya stared at the message on her phone. It was from Connor and had been sent to the Jackrabbit group chat nearly three hours earlier. Riya's phone just hadn't been working to pick it up at the time. The screen kept blinking out before shuddering back, as though she'd dunked it into a bowl of water and it was fighting desperately to stay alive.

She typed back: Got it. There was a fifty-fifty chance the message would actually make it out. Then she slipped her phone back into her bag and set her shoulders back as she took deep, unsteady breaths.

It was just after nine at night, and she was far from home.

Ahead of her was the counter, till, and baskets for various condiments. Beyond those was the dining area. Plastic chair backs and polyester seat covers shone in the fluorescent lights. The black-and-white tile floor was too old to gleam, but at least it didn't look dirty.

Bobby's Pizzeria wasn't a glamorous place to work. But it was a job, and those were hard to come by in Doubtful, and Riya knew she was lucky to get it. A job meant she'd have something to put on her résumé when she left Doubtful. Something to show the world she knew how to work, and was prepared to work hard.

She rounded the counter and began turning out the lights, using the massive switches near the staff area. She started with the prep and storage before rolling forward to darken the dining area until the only lights left were the ones over the serving counter.

If anyone named Bobby had actually owned Bobby's Pizzeria, he'd left well before Riya's time. The current owner was Hirsh, who was good as far as managers went. He paid her on time, ordered restocks on time, and mostly left the pizzeria to run itself.

The only downside was that Riya was often left to close on her own. Especially on quiet nights, like that night. Her coworker had left more than an hour before, and Riya had bounced around the empty space like she was in a pinball machine, scrubbing at old stains on the chairs and wiping dust from the plastic curtains.

They stayed open late for the occasional desperate family who had forgotten to plan dinner or had unexpected guests, but those were few and far between. Most customers ordered their food well before sundown. By the time the massive glass windows overlooking the parking lot turned into walls of darkness, Riya could guarantee the store would stay virtually deserted until the end of her shift.

She didn't mind that busy dinner rush. Her muscles were strong from lacrosse, and she could zip through the prep area and ferry pizzas back to customers faster than anyone else.

It was the part that came afterward that she dreaded. Watching the life fade out of the pizzeria, saying goodbye to her coworkers as they hung their aprons up, and then standing alone, with the store surrounded by darkness on all sides, like a little island of light in an ocean of emptiness.

Riya tied up the final two garbage bags from the kitchen and hefted them as she walked to the rear door. The old metal press handle squeaked as she pushed on it, and she shoved it open with her shoulder as she slipped out.

The dumpster was only ten steps from the rear door, but there were no lights in the alley. Heavy cloud cover was blocking any moonlight, and the darkness seemed to crawl over Riya's skin like cockroaches looking for a place to hide.

She left the kitchen door hanging open so that its glow would seep outside, then jogged to the dumpster and hauled its lid up. She was used to the smell but still held her breath as she swung the bags inside.

A strange rattling noise came from deeper down the alleyway.

Riya hesitated, the lid still held up with one hand. The light coming from the open doorway didn't extend far. Everything from the dumpster's end onward was unreadable.

But were those…eyes?

Cold, unblinking eyes, watching her from the dark?

A deafening bang echoed through the alley. Riya choked on a scream as the light was blotted out.

The kitchen door had slammed closed.

Riya ran for it, her heart in her throat. The door groaned as she wrenched it open and staggered back into the light. She shut it behind herself and turned the lock, blocking out the dark alley and whatever might have been watching her from it.

Breathe in. Breathe out. Breathe in. And then turn.

Wild animals were common in Doubtful. She might have seen one of the raccoons that fought over any scraps that didn't make it into the dumpster. It had seemed too tall for that, and its eyes too wide-set, but... It had been dark. The things she'd thought were glinting eyes could have been anything.

Hirsh trusted her to close because she was responsible. Sometimes Riya wished she had it in her heart to be a *little* bit flaky, just so that she wouldn't be put on closing shift as often.

At least she had one thing to look forward to: her parents would be there at her shift's end to pick her up. They never deviated from this routine. They didn't even want her working at night; picking her up and driving her home was the compromise that had made them relent. A compromise that Riya was very, very glad for.

She checked the wall clock. Five minutes to go.

In the distance, one of the parking lot lights blinked rhythmically, like a lighthouse out at sea. Other businesses shared the parking lot, but there was no life left inside them. They'd all been closed for hours already, their empty windows nothing but dark mirrors.

Riya was very much alone.

She took up one of the cloths and began wiping the serving counter, just to give her hands something to do. As she worked, she kept one eye on the clock, counting down the seconds.

Metal creaked behind her.

Riya turned to stare into the kitchen. A thousand metal surfaces, dulled by age and fire, glittered in the shadows. Slowly, Riya backed toward the light switches. She felt for the stiff plastic levers and pushed on the one belonging to the kitchen.

It clicked as it moved, but the lights stayed dead.

Connor's cryptic message bounced through her mind. *Be careful tonight.* Behind, the blinking streetlight seemed to flash faster, like a siren, or like a warning, or like the thundering of her own heart.

The metallic creak came again. It was the door to the storage room. A door she knew for certain she'd closed, but now hung wide open.

Riya swallowed thickly as she turned every other switch, trying to get any of the lights back on. As she turned the lever for the storage room's lights, the only remaining bulbs overhead fizzed and then burst out.

No. No. No...

She was alone in the dark, a wet cloth clasped in one hand.

Riya's eyes darted toward the prep area, where rows of knives were waiting for the morning staff to arrive. She began edging toward them, her hand outstretched. The darkness was heavy. Oppressive. Enough to swallow her whole.

One of the dining room chairs scraped. Riya swiveled. The tables, which she'd straightened perfectly to burn time, looked almost exactly the same as when she'd last passed them. Almost. A chair had been pulled out from the nearest table, as though it was inviting her to sit.

Or...as though to warn her that she had a guest.

A gasp choked in Riya's throat as harsh, blinding lights doused her. She raised one arm to cover her face. The lights weren't coming from above, but from ahead, through the massive glass windows overlooking the parking lot.

Her mother's car was there, facing the store. She'd turned her high beams on.

Riya didn't hesitate. She threw the cloth toward the sink. It missed, but she didn't go back for it. Instead, she snatched up her satchel and burst out of the door without even bothering to lock it behind herself.

As she slid into the car, she hoped her mother wouldn't see how badly she was shaking. Mrs. Bhatt wasn't looking at Riya, however. She stared straight ahead, toward the store, where her headlights saturated the old furniture and the serving counter in sharp, polarizing light.

"Who was that in there with you?" her mother asked.

Riya, who was pulling her seat belt down toward the buckle, went still. "What?"

"There was someone behind you." Her mother turned toward her, and her pupils seemed tiny in her wide eyes. "It's why I put my lights on. Because someone was behind you, and they were walking closer, and I couldn't see who it was."

They both stared into Bobby's Pizzeria.

The dining room was empty.

"Do you want to see something bad?"

Jessica's voice came hot and trembling. She took Abby's hand as she pulled her toward the stairs.

"It's a secret. Not even my parents know about this yet."

Abby jolted upright, her breathing raw and painful. Bedsheets tangled around her body. She felt dizzy and disoriented, as though she'd plunged underwater and couldn't find the surface.

Slowly, her room came into view, lit only by the cloud-dampened moonlight coming through her window.

It was the second time she'd had that dream in the last week. Not a good sign.

Abby reached for her bedside clock. Even with her eyes adjusted to the dark, it was still hard to see. She squinted at its dial as the second, minute, and hour hands shifted around.

They were moving wrong, all three of them lurching around like insects startled by a sudden light. The hour hand was moving backward in short, sharp jolts.

First, complex technology fails. The cars and smartphones and computers. Then the less complicated machines; streetlights, radios. The simple machines, though…the clocks, the doorbells, the house lights… When they go, it's as bad as it can get.

She hadn't seen her clock malfunction in years. Not since the night her father vanished.

Fear stuck in her throat as she slipped her feet out of bed. The floorboards were a cool balm on hot and prickly skin. She reached for her phone and tapped the power button. She hadn't expected a response and she didn't get one. Instead, she reached into the top drawer of her bedside table and took out the flashlight she kept there.

Flashlights would malfunction too. But they were still more reliable than house lights that relied on wiring and circuit breakers.

Abby nudged her door open and silently moved into the hallway. She'd gone through a lot of bad nights in her house; nights where her mother would howl for hours, nights when storms cut the power and battered the walls so hard that she was afraid the house was about to collapse.

Nothing came close to this night.

The air felt *bad*. Aching. Rotting. As though the whole concept of reality had turned sickly, bulging and bloated with decomposition. She felt it in her lungs, in her bones, in her flesh.

Her house seemed to groan around her as she crept along the hallway. The space near her mother's door was the darkest, and Abby tried turning her flashlight on as she neared it. The bulb flickered, then faded back to darkness. She kept it clenched in her trembling left hand as she tried the handle.

The door's hinges groaned as she pushed it open. Her mother's bed was a mess, even though Abby had changed the sheets earlier that day. It was empty.

The flashlight stuttered, the beam gaining strength again. In the same heartbeat, Abby thought she heard a slow, rattling draw of breath.

She turned, swinging the flashlight in the same motion.

Her mother was crouched on top of her wardrobe. The space between its dusty top and the ceiling was barely two feet high; her mother had hunched, her knees beside her head and her long, bony fingers grasping the edge of the wood as she stared down at Abby. Her face was a mask of pure, ferocious terror.

Even as she fixed the light on her mother, the flashlight faded again.

Abby, her breath held, crept backward and silently closed the bedroom door. Her heart ran painfully fast. But at least her mother was still in her room. At least she didn't have to worry about *that*.

She retraced the hallway to the door with flower decals on its surface. She didn't want to disturb her sister's sleep, so she turned the doorknob carefully and grimaced as it whined. The door crept open an inch at a time, revealing Hope's multicolored room. The computer desk and its equipment, completely dead. The strings of fairy lights on the walls, pinned at careful angles. The quilt, thrown back from the bed.

Abby's heart, which had been running fast, froze.

The bed was empty. One pillow lay askew on the floor.

The window—the window that Hope liked to keep an inch ajar, to feel the night breeze—had been wrenched wide open. The screen was torn into shreds.

Hope was gone.

THIRTEEN

〤〤〤〤

ABBY STOOD IN THE DOORWAY. HER MOUTH WAS OPEN, BUT she'd lost the ability to breathe.

"Hope," she whispered. It came out as a gasp, barely audible.

The empty bed and its scattered sheets filled her vision.

There was a mistake. A misunderstanding. Hope was still here, somewhere. She could be hiding under her bed, terrified but unharmed. Or downstairs, oblivious as she got a glass of water. There had to be a simple explanation.

Abby's eyes were dragged toward the scraps of torn screen that fluttered in the wind.

"Hope." Her voice had strengthened, but barely. Scarcely more than a choked moan. The house maintained its deathly hush.

This was wrong. The Stitcher took people. But not *her sister*.

They were so careful.

They had the rules.

They were so careful.

"Hope——!" This time it was the start of a wail, broken and jagged and raw. Abby crossed the room in three long steps. She bent as she moved and craned to see under the bed. There was nothing there but some discarded clothes and dust. She reached the open window and felt the cooling night air graze her raw skin.

Their overgrown backyard and the partially completed holes were a tangled maze of shadow and moonlight. It was a long drop to the ground below.

What was that?

A branch swayed near the back of the yard, almost as though something had nudged it on its way past. Abby leaned forward, breathless. Her hand gripped the sill. The surface was damp, almost slimy. She took her hand away and saw smears of glistening blood.

Drops of it trailed over the sill and down the wall toward the bed. It was fresh. It shouldn't have been possible, but the patch she'd touched had felt *warm*.

Hope was here just seconds ago. Something woke me, and it wasn't the nightmare.

I heard her being taken.

Abby's pulse was a ferocious, dangerous thing, rushing through her in a torrent as she fled the room. The floor vanished under her feet. She took the stairs three at a time, nearly twisting her ankles as she skidded into the hallway. And then she burst out through the back door, onto the dark porch, and screamed.

"*Hope!*"

Her voice bounced back at her from a dozen directions.

Rocks and fallen branches stabbed into her bare feet but didn't slow her as she shoved her way between the overgrown trees, aiming for the place where she'd caught a trace of movement. She hit the back fence, the rough wood scraping over her outstretched palm.

She still held the flashlight in her other hand. She tried pressing its power button again and again, but it wouldn't respond. She turned, helplessly searching the billowing foliage surrounding her.

"Hope! Answer me!"

Heavy branches swayed in the wind. Moonlight dappled across the ground, a kaleidoscope of motion. Not even the nocturnal insects dared make noise.

She couldn't think. Couldn't breathe. Hope wasn't in the garden any longer, and Abby was gripped by a desperation both wild and terrifying in its intensity. Her legs moved, devouring the ground under her. She'd reached the asphalt roads before she even knew where she was going. And she kept running.

Hope had to be nearby, somewhere in these cold and empty streets. She was *here*, if Abby could just find her.

She screamed her sister's name until her vocal cords began to burn. And she didn't stop screaming. Not when her voice began to distort, not when she began to suffocate from lack of air, not when her own ears began to ring from how hard she was running.

House lights burst on around her like fireflies rising through the night. Abby caught glimpses of forms moving behind curtains in a dark pantomime.

No one left their homes. No one tried to help her.

They knew better than to be outside after dark.

Dead streetlights arched overhead like giant, spindly fingers curled over the road. Her eyes blurred with tears. She called Hope's name again and again, her voice cracking, but the word began to vanish into increasingly frantic screams.

She was losing time and she didn't know where she was going. The town stretched out in every direction, seemingly endless. A thousand places to hide.

Stop. Think!

Her mind was a crackling inferno of fear and misery. She clenched her hands to either side of her head, her teeth gritted, as she slowed to a halt.

You don't have much time. Focus!

A thousand scattered thoughts collided.

Hope had been bleeding. Hot red blood on the windowsill, hot red blood on Abby's palm. If she could find the trail, she could follow it…

It was impossible to see in the dark. Abby hadn't even noticed the blood in the bedroom until she'd touched it. And the flashlight refused to work.

A whine escaped her throat. There was still time. There *had* to be. But it was running like sand between her fingers, and the more frantic she became the faster it escaped.

And then, a sound. Footsteps, pounding over the asphalt. Growing nearer. She swung and saw a figure rise out of the gloom.

Rhys. This was his street. He'd heard her. And, unlike the faceless figures lurking behind drawn curtains, he'd come to find her.

"What happened?" His face was pale, his clothes rumpled. He slowed as he neared, one hand reached toward her, the baseball bat he kept beside his front door clutched in the other.

"Hope," was all she could manage before a scream tried to strangle her. Abby buckled over, hands gripping her knees as she tried to control the emotions that were wrecking her. She drew in a jagged breath. "Hope's gone."

Rhys looked as though he'd been slapped. He turned away, one hand pressed to his mouth.

Think. Focus. There's still time, the desperate voice in Abby's mind pleaded. *There has to be. There's still time—*

As long as I know where to go.

"Vickers," she said.

Rhys's dark eyes flashed toward her. Moonlight splashed over the sharp planes of his face and the crease furrowing between his brows.

"Vickers." The words came out cracked and unsteady on her dry throat, but full of conviction. "We need to go to Charles Vickers's house."

They ran the route to Stokes Lane.

Abby was still in her nightdress, only now it was covered by Rhys's jacket. Rhys brought nothing else except the baseball bat. He typed a brief message into his phone's group chat while they ran. There was no guarantee the message would make it through with technology this unreliable. Or that Connor or Riya would wake to the chiming notification, even if it did. But it felt like something they still needed to do. It was a Jackrabbit rule: *tell someone where you're going.*

If they never came back, at least their friends would know why.

They didn't stop moving until they reached the head of Stokes Lane, then Abby slowed, breathing heavily.

Ahead of her, a thousand strange items shimmered in the moonlight, all lashed to the fences and posts with lines of red thread.

At the end of the street was Charles Vickers's house. Two stories tall and impeccably maintained, it was like a physical manifestation of its master: so plain that it would have been easily overlooked, except for a cluster of small, bad signs. Bars fixed across all of the windows. A padlock sealing the garage door.

Upstairs, a light shimmered in one of the curtained, metal-clad windows.

Abby forced her legs to carry her forward. On either side, the offerings shuddered as a breeze ran through them.

Dolls, their heads rotting and splitting at the seams. Baskets full of broken jars and fruit that had decayed into a thin layer of grime years before. Ribbons, wood carvings, and even fine jewelry that no one was brave enough to take back were slowly tarnishing.

On one fence, tied so low to the ground that Abby could only imagine a young child leaving it, was a plastic bucket and matching shovel used for building castles in the sand. The bucket was half full of rainwater and teeming with mosquito larvae.

The fences along that road were macabre. Rust ran from old nails hammered into the wood. Paint flaked painfully from surfaces that must have once been bright colors. Metal clattered against metal like a dozen nightmarish wind chimes whispering in unison.

Her hands shook. Her breathing was shallow. The houses around them were nothing but abandoned shells except for Vickers's, and the isolation felt like frost creeping into her flesh.

Ahead, an old driveway, run through with paper-thin cracks, led up to the house's front porch.

"Abby." Rhys glanced at her, and he seemed to communicate worlds within that one look. "I won't be leaving your side tonight."

Her heart was in her throat. He dipped his head toward her, his eyes intense as they searched hers.

"Whatever you're planning to do, I'll be with you. But I need to know. How far do you want to take this?"

She understood what he was asking. People who challenged the Stitcher very often never returned. Like Abby's own father. If they tried to get Hope back, the most likely outcome was that all of their lives would be cut short in horrifying ways.

How far do you want to take this?

She knew the answer. It was in the marrow of her bones, in the air she inhaled, flowing through her veins with every beat of her heart. "As far as it's possible to go."

No matter the cost.

He nodded once, a silent acceptance, and faced forward again. Abby took a shallow breath.

Four steps separated her from the porch. The wood had been

recently painted, but it creaked under her weight. Rot lurked beneath a pretty veneer.

She tried to swallow around the lump in her throat. Every window—even the smallest ones—was covered with thick metal bars. But she believed Hope was somewhere inside this building. Which meant Abby needed to get in too.

Keeping their presence quiet wasn't going to help them. She was fairly sure Vickers not only knew they were there but was waiting for them. And she wasn't getting into the house unless he let her in.

She raised her arm and pounded a clammy fist into the door. Four loud beats. The fifth was interrupted. An unseen latch unlocked and the door swept open.

He was here.

"Hello and good evening, Abby Ward. Rhys Weekes."

Charles Vickers loomed into the entrance of his home. A damask dressing gown, the same rust red as his car, was knotted over white pajamas. Slippers, innocuous and tufted, covered his feet. He gave the impression of just having stepped out of bed.

Except he'd opened the door within four knocks.

Abby had been right. He'd been expecting them, likely waiting in the hallway for their approach. And he wanted them to know it.

His glasses glittered in the moon's pale light. When he smiled, his teeth matched their luster. He looked clean, his hair combed, but Abby was hyperaware of how easily the reddish shade of his gown would hide bloodstains. A distant smell—the same damp, cold stench Abby had begun to associate with Vickers—flowed out of the house.

"What can I help you with tonight?" Vickers asked, and his voice was full of that quiet smirk that sent ice through her blood.

He wanted to make small talk. As though everything was normal, as though this was just any night, as though he couldn't see the smear of blood on Abby's hand and the hatred in her eyes.

It didn't matter how velvety he made his words. He'd opened the door. And that was all she'd needed.

Abby lunged forward. Vickers moved with lightning speed to block her path. The door slammed into her shoulder, hard enough to leave bruises.

"Oh, you're feisty tonight, aren't you?" he whispered.

She refused to answer him. Instead, she leaned into the doorway, wedging it open, and filled her lungs with air.

"*Hope!*" Abby yelled. Her voice seemed impossibly loud as it bounced through Vickers's house, echoing through dark and hidden rooms. "Hope, if you can hear me, make a noise!"

"Enough of that," Vickers said. A strand of hair slid loose and draped over his forehead, but his smile didn't fade even an inch as he purred, "You'll wake the neighbors."

He pushed on the door. Abby's muscles strained, but Vickers was stronger. She slid back an inch. The doorway's opening narrowed.

No.

She knew, with awful certainty, that if she allowed him to close the door on her, she would never see her sister again.

A hand slammed into the wood at her side. Rhys, his teeth bared, shoved, forcing Vickers back.

"Go," he hissed to Abby, fire in his eyes. "I'll hold him here."

Abby's heart was in her throat, choking her. She darted through the opening. Vickers reached for her as she passed. His short fingers grazed the back of her nightdress, but she spun out of his reach.

She was in the Stitcher's home. A place no one was ever allowed to see.

A soft rug padded her footsteps as she staggered into the hallway. She hesitated just long enough to glance back at Rhys. He had Vickers cornered next to the door; the bat was held ahead of himself like a barrier to keep Vickers in place.

Sickly yellow light flowed from the hallway's bulb. It reflected off the sweat dotting Rhys's skin. Vickers's smirk had vanished. His face had turned flat and cold, all emotion drained out, his eyes like flint as they tracked Abby's progress into his home.

She didn't know how long Rhys could hold him.

But she didn't need much time. Just a minute or two. Long enough to find one person.

Hope. Where are you?

The house was nearly perfectly dark. Abby didn't know its layout. She moved blindly, rushing and breathless, her hands stretched ahead of herself as she searched for light switches.

Click. A light came on. A living room was ahead of her, two unused couches and one worn recliner facing a small box TV. She kept moving.

Past the living room was a kitchen. Abby pulled up short.

A cutting board was on the counter. Knives had been placed onto it, five of them, lined up with surgical precision.

Abby's blood felt like ice and fire as it rushed through her. Clammy and sick, she called, "*Hope!*"

Still no answer. Hope was either too scared to make noise, or *couldn't.*

There was a muffled cry from the hallway. A thud. The sound of shoes scraping over the floor.

Please, Rhys, please hold him. I need more time.

Abby flew through the house. Her eyes darted over every dim, small detail she could make out, searching for a familiar figure, possibly huddled or collapsed in a corner. Room after room was empty.

A thud came from the hallway, louder now. It sounded like a baseball bat being slammed into the wall.

Ahead, a set of stairs led to the second floor. A faint light shone from its top.

Abby took the steps two at a time, her lungs empty and her heart hammering. Portraits had been hung on the wall; she was so focused on the path ahead that she was halfway up the stairs before she realized the portraits were missing person posters, taken from around town and lovingly framed, each one suspended by a length of red thread.

The house seemed to press in on her, crushing her. She screamed her sister's name again as she reached the upper landing. Downstairs, voices overlapped in short, sharp exclamations. There was a crash of breaking glass.

Rhys needed help. But she couldn't stop her search for Hope. Not yet.

She slammed her hands into doors as she passed them, sparing just seconds to search each room before she moved on to the next. They were spare bedrooms, reading rooms, empty spaces that hadn't been touched in years.

A light glowed from beneath the final door. Abby slammed into it, forcing it open.

Red across the bed. Red across the floor. Red across the walls.

It was Charles Vickers's bedroom. He'd decorated it entirely in crimson. The exact same shade of red that he used to sew up his victims.

The bed was made tidily. The wardrobe doors hung open, revealing rows of sweater-vests and cardigans he loved.

Abby stepped inside, rotating slowly, her gaze darting from crimson wallpaper to crimson carpet.

Her sister wasn't there.

"Hope!" Her voice was hoarse. She felt lost, like a lifeboat cast out at sea, and it didn't matter how hard she rowed because she had no idea which direction to turn.

And then she heard it.

A heavy, angry bang, like a door slammed with enough force to fracture it. The sound set every one of her bones on edge.

She turned toward the doorway, her hands clenched so tightly that the tendons felt like they were about to snap. *Rhys?*

For a second, there was nothing but silence. Then a horrible, sick sound rose from the floor below. Not quite a cough, not quite a gasp, but thin and raspy and delighted.

Charles Vickers was laughing.

FOURTEEN

ᐯᐯᐯᐯᐯ

HER WORLD SEEMED TO FREEZE.

Hope wasn't here.

Rhys was alone, downstairs, with the Stitcher, and the Stitcher was laughing.

And both Rhys and Abby were now trapped in a house with bars over its windows and padlocks on its doors: as impossible to escape from as it was to get into.

Her mind turned blank, every piece of knowledge she'd collated about the Stitcher over the past years of her life vanishing into blinding terror. She fled the bedroom, racing back the length of the hallway to reach the stairs. To reach Rhys. If he was still alive.

There was a distant snapping noise. Every light Abby had turned on during her race through the house vanished in an instant. She put out her hand and touched nothing but inky darkness.

The flashlight was a heavy weight in her pocket. She pulled it free but then hesitated. Turning it on would put a spotlight on her, making her the brightest thing in the house.

But, without it, she was blind, in a building that was completely foreign. This was Vickers's lair. He knew every corner and every nook, and Abby needed every advantage she could get.

She tried the power button. This time, the bulb came on, but it was a weak, fading light, as though the batteries were near dead.

It was enough, though, to press down the hallway.

Eyes loomed out of the darkness. She clenched her teeth as she staggered away from the figure, but it was only a framed poster. A familiar face smiled out at her. Bryce Culling, ambitious entrepreneur. He'd been taken four years before. His remains hadn't been returned for nearly nine months; his reassembled skin had been found wrapped around a tree like a fleshy, rotting layer of bark.

The stairs were ahead. Her flashlight dimmed dangerously as she stepped onto them, and Abby put out her spare hand to hold the railing.

That small bit of contact made her skin crawl. This was the railing Vickers used every day. It was covered by his touch, saturated with the oils from his fingertips. Abby pressed her lips together as she raced down the steps.

She was nearly at the landing when a voice called out of the darkness: "Young Ward girl, what are you doing in my house?"

It took on a singsong cadence, infused with quiet glee, and Abby's insides turned to ice. She swung her fading light across the space below the stairs but couldn't see anything. Vickers's voice had sounded both clear and muffled at once, making it impossible to tell how near he might be.

And she couldn't hear any sounds from Rhys.

He promised to follow me as far as I chose to go. Her eyes burned and her throat ached as she crept onto the ground floor and put her back to the nearest wall. *I shouldn't have let him.*

"It's not nice to push your way into people's homes without asking," Vickers called. It sounded like it was coming from the other side of the wall she was pressed against. Abby skittered away from it, backing into the hall's opposite corner. "If you'd been a good girl and asked nicely, I might have let you look inside."

She was becoming disoriented, but she thought she could see the tan rug that she'd stopped on near the front door, where she'd last seen Rhys. Abby half ran toward it.

She passed the living room with its one used chair. Moonlight came through the windows, but the blue glow was sliced into narrow pieces by the window's vertical bars. Her heart was in her throat as she reached the front entrance.

"But you didn't ask, did you?" The singsong quality was devolving into something colder and angrier, full of grit and ice. "And now you need to face the consequences."

The entrance, the last place she'd seen Rhys and Vickers, was empty. A large mirror hung above a side table had been broken; enormous spiderweb cracks splintered out from its center. Shards of glass sparkled on the floor.

The door she'd come in through was locked. A padlock that was larger than her fist hung from a bracket just below the handle.

She turned slowly, fighting to see through the thinning light. Rhys was gone. But blood had sprayed across one of the white walls. Tears burned Abby's eyes, blurring her vision as she stared at the drops of red as they slowly trailed toward the floor.

"Are you ready, Abby Ward? Are you ready to face your consequences?"

He sounded close. Almost as though he was right behind her shoulder. She swung, light aimed ahead of herself, but all it highlighted was an empty stretch of hall.

If she stayed there, she'd be trapped: cornered between the blood spatter and a locked door. Abby ran.

Her dying light flashed across the round rug in the hall, the cold white walls, and, distantly, another row of framed missing posters. Smiling eyes and bared teeth shone from behind the glass screens.

She swung into the living room. Two large windows overlooked the street. Abby pressed in behind one of the unused chairs to reach the glass. Dark metal bars, old enough that traces of rust ran down them, painted dark lines over the view. She would be able to fit one arm between them, but nothing more.

This was a house designed to contain, and to contain perfectly.

She shone her flashlight through the window. Its glow didn't reach far. And there was no one to see it.

The street was deserted. And Vickers's house was on the outskirts of town. She could scream until her lungs broke and no one would even hear her.

A floorboard creaked in the hallway. Abby, her throat tight enough to choke her, darted away from the window.

The kitchen was ahead. Abby moved into it, her light reflecting off a myriad of cold tiles and chrome surfaces. There was no sign of Rhys.

Ahead was the cutting board. Five knives were still laid out on it, perfectly straight and evenly spaced. Abby's hand shook as she reached for one.

The knife's handle was cold and slightly dusty. It was heavy, too, the blade longer than her hand. She clutched it close to her chest.

She wanted to take the rest of the knives to keep them away from the Stitcher. Keep him from *cutting* anything or anyone with them. But she had no way to carry them all, and nowhere to hide them.

"Abby Ward," Vickers called. His voice floated out of the dark kitchen doorway like the whisper of a ghost. "Abby Ward, where do you think you're going?"

Her flashlight died.

She pressed her back against the fridge. Her mouth was open but she no longer had the strength to breathe.

Shhf, shhf, shhf. Muffled feet brushed over tile, growing nearer.

Fear tasted like acid across her tongue and fire in her nostrils.

She backed away, keeping her body low. There were curtains over the kitchen's windows. They let barely any light through. Only just enough to show the glint of Vickers's glasses as he advanced toward her.

What happens next? Her vision was full of images of red thread, stitched through the creases in her skin, binding her to herself in strange ways.

Would she get to see Hope again while it was happening?

Vickers passed ahead of the kitchen window. She couldn't see any of his details, just his outline. His head tilted as he stared down at the cutting board, transfixed by the gap the missing knife had left.

"Little thief," he whispered.

She fled, racing past him.

She expected him to grab at her. He didn't. Instead, he turned to watch her go, his expression unreadable in the heavy shadows. He was in no hurry. He knew she wasn't going to escape.

She turned as she reached the doorway. The dark pressed around her, drowning her. It was hard to think. She needed to find Rhys. Find Hope. Find a way out. She had no idea how to do any of that. All she could do was keep backing away, her eyes fixed on Vickers as his thick glasses shimmered in the cold light.

She passed through the sitting room and back into the hallway, where she stopped.

She couldn't keep running. This was a maze with no way out.

Abby looked down at the knife clutched in her hand.

Could she actually use it?

Kill the Stitcher? End it, once and for all?

Stronger people had already tried. Braver people. Her father, among others.

But she'd already lost so much; she could risk this bit more. Her life was forfeit, whether she fought back or not.

A heavy hand landed on her shoulder.

Abby felt her world freeze. She swung, knife angled upward.

A blood-streaked face stared down at her. Abby lurched back, pulling the knife away, and narrowly missed slicing it across Rhys's throat.

"You…" She couldn't breathe. Words strangled themselves on her tongue. "You…"

Rhys raised his hand and pressed a finger to his lips. His eyes were large and dark. Fresh blood, shockingly red, ran from his hairline and covered the left half of his face, framing his eye and dripping off his jaw.

But he was *alive*.

He glanced behind Abby, then took her hand and gently tugged. Together, they raced on silent feet through the dark house. Abby wanted to ask him what had happened. She needed to know how badly he was hurt. But she didn't dare speak. Not when the Stitcher was still stalking them.

Rhys stopped at a set of dark doors. He pulled on them, opening a wardrobe. Inside were coats hung from a bowed rail and two umbrellas pressed into the corner. Rhys gestured. He wanted her to get inside.

The thought of touching clothes that had been worn by Charles Vickers made her skin prickle. But they had very few options, and she knew Rhys was right. Hiding was their only real choice. At least until they could find a way out.

She crept into the wardrobe, hunching as the coats grazed the top of her head and shoulders.

As he stepped in after her, Abby saw thin moonlight glint off something in Rhys's hand. A shard of glass, taken from the broken hallway mirror. It had to be cutting into his palm, but he refused to let it go.

Together, they pulled the doors as nearly closed as they could manage. Only a narrow sliver of light showed the gap. They were surrounded by the smell of old coats and mildew. But it was as close to shelter as they could manage.

A game of hide-and-seek in a monster's house.

Rhys leaned toward her. She could feel the heat radiating from his body and could smell the metallic tang of blood. "I'm sorry," he whispered, so softly that she wouldn't have been able to hear him outside of the wardrobe. "I couldn't hold him."

"And I couldn't find Hope," she whispered back.

He drew a breath to answer, but then froze.

Footsteps shuffled along the hallway. They were slow and muffled, but assured. The sliver of light coming through the barely ajar doors was blotted out as a broad form moved across it.

Abby couldn't hear anything over her thundering pulse. Rhys had found her hand. He squeezed tightly, and she pressed back.

The silhouette came to a halt in front of the wardrobe. And it didn't move.

Does he know? Did we leave any trace? A smear of blood on the wood, maybe? Or did he notice the doors weren't perfectly closed?

She didn't dare breathe. It was impossible to see any details, but she was certain that the dark figure outside the door was leaning closer. Looming toward them. The figure seemed enormous as it blocked out the light. Every inch of her body ached with the effort it took to hold still.

Then the form moved away again. The sliver of light reappeared gradually as the Stitcher retreated.

There was a distant, wailing sound, Abby realized. And it was growing closer. Louder. It was accompanied by the screech of tires turning into Stokes Lane.

And as the wails rose and fell in a modulated stream, she abruptly recognized them.

Sirens.

Abby looked up toward Rhys, even though neither of them could see the other. The sirens could only mean one thing.

Riya and Connor had gotten their text message. And they'd sent the police.

Tires screeched again. Car doors slammed. Just seconds later, fists beat against Vickers's front door, accompanied by muffled voices.

There's no chance he'll answer them. Not while we're in here.

But he did. Even huddled in the wardrobe, she heard the unmistakable click of the padlock being unfastened and the door opening. Footsteps moved into the house, spreading out.

Then the narrow line of light was blocked again, and the wardrobe's doors were wrenched open.

Three blinding flashlights shone down at them.

The knife was taken from Abby and the shard of glass from Rhys. Then they were pulled out of Vickers's house, an officer gripping their shoulders. It felt less like a rescue and more like a rebuke.

"He has my sister," Abby said.

Figures moved around her. There were no less than six officers crowding through the hallway and spilling out into the front lawn. No one slowed down or reacted to her words.

She tried again. "My sister. Hope. She was taken. He's got her, somewhere—please, you have to help me find her—"

"Out," the officer guiding her said, shoving her through the open front door.

Police cars filled the empty cul-de-sac, parked at odd angles on dead lawns. Their lights flooded a red and blue halo across the environment. It was eerily similar to the scene on Breaker Street, just days before.

"Riya Bhatt must have called you," Abby said. "Or Connor Crandall—"

"Mr. Vickers called us," an older female officer said. Her tone was clipped, her voice harsh. "He reported a break-in at his house. Wait here, both of you."

The officer guiding them pulled them to a halt in the center of Vickers's front lawn. Most of the other officers returned to the house. Abby had a distant glimpse of Vickers through his open door: the rust red dressing gown, the sleekly combed hair, the curling smile as he spoke to the officers.

He'd called the police. Why? He'd had them trapped.

Why let them go again?

Abby's throat ached. She was on the edge of tears. She looked up at Rhys, but his face was stony, his eyes downcast.

The older female officer returned. Abby knew her from around town. Officer Hewitt, she thought her name was. Gray streaks shot through tied-back hair. She was wiry, her face was full of deep creases, and any friendliness that might have lingered in her eyes was blanketed over by cold anger.

"You're lucky," she said, addressing them both. "Mr. Vickers doesn't intend to press charges. That's a mercy considering some of the damage you caused to his house."

Abby was racked with shivers. She couldn't tell whether they were from lingering fear or building frustration. "Hope's missing. You *know* he has her. Please—"

There was a flicker of something softer in the officer's eyes. Regret? Sadness? "If a relative has gone missing, you can attend the station to make a formal report."

A formal report. That's how all of the others were lost. A formal report, a paper-thin investigation, and a stack of missing person posters to tape across town.

"Whatever you thought you were doing, it was monumentally stupid." Hewitt took a shuddering breath. "I expected better. Especially from you, Rhys."

She spoke to him like she knew him well. He still wouldn't meet her eyes. Understanding clicked: this was one of the officers who had interviewed him repeatedly when his own family was taken.

Hewitt was going to help Abby just as much as she'd helped Rhys. Not at all.

A figure moved past. He wore the same uniform as the others, but she didn't recognize his face. Which meant one thing.

"You're Jen's father." Abby grasped for him, clutching at his sleeve. His eyes widened behind his glasses. He tried to shift back, but she refused to let go. "You have to help me. My sister, Hope, was taken by the Stitcher. Jen will tell you about—"

"Enough," Hewitt said.

"You *have to help*—"

"Enough." Hewitt pulled Abby back with enough force to break her hold on Thompson's sleeve. His face was a blank screen. He gave a brief nod of acknowledgment to Hewitt, then stepped past them, disappearing into the throng of other officers.

Hewitt was breathing hard. She crossed her arms, her features unforgiving.

"You're getting off light tonight," she said. "Considering the gravity of what you tried to do. Forcing entry to a private residence. Property damage. Assault."

"He attacked Rhys." Abby's voice had grown tighter and louder than she'd intended, and she couldn't stop it.

"In self-defense," Hewitt snapped. She took a sharp breath. "Here's what's going to happen. You'll both go home. And you'll stay indoors until dawn. I'll be checking in with your guardians to ensure that's the case. And then, Miss Ward, if your sister hasn't come back, you can file a missing person's report. But you are not to return to Mr. Vickers's house, or harass him if you see him in the street, or disrupt his life any further than you have."

Abby's eyes burned. She felt like she was going to choke on her words if she tried to speak again.

Hewitt leaned closer to them. "You were *very* lucky tonight," she said, and there was an undercurrent of dual meaning to the words. "Now go home."

Rhys held his arm around Abby as he led her away from Stokes Lane.

She didn't think she'd be able to walk otherwise. Her legs, normally so strong, had turned to paper. The shivers wouldn't stop running through her.

There was a park not far from Stokes Lane. It was barely ever used—no one wanted to bring their children so close to Vickers—and rust had begun to consume most of the play equipment. Rhys led her there and eased her into one of the swings.

Inside Vickers's house, she'd been terrified.

But at least she'd been doing something.

This was far, far worse. This was tantamount to surrendering Hope to the Stitcher.

A noise wrenched its way from her throat. A wail, boiling with misery and anger and agony. It felt like a physical thing clawing its way out of her stomach and shredding her insides as it fought for freedom. Once it started, she couldn't stop.

She keeled forward, resting her head against Rhys's chest, and he held her wordlessly, rocking her as she screamed.

Hope was gone.

She'd tried so hard. They all had. The rules, the precautions, the money saved to escape from Doubtful as soon as they were old enough. They'd done everything they could, and none of it had been enough.

Hope is gone.

The screams wouldn't stop, but Abby's ability to lend them voice gave out. She shivered, exhausted, as silence fell over them.

Finally she leaned back so that she could look up at Rhys. Half of his face glistened with drying blood. The other half was wet with tears.

"What am I going to tell Momma?" Abby asked through a cracked throat.

He had no answer for her.

Footsteps crunched over old and dried wood chips. Two figures ran through the moonlight toward them, both clutching phones.

"Abby?" Riya called as she got closer. "Rhys? I got your message. What—oh."

She hesitated as she saw Rhys's face. One hand fluttered toward it then pulled back. "That looks bad. I can call my mom—"

He rubbed his sleeve over the side of his face to clear some of the blood. "It's fine. Just a cut from some broken glass. It doesn't hurt."

"Are you sure? My mom has a first aid kit. She could take a look."

Rhys gave his head a slight shake, ending the discussion.

Connor, slower than Riya, caught up. He bent over, hands braced on his knees, as he breathed heavily. "What happened? Your message said something about the Stitcher. And there are police cars all up and down Stokes Lane."

There was an uncomfortable gap of silence. Abby held her hands limply in her lap, her feet planted in the channels carved through the wood chips beneath the swing. She forced herself to speak. "Hope's gone."

Connor swore. Riya turned aside, her eyes huge, one hand pressed to her mouth.

"We got into Vickers's house," Abby continued. The howling screams churned into her stomach, trapped. "But I couldn't find her."

"Abs, I'm so sorry." Riya clutched her hands together. "The police are there. Are they…searching, or…?"

"They were there to escort us from the property." Abby's jaw ached from how hard she clenched it. "We're under curfew, now. We're supposed to go home."

Riya began pacing in short, sharp loops ahead of the swings. Connor leaned against one of the metal poles, his face slack with shock and his arms folded.

"You're sure the Stitcher took her?" Riya asked, pausing her pacing just long enough to give Abby a sharp stare.

"Her window was open." The memories hurt almost too much to speak into existence. "The screen was torn. Blood on the windowsill."

Connor muttered something and shook his head.

"We knew it was bad." Abby stared down at her hands. They looked foreign, as though they didn't belong to her. "But it was a hot night. And Hope hates the heat. She left her window open. She must have thought… She'd done it so many times before…"

"We thought we were safe," Connor finished for her.

When Abby closed her eyes, she saw the scene again. The shredded screen. The blankets thrown aside, the pillow on the floor. And the blood streaking the windowsill and wall.

Abby lifted her head. "She's not there," she said, realization dawning on her.

Riya stopped her pacing. "What?"

"Hope's not at Vickers's house." She looked back down at her hands. They still bore the streaks of crimson from where she'd touched the windowsill. "Hope was bleeding. But there were no drops of blood inside Vickers's house. None that I could see, anyway."

Riya rubbed at the back of her neck, looking uncertain. "Injuries can stop bleeding quickly, though. Especially if they're superficial."

"No. She's not there. That's why Vickers let us go. And why he called the police. Because he doesn't stitch people at his house." She stood up, her heart running fast. "I was never going to find Hope there. And he knew it."

"Huh" was all Connor said.

Riya frowned as she began pacing again. "No, no, you're right, that makes sense. I can't count the number of times the police have searched his home after someone is taken. And they never find anything. Because there's nothing *to* find."

"He wouldn't have long," Rhys said.

Abby nodded. From the time she woke and heard Hope being taken to the point where she and Rhys had arrived at Vickers's front door couldn't have been longer than twenty minutes. Maybe closer to fifteen. "No, not much time at all. He probably plans for that, though."

"Being at home would be his alibi," Riya said. "He makes sure he's always there after a victim is taken in case the police are called…or in case family members go to confront him."

Exactly like Abby had. She pictured herself racing through the house, calling for her sister, and growing increasingly desperate when there was no answer.

And she remembered the cutting board, covered with five sharp knives.

It was a red herring. She'd picked up one of the knives to defend herself with and had felt dust on the handle. Those knives had been displayed on his kitchen counter for a long, long time.

Waiting…to be found?

Yes. He'd been waiting for someone to force their way into his home. The knives weren't the only items arranged with the intent to shock and confuse. She'd seen the rows of missing person posters, taken from around town and neatly framed, and the bloodred bedroom. They were all there to keep the focus on the one place victims were never actually brought.

"If he doesn't take his victims home, he'd need to hide them somewhere else," Abby said. "Somewhere he could drop them quickly, but where they weren't going to be easily found."

"Somewhere between where he picks his victims up and his own house," Connor added. "Not too far out of the way. Nothing that needs a huge detour to reach."

"An abandoned house?" Riya guessed. "There are plenty of those around."

"And not many people try to explore those abandoned houses," Connor added.

No one wants to go into the empty houses because of how often bodies are found there. Was that deliberate? A way to deter people?

"Okay. We need a plan." Riya's face was pinched with anxiety. "There are too many empty houses to just search them at random and hope we get lucky. For all we know, we have a very narrow window to get Hope back, and we can't afford to waste any of it. Abs, Rhys, which officer told you to go home?"

"Chief Hewitt," Rhys said.

"The chief, huh?" Riya frowned. "Okay, she's a stickler. If she finds out you didn't go home, there'll be hell to pay. No way around it."

"I can take whatever punishment she dishes out," Abby said. "I'm not going to stop looking for Hope."

"No, but you need to be strategic." Riya's glance was quick. "Chief Hewitt has the ability to make your life a whole lot more complicated. Especially for your mother."

Abby pressed her mouth closed.

"You and Rhys will do what you're supposed to do—go home. Give Hewitt and the others exactly zero reasons to doubt that you're behaving yourselves. Connor and I are going to go to Stokes Lane."

Connor craned forward, his eyebrows high. "We...we are?"

"Please." Riya clasped her hands together as she gave him a tense, apologetic smile. "I'd do it myself but I can't be outdoors alone. Not at night."

"That's the rule," he mumbled, then set his shoulders and nodded. "Yeah. Okay. I'm with you."

"Thanks." Riya sagged with relief. "We're going back to Stokes Lane. We won't get close. But we'll find a vantage point. Maybe...maybe the forest behind his house? Somewhere that lets us watch Vickers. For as long as it takes."

"He'll have to leave to go back to Hope," Abby realized.

"Exactly. If we're right—if Hope is being kept somewhere else—then she won't be hurt as long as Vickers stays inside his house. And when he leaves..."

"We follow, and we find out where he's keeping her," Connor finished.

"Dangerous," Rhys muttered. He glanced aside, frowning, then turned back to them. "Keep your phones active if you can. Message me every twenty minutes so I know you're safe."

"Understood," Riya said. She was already turning back toward the park's exit, and the road leading to Stokes Lane. "Go straight home. While we're keeping lookout, you two need to figure out what we're going to actually do when the Stitcher decides to move."

FIFTEEN

RIYA STOPPED AT THE HEAD OF STOKES LANE AND STARED DOWN its length.

Red and blue lights blinked across the rows of empty houses. There were still police cars outside Charles Vickers's house. Not as many as when Riya had passed them while looking for Abby and Rhys, but a couple. That was good. Vickers couldn't leave his home while the police were there.

Connor staggered to a halt behind her. His face was strained and bloodless. He didn't want to be here.

Neither did she.

Stay away from Charles Vickers was their first rule for a reason.

But she'd seen the blinding terror in her friend's eyes. Abby would never be the same after this.

Probably none of them would.

So they had to at least *try*. Riya didn't think she could live with herself if she didn't.

Two officers stood on Vickers's front lawn, surveying the houses. They stared toward Riya. She cleared her throat and then tugged on Connor's arm, leading him on past the street.

They needed a vantage point. Somewhere they wouldn't be found— not by the police, and especially not by Vickers. She'd had the thought of hiding out in the forest. Stokes Lane was at the edge of town, and its back faced the tangled trees that formed Doubtful's border.

But, as she neared the woods, that began to seem less and less viable. She and Connor would be exposed to the elements, and their clothing was neither thick enough nor waterproof enough to ward off rain and dew. Some height would be an advantage, too, and while Riya was confident she could climb a tree, she didn't know if Connor would be able to follow. Which meant...

The houses. That thought chilled her, but it seemed like the only option. The entire street was composed of empty homes. And some of them—especially the ones closest to Vickers's—would have windows that faced toward him.

She hated going near empty houses. The rotting floorboards and mold were the least of her worries.

Her parents wouldn't like it either. She could already hear her mother's lecture and see her father's baleful stare. But, then, she was already going to be grounded for infinity if they found out she'd snuck out after dark, and infinities couldn't exactly be stacked.

"This way," she whispered to Connor, and led him down through the space between the forest and the fences surrounding the empty houses.

It wasn't hard to find a gap. Most of the buildings had been empty for well over a decade, and the wooden boundaries had been left to rot and collapse. Riya crept through a hole in the wood and onto a lawn that had grass and weeds growing up to her hips.

The house was riddled with broken windows and peeling siding, but it was two stories tall, and next door to the Stitcher's house. Which was about as good as they could hope for.

Connor made a faint whining noise when she pointed up toward the house, but then set his jaw and nodded.

Riya found an empty window frame within reach. Dust billowed around her as she slid through it. The kitchen door was swollen from moisture damage, and she had to put her shoulder into it to force it open for Connor.

Most of the house's furniture was gone, which meant it had most likely been vacated by choice, not through death. Scraps of the old family were still left, though. Two broken chairs against the kitchen's far wall. Plastic buckets and a used broom. Riya moved on quiet feet into the house's center and found herself staring up at a staircase. *Up there*, she thought. One of the rooms up there would give them the best view of Vickers's house.

She just had to hope that none of the floorboards broke and sent her plunging to her death. And that none of the rooms contained any of the telltale red thread to mark the resting place of a resewn body. And that the mold wasn't the toxic kind. And…

Riya swallowed the doubts as she stepped onto the stairs.

They were doing this for Hope. For Abby. And for the rapidly fading dream that their small friend group might be able to survive Doubtful.

––––––––––––

Rhys's phone chimed. He pulled it out, read the message, and then showed it to Abby. The text was from Riya: We found a vantage point. House 14, second floor. Police are still at Vickers's. Might be searching it? Lots of people moving through rooms. Will keep you updated.

She nodded.

Riya had been efficient. She and Rhys were still navigating the roads back to his house. He'd suggested they stay there together until morning, and she hadn't argued. Chief Hewitt wouldn't be able to criticize her for it, she was sure. One ugly, painful question kept circling around, burning her on every pass.

What will I tell Momma?

Abby had been holding her family together like she was clinging to her loved ones in a hurricane. And now she was on the edge of losing them all.

Rhys's house came into view. His street was in an older part of town, and influences from its mining history were everywhere. The houses were smaller and sturdier, most built of brick instead of wood. They were dwarfed by the trees around them, some of which had been planted more than a hundred years before. It left the area feeling wild and untamed. There were no lights on in the street.

Rhys unlocked his front door and held it open for Abby.

"Is that you, Rhys?" a voice called.

After his parents were taken, Rhys moved in with his grandmother, Alma. She'd always struck Abby as a gentle, kind person, but there seemed to be less and less of her with each passing year.

Muffled audio came from a television. Rhys led them toward it, and as Abby stepped into the open doorway to the living room she saw Alma was huddled in a high-backed chair. The blanket draped over her legs seemed to swallow her. She looked tiny and bird-thin.

"It's late, Nana." Rhys spoke softly. "You shouldn't have waited up for me."

It was more than late. Abby's best guess put them somewhere shy of three in the morning.

"I'm just waiting for my show to finish," Alma said.

Abby took another step forward, and finally saw the television.

It was a small, old-fashioned box set with an antenna angled on top. Images merged across the screen. Two separate shows tangled, their audio and visuals blending horribly. Faces and shapes fused into one another. Digital artifacts infected the screen. The audio tormented, not quite music or dialogue or background sounds, but a ragged blend of all three.

Abby was certain she could see a screaming face off to one side, howling at the audience beneath layers of jarring color and texture. She turned aside.

"Abby Ward is staying with me tonight," Rhys said. As he watched his grandmother, a mix of tenderness and heavy sadness slipped into his expression. "A police officer might call you tomorrow to check she was here."

"A friend," Alma said, and a smile entered her voice. "Oh, that's lovely. A friend has come to visit you."

"We'll be in my room if you need me."

"Of course." Her thin, bony hands twitched on her lap. "I'm just waiting for the end of my show."

The face in the corner of the television screamed, and screamed, and screamed.

Rhys led Abby back toward his room. It had been a long time since she'd last seen it. If the group spent time together, it was usually at Riya's house—the most central part of town—or at the lakeside.

While Riya's bedroom was filled with sports trophies and memorabilia, and Connor's was decorated with posters from the shows and movies he liked, Rhys's bedroom was bare. A bed was pressed to one wall beneath the window. A bedside table and a stark desk were the only other pieces of furniture. The only real trace of Rhys and his personality was a small stack of books beside his bed.

He kept it clean, but otherwise, it might have been a hotel room.

Abby couldn't suppress the rush of sadness she felt looking at the space. She sat on the edge of the bed, fingers picking at the blue quilt. Most of them were trying to avoid tying themselves down to Doubtful, but Rhys most of all. "You're staying for Alma, aren't you?"

He glanced at her quickly. "Yes." A pause, then he added, so quietly that she almost didn't hear, "And for other things."

Her heart did the strange flopping motion it something did around him, but there was no bittersweetness about it this time. Just aching, grinding pain.

Rhys turned to the stack of books. "There are things we can do, even if we can't leave." He crouched to pull a title out from the stack. It was small and worn and leather bound. "I've been keeping notes. Everything we ever discussed about the Stitcher—every theory, and every detail—is in here. We might find something if we go through the notes together."

She knew what he was doing. He was trying to keep her occupied, trying to distract her from the pain. But it wasn't going to help get Hope back. Their years of collecting scant scraps of information about the Stitcher's patterns hadn't brought them any major breakthroughs, and revisiting those notes now wouldn't save them.

Rhys turned back to her, holding the book out. He still bore streaks of red down one side of his face. Abby found herself staring at them. "Do you have a first aid kit?"

A flash of panic moved across his guarded features. "You're hurt?"

"No. I'm not." She stared pointedly at his forehead until he understood. He relaxed a fraction.

"In the bathroom."

She found a small box in a cabinet above the sink. As she closed the cabinet's mirrored door, she found herself staring at her reflection.

A stranger looked back. Her skin was bloodless and drawn. Shadows clung under her eyes.

Focus on what's important. She fumbled for a clean hand towel in a basket near the sink. *You can't afford to crumble now.*

Rhys had tried to distract her with work. Retracing ground they'd already covered a dozen times would still be better than doing nothing.

And maybe he was right. Maybe there was a vital clue buried in their notes that they'd missed. They wouldn't know unless they looked.

Abby wet a hand towel in the sink, then carried it and the kit back to Rhys's room.

He was waiting on the bed, the notebook clasped in his lap. Abby shuffled onto the quilt next to him, on her knees so she could reach his forehead. "You read, I'll clean," she said.

As Abby dabbed the dried blood from his face, he sorted through the notes. He'd used the book to record everything he knew about each disappearance, as it happened: when and where they were taken, whether there were people nearby, how long it took for their remains to be found. *If* their remains were ever found.

She caught glimpses of the scrawling words. The earliest pages were written in the painstakingly tidy hand of a young boy. He'd been keeping these notes ever since his parents were taken, Abby realized. Back then, he hadn't even been able to talk to Abby about it. But he'd written. And those earliest notes had helped build the foundation for their current set of rules.

They kept Rhys's phone beside them. Every twenty minutes, it pinged, which sent them both grasping for it. Each time was always Riya, checking in and sending an update.

They're definitely searching his house, she wrote, and twenty minutes later, Final police car just left. No sirens or lights this time. They can't have found anything. And, still later, Vickers is still awake. I can see him moving behind his curtains. Going from room to room.

Occasionally they also got messages from Connor, along the lines of: I made friends with a cool bug. :)

Abby fought to keep the disappointment from bleeding into her expression as Rhys sent a quick acknowledgment. Her friends were putting everything on the line to help her. Without them, she'd have nothing.

And, at that moment, no news was probably as close to good news as she would get.

She cleaned and disinfected Rhys as well as she could. He'd been honest, at least: the cut probably hurt, but it was shallow. She put the kit aside, then leaned next to Rhys, their shoulders pressed together, as they read.

Certain phrases appeared repeatedly across multiple entries.

Doors unlocked.

After dark.

Near the outskirts of town.

And one phrase, over and over again: Victim was alone.

I was so close. Abby's whole body ached. *Across the hall. Asleep. So near, but not near enough to make her safe.*

Why didn't I hear her?

"Hope didn't make any sound," Abby said. It hit her like a jolt. She'd been woken by a noise, yes—but not her sister's voice. Not a scream or a cry for help. If she'd heard that, she wouldn't have lost time checking her phone or watching her clock or wandering along the hallway to her mother's room.

If Hope had just called to her.

Rhys took a slow breath. His brows dug deep grooves between his eyes. "That's a pattern."

She stared at him, and he turned the journal's pages to find specific entries, then held them out for Abby to read.

Jacob Sutherland: taken less than a block from a bus station where multiple people were waiting. No one heard anything. Sadie Bajer: vanished from the alley behind her workplace while her colleagues were inside. No one heard anything. Maxine Strome: taken while playing in her backyard at night. Parents and siblings were getting ready for bed inside the house. No one heard anything.

"There are never any witnesses," Rhys said, speaking carefully, "Even when others are nearby."

"Because there aren't any calls for help," Abby muttered, frowning. "No screams. How's that possible? I could understand it in *some* cases—people freezing, or panicking, or being too frightened to speak, but..."

But in every case? No one, no matter their personality or temperament, ever made a sound?

She met Rhys's eyes and saw her thoughts reflected there. His parents vanished, one after another, on a storming afternoon while he was locked in his car. And he didn't hear anything.

How had Vickers been able to silence so many people?

"You have all of the addresses," Abby said, staring down at the open pages of the journal between them. "We should mark them on a map. There might be a pattern."

They'd tried something similar before: building a map of where people vanished, to see if there were certain sections of town that were more dangerous. The locations had seemed too scattered, though; too random. They'd given it up as a false lead.

Now was different, though. They weren't looking for areas to avoid. They were trying to pinpoint the one place they needed to *find*. If Vickers truly did have a separate area that he used to contain, dismember, and restitch his victims, it might be possible to zero in on it.

"Good thought," Rhys said, jotting down a note on the journal's final page. "He might be using multiple locations. But he can't be moving his victims far; we should be able to create something like a heat map to narrow down to certain streets."

Abby's focus drifted toward the window. Dawn wouldn't arrive for hours. When it did, she'd begin her search. Whether Charles Vickers left his home or not.

The Stitcher's victims didn't always die immediately. Sometimes he kept them alive for a while. Sometimes small body parts were found around town weeks before their official deaths.

She'd always found that the most horrifying thought. Now, it was all she was clinging to.

Stay alive, Hope. No matter what. Give me enough time to find you.

Riya watched as color bled into the horizon an inch at a time. She was tired. Her eyes felt like grit had become caught behind the lids, and her mouth was tacky. But she'd made it through the night.

They'd ended up on the house's second floor. The floorboards had *not* collapsed, not yet, but Riya still didn't fully trust them. She'd spent some of the early morning hours trying to remember who had once lived here and how long it might have been abandoned, but all she'd managed to recall was it had been decrepit and empty even when she was a child.

Most of the rooms they'd passed still had a few pieces of furniture in them, turning moth-eaten and sun bleached and dusty. The room with the best view of Vickers's house had been left completely bare, though. Like the owners hadn't wanted to spend any part of their day facing toward him. It was home to a small number of beetles, both dead and alive, and not much else.

The space had worked well for the vigil, though. Gauzy curtains had lost most of their color but gave Riya something to hide behind if she needed it. She'd watched Vickers's house obsessively, very aware that if he left, it would probably be discreetly and possibly through the back door.

He'd stayed up for hours, even after the police had driven away. She'd watched him move like a phantom from room to room, always shielded behind the metal bars and his own curtains. She hadn't been able to see what he was doing, only that his movements were unhurried and he never stayed for long in any one room.

Eventually, he'd turned out the lights one by one, finishing in one of the upstairs rooms. That had to be his bedroom. He hadn't stirred since.

Connor was tucked into the nearest corner. He'd dragged an old wooden chair into their room and had coiled up in it, his head resting on the wall, and faint, wheezing snores came from a throat crimped by the bad angle. Connor had always been up front about being comfortable with perfectly average grades. He'd never gotten practice staying up all night to cram for exams.

She took her phone out. The Jackrabbits group chat was full of a long string of updates sent to Rhys, and Rhys's replies. He and Abby were making plans to search abandoned buildings near Abby's own house.

She sent him the final message of the vigil:

Still quiet. Expecting Vickers will probably sleep in late to make up for last night.

Connor shifted in his seat against the wall. Riya reached out her foot and nudged him, then nudged him again, harder, until he finally woke. "Uh," he managed, and half slid out of the chair before he caught himself with a grimace. "Sorry, what?"

"It's morning," Riya said. She nodded toward the house outside their window. "He hasn't stirred for hours. Do you think you could take over the watch for a while?"

"Can I—" His eyebrows shot up. "Uh. Watch the house. Right. Okay. You're not staying with me?"

"We need to make the most of whatever time we have." She stood up, careful to stay out of view of the window just in case, and ran her hands over her jeans as she tried to clear some of the dust off. "It should be safer now. It's after dawn. Keep texting the group chat, though, and try not to let him see you."

Connor looked terrified even as he gave her a thumbs-up. Riya felt a pang of guilt. She wouldn't want to stay alone in the house next to Vickers either. But Connor shuffled his chair a few inches closer to the window and leaned forward, and Riya gave him a final goodbye wave before sneaking out of the room and toward the stairs.

She fired off more messages as she left, letting Rhys know that Connor was taking over the watch. Then she slipped through the open back door and out into the high weeds surrounding the house.

She had damage control to do. She spent a solid minute carefully constructing a text to her parents, who were due to wake within the next half hour and would *definitely* not enjoy finding their daughter's room empty. She told them the lacrosse team was meeting for an early-morning practice and she'd go straight to school afterward.

She'd have to cross her fingers that they didn't find the story too suspicious. If they called the lacrosse team captain, or checked her room and found her school backpack still there, she'd be in a world of trouble.

Lying to them felt horrible. But telling the truth would be like setting off a bomb. Riya was certain they'd be *less* mad if she'd spent the night at a wild party full of underage drinking. Her family almost never talked about the Stitcher, as though speaking the word might somehow invite him into their lives. But his presence permeated their home and their habits. Riya's childhood had been punctuated by self-defense classes and pepper spray as birthday gifts. Her parents picked her up after school and work with unflinching regularity. It might have felt smothering if Riya herself hadn't dreaded the thought of walking home alone so much.

So she lied, switching a bomb filled with shrapnel for a guilty little ache that would probably persist for weeks.

She'd swallow that ache, though. Because, even though she could probably get back to her house before her parents even woke, she wouldn't. There was work to do.

Jen could smell toast as she climbed downstairs. Toast was her father's last resort for breakfast when he was running late and couldn't lose time frying eggs.

Sure enough, when she turned into the kitchen, she found him standing behind the counter, absentmindedly eating a slice while he stared down at the stack of papers that only seemed to multiply with each day. "Mm," he mumbled, a distant acknowledgment of Jen.

"Mm yourself," she said, heading for the fridge. The shelves were nearly empty. Apparently, the toast wasn't just a sign of a time shortage, but of neglected grocery shopping. "Guess crispy bread's on the menu for both of us."

"Jen. I actually wanted to talk to you." Her father seemed to break out of his trance. He put the slice back on his plate. Jen turned, her back to the fridge, as she waited.

"Do you know a girl called Abby Ward? Lives on Sycamore Avenue?"

She had no reason to grow tense, but she did anyway. "Yeah. I met her at school."

"Ah." Thompson rubbed at the back of his neck. "I had an encounter with her last night. And she claimed you were friends."

"That was bold of her."

"Look…" Thompson dropped his hand, but the careful tone didn't falter. "I asked some of the other officers about her. Apparently, there's something strange going on with her family. Something about her mother. I never want to tell you who you can and can't be friends with, but…maybe keep some distance from that girl."

"That was already the plan," Jen said, and it was the truth.

"Really? That's good." He seemed strangely relieved. "You've always been a good judge of character. I'm proud of that."

"She says she never leaves her home after dark," Jen said, tilting her head. "How'd you cross paths with her?"

"She was making a fuss at one of the residents' homes." Thompson was beginning to drift away from the conversation as his attention floated back toward the paperwork on the kitchen table. "She said her sister was missing, but when we invited her back to the station to make a report she refused."

Hope?

Images of a brightly colored girl and a slightly-too-large smile flashed through Jen's mind. Out of the five friends sitting around the bonfire, she'd been the only one without that hunted look in her eyes.

Hope was taken?

Her father must have heard it wrong. Maybe Abby was rambling about the Stitcher snatching people and he got confused. Or maybe she was lying, a ploy to get attention, just like she'd lied to Jen at the lakeside.

She blinked and saw the intensity in Abby's eyes as she talked about the Stitcher.

Nothing about this felt right.

Nothing about *the town* felt right.

"I'll walk to school today," Jen said, glancing toward the paperwork. "Give you some extra time with that."

He hesitated. "No. It's okay. I can drive you."

Human remains found in empty houses. Human remains found in the woods behind their yard. He was nervous, and probably with good reason.

"I want some exercise," Jen said, taking up her bag. "And if you're worried about me skipping school, you can relax. You know I've never skipped in my life."

"Right." He sighed. "Keep your phone on you and call if there's any trouble, okay?"

"Will do." She snatched up one of the pieces of toast on her way out.

Jen could feel her father's eyes following her through the window, so she kept her pace relaxed as she turned left, along the road that would take her to school. She waited until she was out of sight of the house before turning down a side road and doubling back on herself, to walk toward Sycamore Avenue.

Her father knew her well, but not completely. She *rarely* skipped school. And today seemed like the kind of day when she needed to make an exception.

SIXTEEN

ʌʌʌʌ

IT WAS DARK. ABBY TRIED TO BREATHE BUT THE AIR CAUGHT IN her throat. It was laced with moisture and a smell that felt familiar but that she couldn't place.

She reached forward. She couldn't feel anything, either, except she was on some kind of hard surface.

And she was cold.

There was a faint noise behind her. A skitter, like something moving across loose stones. Abby turned toward it, moving on her hands and knees. "Hello?" she called.

The reply came from a long way away. "Abby?"

She knew that voice. A surge of longing rushed through her as she began crawling forward, her arms reaching blindly into the dark. "Hope! Hope, it's me! Where are you?"

There was a soft scrape, then a hiss, followed by a flicker of light. A lit match was held in thin, pale fingers. Abby knew that hand. She began moving faster, crawling toward the distant form. She only stopped when the voice spoke again.

"Why did you leave me here?"

It didn't sound right. It was Hope's cadence, yes, but blurred and damaged. Abby could see the hand that held the flickering match, but not much more. Her sister was hunched over, and the hair that hung over her face was drained of color.

"I tried to find you," Abby whispered. She reached forward. The match was burning out fast. "I chased after you."

"And when you couldn't find me, you gave up on me." The hunched form shifted, the head rising. The curtain of hair began to part, revealing bloodless skin. "You forgot about our father. And you forgot about me."

Tears stung Abby's eyes. She could barely breathe. "I didn't, Hope. I swear I didn't forget about you."

The head came up to stare at her. Only, there were no eyes. Empty sockets had been sewn closed with loops of red thread.

"You forgot me," Hope said, and the threads stitching her lips together strained as she fought to speak. "You forgot me."

The match held between her dead fingers burnt out.

Abby screamed as she woke.

She was no longer in the dark. Sunlight flooded through a window above a bed that wasn't her own. She sat up, her heart thundering, as she stared wide eyed at her surroundings.

"Hey," Rhys said, reaching toward her. "You're safe. I'm here."

Rhys's house. Rhys's room.

She'd fallen asleep. It was well past dawn.

Terrible shame washed over her. Hope was being held somewhere, terrified, possibly hurt, and Abby had still managed to fall asleep. She shoved herself off Rhys's bed and began grabbing, with shaking hands, her belongings off the floor. "Did you fall asleep too?"

"No," he admitted. "But sleep's going to be hard to come by for a while. I wanted you to get what you could."

The shame only thickened. She could barely think as she stared at the things she held: the map they'd been working on, dotted over with red *X*s, and the jacket Rhys had lent her.

"I was supposed to start searching at dawn." The icy accusation from the dream rang in her ears. *You forgot about me.* "And I've lost hours."

"The sun hasn't been up for long. Here." Rhys held some items out to her: a plain black T-shirt, and a pair of jeans with a belt. "They're clean. And they'll save you having to make a trip back home."

She was still wearing the nightdress, Abby realized. She grabbed the clothes from him and rushed into the bathroom to change. They were too large for her by several sizes, but the belt cinched the jeans tightly enough to stay in place, and she kept her nightdress on under the top to help disguise her lack of a bra.

Her pale, blotchy face stared back at her through the mirror. She glared at it, challenging it.

Focus. Don't fall apart. It's not too late to save this.

She took a short, harsh breath, then folded the map under her arm as she moved back into the house's central rooms.

Rhys was in the kitchen. He moved quickly, but he'd laid three bowls on the kitchen counter and was filling them with cereal.

"I need to go," she said, and barely managed to keep the tenseness out of her voice.

"Thirty seconds," he said, snatching milk out of the fridge. "Alma hasn't had breakfast."

Footsteps shuffled behind them. Alma emerged from the living room. She wore the same clothes she had worn the previous night. Distantly, Abby thought she could hear the television playing the same horrific spliced audio.

"Stay for breakfast," Alma said, and placed one gentle hand on Abby's arm.

"Thanks. But I can't." It hurt to talk. "I can't lose any time."

"Oh?" Alma's head tilted up to blink at her. "Why's that, sweet girl?"

Abby couldn't answer. She shot Rhys a glance as he placed the bowl of cereal and a quickly sliced apple on the small dining table.

Rhys saw her look. He cleared his throat as he answered. "Abby's sister was taken last night, Nana."

"Ohh," Alma sighed. She pressed one hand on her heart as she turned away. "Oh, the Stitcher. That's bad. That's so bad. The Stitcher takes so many. I'm sorry, sweet girl."

The platitudes. They rained down on the unfortunate who had lost loved ones. Abby had felt them before, when her father went missing, but she still knew it was nothing compared to what Rhys had heard when his family was found.

She didn't blame Alma. What else were you supposed to say? Abby herself had given her share of *I'm sorry*s to others.

It didn't matter. She just wanted to get outside. Searching the empty houses was a long shot, but at least it had better odds than doing nothing.

Alma, slowly pacing away, continued to murmur to herself. "So sad. He takes so many. And only one of them ever came back."

Abby froze at the door. Slowly, she turned toward Alma, who stood at the window and stared out into the morning light.

"Did you say…" Her voice caught. Every hair rose as gooseflesh covered her. "Someone came *back*?"

PART THREE

LEGENDS

SEVENTEEN

〰〰〰

THOMPSON HAD SAID ABBY WARD LIVED ON SYCAMORE AVENUE. It didn't entirely narrow Jen's search down, but it was a start.

Houses spread out ahead of her, all of them in various stages of aging, much like the rest of the town. She caught sight of bikes and scooters tangled over with weeds, of cars rusting beside their buildings, and of windows that had shutters sealed tightly across them.

Jen walked along the center of a street that seemed to rarely carry cars. She scanned the houses she passed. It was breakfast time. Kids should be leaping out of doorways as they raced the clock to get to school; adults should be mimicking their urgency as they raced the clock to get to work.

There wasn't any sound. No movement. The whole area seemed to be holding its breath.

Something crunched under Jen's shoe. She pulled back and felt her stomach turn. She'd stepped on a bird. It lay chest-down, head twisted at an angle, wings limp on the asphalt.

Guilt surged up, then faded again. The bird had already been dead. Probably for a while. Its eyes had been eaten out by ants, leaving just ragged hollows.

It wasn't the only one, Jen realized as she lifted her gaze. Another feathered body lay in a gutter close by. Another on a nearby lawn. Two more further down the road, only visible because their pinions quivered in the breeze.

Animals die, she told herself, but the sentiment rang hollow.

Part of her wanted to turn around and hike straight to school, like she'd promised her father she would. She squashed the instinct.

A flutter of pastel pink caught her notice.

There's no color in Doubtful, she realized as she stared up at the curtains floating out of an open bedroom window. It was like the town had been drained over decades. Everywhere else was muted browns, faded earthy greens, and grays. Everywhere except for Jen's own body, which sported a striped blue-and-black shirt…and the curtains. They reminded her of Hope and her tinted hair.

Jen's eyes followed the lines of the house toward its front door. There, tucked near the welcome mat, was a handheld lantern. She'd seen it before, by the lake, used to form part of a circle of light.

"Found you," Jen whispered.

She hitched her backpack higher on her shoulder as she swung into the open driveway. She was only halfway to the door when she saw movement inside one of the windows.

A woman paced through the living room. She looked like she might be nearly forty, but it was hard to tell; creases ran through her face, and her skin was blotchy and pallid.

There was something familiar about the angle of the woman's brows and the shape of her nose. There was more of Abby in her face than Hope, though. Especially around the eyes. She had that same hunted, haunted look, like a bruise that would never fade.

The woman stopped pacing, as though she'd felt Jen's eyes on her. Then, very slowly, the woman turned to look at her. She didn't turn her head, though. Her whole body rotated in small shuffling steps until she stood directly facing the window, her arms limp at her sides.

Jen forced a bright smile and raised one hand to wave.

There was no response. The woman just stared, and stared, and stared.

There's something strange about the family, Thompson said. He wanted me to stay away from them.

Jen's smile began to falter. Still, the woman kept staring at her. No, not *at* her. *Through* her. As though she was looking at something that no one except for her could see.

There was no one else in the house, Jen was certain. It was as deathly quiet as every other building in the street. As deathly quiet as a grave.

"Hello?"

Jen swung. At the start of the driveway, just a dozen paces away, stood Riya. The relief was overwhelming and unexpected in equal parts.

"Hey," she managed, but it came out breathy and thin. She cleared her throat. "I—I heard some rumor about Hope going missing and, uh—I know it's weird, but I wanted to check she's okay."

Riya hurried closer, her arms crossed over her chest. She was dressed for exercise: sweats and a shirt that was stretchy and breathable.

"It's not a story." She looked tense and tired, as though she'd barely slept. "Hope was taken last night. Abby and Rhys are searching for her. I wanted to check that Mrs. Ward is safe, then I'm going to join them."

There was a break of a few seconds where Jen couldn't speak. Her mind turned empty, like someone had pulled a plug and drained all rational thought. All she could manage was, "You're not lying to me, are you?"

"I wouldn't. Not about this."

"Oh."

Hope was taken. That thought had seemed like a curiosity before, but now it hit her like a sledgehammer. *Hope was taken, and she's going to turn up like that body they found in the woods behind my home. She's going to be sliced up and sewn back together wrong.*

The shock and the sickness and the disbelief formed a poisonous concoction inside. Her mind kept chanting, *it's not real, it's a joke, it's not real,* but the sincerity on Riya's face was enough to silence that thought.

Riya was telling her the truth. The brutal, aching, ugly truth. It was up to Jen to believe it or not.

Jen swiped the back of her hand across her jawline, which was growing clammy. She turned aside so that Riya wouldn't see and found herself staring back at the house's living room window.

Just feet away, Mrs. Ward pressed limply against the glass, staring down at her.

Jen fought to put her words into order as she shuffled closer to Riya. "Uh. Do you know Mrs. Ward well?" At Riya's nod, she continued, "Is she okay?"

"She's sick," was all Riya said. "She has been for a while. Abby's looking after her."

Jen looked back toward the window. Mrs. Ward's eyes were fixed on Jen, and yet, stayed unfocused.

"Let's head back," Riya said, a tentative smile flitting up and then fading again. "Mrs. Ward gets stressed by strangers. She'll be calmer if we give her some space."

As they moved back along the driveway, Jen couldn't stop herself from speaking. "I know it's not my place, but…"

"There are no psychiatric hospitals or clinics in Doubtful," Riya said, as though she could read Jen's mind. "And Mrs. Ward can't leave the town. Not anymore."

Jen shot her a quick glance. "Why not?"

"This town…" Riya seemed to be struggling to put her thoughts into words. "It's like it plants hooks in you. And the longer you live here, the more hooks start to embed themselves, and if you try to pull free you'll only hurt yourself. If people are taken away from the town— if they're forced to leave their homes when they're not ready—they don't usually make it. Most patients who are transported to hospitals or care facilities don't live past six months."

Jen felt a chuckle begin to grow. It was reflexive, a guard against obvious lies, and yet, again, Riya showed no signs of mockery or deception. It actually seemed to be hurting her to explain. Jen clamped down on the laughter before it could break out.

"Abs is trying to care for her mother at home for as long as possible," Riya continued. "But if the wrong people knew about her mother's situation—if people wanted to hurt Abby—then they could have Mrs. Ward taken away. And Mrs. Ward wouldn't survive it."

This wasn't just an explanation. It was a warning. Riya's soft eyes pleaded with her: *Don't talk about this with too many people. Don't put this into the wrong hands.*

But then Jen flashed back to Mrs. Ward's limp hair and sallow skin.

"She's sick," she said. "Physically, not just psychologically. And unless Abby moonlights as a trained nurse—"

"I know, I know," Riya whispered, and she sounded utterly miserable. "My mom helps when she can. Mrs. Ward has good weeks and bad weeks. You saw her at her worst. In her good weeks, everything gets better. But she's influenced by whatever makes things go weird around here."

"The Stitcher," Jen guessed.

Riya nodded.

Jen stared along the street's length, at the stiff birds laying on the asphalt and the houses that refused to stir. "You talk about the Stitcher like he's some all-powerful supernatural entity, but in the next breath you try to tell me he's just some guy who lives nearby. It doesn't make sense."

"No," Riya agreed. "There's a lot we still don't understand. But this is as close to the truth as we've been able to get. And maybe as close as we ever *will* get."

Jen sighed. She rubbed at the back of her neck. Then she said, "I need to go to school; I promised my dad I would. But is there anything I can do to help? With what's happened to Hope?"

"Probably not right now." Riya smiled tentatively. "But thank you."

"Okay." Jen pulled out her phone. "Give me your number."

"Uh—"

"So we can keep in touch if that *not right now* changes to a *yes, urgently.*"

"Right." Riya swallowed. She recited her number.

"There," Jen said, firing off a winking emoji. "Now you'll have my contact too."

Riya scrambled for her phone as it pinged and stared at the notification.

"I got the cool girl's number," Riya said, and she sounded faintly shocked. Then she immediately grimaced. "Oh, nope, not appropriate. Not right now. Sorry. And also sorry for calling you *the cool girl.* I know your name, I swear."

"It's fine. I like being Cool Girl." Jen found herself smiling in spite of everything. "Put that as my name in your phone."

Riya's face had turned an intense scarlet as she squeezed her lips together and typed in the moniker. "Thanks," she managed.

"Keep me updated," Jen said, as she turned back to the path that she was pretty sure would eventually lead her to school. She'd promised her father she wouldn't skip. Arriving late would keep that promise… mostly. "I want to know how this turns out."

Riya's stomach was a ball of tension as she watched Jen leave.

Maybe she should have said yes. Maybe she should have taken the help that was being offered. She knew, better than anyone, that they needed every slim advantage they could get.

But saying yes would drag Jen into a world she didn't know, and wasn't prepared for. Riya *herself* wasn't prepared, and she'd lived in Doubtful for her entire life.

She'd heard that drowning people would clutch at anyone trying to rescue them, and very often pull them under as well.

Right now, Abby was drowning. And Riya could feel herself teetering on the edge of it too: wanting to grasp at anyone who could help, but knowing she'd just be spreading the damage.

Her phone chimed a second time. *Jen again?* But the taller girl was still walking away, and about to turn the corner and vanish from view. Riya pulled her phone out and stared down at the message. It was from Rhys. Riya's breath caught as she read it.

Someone survived the Stitcher. And she still lives in town. We're going to meet her now.

EIGHTEEN

〤〢〢〢

her friends lived there, and the one park and handful of small businesses it housed weren't as good as the ones closer to Abby's home.

The plants all seemed thinner and sicker. Dark, brittle branches encroached on the pathways, threatening to scrape her skin if she walked too close. Street signs listed, and the names were faded so badly, they almost missed their turn.

The path they walked down felt darker and colder than the main roads. Brick fences ran along the edge of the sidewalk, occasionally interrupted by rusting steel gates or open driveways.

They stopped in front of a house that stood set back from the road, almost as though it wanted to hide. Its windows were dark. A frosted glass pane in the front door should have given them a glimpse inside but only reflected the outside world back at them.

Tarnished numbers on the mailbox read *26*.

"This is it?" She asked it as a question, even though she knew the answer.

Rhys gave a short nod without taking his eyes off the frosted window.

Alma had only been able to give them a name: Bridgette Holm. Rhys had torn though the house's cupboards until he found an address book that looked at least two decades out of date. They'd knelt on the floor, flipping through the thin pages, until they found her.

The address was in Doubtful. And it was only a twenty-minute walk from Alma's house.

"She might not be there any longer," Rhys had cautioned.

Alma had made a faint noise in the back of her throat. She sat under the window, faded light streaming over her as she watched them, her cereal sinking into the milk. "She'd still be there. She never left."

Abby had lifted her head. "How have I never heard of her before?"

"People don't like talking about it, I suppose." Alma had narrowed her eyes as she stared into the distance. "It caused a big stir when she came back, but almost as quickly as people started talking, they stopped. I suppose… People feel like it's dangerous to speak about it too much. Like it might draw it to them."

Abby knew what Alma was saying. A lot of people didn't want to be around someone who'd come so close to the Stitcher. As though it tainted them by proximity. As though being too near them might draw the Stitcher's attention, somehow.

Rhys had felt that acutely. No matter how many jobs he applied to, he was never called back. People he'd never even met would stare at him on the street. Once, years before, he'd thanked Abby for staying his friend, and she'd been shocked by the idea that he'd thought she would ever *stop*.

Abby had been spared a lot of that. Her father was only *missing*, not a body in a coffin. People didn't picture the remains when they looked at her.

That might change now.

She'd grimaced, clenching her hands until her fingernails bit into the skin.

She couldn't think like that. Hope was going to come home, and come home intact. She just needed more time. And more knowledge. And she hoped Bridgette Holm would be able to give that to her.

"I'm here!" Riya called. She ran toward them, a backpack bouncing on her shoulders, and by the sheen of sweat coating her, Abby knew she'd been running for a while. She slowed down at their side, breathing deeply as she stared at the house. "This is it? This is Bridgette's?"

"We hope," Abby said.

Despite what Alma had said, she couldn't stop the doubt. A lot could change in two and a half decades.

"Any news?" Rhys asked.

"Connor's still watching the Stitcher house. He keeps stressing me out by being late on his check-ins." She frowned, downing gulps of air between words. "I already dropped him off some food, bottled water, and a battery pack for his phone, and he says he'll be okay to keep watch for a while longer."

"You've been busy," Rhys noted.

"You have no idea." Riya pulled a towel from a side compartment of her bag and used it to wipe down her face and neck. "Let's do this."

Abby had already begun moving forward. She was terrified of what might be on the other side of that door. Answers. Or emptiness. She ran the final steps to the door and lifted the heavy knocker, slamming it into chipped wood three times before taking a step back.

Something moved behind the frosted glass. Three painful heartbeats of silence passed, then a woman's voice called, "Who is it?"

"Ms. Holm?" Abby clenched and unclenched her hands at her sides.

Another pause. "Yes."

Relief beat itself to life in Abby's chest like a frantic bird. "My name's Abby Ward. Last night, my sister was taken by the Stitcher. I… I heard something like that happened to you, once, a long time ago, and that you survived. I need you to help me."

The dark shape beyond the glass shifted out of view. Abby waited, her breath held. The silence stretched, and stretched, and stretched, and still no answer came.

Tears built a horrible pressure behind her eyes. "Please. I haven't got much money, but I'll give you everything I have. I just want to know what happened, and how you got away. *Please*."

Still silence.

She turned to Rhys and saw her own desperation reflected in his eyes.

Floorboards inside the house creaked, and it sounded like the old building was sighing. The blurred shadow shifted back into view. Then a lock clicked open, followed by a second and third lock, and finally the scrape of a latch, and the door crept open a few inches.

Abby strained to see Bridgette Holm. She was tall and thin with curling black hair pinned back from her face, and her large eyes traced over them, as though measuring them up.

"Your sister," she said. "Taken last night."

"Yes. Hope. She's only fifteen." Abby clenched her hands together until the knuckles turned white. "If you can tell me anything, Bridgette, anything at all—"

The door opened further, just barely wide enough for a body to step through. "I'm not Bridgette," the woman said, her voice low. "I'm Vivian, Bridgette's sister. She's agreed to talk to you. This way."

Sisters. They still lived together, even decades later.

Abby had to turn sideways to slip through the barely open door. Rhys and Riya followed, introducing themselves in muted voices. Something about the house seemed to call for quietness. Inside was dim and dusty, the furniture all made of dark, scratched wood, and the walls decorated with heavy peeling wallpaper. It made the space feel more cluttered and crowded than it actually was.

Vivian didn't speak but led them to the right. There was a room there, decorated in the same dark, muted shades of reds and browns. A woman sat in a chair beside the window. The resemblance was immediate: dark, curling hair, and dark eyes that turned down at the outer corners.

Based on the timeline Alma had given them, Bridgette would have been just shy of forty, but she looked at least a decade older. Her skin was turning thin and crepey, especially around the hollows beneath her eyes. She wore a thick cardigan despite the mild weather, and a thick blanket was draped over her lap, trailing down to the floor.

Bridgette had been reading, but placed her book on a side table that already held a mug of coffee that looked to have gone cold. Her lips seemed bloodless. She didn't smile, but she nodded toward the faded couch opposite her chair. As they sat, Vivian disappeared deeper into the house.

"I'm sorry about your sister," Bridgette said. Even her voice sounded husky and cracked. "But the kindest thing I can tell you is to give up now."

Abby swallowed around the lump in her throat. She leaned forward in her chair, reducing the distance between them. "I can't do that."

"No," Bridgette agreed, and her eyelids fluttered down. She had very long lashes. They, along with the downward turn of her eyes, gave her the impression of being eternally sad. It was only balanced by the hardness and durability carved into the creases across her face. "Not many people can. But whatever path you're trying to follow is only going to hurt you and everyone you love. It's important you know that."

Riya shifted uneasily at Abby's side, but Rhys was as still as a rock. Something small and pale moved across the room. Abby was mesmerized by Bridgette, and only tore her eyes away when the small shape wove around her legs. It was a cat, its long fur a pale moonlight color. She reached down to stroke it, and as it lifted its head she saw it was missing both eyes. Skin filled the concave hollows of its eye sockets.

"Newborn animals come out wrong when the Stitcher surfaces," Bridgette said, her voice cold. "Most people have them put down immediately. I take whatever ones I can. People are scared that getting too close to those touched by the Stitcher will expose them to the so-called curse."

"There's no curse," Abby said reflexively.

Bridgette's bloodless lips twitched into something like a smile. "No.

There's no curse. Leaving those offerings won't save you, and living with those who have been touched won't harm you. When the Stitcher decides to take someone, it's all empty, hopeless luck."

Abby nodded. She'd known that for a while. But, still, people would hold on to whatever superstitions they thought could spare them from the nightmare.

"I want you to tell me everything you can," Abby said. "Do you remember where he kept you? How did you escape? Did the police ever interview you? Why wasn't he arrested?"

"He..." Bridgette murmured, and Abby felt like she'd said something wrong. Then the smile cracked Bridgette's dry lips again. "Yes. I suppose it is a *he*, isn't it?"

Abby didn't know what to say. Her hand was still reached downward, and the blind cat pressed against it, asking for attention.

"I'll tell you what happened to me," Bridgette finally said. She laced her hands over the blanket covering her lap. "And I'll tell it as completely as I can. You can do what you want with the information, and after this final warning, I won't try to influence you again. But, if you have any sense of self-preservation left in you, grieve for your sister. Build a little monument for her in your yard and place flowers there and tell yourself she died quickly and made it to heaven. Don't try to get her back. Don't go digging. Because there's no good outcome for you if you do."

"I understand," Abby said, and her blood was ice in her veins. "Tell me what you know."

NINETEEN

BRIDGETTE'S STORY

SOMETIMES THE WORST THINGS THAT HAPPEN TO YOU COME from the smallest decisions. You lean on the accelerator instead of the brake. Or you shift your weight on the ladder. Or you leap into the pool headfirst without checking how deep the water is. Tiny, tiny mistakes that would have been inconsequential any other day. But for some reason, the universe's gears get jammed at that exact second, and your tiny mistake permanently changes the remainder of your life.

For me, that mistake was forgetting my bag. I was about your age. My friends and I always hung out for a while after school; even back then, our parents wouldn't let us leave our houses after dark, so that gap between school and home was our only real chance to relax together.

We had a soccer ball that we hid in the bushes just down from the school gates. They were big, bushy plants. Are they still there? Yes? I like that. They made a good hiding place. It was a hot day, and when we got the ball, I left my backpack under the branches so that it wouldn't feel so warm on my back for the walk home.

The street beside the school was always quiet in the afternoon, and we used chalk to draw temporary goalposts as we played. We can't have been there for more than forty minutes when Jackie's mother marched toward us, yelling about how it was nearly dusk and we needed to go home. It *wasn't* nearly dusk. Wouldn't be for another hour, hour and a half. But Jackie's mother scared us when she was angry, and she was angry that day.

She would have been frightened because the Stitcher was growing active. Everyone could sense the signs—their radios stopped working, the streetlights died, late at night you could hear animals screaming as though they were in the most unimaginable pain. Even my friends and I felt it, no matter how hard we tried to ignore it. That was why Jackie's mother was so stressed. We weren't late. She just wanted her daughter to be indoors, where it was safer.

Jackie left with her mother, and the rest of us scattered. Vivian and I headed home. We were nearly there when I realized I'd forgotten to get my backpack.

That was when I made my choice. I could have left the backpack hidden in the bushes and picked it up the next morning, except I had homework and didn't want to fall behind. I could have asked Vivian to walk back with me. She even offered to. But instead I called out, *it's fine, I'll be back in twenty*, and jogged the path to school alone.

That decision was made in a split second, and it's one I'll never forgive myself for. People say I'm lucky that I came back. That I was blessed, that I had a guardian angel watching over me.

I think I'd consider myself luckier if I'd never been taken at all.

The path to school took me through one of the parks. Usually there were at least a few other people there—joggers, or mothers with little kids that they pushed on the swings. That day, there was no one. Everyone was nervous because of the way things were going bad. They all wanted to stay indoors.

I'd always liked that park before, but crossing it when it was so empty felt different. As though it was no longer a safe place. I began to walk faster and faster, just trying to get out the other side.

And then I heard a sound coming from behind. I turned. There was a swing set, and one of the swings was rocking back and forward as though something had brushed past it, even though the park was still empty.

For most of my life, I'd tried to ignore the Stitcher's presence in our town. It had seemed like a waste of a life to spend my time cowed by fear. But, at that moment, I felt the Stitcher's existence more acutely than I ever had before. The air was electric. Every hair on my body stood stiffly up. My bones began to ache and my teeth felt too big for my mouth. It became hard to think—almost like I was falling into a dream.

And then I looked down at my shadow. It was growing bigger. And that was such a strange thing that I couldn't tear my eyes off it. It kept ballooning out and changing shape until I finally understood what was happening.

It wasn't my shadow growing bigger. It was a second shadow, much larger than mine, falling over me as the Stitcher approached from behind.

I don't remember much of the next bit. Just flashes. I remember being dragged across the road. It scraped a patch of skin off my left shoulder. I remember seeing flashes of houses, and begging the people inside to look out their windows, to see me, to *help* me.

Then everything faded away. I don't know if I passed out or if my mind just refused to hold on to any memories of what happened next, but when I woke up, I was alone, and I was somewhere very dark.

At first I thought it was night. But it was so much darker than any night I'd ever seen before. There's always *some* kind of light, no matter how scarce it might be. But this—this was pure emptiness. A void.

And I felt the rocks under my hands and I heard the drip of falling water and I stared into the blackness and I realized: I was in the mines.

They were supposed to be closed up. The entrances were all boarded over, the passageways collapsed. It had been that way for not only my entire life but my parents' lives as well.

But, somehow, the Stitcher had found a way into the mines. Or, maybe, he had found a way *out*.

Some of the Stitcher's victims die quickly. Some stay alive for a while. Until then, I'd always imagined the Stitcher had ways to contain them: cages, or tying them up with ropes, or locking them in his basement.

But I wasn't trapped at all. I could move in any direction I wanted. And that was the beauty of the mines. I could crawl for weeks in that empty blackness and still not find any way out. I could scream until I was hoarse and no one would hear.

In darkness that intense, you lose the ability to tell time, to judge distance, or to even know where your arms and legs are in relation to one another. It's oppressive in a way that breaks spirits and crushes hope.

It was down there with me. The Stitcher. Sometimes I heard it creeping through the passageways. Unlike me, it seemed to know the darkness intimately.

If it had ever known how to speak, it had forgotten by that point. All it knew was the darkness, and the threads. Those little red lines that it uses to stitch up its bodies were strung all through the mines. They were like spiderwebs, and I think it even used them in the same way, to sense where its prey was, to feel when they stopped wriggling.

Crawling was my only option, so I crawled. And I didn't stop crawling. Sometimes I found pools of sour water and I drank them without knowing what might be in them. Very often, I hit dead ends and had to turn back.

I lost track of time. Later, at the hospital, I learned I'd been gone for three days. In the dark of the mines, it felt like weeks. Weeks of numb limbs and pain that wouldn't fade and exhaustion that I had to fight through to keep crawling.

Twice, the Stitcher came for me. Twice, I survived it.

All I could do was keep moving. It was the only thing left that I had any control over: one hand at a time, dragging myself forward.

Then I saw light. At first, I thought I was imagining it. The dark does things to you like that: deprived of their ability to see, your eyes will create phantom shapes from the emptiness. But I still crawled toward it. And the light got bigger. And brighter. And the tunnel led upward for what felt like forever, and then I crept out through an opening and into the light.

I survived the Stitcher not through cunning or preparedness, but through pure chance. Later, when I learned how expansive the mines truly are, I realized how unlikely my escape had actually been. Across countless scores of victims, I was the only one who'd managed to find an exit.

I was taken to a hospital. The police asked me endless questions. I asked them some back. When were they going to open up the mines and search its depths?

Only one officer seemed to believe my story. He would listen intently and take notes as I told him everything I remembered. And he told me what he knew in return. Out of everyone I spoke to, he was the only one who actually seemed to want to know the truth.

I heard he'd been let go from his job a few years after my rescue. Isn't that a polite way of putting it? Let go? As though they'd been clinging to him and finally lost the strength to hold on any longer. They probably thought they were *letting go* of a problem, but I suspect the station felt his loss. He was likely one of the most effective officers they had.

But maybe it's for the best.

Maybe the thing in the mines should be left undisturbed.

A dozen glinting eyes stared at Abby from every corner of the room. She saw dogs and cats, their bodies misshapen. Limbs missing; extra limbs grown where they shouldn't. Recessed and missing jaws. An eye with two pupils.

Bridgette leaned back in her chair as she finished her story. She looked older than when they'd arrived. The skin under her dark eyes seemed thinner.

"That officer," Riya asked. "Is he still in town? Do you remember his name?"

Bridgette hesitated for a second. "No. He gave me his card in case I could help further but… No. I threw it out. I didn't want to think about the Stitcher, or the days I spent missing, anymore. Even though those two things have gone on to shape the entirety of my life."

Abby's breathing was shallow. *The mines.* Everyone in Doubtful knew that their town was built over a network of abandoned tunnels, but she'd been told they'd all been collapsed and flooded decades before she was born.

Apparently, someone had lied.

If the mines truly still existed beneath them, and they were being used by the Stitcher, it would answer so many questions. Like how Vickers was able to contain multiple victims at a time. How no one had ever heard them calling for help. And how no location for where the bodies had been butchered and sewn up could ever be pinpointed.

The mines were the ideal location for Vickers to hide his crimes. They'd been under Abby's feet this entire time, and she hadn't even known.

"Ms. Holm…" Rhys hesitated. "You talk about the Stitcher as though it's a monster. We… I…grew up believing it was a man. Charles Vickers."

"Mm." Bridgette's eyes fluttered closed. "A lot of people believe that. The caverns were dark. I can't tell you what the Stitcher looks like, but it wasn't a human."

Abby's hands ached from how tightly they were clenched. "You found a way out of the tunnels. Where was that? What part of town did you emerge into?"

Her eyes opened, and the stare she gave Abby was piercing and shrewd. "The lakeside. There was a wall of what looked like fallen rocks. Behind that was an entrance to the mines. It had been boarded over long before, but the boards were old and crumbling and left just enough room for a body to get through."

The lakeside. The place they'd visited so often and spent so many hours at. Abby knew the rockslide Bridgette meant. They'd walked past it a dozen times and never once noticed the mine entrance.

But then, they'd never been looking for it.

"Thank you," she said, standing. Rhys and Riya followed her lead. "If there's anything else you can think of—"

"Don't go into the mines." Bridgette took a slow, deep breath, then let it out carefully. "But, if you do, crawl *away* from the threads. The denser they are, they closer you are to the heart of its lair. And that's not somewhere you ever want to be."

Abby nodded stiffly as she turned to go. "Thank you."

Riya tugged at her sleeve, stopping them before she could reach the doorway.

"Ms. Holm. Bridgette." Riya turned back to her. "You said the Stitcher came for you twice while you were inside the mines, but you survived both times. What does that mean?"

For a moment, Bridgette was silent, her dark eyes inscrutable. Then, slowly, she reached for the blanket draped across her lap. Her long fingers curled into the fabric as she pulled it up.

The space underneath was empty. Her legs had been carved away, one at a time, above the knees.

"Go home," she said, as the blanket fell back over the empty space. "Forget this conversation. Forget your sister, if such a thing is possible. Stay indoors and seal your locks. The Stitcher isn't done yet."

One of the dogs in the room's corner began to growl, its ears pinned back.

"But…" Riya had gripped Abby's arm. Her fingers were shaking.

A cat's throaty, groaning yowl joined in with the dog's warning.

Something moved in the doorway behind them. Abby flinched as Bridgette's sister stopped inches from her back.

"The animals feel it," Vivian whispered. "They were touched by him in the womb, and now they feel when he draws near. One new bauble for his collection is not enough. He still intends to hunt."

A second dog began to growl. Glinting eyes flicked through the gloom, wide and tense.

"Go home," Bridgette said, her voice low and cracked. "I have nothing more to offer you."

A cat hissed at them as they fled into the hallway. Vivian watched them until they were out into the old, crumbling garden. Then the door snapped closed behind them. Abby saw Vivian's silhouette move beyond the glass as one, two, and then three locks were fastened.

Then even the silhouette faded away, leaving them completely alone.

TWENTY

〰〰〰

CONNOR SWUNG HIS LEGS. HE WAS TIRED. TIRED OF SITTING, tired of waiting, tired of staring at a house where nothing actually happened. Tired of getting texts from Riya asking him to check in and say he was still alive. Tired of getting updates about everything the others were doing without him.

Someone had to watch the Stitcher's house. He knew that. He just kind of wished that someone wasn't *him*.

The house's back door opened, and Connor snapped out of his slump. He'd seen Charles Vickers move through the building before—vague shapes passing behind dark windows, wandering the rooms almost like a specter—but this was the first time he'd actually come outside.

He carried a large black garbage bag. Connor fumbled for his phone, switched it to camera mode, and took several hurried photos. There was a high chance they wouldn't come out right. Technology was still jittery; most of his texts took at least two minutes to send. But he'd get what he could.

Vickers dropped the bag into the bin behind his house. Just regular trash, most likely. Even a serial killer would need to throw his garbage out occasionally. But Vickers didn't return to his house afterward. He paused, standing in his backyard, in the space between his back porch and the trees of the forest. Then he looked around, glancing toward the house Connor hid in.

Connor flinched back, pressing into the wall, willing himself to be invisible. The room was dark and the sun was at a bad angle to reveal its contents. That's what Riya had said, at least. She'd told him, as long as he didn't let his phone's light give him away, he'd be nearly invisible there. Connor pressed his phone into his shirt to blot out the glow.

Slowly, Vickers took his glasses off, folded them neatly, and placed them on the edge of the porch. Then he picked up a tire iron. The metal looked old and too dented to be very reliable at its job anymore. But Vickers carried it as he approached the tree line.

He stopped in front of an old pine. For a second, he just stared at it. And then he raised the tire iron and swung it with incredible force.

Chips of wood slashed off the trunk as the metal dug into it. He swung again and again, putting his whole body into it, slashing at the tree with such intensity that pine needles above shivered and fell loose.

Vickers screamed. It was brutal, furious, animalistic. His attacks on the tree intensified. Connor had a horrible sense that Vickers was picturing a face there, instead of the foliage he was shredding.

When he finally stopped, a whole section of the trunk had been stripped bare. A patch of pale white flesh oozed beneath the darker gray rind.

Vickers stood still, the tire iron hanging at his side, and stared at his work. Then, slowly, he turned back to his house. Placed the tire iron on the edge of the porch. Picked up his glasses and slid them onto his sweaty face. Then slowly, calmly, returned to inside his house.

"What the hell," Connor whispered, still clutching the phone to his chest. "What the hell, *what the hell*."

"She seemed really certain it was a monster," Riya said. "It's just… It's weird, right?"

Abby could barely keep up with the conversation as she forced her way through low branches to take the most direct route through the forest to the lake. Every fiber of her being was focused on their destination, and the conversation felt too much like a delay. "She didn't see him clearly. I'm sure, in the dark, he must have *seemed* like a monster."

"Maybe that's where the rumors started," Riya continued. She was smaller, and ducked and wove through the trees easily. Rhys, the largest of them, was unexpectedly quiet as he followed behind. "Even if people didn't talk about Bridgette's experience much, maybe her comments about it being a monster stuck in the public's conscience."

"My Alma said the same legends were around when she was a child," Rhys said.

"Ah." Riya huffed out a breath. "Okay, that's that theory gone."

Sunlight flashed through the branches ahead. Abby broke into a sprint and burst out from the forest, breathless, onto the sandy dirt ring surrounding the lake.

The sun was approaching its zenith. It shimmered off the lake's surface, forming a sparkling horizon. It should have been beautiful, but Abby couldn't bear to look at it. She turned right.

The remnants from their last bonfire were still there: a pit of char and ash, surrounded by the logs they used as makeshift seats.

She jogged past the bonfire and along the lake's edge. In the distance, the ground rose up into a steep mountainside forming one edge of the lake.

Bridgette said the entrance was behind the fallen rocks.

Huge boulders formed a natural barrier that came nearly to the lake's edge. Abby couldn't even spare the time to check her friends were following her as she sprinted around them.

She came face-to-face with an old rockfall. It created a steep slope of boulders and smaller shards of stone, running from the stony walls and ending at the water's edge.

This was the place Bridgette had directed her to. It *had* to be. No other part of the lake's edge matched her description. And yet, there was no visible mine entrance.

Panic swelled. She began clambering over fallen stones that threatened to twist her ankle with every step.

"Abs?" Riya called from somewhere behind. "Abs, slow down a minute."

"It has to be here. It's the only place Brigette could have been talking about. It has to be here—"

"It was," Rhys said, quietly.

Abby stopped. He was gazing up to a space just above her; she followed his eyeline. A bar of old, decayed wood was barely visible behind the rocks. If the stones were cleared away, it would have been just slightly higher than their heads.

Realization crashed over her. That had been the ceiling of the mine's entrance: the highest piece of wood used to brace the tunnel.

Her gaze dropped down, to where the entrance had once been. Now there was nothing but rubble. Some pieces were the size of a car. Some were as small as her fist. But they formed an impossibly dense, impossibly heavy barrier.

"No," Abby whispered.

She could still get in. The entrance was there, if she just cleared away enough of the stones. Abby began clawing at them, dragging rocks away and letting them tumble down the slope.

Rhys came up beside her. He bent forward and joined her in trying to move the stones.

Abby's pace was frantic. Each shifted stone made a cracking noise as it rattled away. Some splashed as they hit the water. She moved faster, and then faster still, her nails chipping and her fingertips aching.

Riya, standing at the lake's edge, called her name tentatively. Abby ignored her. Skin scraped off her palms as she forced them between rough stones, looking for purchase.

She didn't need to make a big opening. Just a gap, wide enough to squirm her way through. Just enough to get Hope back out of.

"Abs," Riya called again, and she sounded impossibly frightened. "Abs, I don't think it's going to work."

Her breathing was shallow. A whistling noise filled her ears, dampening everything else. She bared her teeth, her movements becoming more desperate, more urgent. Every rock she shifted just brought down a rain of other stones to fill the gap.

Rhys continued to work next to her. Abby glanced at him. His expression was unreadable, but she knew him well enough to understand what he was thinking. The realization came with a crushing amount of grief.

He was doing this for her sake. And he was going to dig for as long as Abby wanted them to. Even though he knew.

They were never going to get through.

She slumped back, collapsing onto one of the larger boulders, and stared blankly at the rockfall. After a second, Rhys carefully sat at her side.

Riya was right. The wall of fallen stones was too thick. They weren't going to shift it with their hands. Even heavy machinery would struggle with it.

She wanted to scream. She could barely muster the energy to breathe.

There was a soft rattle of loose stones behind them as Riya climbed the pile. She came up to Abby's other side and carefully tested a rock before sitting on it. For a moment, the three friends simply stared at the pile of rubble and the small glimpse of wood visible through it.

"Maybe the old stories were right," Riya whispered. "Maybe the mines were all collapsed shortly after they closed."

Abby squeezed her eyes closed. "No. Bridgette had no reason to lie to us. She came out through here—she must have—"

"Look," Rhys murmured.

They followed his nod toward the beam of wood. It was old and weather-bitten. Tinges of something dark seared its underside, like stains from oily smoke.

"Oh," Riya whispered, craning to see better. "Those are scorch marks. Maybe…maybe from dynamite? But…"

"They're more recent than the mine's closing," Rhys said. "From within the last decade or two."

It took a second for that to sink in.

"They collapsed the entrance after Bridgette came out," Abby said, her heart thundering. "She escaped the mines and showed the police where she'd gotten out and their only response was to collapse it." *Which means…* "The mines are still back there. Still open. They only sealed the entrance."

The tinge of hope crumbled into frustration. The tunnels were probably no more than ten or twenty feet past the blockage, but getting through was effectively impossible.

"I'm sorry," Riya said. She swallowed, then pulled her backpack off her shoulders. "You haven't eaten yet today, have you? Here."

Abby found her scraped and numb hands being filled with a bottle of water and a banana. She stared at them, mute, while Riya passed another set to Rhys.

"I ran some errands," she explained, almost apologetically. "Food and stuff for Connor while he watches the Stitcher's house. Food for us. I stopped by your house, too, to make sure your mother was still okay."

"You've been busy," Rhys noted.

"Well, yeah." She made a face. "Someone's got to be prepared. I just wish I'd had time for more. Especially if we're trying to get into the mines. You'd need lights, maps, a way to mark your path, maybe even a weapon. Without all that, you'd just end up like every other victim who's been taken down there."

Abby's mouth was parched; the bottled water looked too tempting. She unscrewed the lid and tilted it back, drinking deeply. Thoughts of how thirsty Hope must be stabbed through her.

She squeezed her eyes closed as she lowered the bottle. *Focus. Use your time wisely. The path's blocked; what's next?*

"There'll be other mine entrances," she said. "There has to be. If Vickers is keeping his victims underground, then he'll still have a way to get to them."

"Good point," Riya said. She stood, scanning the rocks and the lake's shore around them. "Even though Bridgette got out through here, it's hard to imagine this was ever Vickers's main entrance. There's no way to get a car through the forest, and it's a long way to carry a person, even if they're unconscious."

Abby stood as well. She'd drank the water, but she couldn't stomach the banana. "It would be somewhere closer to town, probably."

Riya nodded. "I did a school project on the mines when I was eight. The tunnels ran everywhere. They all connect underground, but there were dozens of entrances scattered across the town and its fringes. Of course, they also said the tunnels were permanently flooded. Probably to keep curious people from trying to explore them."

"I know of two entrances," Rhys said, and Abby snapped toward him. He held up a hand to quiet her anticipation. "I've *heard* about two. Supposedly they're both closed, though."

"They're worth checking out, at least," Riya muttered. She chewed on her lip. "The library should have historical records of the mine layout and any other entrances."

"That's our plan, then," Abby said. The thrum of tension was back in her limbs. She nearly shook with it. "Riya, you'll go to the library. Find anything you can; pass it to Rhys and I. We'll split up and start on the two passages he knows about. If they don't work, you can give us more places to search. There *has* to be a way in; Vickers probably knows the mines well enough to have all of the exits mapped."

Riya worked her jaw. "We shouldn't be splitting up. Bridgette said the Stitcher wasn't done yet."

"We left Connor on his own," Rhys noted.

"And he's watching the house. We'll have warning if Vickers tries to leave," Abby said.

"Mm." Riya still didn't look comfortable. "Fine. But you have to promise: if either of you find an opening to the mines, you won't go in. Not without giving us a chance to prepare first. Promise me."

Rhys answered easily. "I promise."

"Abby?" Riya pressed. "I need to hear it."

Hope's in there. In the dark. She'll be thirsty by now. Hungry, too, and cold. She only wore a singlet and shorts to bed. How cold are the mines? How long does it take someone to succumb to exposure?

Abby took a slow breath. "I'll text you if I find a way in."

"That's not what I asked."

Abby met her friend's eyes, and she held their gaze, unblinking. Three seconds. Five. Eight. Riya broke the stare first, shifting uncomfortably as she looked away. "Fine. Okay. If this is what it takes. But *please* remember: Hope will have the best chance if you go in there prepared. Okay? I'm not trying to be the bad person here. I just want to keep us *all* alive."

"Okay." Abby grimaced. "You're right. Sorry. I'll... I'll do my best."

What if she got wet? Bridgette said there were pools of water in the mines. How long until hypothermia sets in if her clothes get wet and she can't dry them?

Riya and Rhys were watching her, waiting for her go-ahead. She glanced up at the sun to judge its angle. Past midday. Their time was running out.

"Let's go."

TWENTY-ONE

⋀⋀⋀⋀

AS IT TURNED OUT, JEN WAS GLAD SHE HADN'T COMPLETELY
skipped school. Thompson was waiting in his cruiser outside the gates
when classes let out, which meant he'd left work early specifically to
pick her up.

"Hey," she said, sliding into the passenger seat and pulling her
belt on. He gave her a smile, but it was small and tight-lipped. She
narrowed her eyes at him. "Am I in trouble?"

"No? Of course not." His glance was quick. "Why, what have you
done that you think you'd be in trouble?"

He knew her well enough to know she had something to hide. She
weighed her options and went for an easy white lie. "I ate the last of the
ice cream without telling you."

"Oh." He relaxed. "Well, that's fine. It could certainly be a lot worse."

The car rumbled under them as he pulled away from the school
slightly too sharply. He grunted, apologetic, as Jen straightened herself.
Something was bothering him.

"What's happened?"

Thompson grunted again, apparently working his phrasing over in his mind.

"Come on, spit it out. The drive home is, like, three minutes tops, so we're going to have to fast-forward this heart-to-heart if we want to get it done in time."

This time, his smile was more genuine. "You're so much like your mother," he said, and it was impossible to tell if he said it as a complaint or as a compliment. Then he sighed, and his smile faded. "Things are bad at the station."

"Bad how?"

"When I arrived, my desk mate was drinking. He wasn't even trying to hide it in a coffee mug or anything; the bottle and label were both in plain sight. The chief walked in, took one look at him, and just walked past."

"Huh," Jen said.

"And then I found…" he cleared his throat. "There was a white-board up in the break room. Names were written on it. I sat there at lunch, staring at it for a full fifteen minutes before I realized what it was. The other officers were taking bets."

"About?"

"About whose body they were going to find next."

They pulled up in the driveway outside their house. Jen, stunned, could only stare at her father. He didn't try to turn the engine off, but sat there, gazing up at their new, spacious house, the one they'd barely unpacked into.

"I think it was a mistake to come here," Thompson said at last. He cleared his throat. "I thought I'd seen every kind of corruption and every level of jadedness in my time in the force, but this is something entirely different. And I don't think I can continue to respect myself if I stay working here. I'm… looking for another transfer. For as soon as I can."

It should have come as a relief. It just felt like an ache forming deep in Jen's chest.

Thompson finally turned the car off and opened his door.

"Wait," Jen said. He paused, one leg out of the car. The question hung on Jen's tongue. She wanted to know the answer *badly* even though she didn't want to actually ask it, but it tumbled out of her before she could stop the words. "Was Hope Ward's name on the board?"

"Yes," Thompson said, and climbed out of the car.

Abby faced the mine shaft that had been carved into the cliffside. Unlike the entrance at the lake's edge, she could see the form of the original mine opening: solid wood beams created a rectangular door wide enough to shift mine carts through. Even some of the track remained visible, though most of it had grown rusted and twisted.

That was where her luck ran out. Ten feet inside the mine was nothing but a wall of rubble. She'd already tried crawling over it, searching for any small gaps she could squirm her body through. There were none. It was sealed just as thoroughly as the lake-edge exit.

She typed into the group chat: No way in.

Their conversation sprawled behind them, a back-and-forth

between Abby, Rhys, and Riya at the library. It formed a pattern she couldn't stand to look at.

No way in here.

Try the wooded area behind McPherson Lane...

No access.

Go to...

No luck.

Turn down...

It's blocked too.

She watched the phone, waiting for her next set of directions. The sun was growing low. That was fine, though; she'd stopped by her home to pick up both her phone and her bike, and now she could traverse the empty expanses at the outer edge of town far faster than she could by foot.

They would find a way in. She had to believe it. Hours were trickling away, but all they needed was one gap, one tunnel that was only partially collapsed, and it would all be worth it.

Rhys's message came first. Mine is blocked too.

"Come on," Abby whispered. She leaned her back against the stone wall next to the mine, her bike propped next to her, as she waited. "Where to, Riya?"

Her heart plunged at the message.

It's 5:10. I'm calling it. We need to get indoors before nightfall.

Abby tasted sharp fear as she typed furiously. Not yet! Give me at least one more!

Her phone pinged with Riya's reply: I can't... That was the last mine shaft. The maps don't show any others.

Abby's legs gave out. She slid down the stone wall, her body shaking and her eyes burning. Then she dropped her phone into her lap. Ahead, Doubtful stretched across the horizon. The sky was turning an angry red at its edge as the sun fell.

There was nothing else she could do. She had to go home.

Riya hunched at a study table near the back of the library. In front of her was a stack of books on the history of Doubtful's mines, and a printout of the mining system overlaid with a rough guide of the town. It had taken a lot of time to put together, and the results were crushing. She'd dotted her map with circles, then covered each circle with a large red *X* when it was discovered to be a dead end.

"Library's almost closed," Mrs. Claver called. Riya gave her a tight-lipped smile. She was a regular at the library and frequently got that last-minute warning, but it usually left her feeling satisfied, not helpless.

She folded up her printed-out map and placed the guides back in the book cart for reshelving. Her phone vibrated when she was nearly at the door. It was Abby, responding nearly five minutes late with a single word: Ok.

"Sorry," Riya whispered. She stopped on the sidewalk outside the library and took a long, slow breath. The exhaustion was crushing her. On any other day, this would be when she went home and crashed into bed. Now, there was only more work to be done.

Abby climbed off her bike as she reached the fence line of her house. The building was dark, even though dusk was setting in. Any other day, Hope would be inside, rushing through her homework—or neglecting it entirely—so that she could throw herself in front of her computer and begin recording the video she'd been thinking about all day.

A tiny, irrational, delicious thought entered her mind. What if she opened the door and found Hope inside, tired from school and asking where Abby had been all day?

It wasn't impossible. Abby had never searched the house thoroughly after discovering her sister's window open. She could have whipped her friends into a frenzy over nothing.

Wouldn't that be embarrassing? Abby parked her bike beside the front porch with shaking fingers. *I'd never live it down.*

Then she climbed the steps and opened the front door and called out with an unsteady voice, "Hello?"—and was answered by only silence.

Fresh pain began to seep out through the cracks in her armor. She folded her arms around herself as her chest walls threatened to split.

She climbed the stairs. Her mother was in her room at the end of the hall, muttering, and refusing to open the door. That was probably for the best. Abby had no idea what she was supposed to say to the woman who'd raised her. Or how much her mother would even understand.

The door to Hope's room still stood open. Abby entered, and her burning eyes traced over the familiar furniture. The bed, left in disarray.

The window, wide open, letting the cooling air rush through. The drips of blood trailing from the windowsill and down to the floor, now dried.

Abby sat on the floor, with her back to the bed and Hope's pillow clutched to her chest, and closed her eyes as she held on to the last traces of her sister.

She didn't try to shut the window. Part of her wished the Stitcher would come back and take her too.

With every degree the blue sky cooled, Connor's nerves ratcheted up another notch.

Being alone during the day was bad enough. He absolutely couldn't be alone after dark.

But he also couldn't leave his post. Not without effectively abandoning his friends to the worst fate imaginable.

He pulled out his phone and began mashing out messages to Riya.

not gonna lie

its getting kinda late

and im getting kinda nervous

is the plan for me to stay here tonight ooor...?

A floorboard creaked in the lower half of the house. Connor's head snapped up, his fingers flying over the phone's keypad.

i think im about to die

The door to the room burst open and Riya plunged through, bathed by the dying daylight. Connor staggered back, shock quickly turning to relief. "Oh," he managed.

"You're not going to die, you fool," she said, reading his message even as she crossed to him. "I'm here. Did you really think I'd forget about you?"

"I dunno, I feel pretty forgettable some days," he said, and managed to chuckle. "You've had to run, what, three marathons' worth of circles just to keep your parents off your back, meanwhile mine still haven't called to ask where I am."

He's said it as a joke, but Riya instantly looked guilty. "I'm sorry."

"Don't be." He shrugged, slumping back in his chair. "I wouldn't trade them for your helicopter parents for the world. What's the excuse right now?"

Riya snorted as she unzipped her backpack. "I'm at an all-night study session with Casey James to prepare for next week's test. She owes me for covering for her when she went to an out-of-town party last month. Which is good. My parents already called her to confirm I was there."

She opened a message on her phone, then held it up so Connor could see.

Just lied my butt off to your parents about you being in the bathroom. Whichever guy you're with, he'd better be damn cute.

"Not sure if Charles Vickers hits *anyone's* definition of cute," Connor said, "but sure."

"How's our subject doing, anyway?" Riya nodded to the window. "Other than the tree mauling?"

They were both making sure to keep to one side of the room, out of view from Vickers's house, but Connor still grimaced as he glanced toward it. "Yeah, not much. I'm pretty sure I saw him eating an early dinner about half an hour ago. Real, uh, thrilling action."

"Honestly, I'm just grateful he *hasn't* tried anything dramatic." Riya pulled takeout sandwiches out of her backpack, plus a stack of extra bottles of water. "Here. Dinner. Sorry it's not much."

"Ah, I see you went for the decadence of deli turkey slices," Connor said, holding the sandwich up in both hands like it was a trophy. "I'm normally more of a highly processed ham person myself, but deli turkey slices have a certain rubbery quality that's hard to replicate in any other reconstituted meat."

"Just eat it, you goof," she said, grinning. "Then you can take a break from watch duty and get some sleep, if you want. We can swap over halfway through the night."

He lowered the sandwich. For the first time, he realized how exhausted she was. Her eyes seemed to droop from it.

"You know, I feel like I'm on a roll," he said. "Why don't you sleep first?"

She gave him a dubious look. "You've been here alone all day. You must be sick of it."

"Nah, it's fine. I'll give you a gentle kick or two if I feel like I'm getting dozy."

"I'll hold you to that," she said, unfastening the bedroll from the backpack. She must have pilfered it from her parents' rarely used camping supplies while they were still at work. "Good night, Connor. And thanks."

"Good night," he said, then unwrapped the sandwich and bit into its soggy bread as he turned his gaze back to the Stitcher's home.

***

"You forgot about me." Hope's voice barely sounded like her any longer. It was distorted, wavering at the edges, touching on three tones at once like one of the televisions that had become scrambled. "I was too much work and so you let me go and forgot about me."

"No," Abby whispered, even as Bridgette's voice played in the back of her mind. *Forget about her…if you can…forget about your sister…*

She knew where she was, now, surrounded by the cold and dark and the damp, sickly air.

She was with Hope, in the mines.

"You forgot me." There was the hiss of a match being lit, and a tiny circle of light formed ahead of Abby. Something moved on the other side of it. Something malformed, reshaped. Crisscrossed over and over by trails of red stitching threads.

"You forgot," Hope said, a hand where her shoulder belonged, a halo of ribs protruding like feathers from her back, her face half carved away, every part of her body stitched so tightly that she had to squirm to move closer. "And now look at what he's done to me."

"*No*," Abby screamed.

The echoes of her fading voice reverberated through their family home. She sat with her back against Hope's bed, drenched and clammy. Her chest ached like she'd taken a punch.

"No," she repeated, this time as a whisper.

Every time she blinked, she saw the misshapen dream-Hope again. It didn't help to tell herself that it was just a nightmare. The truth was, Hope had been taken, and Abby had no way of knowing what might have already been done to her.

She swiped her sleeves over her cheeks to clear away tears. Ahead of her was Hope's computer. Abby pushed the chair aside as she crawled to it and switched it on. It only took a minute to boot up. Abby stared at the screen, eyes glancing across the icons, searching for a folder that might hold photos.

There, near the bottom-left corner: Edited videos.

Abby opened it. Dozens of files were inside. Hope's beautiful face smiled out of nearly every icon.

She clicked on one at random, then unplugged the headphones from the computer. Hope's voice flooded the room, tinny from the speakers, but more real and alive than the dream's broken vocals. It was Hope reviewing a game she'd purchased.

The words washed over Abby like a soothing wave. Before she was ready for it, Hope was waving as she said goodbye, and the video ended. Abby clicked on a different clip, and then another, and another, as her knees began to ache from where she knelt on the floor, and gazed up at the screen.

When Abby clicked on the last video, she saw Hope was wearing her blue blouse with the lacing. She'd only borrowed that recently.

Abby leaned forward, arms folded on the tabletop and her chin resting on her hands.

It was a dance routine, recorded in their own backyard. Hope moved with grace, the smile never leaving her face as she swung and hopped to a pop song. Abby felt herself smile even as tears trailed down her cheeks.

Then her smile faded. There was something in the background of the video. Something that didn't belong.

The song finished. Hope's digital clone grinned as she jogged forward to turn off the recording, the screen going black. Abby clicked to replay it.

Hope threw her arms up as the routine began. The upbeat song played. Behind her, their yard looked like a forest. Trees and bushes and coiling vines overlapped. And in between them, just visible behind Hope's shoulder, was a man.

A man, in their house's backyard, watching Hope as she danced.

Abby's blood turned to ice as she paused the video and enlarged it, zooming in as far as possible, until the pixels formed distinct edges and the shape was as large as she could make it.

Then she sat back, her mouth dry and her eyes burning. There was no mistaking what she was looking at.

The quietly smirking face of Charles Vickers.

TWENTY-TWO

〜〜〜〜

RHYS WOKE BEFORE THE FOOTSTEPS EVEN REACHED HIS WINDOW.

Sleep never came easily. When it did, the dreams overlapped, frantic and stressful. He'd snap awake when he heard Alma move through the house to turn the television on, or when a car drove by, or when the neighbor's dogs barked.

There was nothing to fear about any of those sounds, but in the depths of night, they felt like the first warning that it was going to get bad again. The car could be a police cruiser, just like the ones that kept parking outside his house when his parents were taken. The dog could be warning him that something was nearby. Alma's footsteps might not actually belong to Alma.

That night, there was no dog or click of the television. He was woken by the crunch of feet on dirt, creeping toward his window.

He sat up, one hand reaching toward the phone on his bedside table. No clouds covered the moon, and its light was strong. He could see the visitor easily, even though she was still hidden in the shade of the trees.

Abby looked ethereal. As white as a ghost, her pale hair streaming around her drawn and intense face, her eyes blazing like coals.

Rhys unlocked and unlatched his window, and slid it open. He leaned through it as Abby reached him on the other side.

"Sorry," she whispered, as though the night was something too sacred to disturb. "I didn't want to risk frightening Alma by knocking."

"What are you doing outside?"

He tried not to let it sound like a recrimination. All the things he could say—*it's not safe, the Stitcher is still prowling, you can't be out at night*—were all things she knew just as well as him.

She held up her phone. On the screen was a photo. It was blurry and zoomed in, but Rhys could still make out a familiar flash of pink and lilac hair. Hope, just off to the side of the screen, barely visible.

"She recorded this just days before she was taken," Abby said. "That's Charles Vickers behind her."

Rhys's eyes slid to the shadowed, blurred figure in the background.

"He was stalking her," Abby continued, her whisper angry and aching and raw. "Do you still have the map we put together? The one where we marked possible locations to search?"

He nodded once.

"We went to every single known mine opening," Abby said. She leaned forward, her hands gripping the windowsill, her cool skin barely grazing Rhys's. "Which means he's getting in and out through one we don't know. Maybe even one he dug himself. I want to start looking for it. And I want to start looking in the abandoned houses."

He glanced up. The moon was still strong, but the moment clouds cut across it, they'd lose all visibility.

It was risky to go out at night. But, then, doing nothing carried a slate of risks of its own. And he knew, from experience, which one would hurt more.

"Okay," he said, and reached for his jacket.

"Huh," Jen said.

It was just after four in the morning. She stood at the kitchen window, a glass of water in one hand, her mind still feverish from the bad dreams that had woken her.

Two shapes moved through the trees that formed the edge of her backyard, both walking bikes at their sides.

It seemed impossible, but she thought they were two of the bonfire group: Abby Ward and Rhys, the boy who rarely spoke.

She felt a twinge of curiosity, calling her to slip outside and follow the pair. With very little effort, she squashed it.

Investigating creepy occurrences in the middle of the night in a weird town felt like the kind of scenario you'd only find in a horror movie. Specifically, a scenario that would fast-track the participants to the morgue. Whatever they were doing, they could do it on their own.

Jen finished her glass of water, switched the light off, and climbed back upstairs.

Do you want to see something bad?

Abby stared up at the house that had once belonged to Jessica Price. Two stories tall and wide enough to sprawl, it cast a heavy shadow over her.

It was growing harder to remember Jessica's face. That almost-forgotten experience—the overcast autumn night when she'd arrived for a birthday sleepover where she was the only attendant—felt like it belonged to a different lifetime.

But, for a few short years, Jessica had been one of her best friends. She remembered them braiding each other's hair and sliding small wildflowers into the gaps. She remembered playing games that were full of whispered secrets and dares.

More than that, though, she remembered sitting alone at Jessica's dinner table, feeling small and frightened. Jessica's parents weren't home. None of the other girls had arrived for the sleepover. And Jessica seemed *odd*.

And then came that breathy whisper: *"Do you want to see something bad?"* The words were full of tremors and dread and a strange, electric excitement. *"Not even my parents know about this yet."*

Abby had nodded even though she'd wanted to say no. And Jessica had taken her hand and led her up to the second floor, and then onto the smaller, thinner ladder that reached into the attic. There was a door up there, and Jessica had turned the handle and let it glide open.

It was Abby's first time seeing a dead body.

"He was gone for months," Jessica had whispered into Abby's ear. "But the Stitcher brought him back."

And Abby had remembered how Jessica had been missing from school for a week and how people had murmured that her uncle, who was living with her family, had gone missing during the night.

Then Abby had stared up at the mangled body suspended from the rafters by endless lines of red thread and she'd wanted to scream.

They'd stopped being friends after that night. Abby still felt guilty about it, even though Jessica had been the one to sever the relationship. From that night on, all Jessica had wanted to talk about was the Stitcher. During recess she drew pictures of what she imagined he might look like—not Charles Vickers, but the monstrous, inhuman thing unleashed from the mines—and passed them around. She recited the singsong rhymes so quickly that the words blended together. She threatened to send the Stitcher after anyone who hurt or upset her.

Less than a year later, Jessica's parents failed to show up to work one morning, and Jessica herself was absent from school. Their unofficial fate was very similar to that of Abby's own father: listed as missing, possibly having left town, or possibly victims whose remains had not yet been found.

Their disappearances remained a mystery. And their house remained empty. Abby gazed up at it and found her eyes drawn to the small window in the attic.

The body would have been taken away a long time ago. But the hairs on her arms rose just from looking at the roofline's silhouette.

"Are you certain you want to try here?" Rhys asked.

They stood in the center of the street. It was still well before dawn, and the houses around were all silent.

She didn't know how to answer him, or how to confess that she took longer routes to avoid going near Jessica's house, or how to explain the sheer deluge of emotions she felt while looking up at it. Enormous guilt, for abandoning her friend during her trauma. Curiosity, to revisit the inside of the house that had shaped so much of her life. More guilt, for *feeling* that curiosity.

But they'd used Rhys's map to mark locations that were worth searching, based on proximity to where victims were taken. And Jessica's house was surrounded by red dots. As much as Abby wished she could avoid the place, Hope had to stay her only priority.

"Yes," she said, and led the way toward the building.

They left their bikes leaned against what had once been a fence before a vine had swallowed it. They each had a flashlight, and pulled them out as Abby led the way to the front door.

It wasn't locked. The hinges were old and groaned when she nudged the wood inward.

Inside was like revisiting a long-lost memory, only the memory had been corrupted into a nightmare during the years it had wandered. Familiar wallpaper hung down in shreds. The couch Abby and Jessica had crawled over while watching television was still there, but badly faded, and the cushions and padded seats had been pulled off and discarded onto the floor. Everywhere was coated in dust and cobwebs.

Rhys glanced at her and gave a quick nod. They were working with a plan. A quick loop through the house and then the backyard. They were looking for anything out of place: footprints through the dust, trampled plants in the backyard, areas that seemed to have been visited and visited recently.

But, even as Rhys vanished into a dark kitchen full of broken tiles, Abby found herself gazing up at the stairs.

Do you want to see something bad?

A single red thread had become caught around one of the banisters. It was only a few inches long, but a loose end dangled down, almost as though asking to be pulled.

Abby reached up. She took hold of the thread's end and gave it a light tug. It pulled taut.

Not caught around the banister, then, but tied. Deliberately.

Rhys had appeared in the doorway. He watched silently as Abby began to climb the stairs.

The thread had probably fallen there during the investigation into the Price disappearances, Abby told herself, even as their rules played through her mind like a recording she couldn't escape. *Red thread means a body is nearby.*

The stairs groaned under her weight. The house had never seemed this old or this weary when Abby had played in it as a child. She reached the landing and saw another loop of red thread, this time laying on the carpeted hallway. She raised her flashlight. More glimpses of red spread out ahead of her: looping over doorknobs. Crossing the hall in sweeping arcs. Trailing from the lights like cobwebs.

Dozens of feet of it, concentrating as it grew closer to the furthest room.

The light in Abby's hand shook as she ducked under the first loop of thread. Rhys had followed her up the stairs, but he stopped at the landing, silently watching her.

The hallway must remind him of the scene in the forest where his parents were found, Abby realized. He'd told her about it, in halting whispers: the lines of overlapping red, leading up to the dripping flesh parcel suspended so high above the forest floor. Threads exactly like these. She should turn around, usher him back down the stairs. Shield him, the way he'd tried to shield her.

But the final door was close. And there was an urgent, crawling fear building in her chest that her sister had been returned to the world sooner than Abby had anticipated.

Do you want to see something bad?

She stepped over a low-hanging line of thread. It swayed slightly as her shoe brushed against it, and that small touch seemed to send shivers through every other thread in the hall, as though calling them to life.

Thread had been tied to the handle of the final door. Abby knew this room. It had been the craft room; expensive fabrics and jars of buttons lined shelves around the walls. She and Jessica hadn't been allowed to play in it.

She touched the door. It already stood ajar an inch. She was afraid the looping thread around its handle might hold it closed, but the dozens of lines seemed to stretch endlessly as the door drifted inward.

A naked dress form stood in the room's center, its blank face pointed toward Abby, its arms reaching toward her as though to pull her into its embrace.

The room was almost exactly how she remembered it. The bolts of cloth piled up. The boxes of needles and thread. The stacks of patterns used to construct dresses and pants and jackets.

Two more mannequins were positioned behind the first. They'd been contorted, bent over, limbs jutting out awkwardly.

The house groaned, as though its burden had become heavier.

Abby raised her light back toward the closest dress form, and felt her heart miss a beat.

Its sightless face stared back at her.

It had never had a face when she was a child.

In the few occasions she'd been allowed to see into the room, the dress mannequin had been a bare cloth torso, nothing else.

Human arms reached out of it, the fingers contorted as though to grip her. A human's face gazed at her from where it had been sewn into the cloth. Its eyes and mouth were stitched shut. Patches of skin had been pulled up and sewn in around the jaw and the neck to make it fit on top of the model. The arms each had one joint too many.

The two mannequins behind it were worse. Limbs had been constructed out of body parts that had never been limbs during life. A head was attached the wrong way, staring at its own back. One had four legs.

Abby opened her mouth, then closed it again. Fear and shock and grief stung her eyes as she blinked. The bodies were all old and desiccated. Dry skin threatened to tear around the stitches.

She'd found the Price family, she was fairly sure.

A floorboard groaned. Abby stared downward, even though there was nothing to see except dusty floor. The sound seemed to have come from the level *below*. But both she and Rhys were on the second floor…

Light fingers touched her back. She flinched, then gasped. Rhys's face came into view. He raised a finger and pressed it to his lips.

He'd heard the sounds too.

They weren't alone in the house.

She and Rhys held still as they listened. She could feel his pulse beating through the fingers resting on her shoulder. His dark eyes were fixed and unseeing.

Whatever was below them shifted through the house. Abby fought to remember the building's layout as she tracked it: through the living room, past the kitchen, back into the hallway. Boards groaned under its weight.

The house wasn't this loud when we moved through it.

The building groaned like its life was being squeezed out of it as the unseen figure shifted its weight. Abby glanced at Rhys and knew he was thinking the same thing.

A person shouldn't sound this heavy.

Abby's flashlight burst bright and then died. Darkness rushed around them.

Fear came like a sharp stab through her chest. Flashlights were simple technology. They almost never went out, not even when things got really bad.

The Stitcher was here.

The footsteps were carrying him away, though. Toward the front door. Then through it.

Abby's body moved before her mind could even process what she was doing. She darted past Rhys and along the hallway, her feet light as she ducked and wove around the threads. He grabbed at her, trying to stop her, but she slipped out of his grip.

She took the stairs fast. At the back of her mind, she knew she needed a plan—some idea of what to do if she caught up to him, some kind of weapon—but there was no room for it between her thrumming heartbeats and the rushing fear.

The Stitcher was here.

She couldn't lose him.

Abby landed in the downstairs hallway. The front door hung open. She ran for it, but stopped short on the front step.

When she and Rhys had arrived, only two of the streetlights had been working. Now, they were all dead. She couldn't see anything. No glimpse of movement. No sign of which direction he might have gone.

Her flashlight flickered, then came back to life, like a dead body being revived. She stared at it, mutely, and at the patch of pathway that it illuminated.

Rhys came to a halt next to her. His face looked bloodless, his lips pulled back from his teeth.

"Don't," he whispered, and his voice was hoarse. "Don't you dare leave me."

Abby didn't know what to say. Or how to apologize when every fiber of her body wanted to keep running until she caught up to the man who had taken her sister. Instead, she found Rhys's hand and held it tightly. He squeezed back, his fingers shaking, and for a long moment, they stood together like that, staring along the dark road laced with predawn mist.

Abby's light lingered over the patch of pathway that had caught her eye. There was a footprint there, formed from lingering dew. She knew it wasn't either hers or Rhys's. It had been made by a bare foot; the curving sole and the toes left clear impressions.

And it looked far, far larger than either of their own shoes.

She didn't need to draw Rhys's attention to the print. He'd already seen it. They were both silent for a long time, then Rhys spoke the question they were both dreading having to ask.

"Are we certain the Stitcher's human?"

Abby had no idea how to answer him.

TWENTY-THREE

∿∧∧∧∿

CONNOR TILTED BACK IN HIS CHAIR, BALANCING IT ON ITS TWO
back legs, his own foot nudging against the wall to keep him steady.

Day Two of guard duty was far less exciting than Day One. And
Day One had already been painful. There were only so many hours you
could spend staring at a house before your mind began to scream from
sheer lack of stimulation.

Technically, he had everything he needed. Food, water, power banks
for when his phone's battery drained. Only, he couldn't even use his
phone to distract himself. Riya had been clear on that: If Vickers left,
there was a good chance he'd do it quietly and discreetly, and even a
minute of lost focus could cost them everything.

So he just had to sit, surrounded by a hundred things more inter-
esting than watching the Stitcher's house—he would have even been
thrilled by the chance to peel some of the flaking paint off the walls at
that point—and do his best not to fall asleep.

Riya had been good to him, though. She'd gone on a supply run early that morning, and now his temporary home held a stash of soft drinks and chips and sandwiches. Riya had even brought him with some jars to, in her words, *take care of business*. He'd left the jars empty and stacked in the corner. The house might be old, but it still had two bathrooms and two intact toilets. Neither of them actually flushed, but Connor had decided that was going to be someone else's problem.

The front door on Vickers's house moved. Connor, who'd been balancing the chair on its two back legs, threw himself forward. He clutched at the edge of the windowsill and sunk down low so that only the top of his head would be visible, as he watched.

Charles Vickers stepped outside. He was wearing one of his red sweater-vests over a long-sleeve shirt and a pair of brown slacks. The last time Connor had gotten a good look at him was in the aftermath of the tree massacre, and he looked like an entirely different person. The red, sweating face and bared teeth had vanished back under Vickers's immaculately manicured mask. His hair was combed. His fingernails trimmed short and kept clean. The small, persistent smile lingered around his thin lips as he locked his front door behind himself, then bent down to touch the potted plant beside his front door. He straightened, the smile unflinching, and Connor sank back as Charles Vickers stepped off his front porch and walked the short path to the street.

He's leaving, Connor realized, and that thought was followed by a wave of pure panic. *It's actually happening. He's leaving.*

What am I supposed to do?

"Don't do this to me," Riya whispered.

It was after ten. The sun had been up for hours, but every text she'd sent to the Jackrabbit group chat had gone unanswered.

Abby hadn't been at her home. Rhys wasn't at his. And she didn't know where else to look for them.

A long series of messages to her classmates and classmates' parents had brought back sparse results: a handful had replied saying they hadn't seen either Abby or Rhys that day, but most didn't even give an answer.

That meant technology was going jittery again. Riya's old-school phone still seemed to be working, but it was getting harder and harder to contact anyone else.

That, or…

Word would have spread about Hope. Riya had never felt the ostracization that came from being close to a Stitcher victim before, but she thought she was getting a taste of it now. Especially since she was asking about where to find Abby Ward. People would see that message and delete it, as though the name alone was able to attract something malevolent into their lives.

Leafy trees shaded the path. It was a quiet part of town. Riya had already biked through most of the central streets without luck; she was now trying the outskirts. Questions bounced through her mind like a one-woman game of table tennis; should she go back to Connor? He wasn't answering her texts either. Should she try Abby's home again? Rhys's?

Riya's breath caught. Her thoughts had been too loud, too frantic. They'd distracted her from her surroundings.

And from the slow, steady thud of footsteps approaching from behind.

Riya's skin crawled. She came to a halt. The trees shaded her, but she felt her core grow hot even as her extremities turned cold.

Rule Two. Don't be alone.

The footsteps continued to move toward her, steady, unhurried. Following her down this path, a path she very well knew was never used.

Riya swung.

The dirt trail behind her was empty. The bushes on either side rippled in the wind, then fell still again.

A lump formed in Riya's throat. She pulled her phone out again and switched it on. Pixels flickered, threatening to bleed out to white, before stabilizing again.

She didn't know what else to do. She opened the newest number on her phone, the only one she thought might still answer her. And might still want to help.

"Huh," Jen said. She lay on her back on her bedroom floor, phone held above her head and silhouetted by morning light. She'd made a small start unpacking the boxes before realizing the futility. Not much point trying to settle in when it would all need to be boxed up again.

Riya's message was an enormous paragraph of apologies and explanations and pleas, and Jen had to skim read it to get the gist. She was looking for Abby and Rhys. "Huh," she repeated to herself, and typed out a reply. Saw them last night, about 4am. Walking through the trees behind my house.

Thompson moved through the building below her. It was Saturday, which meant they both had the day off from their respective institutions. His footsteps paused, and he called up the stairs to her. "It's a nice day. Don't you want to head out? Enjoy the sun?"

She thought about the red threads she'd found. About the haunted look in the others' eyes. About how, when she'd arrived at school the previous day, people had whispered Hope Ward's name in frightened tones, but then by lunchtime, no one was willing to talk about her at all. "Nope," she called back.

Her phone pinged. Riya: Thanks

It was only a single word, but it felt dejected. Slightly desperate. Jen flexed her jaw.

If you get involved now, you'll have to be prepared to go the whole way. This isn't the kind of thing you can do in half measures.

She thought of Riya's gentle eyes. Her long fingers, clasped around one another as she tried with intense sincerity to warn Jen about the town. She wasn't sure how much goodness existed in Doubtful, but the bulk of it had to be concentrated in that one girl.

"Damn it," she muttered, and rolled to her feet. She jogged down the stairs to find her father.

He was drifting between the kitchenette and the room that was supposed to be his study but only really held a desk, an old computer, and an empty bookcase. Unlike Jen, he didn't have the luxury of leaving his things in boxes until he was able to transfer.

"Hey," Jen said. "Is there any way you can plug into your secret surveillance system and find Abby Ward?"

The secret surveillance system was their joke. Jen liked to pretend Thompson was decked out like a first-class spy. In return, he would sigh longingly.

The request was at least enough to snap him out of his distracted fugue. His eyes sharpened as he stared at her. "I thought you were staying clear of her."

"I am." Jen held up her phone. "I'm doing this as a favor for a friend."

He watched her, dubious. Jen wiggled her phone. "You know, friendship? That thing teenagers are expected to form?"

Thompson sighed and turned toward his office. "I'll see what I can do."

Jen waited in the hallway, scuffing her boots across the old wood and watching tiny dust motes form, while Thompson spoke to someone on the phone. He came back a few minutes later, looking weary. "An officer saw Abby Ward and a companion traveling down Breaker Street twenty minutes ago."

"That's perfect. Thanks." Jen tapped out a quick text, then glanced along the hallway, toward the front door.

I decided I was doing this, didn't I? No half measures.

"You know, you were right. I should get out and enjoy the weekend."

Thompson's whole face soured. "You're going to Breaker Street, aren't you?"

"I'm going to meet up with my friend," Jen deflected. "Who knows what we'll do? We might go to the pool. Or play lawn bowls. Does this place even *have* lawn bowls? That's something I'll have to find out."

"Jen…" He took a deep breath, then sighed heavily. Jen waited, one hand on the door. In the morning light, it was hard not to notice how old he seemed, and how many new creases had formed around his face. "You know I trust you. You've always been bright and you've always had a good sense of self-preservation. And I'm trying to trust your judgment now too. Just... Be safe, okay?"

"I will," she said, and as she stepped out of the house, she hoped that was a promise she could keep.

Things were about as bad as they could get.

Connor's teeth rattled as he jogged down the stairs. Charles Vickers was on the move, and Connor didn't know what to do about that.

Riya wasn't answering his frantic texts. None of the Jackrabbits were. Which could only mean one thing: the phones had gone on the jitter again.

Technically, it could mean two things, Connor reasoned. There was the possibility that they weren't replying because they were all dead.

He tried not to think about that too much.

He landed in the empty downstairs hallway. Furniture, covered by discolored sheets, stood like ghosts in the corners. Connor held his phone in one hand, staring at a screen that showed his last three messages and nothing new, while he rubbed the back of his other hand across his forehead.

What would Riya do?

She'd follow Charles Vickers. That was obvious. That was the *plan*. Follow him, because odds were he would lead them to where Hope was being kept.

But then?

What was the plan when Vickers arrived at his destination? At, say, an empty house? Was Connor going to rush in, all heroic, and try to save the day? He'd die. He wasn't strong like Rhys or fit like Riya. If he threw his fist too hard, his shoulder would dislocate. Knowing him, he'd trip on the first stair and impale his head on a rusty spike and do Vickers's job for him.

Calm, he recited to himself. *Stay calm. Panicking won't fix anything. Stay present. Stay focused.*

He'd figure out the heroic-death hurdle when he reached it. For now, he only had one thing to do.

Not lose Charles Vickers.

The abandoned house's door creaked as Connor opened it, and he grimaced. *Stay hidden.* That was the other most vital instruction. They couldn't let Vickers suspect he was being watched. Which meant, if Connor was going to follow him, it would have to be at a far distance, and very quietly.

He crept around the house's side. The long grass hid him when he crouched in it, even though he was pretty sure he was gathering a collection of small insects as he moved through the stalks. He reached the house's fence and raised himself up just high enough to see over the strings of handmade bead necklaces and the teddy bear that had lost most of its stuffing through a hole birds had picked in its foot.

Vickers had moved faster than he'd expected. He was already at the street's end and turning right.

"Okay," Connor whispered. "Okay, okay, we can do this, okay."

He moved through the houses' yards. There, at least, he'd have enough cover to duck behind if Vickers turned around. It was slow going, and he felt the ligaments in his wrist and shoulder twist uncomfortably as he pulled himself over a fence.

Finally, though, he was at the street's end. Vickers was in view, about forty yards ahead, walking briskly and with his hands in his pockets.

Riya had theorized that Vickers would take a hidden path to get to his secondary location. Either traveling through the woods, or taking a back lane where there wouldn't be any eyes to watch him.

Apparently, she'd been wrong, and Vickers wasn't afraid to walk directly through town.

Connor climbed through a hole in the final fence, then dusted himself down before settling in to follow his target.

He hung well back and kept his phone out, hoping that, if Vickers turned around, Connor could act as though he was out on a casual stroll and absorbed in his technology. They were far enough apart that Vickers wouldn't see how shaky he was, at least.

Vickers didn't turn, though. And his path led them further and further toward the center of town.

Maybe he's not going to Hope, after all. Maybe he's just out to run some errands. Even serial killers need to buy groceries.

Or maybe he really does keep his secret secondary location in the heart of town. I wouldn't even be shocked. Everything he does is right under our noses because he knows there are never any consequences.

Connor kept typing notes into the group chat, updating the others about which streets Vickers turned down. The texts still weren't going through, but at least they'd have them as a record if Connor abruptly vanished.

Just another thought to try not to dwell on.

They reached the main streets. Vickers paused a few times to read fliers posted in windows and to stare into the town's café, as though contemplating interrupting the diners there. It was a Saturday morning and the streets held a handful of shoppers, but they all turned aside—either entering shops, or crossing the road, or even turning around and going back the way they'd come—the moment they saw Vickers. It meant that there was almost no one around to help hide Connor's presence.

And then Vickers arrived at his location. The movie theatre.

The old marquee above the doors announced a lackluster run of films. Like most parts of the town, the theatre was slowly dying, and symptoms were everywhere: the seats were flat and tacky, the concessions stale, and the movies offered always weeks behind what arrived in the bigger towns. Vickers stared up at the advertised names as though fascinated, and then stepped through the doors.

"Okay," Connor whispered, tapping out a final text that he already knew wouldn't be answered. "The theatre. He just wants a fun day out. A distraction from the horrors, maybe."

He pressed the button to send his message, Vickers into theatre, then paused.

It would be easy enough to hang around the shops for an hour or two until the movie finished and Vickers came back out.

But what if that was a mistake?

Riya had believed the Stitcher would take some kind of hidden path to his holding location, just in case he was spotted on the way.

What were the odds the theatre was a part of that path?

It had doors that led out into the back alleys, the narrow spaces between shops that were always crammed with dumpsters.

Or, worse, what if there was some kind of basement in the theatre? What if Vickers had found a way into the mines right in the town's center?

It was starting to feel like paranoia. But, then, paranoia might be warranted. His friend's life was at stake, and the others had trusted him not to lose sight of Vickers. No matter what.

He wished he had Riya with him. Even Abby would have been grounded enough to act as a common sense filter. But all he had was himself and a brain that was on the edge of panicking.

Only one clear thought rattled through him, like a moth beating itself against a flame: *Don't let Vickers escape.*

He bounded up the stairs and shoved through the theatre's doors. The foyer smelled of old popcorn and spilled soda. Vickers was alone in line, buying his ticket from a girl at the counter who had shrunk back as far as she possibly could while still completing the transaction.

Connor hung close to the doors, pretending to examine a rack of fliers advertising their current offerings.

Finally, Vickers left the counter, a box of popcorn under one arm. He glanced around the foyer, his cool eyes and cold smirk landing on Connor for just a second before he wandered down the hallway to the theatres.

Connor rubbed his hands on his pants to wipe the clamminess off them as he rushed to the counter, ignoring the other attendant who'd raised his hand to greet him, and went straight to the teen who'd served Vickers.

He knew her, he realized. They had history class together. "Hey, Kelsey," he managed. "Weird question. What movie was that guy before me going to see?"

"Not a weird question at all," she returned, her bleached hair like a halo around her face as she grimaced. "He was going to *Snap Decision*."

He'd picked a comedy. It felt like such an odd choice, and yet, very on-brand.

"Yeah, that's the one I want to see too," Connor said, fumbling for his money. Would he look obvious if he went into the theatre alone, with no concessions? Probably. "And, um, a small popcorn and lemonade."

Kelsey made a weird face at him but wordlessly put the transaction through. She even gave him a friend's discount, possibly out of pity. Connor snatched up his snacks and ticket and half jogged along the dark hall to Theatre 4, the final door.

The room was already dimmed and the trailers playing when he entered. Only one seat was taken. Vickers, sitting in the center of the row at the back of the theatre.

Connor had wanted to sit behind him so that he could watch him without being visible. Instead, he was forced to choose a seat in the front section, closest to the screen. He placed his drink in the cup holder, the popcorn on the floor by his feet, and took his phone out as a jarring laugh track blared through the room.

In theatre with Vickers. Wish me luck.

Then he switched his phone to vibrate and turned it off. Its blank screen was just barely reflective enough to act as a dull mirror, showing him a distorted and desaturated version of the room behind him. When he held it just right, he could see Vickers's form, nestled in the back of the room. His glasses glinted in the low light.

Wish me luck, he thought again, and hunched down for a long wait.

————————

It was all Riya could do to keep breathing as she biked through town. Jen had come through for her. Jen, who'd somehow cared more than the dozens of classmates and studymates and attentive parents who were ignoring her texts.

She hoped Jen would leave Doubtful, and quickly, before the town began to poison her too.

Her bike skidded as she ground to a halt at the start of Breaker Street. This was where they'd watched the covered stretchers being removed from the abandoned home. Long strips of police tape still fluttered in the breeze, not yet dusty or sun bleached like the other lengths scattered through town, but already just as forgotten.

They'd been here twenty minutes before, Jen had said. Which meant they could have very easily vanished into another part of the town already. But at least it was a start.

Footsteps crunched over gravel behind her. Riya's heart kicked up a notch. She turned.

A figure stepped out from the shadows of the abandoned commercial signage store. Jen's bright yellow top was like a gasp of color in the otherwise faded town.

"Hey," Jen said. She thrust her hands into her jeans pockets as she shrugged. "Hope this is the kind of party I'm allowed to crash."

"Any time," was all Riya could manage. Her jaw quivered, and she reached toward Jen. Jen reached back, and they somehow ended up in a tangle halfway between a hug and shaking hands.

"Thanks," Riya said, clearing her throat as she patted Jen's arm. "I just… I just need to find them."

Jen gave a short nod, and turned toward Breaker Street. "We will."

The houses felt uncomfortably quiet as Riya and Jen followed the street, Riya pushing her bike. A new *For Sale* sign had gone up since she'd last been there. Birds fought in a tree, their wings beating in sharp gusts, but that was the only sound Riya could hear.

"Hey," Jen said, nudging her. "Bikes."

Riya recognized them. Abby and Rhys's bikes were parked down the side of an abandoned house. The same house they'd seen the bodies removed from.

"Okay," she muttered, then sucked in a breath and hopped the fence in a lithe movement. Strands of loose police tape whipped around her. The house's front door still stood open, the way the paramedics had left it. Inside was heavy with shadows.

"Abs?" She didn't dare call loudly, but kept her voice at a stage whisper. "Rhys?"

Something shifted inside the building. She heard the distinct crackle of broken glass being crushed. The scrape of heavy feet across the floor.

Jen was at her shoulder, her breathing shallow. "Don't go in," she whispered.

Riya's eyes trailed toward the doorway. Dark stains were smeared across its edges. Her stomach turned as she recognized old blood.

More glass crunched as something moved through the house. At the end of the hallway, Riya thought she could see a faded handprint on the discolored wall, made of the same rust red color that crusted the doorframe. It smeared to one side, as though someone had been grasping at the wall while being dragged away.

A shape moved ahead of the handprint, blocking it from sight. The hall was too dark to see anything except an indistinct outline. It stared at Riya, eyes glinting in the low light, then it began to move toward them.

Jen's grip pinched her arm as she began to pull Riya back, away from the house.

The figure was moving closer, rocking uneasily as it trailed the length of the hall. Its pace was growing faster. Riya's heart was in her throat, choking her.

And then the figure lurched forward and into the light.

It was Abby. She looked bad; sickly and tired and no longer the careful, calculated girl Riya had grown up with. Her normal poise was gone. She looked ready to sink her claws into anything that moved.

"You terrified me," Riya gasped, pressing a hand to her throat as she bent at the waist. She gave herself just long enough to pull fresh oxygen into her lungs, then said, "I've been searching everywhere for you. Why haven't you been answering my texts?"

Abby pulled her phone out of her pocket. She stared at it for a second before turning it to face Riya. Her phone's screen was a trailing mess of symbols and flickering lights, full of strange phrases that blended into one another before vanishing entirely.

"Sorry," she said. "Jitters."

"Mine as well," Rhys said. He moved out of one of the side rooms, tucking his own phone away. "What's happened, Riya?"

Too much. Riya braced her hands on her knees. "Connor's gone quiet again. I needed Jen to even find you. I spent part of last night trying to research the mines online, but there's almost no information about them."

"I didn't realize how late it was. We've been searching for entrances," Abby said, and she sounded slightly numb. "We must have crossed half the town by now."

Riya grimaced. She should have guessed her friend would break curfew. It had been too much to ask her to stay put for two nights in a row. "As long as you're both still safe. But I don't think we're going to have much luck just by searching randomly, or else we would have heard about people finding ways into the mines well before this."

"That's why we've been looking in areas where people don't normally go," Rhys said when Abby failed to speak. "Houses where victims were found. Wooded areas. Places that are difficult to reach."

Riya nodded. It wasn't a bad plan. It was what she'd do if she was out of options and getting desperate.

"You're trying to get into the mines, huh?" Jen asked. She leaned against the house's wall, eyeing the fluttering police tape coldly. "If I was trying to get somewhere restricted, I'd look for someone who knew more about it than I did. Do you have any local historians or mine experts in town?"

"As far as we know, the only living person who's been inside the mines is Charles Vickers," Riya said.

"Not quite." Abby's voice sounded faint, but her eyes had turned hard. "There's someone else who's been into them. And I think she knows more than she told us. We need to visit Bridgette Holm again."

TWENTY-FOUR

∿∧∧∧

THE MOVIE PLAYED. CONNOR SAW VERY LITTLE OF IT. IF SOMEONE had asked him about the plot, he'd have nothing to tell them.

He held his phone carefully, just one corner exposed and angled so that it caught Charles Vickers's shadowed form in its reflection.

Vickers was unnervingly still. Only the glints of his glasses highlighted where he was. He never laughed, even when there was a pause in the film's audio to allow for it. Maybe the movie wasn't very funny. Or maybe Vickers just didn't have a sense of humor.

Slow, creeping paranoia grew, infecting Connor like a sickness.

The more he watched Vickers, the more convinced he became that Vickers's glinting glasses weren't pointed at the screen. That they were aimed toward Connor himself. Fixated on the phone, watching Connor just as closely as Connor was watching him.

He couldn't take it any longer. He lowered the phone, hiding it.

Above, two characters on-screen were having an argument in a restaurant, and it was escalating. The beats in the audio and the reactions from the background actors suggested it was supposed to be funny, but all Connor could hear were increasingly angry voices, rising to yell at one another.

Yelling, and footsteps.

Not coming from the cobwebbed speakers at either side of the theatre, but from behind. Descending toward him.

Connor fumbled for his phone. He aimed the reflective screen toward the back of the theatre. Vickers's seat was empty.

A hand landed on his shoulder just as one of the actors on-screen screamed. Connor jolted like electricity had passed through him. He wasn't sure his heart was even still beating.

"Are you enjoying the movie, Connor?" Vickers asked.

Vickers wasn't an especially tall man, but he seemed enormous at that moment.

Connor's eyes watered. His body had turned icy cold. He didn't know what else to do; he forced a tight smile as he nodded.

"I'm not," Vickers said. His hand was still resting on Connor's shoulder. Lights played off his glasses, and it was impossible to see his eyes behind them.

"Oh," Connor choked out. "Sorry."

Characters furiously yelled above them. A fist slammed onto the table. Vickers's fingers dug in, not quite pinching but coming close. He leaned closer. His voice was almost drowned out by the movie's audio. "I know you're following me." The fingers twitched, just hard enough to hurt. "I know what you're doing."

Connor didn't dare speak. He didn't even dare breathe.

Vickers's lips peeled back into a smile. He was so close that Connor could see the screws in his glasses and the staining at the edges of his teeth. His voice was velvet and poison. "She's not coming back."

Connor's heart felt like it was going to burst. The characters above them yelled and yelled and yelled, their words overlapping.

A soft chuckle escaped Vickers. He squeezed again, hard enough to hurt, then let go. "Enjoy the movie, Connor Crandall. Life is short. Borrow joy where you can."

Abby's hair stung her face as they flew through town on the backs of their bikes. Jen balanced on the back of Riya's, apparently a temporary addition to their group.

Tiny scrapes and cuts ran across Abby's shins and hands, mementos from hours searching crumbling buildings in the dark. It was almost a relief to feel those aches, though. They helped distract her from the way her mind hurt every time it circled the impossible problem of getting into the mines.

She and Rhys had searched through so many houses. So many abandoned yards. So many sparse patches of trees. Rhys's map was a wash of red ink, marking the locations they'd covered.

And she was still no closer to getting Hope back.

They slowed to a halt outside Bridgette Holm's house. The building seemed colder and more recessed than when they first visited it, as though it had shrunk in on itself. Abby let her bike collapse against the brick wall as she approached.

The frosted glass pane in the front door seemed to watch them like an enormous eye. A small rectangle of paper had been taped to the wood. Abby lifted the knocker and dropped it against the door five times, and each bang seemed to echo around them like a massive, pulsing heart.

There was no response.

Riya reached past her. She peeled the small rectangle of paper off the door. It looked like it might be a business card of some kind. Riya took a step back, and her lips twitched as she read the narrow, faded printed name.

"Bridgette!" Abby called, this time using her fist to knock on the wood. "Vivian!"

Someone shifted on the other side of the glass. Abby had the impression of an impassive face staring out at them, but then the form faded backward and vanished into the darkness.

She knew, instinctively, that she could knock on that door for an hour and it still would not be opened.

"Abs," Riya said, holding the card up. "I think this is him."

"Who?" She took the paper. It was thin and creased at the corners, as though it had been jostling around the bottom of a drawer for years. A name stood out on the card's front: Nicholas Rigney. There was no listed occupation: just a phone number, which had been crossed out with an ink pen, and an address in Doubtful.

"I bet it's the police officer who knew the most about Charles Vickers and the Stitcher," Riya said, pointing to the name. "When we asked her about him, Bridgette said she'd thrown out the card.

But that was a lie. She knew we'd be back, so she found it, and she left it for us."

Abby glanced back to the front door, where the card had been taped. "How did she know we'd be back? Anyone could have taken the card before we got here."

"No one else visits," Rhys said, simply, and Abby knew that was the crushing truth.

The edges of a dark silhouette were barely visible, watching them through the window.

"Let's go," Abby said, and turned to retrieve her bike.

Nicholas Rigney's card listed an address on Cawley Avenue, which was only a few streets away from Abby's home. The house number was familiar. Her heart skipped a beat. They were being sent to the old, strange building that was surrounded by hedges that were at least twenty feet high.

There were a few houses in town, other than Charles Vickers's, that people tended to avoid. And this was one of them.

The hedges were grown so high and so densely that only one part of the house was still visible: the third-floor attic. And the attic held a single, circular window.

Abby had never seen it for herself, but she'd heard rumors that, at night, a light would come on in that attic room and a man would stand at the window to stare down at the streets. People said he was only visible as a backlit silhouette, but that he would sometimes stay there for hours, so unmoving that he could be mistaken for a statue.

She very badly wished the card would direct them to any other house in Doubtful. That still didn't stop her from pushing her bike faster and harder as she wove through the town's wide roads.

The hedges were visible before they even turned onto Cawley Avenue. Abby didn't slow until they were right outside the house.

The hedges were old and brittle, and dusty spiderwebs spanned any gap they could find. Only two things interrupted the perfect barrier: a metal mailbox extruding from between tightly wound branches, and a wooden gate that seemed to have carved a gap in the green. Even when she leaned close to its edges, the gaps were too narrow to see through.

Instead, Abby took a step away and tilted her head back to see the high attic and its round window. It was dark and empty.

"I saw him, once," Riya whispered. "When my mother was driving me back from work. The path we normally took was blocked, so we had to drive down Cawley Avenue. And he was up there, at the window, and I'm certain he was watching our car as we passed."

Abby couldn't stop herself from asking, "What did he look like?"

Riya only shook her head. "I couldn't see much. All I could really make out were…angles."

A gust of cool air blew past them. Abby thought she caught a jarring jingle, like metal rattling against metal.

Stay focused. You need to do this. For Hope.

She shoved on the wooden gate. It creaked as it swung inward. That wasn't the only sound: it was joined by a scattered cacophony of rattling metal.

Bells, she realized as her shoulder brushed the hedges on the way past, and the sound repeated. *He's strung bells all through the hedges. They're rusted now, but there's no way through without disturbing them. Are they to warn him about intruders?*

Or about the Stitcher?

Inside, the hedges felt dimmer than the outside world, as though what little saturation and warmth Doubtful managed to cling to had been sapped away. The lawn was a crosshatch of dead and dying grass. Only a few plants existed inside, grown close to the building, but the hedges had starved them of sunlight, and they grew stunted.

She gazed up at the building. It was plainer than she'd expected. The round window set into the attic was the only really notable feature. The building was old but seemed maintained: none of the paint peeled, and none of the windows were cracked. It reminded her faintly of Charles Vickers's home and the way he persisted.

Abby left her bike against the hedge, out of sight of the road. She crossed the old paving stones dotting the dying lawn before she could second-guess herself, and knocked hard at the door. The booming echoes seemed to linger in the air for a long time.

The others gathered close behind her. Rhys's arm brushed against hers. Riya pressed close to her other shoulder. She was unspeakably grateful to not be alone.

Shuffling footsteps approached the door's other side. "Hello?" a voice called.

Abby swallowed, the business card clutched in her hand. "I'm looking for Nicholas Rigney. I was told he might be able to help me."

There was a second of silence, then a lock clicked. The door opened, and Abby had to tilt her head back to see the man standing before her.

He was enormously tall and thin. His shoulders hunched, as though he was self-conscious of his height. His shirt looked old but immaculately ironed. All of the buttons were done up, even the ones at his throat. Gray hair was combed neatly over his head. She guessed he was at least sixty. His long, thin face held sunken cheeks and watery gray eyes.

"I'm Nicholas," he said, and a very small smile flitted over his thin lips before vanishing again. "And I already know you. You're Abby Ward. Your sister was taken yesterday."

Chills ran through her. *I've never seen him in town. I've never known anyone who's so much as spoken to him. But he still knows about Hope.*

She held out the card, and hoped he wouldn't notice the way the paper trembled in her grip. "Bridgette Holm sent us. She thought you might be able to help."

His gaze flitted over the rest of the group: Rhys, Jen, and Riya. He stepped backward, one long arm stretched behind himself to beckon them in. "My office is straight ahead, first door to the right. Please leave your shoes outside. I'll get you some drinks."

She was past the point of being able to turn back. Abby scrambled to pull her sneakers off while Nicholas vanished deeper into the house. Her socks padded over clean wood boards as she followed the indicated path, the others close behind.

The hallway was sparsely furnished, but the office was its opposite. A dark wood desk was positioned in front of a covered window, two seats already waiting ahead of it. Bookshelves covered most other walls. About half of them were filled with books, but the rest held display items: taxidermized birds hidden under glass domes, dried plant samples next to scientific sketches, fossil specimens, and pieces of age-stained paper with ink writing sealed behind glass.

Extra seats were set back against the far wall, and Rhys carried two of them forward so that they could all sit.

They waited, and Abby counted the seconds as they ticked out of the antique clock on the wall behind them. Jen paced along the shelves as she examined the display items. She stopped in front of a display holding an old clothbound book that was falling apart at the seams.

"That's a diary kept by one of the town's founders," Nicholas Rigney said. "I inherited it from the town's previous historian. The current one believes we don't need to keep those kinds of artifacts."

He entered behind them, carrying a tray. On it was a coffeepot with fresh-brewed, heavily dark liquid in it, plus a pitcher with what looked like lemonade. Apparently he hadn't been able to decide what to get them because there were five small coffee cups and five glasses neatly stacked next to the drinks.

"Please, help yourselves," he said, placing the tray on the desk. Instead of sitting behind the table, he pulled his office chair around so that he could form a circle of seats with them. Jen left the display and folded herself into one of the hard-back chairs.

Now that she was here, Abby didn't completely know how to start. She threaded her fingers together, then loosened them, then clenched them in her lap.

"Your sister was taken in the middle of the night, through her bedroom window," Nicholas said. He sat forward in his chair, his hands resting on the crease lines of his tan pants. "I hope it's not presumptuous to jump straight into the core of the matter."

Abby's mouth was dry. "Not presumptuous at all. Bridgette Holm said you used to be a police officer, Mr. Rigney."

"You can call me Nick, if you like," he said, and the small twitchy smile returned for a second before vanishing again. "And I was. For twenty-one years. It wasn't an easy job."

"Bridgette said you were the only officer who seemed to truly care about her story."

"That was nice of her." He scratched long fingers over his forearm, glancing aside. "There was a culture in the station of…not asking too many questions about the Stitcher. I wasn't very good at abiding by it. As you can see from my collection."

Abby couldn't stop herself. "Why don't they arrest him?"

"Him?" Nick's thin gray eyebrows rose. He seemed to consider her question for a second. "I suppose you mean Charles Vickers."

Abby let the silence hang. Memories of the enormous footprint outside the Prices' house clung to her.

Riya spoke instead, her voice tentative. "The Stitcher *is* Charles Vickers, isn't he?"

Nick clasped and unclasped his hands. He chuckled, nervous. "That's a complicated question. No, he's not exactly. But you're also not terribly far off the mark."

Something inside Abby felt like it was collapsing, like a balloon with a hole. She crumpled back in her chair, her breathing labored.

"Here," Nick said, reaching for the untouched tray of drinks. "I'll tell you everything I know. But please be patient with me. Nothing about Doubtful is quite as simple as it seems."

A glass of lemonade was pressed into her hands. She didn't think her knotted stomach would hold it.

"I've been aware of your group for a couple of years," Nick added as he continued to serve drinks. "You ask questions. You've pulled up old records at the library. It's rare to find people this curious about the Stitcher. Only, Connor Crandall is normally a part of the set." He glanced at Jen. "You're new."

"I'm just here for the ride," Jen said, and flashed an off-center smile. "It's a lot wilder than I expected when I got on. Coffee, please."

"You knew about us?" Riya asked, frowning.

"Of course. I'm retired, but I keep as close a watch on the Stitcher situation as I can manage. I still have a precious few friends at the station who share what they know, particularly Chief Hewitt. Otherwise, I scavenge knowledge where I can."

An image surfaced in Abby's mind: the silhouette of a man standing at his attic window, the one window in his house that offered the best view of the streets below. Standing, for hours, staring.

"Why didn't you try to talk to us?" Riya sat forward. "We've been *fighting* to get information out of people—no one wants to answer any questions—"

"Yes, and perhaps it's better that way." He passed the coffee to Jen, then sank back into his chair. "Knowledge does not always equal wisdom, as I've learned through my own repeated failings.

If you knew the truth about the Stitcher, how could you have protected yourselves better? What could you have done differently? Nothing."

"But…"

He let go of a small sigh. "For too many years, I tried to share what I knew with as many people as I could. It was never welcome. It cost me family. It cost me almost every friend I'd known. It cost me my job. When people about town stopped talking to me, I made a decision. I could no longer try to force the truth on people who didn't want to hear it. If anyone wanted it, they could ask. And I would be here for them, waiting."

Abby's throat burned. Her whole life she'd been told the man behind the high hedges was dangerous. A recluse. Someone she didn't want to cross.

People feared anyone or anything that got too close to the Stitcher. And that seemed to include Nicholas Rigney.

She glanced behind herself, toward the crumbling journals and scraps of paper fixed behind glass. He'd been holding on to the town's secrets all of this time, ready and waiting to share them with anyone who asked. She just hadn't known.

"Tell us everything," Abby said, and her tongue felt so leaden that the words barely sounded like themselves.

"I will." He drew his own coffee closer. "Where do we start? With Charles Vickers? No, he's only important later. We'll need to go further back. Much further. To the town's very beginning."

TWENTY-FIVE

NICHOLAS'S STORY

THIS TOWN WAS BUILT AROUND ITS MINES. THE GROUND HELD seams of coal that ran deep and far.

When Doubtful began, it was barely more than a cluster of shacks to accommodate men who had come in search of work. It was hard labor, with long hours spent deep underground. Most days, they would barely see the sun on either side of their shifts. Their time was spent in the dark and the dust, picking away at the walls with only lanterns to light their paths.

But the mines were rich, and the tunnels burrowed deeper. Men brought their wives to live with them. Those wives bore children. Businesses sprang up to accommodate the growing needs. Streets spread out from the town's center like rivers, filling with houses that grew larger and more expensive as Doubtful prospered.

Gradually, the mines began to wear out. Veins of coal could only be followed for so long until they were exhausted. The companies in charge pushed their workers to dig deeper, to search harder.

Flaws in the mines' construction began to show under this new pressure. Safety precautions were minimal at the time; cave-ins, gas leaks, and deaths were not unheard of. As the mines grew older and their limits were pushed, the walls became increasingly unstable. Many men complained that sections of the mines were too dangerous to continue working in, but the company owners, seeing their profits drying up, were unwilling to lose money in attempting to fix the multiplying problems.

And this is when the central character of our story is introduced. Silas Wright, like most men in Doubtful, worked in the mines. He was described as a tall and thin man, with a patient and gentle temperament. He drank, as many of the miners did, but was not accused of being a drunkard. He smoked. And he had his wife and mother boarding in his home, and three adult children, all who lived close to him.

Please excuse the banal trivia, but very little is known about Silas when he lived. I have only found one surviving photo of him, and it is a group picture where he stands in shadow and cannot even be clearly seen.

However, for all of his obscurity during life, he has become perhaps the most important figure in Doubtful's history.

Silas was fifty-four when the cave section he was working in collapsed. Eight men were swallowed in the rubble some fifty feet below the surface close to half a mile from the nearest open entrance.

When men approached the cave-in, they heard a tapping noise coming from behind it. That led them to believe at least some of the miners had survived, possibly in a pocket inside the rubble. Urgent efforts were made to save them.

The cave-in was more dire than at first believed, though. A dozen men worked day and night moving rocks. Three days passed, and then four. Still the tapping persisted, and so did the rescue efforts.

All of the while, one figure stood outside the mines, patient and stoic as she waited for news. She was Silas's mother, Florence Wright.

Even less is known about Florence than about Silas. She never kept her own records that I've been able to locate, and so everything I have has been cobbled from letters between neighbors, journals from the time, and newspaper clippings. Many of these treasures were gifted to me by the town's old historian, who had an academic interest in the events. Others I've salvaged from estate sales and official town records. Too many have been destroyed or lost over the last hundred years: my efforts have been extensive, but still vastly incomplete.

What we know for certain, though, is that Florence loved her son dearly. No tears were shed while she waited, but she remained there, day and night, for her child to be brought back.

Finally, on the dawn of the fifth day, the bodies were reached, and the tapping noise fell silent.

There were no survivors. The bodies had not only been crushed but had been torn apart by the force of the collapse. To this day, no one has been able to explain the tapping noise that persisted until the tunnel was opened, and then immediately ceased.

Silas's body was brought out of the mine in pieces. A section of an arm; half of a foot; the scalp from his head. Silas's wife wailed, but his mother, Florence, voicelessly took the scraps of her son as each was given to her.

Funeral parlors had only just started to gain prominence in America; many funerals were still conducted in homes, and it was common for bodies to be kept with the family for several days until burials could be arranged. And so, Florence brought the pieces of her son back to their family home and laid him on the dining table.

And then, she took out her thread and started stitching.

Florence Wright brought in extra income for the family as a seamstress. Even though she was in her seventies at the time, her fingers were still dexterous. She took her decades of practice and love and poured them into her son as she rebuilt him, a scrap at a time.

Neighbors believed she was trying to make him presentable for the funeral. They tried to dissuade her, telling her to at least not use red thread, but Florence was adamant. Her son had worn red nearly every day of his life. He would wear red now.

His body was reformed over the course of three days. Scant reports from curious visitors describe the results as horrifying, macabre, and brutal.

But, from what we now understand, Florence never intended to display her son for his funeral. She had entirely different intentions, and even more remarkably, she achieved them.

Silas's wife returned to the home one morning to find her mother-in-law sitting at the table where Silas's body had been. Her journal describes Florence as appearing exhausted, as though she had not slept for even a minute of the last three days, and covered in drops of vivid red blood. She smiled, though, with the satisfaction of a woman who had cheated death.

The table was bare except for a bloodied sheet. Silas's body was missing.

When asked where he had gone, she simply said, *back to the mines.*

His remains were never formally recovered, but, from that day forward, there were increasingly frantic reports of someone or something moving through the tunnels. The miners who encountered it described the presence as tall and thin, unclothed, and threaded over with yards of tightly stitched red threads.

And then men began going missing. Their bodies weren't found; they simply seemed to vanish in the time between entering the mines and the end of shift. At first the mining company tried to claim they had left town, but soon it became apparent there was some larger, more pervasive problem.

It's hard to know what the final blow to the mines was; the deaths caused by the cave-in, the dwindling profits, or the ongoing issue of vanishing workers and increased reluctance in those who remained. It could have been that all those factors together made it impossible to continue. Regardless of the reason, Doubtful's mines were closed five months after Silas's death.

What's significant is that the entrances to the mine shafts were barricaded. Abandoned mines from the time were often left open and unattended; whatever the mining company's official stance, it spent a not inconsiderable amount of money to board up every single one of the mine's many openings.

For a while, nothing remarkable happened. At least, not of the unnatural kind. The town struggled with the abrupt and brutal loss of jobs. Many turned further to drink; others turned further to religion. Still others abandoned their homes and left town for better prospects elsewhere.

It was nearly six months before we hear from Silas, or his family, again. Silas's wife had moved out of her family home to live with one of her adult children, leaving Florence in the house by herself. I can only imagine that what had happened to Silas played some part in that decision. As far as I can tell, Florence never spoke to her daughter-in-law again.

Neighbors began to complain of a foul smell coming from the house. It appeared that no one had seen Florence for upward of a week. The town's elders forced entrance to the building and what they found inside was described as unimaginable violence.

Florence had been murdered. Her body had been dismembered, and pieces of it were scattered through both floors of the building. Her sewing supplies had been scavenged, and trails of red thread were soaking in the pools of blood.

Most notably, not all of Florence could be recovered. Although there appeared to be pieces of her in nearly every room, once the undertaker arranged those parts in her coffin, he found at least a third of her body was missing.

There was one more discovery to be made in Silas's former home. In the center of the hallway, less than a dozen feet from the front door, was a hole. The floorboards had been taken out, and then foundation, dirt, and stone alike dug through. The hole descended straight down and was just large enough for a man to climb into.

The mine shafts extended under the majority of the town. The hole had been connected to one of them. No one could answer exactly when it had been added to the house, but its purpose appeared clear: to grant direct access to the mines.

Here is where we leave facts and enter my own suppositions. These are the things I believe to be true:

The creature that was once Silas lived in the mines, killing anyone who strayed too close to his new domain.

His body was malformed, however, the skin shriveled and rotted in the damp. Either with his mother's help or by his own hand, he began taking replacement body parts from his victims to repair the sections of himself that were failing.

When the mines were closed up, his source of supplies was lost, and so his mother granted him access to the town through a tunnel she had carved into her own home.

And because of that, she became one of his victims—whether willingly, or by accident, she was killed by the monster she had created. Like every other victim, parts of her were added into Silas's crumbling husk.

Silas continues to live beneath this town. He continues to take victims. Patch by patch, he repairs himself.

And no one, not in the hundred years we have been given, has found a way to kill him.

TWENTY-SIX

\/\/\/\/\/\

NICK DRAINED HIS CUP AND SET IT ASIDE. HE LOOKED TIRED—NOT just physically, but emotionally.

Abby clenched her hands in her lap. "A monster," she said, and it wasn't an accusation or a question, but simple helplessness.

"A monster born of man, yes." He nodded. "I suspect there is very little, if anything, of Silas's mind left at this point. It's my belief that the gentle and patient man described in the accounts I've read died in the mine collapse."

A thin chuckle escaped Jen. "This is wild," she said. She glanced at the others as though she was seeking support from them. "You know, I'd barely started believing in a serial killer called the Stitcher, and now you're asking me to accept that the killer is a monster instead."

"You can see why I don't share this information often." Nick shrugged. "Even people who are predisposed to believe in the super-natural don't want to hear the story I just told. It becomes hard to fall asleep when you know what lives underneath your town."

Jen chuckled again, then sank back into her chair, looking uncomfortable.

"So..." Riya seemed to be trying to clutch threads together. Her eyebrows were low and her skin ashen. "The police..."

"They know," Nick said. "Perhaps not your father, yet, Miss Thompson. New officers are eased into it. They're exposed to the evidence a piece at a time, until there is too much for any doubt left to exist, then they're given the complete story. At least, that was how it was done when I worked at the station."

Abby had felt like she was deflating before, but now it was like she was going to explode from the sheer weight of what Nick was trying to tell her. "And they just...let the monster take whoever he wants?"

"There have been many, many attempts to stop the Stitcher." Nick exhaled slowly. "And many deaths in the pursuit of it. Men and women, braver than I, who laid down their lives in an effort to buy the town salvation. Nothing has worked."

"What have you tried?" Jen asked. She had her head propped up in one hand, and looked somewhere between dubious and enthralled.

"Everything. Officers have gone into the mines with guns and incendiary devices and never come out again. Traps were laid but it never took the bait. Do you remember the CCTV cameras?"

Abby shook her head.

"Of course, they were all uninstalled when you were still very little. But, for about a year, every street corner had a security camera monitoring it. The police chief at the time, Rogers, thought it might be possible to install an early-warning system: sirens or a prerecorded message telling townspeople to get to a secure location when the Stitcher was seen. Of course, it never worked. The monster disrupts technology. The sirens failed the moment the Stitcher began hunting, and none of the cameras were able to catch it on film."

Abby frowned at her shoes. A memory teased at the edge of her mind: of being in a stroller and pointing up at a man unfastening something from a light pole. The CCTV monitoring system?

Nick continued: "Shortly before I started working at the station, they attempted to block the mine shafts, believing they could trap the monster underground and let it slowly starve. The mine entrances were all collapsed with explosives, but the disappearances continued. We've since discovered that the monster has been able to dig new entrances for itself. They're little more than holes, and they're difficult to find. For every one that's sealed, another one is formed."

"So…" Riya rocked, one foot tapping on the floor with increasing agitation. "You just…let it roam? Let it take people? Record the disappearances and put up posters asking for information and then wait for the body to show up?"

Nick's eyes were impossibly sad. "Yes."

"How…" she seemed to be struggling to breathe. "How can you—"

"Please understand. We would stop this if we could. In the absence of that, all we were able to do was provide comfort for the families to the best of our abilities. To give the impression that something was being done for their loved one, even if we knew it was already too late. It's not much, I admit."

"No," Riya choked. "It's not."

"It's why the station has such a high turnover rate. Few can stomach it." He turned to stare out the window. The angles of the shadows had changed, and Abby had the horrible realization that their daylight hours would be running out soon.

"What about Charles Vickers?" she asked. "You said he was still tied to all of this."

"Of course." Nick chuckled. "Yes, you were not wrong to believe he was connected to the Stitcher murders. Silas Wright had children. And his children continued the family line. The surname was changed, but…"

"No," Abby said, realizing what he meant.

"Charles Vickers is the last descendant of Silas Wright. He has a bond with the monster that defies understanding. I haven't fully been able to grasp his mental state toward it, but he seems to treat the creature's presence as something precious, like a family heirloom. He watches over its activities. And, in return, he's kept safe from harm."

Abby pictured Charles Vickers's smirk: the coldly delighted little tilt to his lips that suggested he knew something no one else did.

"We could never arrest Charles Vickers," Nick said. "Technically, he has committed no crimes. There is no DNA evidence on any of the bodies and no fingerprints. The only thing tying Vickers to the victims is the red thread—and it's a common brand that anyone could purchase."

"Isn't there some way to put pressure on him?" Riya asked. "Keep him in holding for a few nights. Arrest him on a technicality. Something!"

"Vickers is very much aware of his rights." Nick shook his head. "We can only do what's allowed within the law. If we have suspicion that he might be involved in a crime—if someone reported him—we could search his home or bring him in for questioning. And we did, frequently. He knows the game well by this point. I had the sense that he even enjoys it."

Abby remembered the night she and Rhys had been trapped in his home. The walls were covered with framed missing person posters. A row of knives had been laid out on the kitchen's cutting board.

The home had been staged, as though to provoke a response from anyone who got inside. But none of it was in any way illegal. And the police had stayed for hours, Riya said, combing the building on the night Hope went missing.

"Twice, a police officer tried to get more aggressive with him. Each time, within a day, that officer had been taken." Nick's thin shoulders shifted in a shrug. "It's a horrifying fate, and it's one Vickers wields as a threat over us all. Or anyone else who inconveniences him."

"So he can control the monster?" Abby asked.

"From what I can gather, yes, sometimes. It's a symbiotic relationship. Vickers shields and enables the creature; the creature can be persuaded to take certain people in return. I should add, though, those occasions are rare. Most victims are taken by the monster's own volition. The Stitcher…" Nick paused, seemingly casting around for the right words. "It picks its targets with care. Sometimes it will watch or stalk multiple opportunities before making its selection. I've spent years trying to look for a pattern in its choices, but if one exists, I can't find it."

Riya swallowed thickly. "You said he's taking body parts to rebuild himself."

"Yes, that is my supposition." Nick gestured vaguely, then folded his hands. "I have never seen the Stitcher myself, and I have no conclusive proof, but my research suggests you're correct. The Stitcher is not alive, and therefore its body doesn't heal itself. Over time, parts decay, they fall off, they cease working. And it's my belief that the Stitcher takes people to harvest parts to fill the gaps."

The silence that fell over them felt impossibly heavy.

"The bodies that are returned to us are so altered that they are nearly unrecognizable," Nick continued. "And the remains are rarely shown to the families—at least, not for more than a glimpse. It's not often that someone has the chance to notice that parts of their loved ones are missing in the coffin, but that's exactly what the coroner finds, again and again. You wouldn't remember me, but I was at your family's funeral, Mr. Weekes. And I can tell you there weren't three complete bodies in those caskets."

Rhys's face was pale. He refused to make eye contact with any of them.

"Wait, *three*?" Jen asked.

Abby shot her a furious glare to silence her.

"I'm so sorry," Nick said. He reached toward Rhys, then pulled his hand back. "I shouldn't have said that—I shouldn't have presumed you'd want to know—"

"It's fine," Rhys said, his voice barely audible.

"Forgive me." Nick seemed genuinely apologetic.

Tingling had spread through Abby's fingers. Stress, or shock, or fear, she wasn't sure. One question had been echoing through her mind through the conversation, and it was growing impossible to ignore. "How do I get into the mines?"

Nick watched her carefully. "If you go into them, you'll die."

"I understand."

He glanced at the others, apparently seeking some sign that he should stay quiet. He met a row of hard, hungry eyes. Nick drew a deep breath and held it, before letting it out as a sigh.

"The creature sometimes digs its own exits around town. But they *are* hidden, and the police collapse them when they can find them. I'm sorry that I don't know of any that haven't been blocked."

Abby clenched her teeth, willing herself not to scream.

"There's *one* path into the mines that's still open, however," Nick said. He closed his eyes, as though he already regretted what he was about to say. "It's inside Charles Vickers's home."

She lurched forward in her chair, gripping the fabric seat. "What?"

"Silas's descendants continued to live in his home, even after Florence's murder. The building was rebuilt and renovated several times in the ensuing years, so it's no longer recognizable as the home from back then. But it's still in the same place, and housing the same family, even if they hide it well."

A hole in the hallway, near the front door, leading straight down to the mines.

All of this time, we thought Vickers would have to leave his home to get to Hope.

He's had access to her the whole time.

"So I need to get back into Vickers's house," she said.

Nick's smile was very small and very sad. "There's nothing there for you except death."

Death, and my sister. Abby stood.

Whatever waited for her in the earth beneath the town, she would meet it.

She would meet it with fire and teeth.

PART FOUR

THE

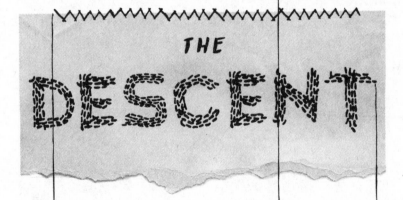

DESCENT

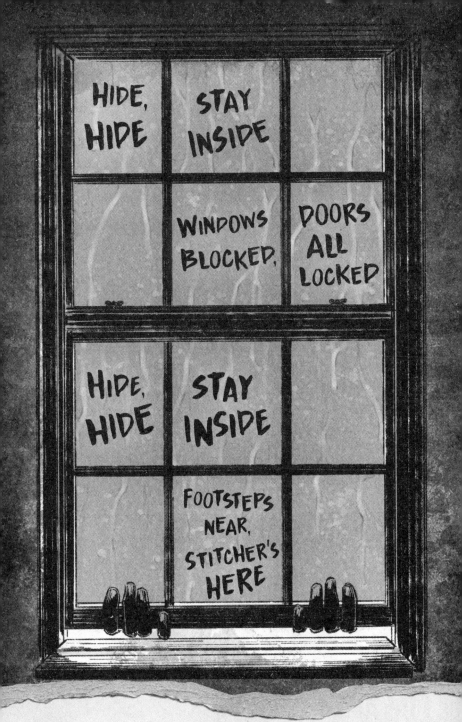

RULE #4 KEEP YOUR HOUSE LOCKED UP TIGHT, OR THE STITCHER WILL COME FOR YOU.

TWENTY-SEVEN

‿⌁‿⌁‿

THEY SPILLED OUT OF NICHOLAS RIGNEY'S HOUSE.

Riya felt sick to her stomach.

No one else around her was doing well. Rhys was withdrawing even further into himself. Abby looked half wild, and Riya knew Abby was on the verge of doing something very reckless and very, very dangerous.

Even Jen, who'd been nothing but calm and collected until that point, seemed shaken. This had to be a lot for her to take in.

It was a lot for *all* of them.

They'd thought they'd understood what they were facing. They'd spent their lives guarding themselves against Charles Vickers. The town had always been split, with some of the population believing in an inhuman monster that had come from the mines.

Superstition, Riya had thought. Paranoia, manifesting into a belief in the supernatural. She'd actually felt proud of her ability to face the truth.

According to Nicholas Rigney, she was the one who'd swallowed an easy delusion.

This isn't how reality is supposed to work.

"How can we know if he's telling the truth?" Riya asked before she could stop herself. "About the Stitcher being a monster? Or, or is it possible he's wrong? He told us the town's history, sure, but he couldn't offer any actual proof—"

"I don't care," Abby said as they stepped past the wall of protective hedges and into the street. There was a stony finality in her voice. "Monster or not. I have a way into the mines. Nothing else matters."

She seemed to actually believe it.

Riya pressed one hand into her side, where an ache was forming in her stomach.

They could fight a man. Riya had no idea how they were supposed to fight a monster.

Then Abby's phone pinged, followed quickly by a chime from Rhys's and Riya's own phones. She pulled hers out and stared at the screen with growing horror as a trail of nearly twenty undelivered messages arrived at once.

"Oh," she moaned. "*Connor.*"

Abby saw Charles Vickers, and she braked so hard she nearly lost grip of her bike.

They'd been rushing to meet Connor in the town's main shopping street. The route was so familiar she could follow it in her sleep, and she'd been so focused on their meeting spot—outside the Bridges' store—that she'd forgotten to be cautious in case of Vickers.

They'd swerved around a corner only to find Vickers standing barely twenty yards ahead of them. He faced a bulletin board. Aged missing person posters rattled like dried leaves in the wind, their smiling faces so washed out that they almost looked as though they were screaming.

Vickers's lips twitched as he scanned the posters. With a sickening lurch, Abby realized he was looking for any he might have missed from his collection.

Riya grabbed her arm and pulled her back behind the corner they'd just rounded. Rhys was already there, his shoulder pressed against the laundromat's brick wall.

"That's him, huh?" Jen asked, climbing off the back of Riya's bike.

She'd never even seen Charles Vickers before, Abby realized, and she almost laughed. He'd been such an ever-present part of her life she'd forgotten that not everyone would recognize him on sight.

"That's him," Riya confirmed, then turned, scanning the shadows behind her. "And here's Connor."

He jogged toward them from the alleyway's darkness. He looked bloodless. His freckles, normally pale, stood out like spots of color on his gray face, and his smile was both reckless and terrified.

"He knows I'm following him," he said, panting, as he joined their circle. His Adam's apple bobbed as he swallowed. "And I don't think he's happy about it."

"That's fine," Riya said. "There's been a development."

Very quickly, she outlined what they'd learned at Nicholas Rigney's house. Connor's eyebrows rose higher and higher the more she spoke.

When she finished, he simply said, "I can't believe my mom was right. Does… Does this mean I need to apologize to her?"

"Not really the priority right now," Riya said with a grimace.

"Yeah but… She was so adamant it was a monster. We couldn't even talk about it over dinner because the whole house would start to argue. I'm going to have to eat so much crow over this." He sighed, then glanced at Abby. "So… What's the plan?"

"I need to get into his house." She'd already run through her memories of the building a dozen times. Barred windows. Locked doors. She hadn't been able to escape on the night she'd been trapped there, which meant there would be no easy way inside either. "I'll need to wait and watch him until he goes home and unlocks the door. And then figure out some way to get past him."

Connor's lips twitched, then he broke out into thin, panicked laughter.

"Shh," Riya hissed. "He's close."

"Sorry—sorry—but… I think I can get you in. Right now. Without Vickers knowing."

They stared at Connor. Then Riya asked, her voice husky, "Are you sure?"

"Yeah." He shrugged. "At least, mostly. I'm pretty sure."

"Okay." Abby ducked to look around the brick corner. As she watched, Vickers reached up and unpinned one of the fliers. He admired it for a second before tucking it into the satchel he wore over his shoulder. She leaned back before he could catch her watching. "That changes everything. We need to get to his house *now*, before he does."

"Hold on." Riya grabbed her arm, pinning her in place. She beckoned, and the group—Connor, Rhys, Jen, Abby, and Riya herself—pulled in closer. "When Vickers walks to town, he usually stays out until dusk. Which means we'll have at least an hour. And I refuse to send anyone into those mines unprepared."

Burning frustration scorched through Abby's insides. "I can't waste time—"

"*Please*." Tears shone in Riya's eyes. She held Abby's arm so tightly it ached. "If I've meant anything to you as a friend, give me this. Fifteen minutes to prepare. That's all I'm asking. If you're going to have any chance of getting Hope out of there, you'll need every advantage you can get."

She felt like she was being torn in half. Every minute she wasted was another minute Hope was trapped in a labyrinth with a creature that felt nothing except hunger.

But Riya was right. As badly as she needed to get to Hope, she couldn't stop there. She needed to get Hope *out*, and alive.

"Okay," she said, bracing herself. "Fifteen minutes."

"We can't lose sight of Vickers in the meantime," Riya said. "We'll need someone to follow him and alert us when he's heading home. He's already warned Connor once, so that means—"

"I can do it," Jen said. They all looked at her, and she shrugged, her jacket crinkling around her shoulders. "I've never seen him before. And vice versa. He won't know that I'm with you."

"Are you sure?" Riya asked, and there was a flash of real fear in her expression. "You'll need to stay out of his sight, if possible. Even if he's not the Stitcher, he's still dangerous. Do you know where his street is?"

"Can do, I know, and yes." Jen's smile was only visible for a second before it vanished again. "Look, I'm going to be honest—we barely know one another. And listening to that ex-officer talk was like listening to a respected professor explain that yes, fairies are real, and they live in his backyard. It's... It's a stretch."

"I know," Abby said, and the others nodded with her.

"Right." Jen shrugged again, then glanced aside. "But it's impossible for you to be faking any of this. It's... It's more than scary campfire stories. You're in real pain right now. I can see that. And... I want to help, if I can."

"Keep in contact with me," Riya said. She reached toward Jen, and Jen reached back, and for a second their hands touched before they separated again. "Text me every five minutes so I know you're still safe."

"I'll do that." Jen's smile was quick and hard and full of intensity. "Good luck, all of you, with whatever you need to do."

She stepped out of the alleyway and began walking down the main street.

Riya took a breath that seemed to hurt her. Then she straightened her back, her neck long, and clenched her hands into fists at her side. "Okay. Fifteen minutes to prepare. Let's go."

The four of them piled into the Bridges' general store. The prices weren't as good as the grocer a few streets over, but the packed shelves held far, far more. Mr. and Mrs. Bridges were behind the counter, and watched curiously as Riya led them through the shelves, shoveling items into baskets with what felt like practiced precision.

She knew exactly what she wanted to get, Abby thought as she watched her friend work through the rows methodically. *She's probably reviewed the list over and over in her mind as she watched Charles Vickers's house.*

They placed their bounty by the checkout, then all four of them reached into their pockets, emptying whatever money they had and dropping it onto the counter. Abby still didn't know if it would be enough.

Mrs. Bridge's gaze trailed over the heaped supplies, and her face seemed to deflate, the smile vanishing under heavy sadness. "Oh," was all she said. She lifted her eyes to meet each of them in turn, then she reached forward and pushed the piles of money back toward them. "No charge," she said. "Not for you."

They whispered muffled thanks as Mr. Bridge helped them pack the supplies into bags. "Good luck," he said as they left, and to Abby, it felt more like a goodbye.

Riya's phone pinged as she stepped out of the store. She read the message without breaking stride. "Jen's got eyes on him. He's stopped at the bakery."

That meant they had a clear path to Vickers's house. Abby tried to temper herself, to slow down, but she found herself moving faster and faster as they biked out of the main street.

The others quickened pace to keep up with her. Vickers's house was on the outskirts of town, but they knew all of the shortcuts. Their bikes brushed against store walls and trees, skittering over gravel and dirt and asphalt as they raced time.

Within five minutes, they'd reached Stokes Lane.

Abby skidded to a halt, one leg out to balance, as she stared along the rows of rattling offerings affixed to abandoned fences. At the end of the street, Vickers's house was cold and dark, its bar-covered windows like black eyes watching them.

Riya nodded to one of the empty houses beside them. "We need to take a moment to prepare. Somewhere no one will see us."

Connor chuckled as they walked their bikes into the overgrown yard and rested them against a tree so old and cracked that it seemed near to crumbling entirely. Vines grew thick along the fence, hiding both them and their bikes from the view of the street. "Except for our hideout, I don't think any of these houses have had a person inside them in years."

"Still." Riya dropped her backpack from her shoulders, and the others followed suit. "I'm not taking chances. Not now."

They tipped their shopping haul onto the ground and crouched in a circle around it. "We'll need four backpacks," Abby said. "And we should divide everything equally. Just in case we get separated down there."

There was a beat of horrible, lingering silence.

Abby looked up. Riya was no longer meeting her eyes.

"Abs…" Riya clasped her hands. "I want to help. I want to help so badly. But…"

"I have my family," Connor said. He sat back on his heels, his long arms crossed over his knees. His eyebrows hung low. "Both Bridgette and Nick said it was going to be a death sentence down there. I can't do that to my folks."

"Oh," Abby managed.

Riya seemed to hunch in on herself, her lips going pale and pinched the way they only did when she was miserable.

"Look," Connor said. "I've spent the last two days in an empty house surrounded by beetles. I followed Vickers into a movie theatre and sat there alone for hours. I'd walk over burning coals for any of you guys. But... But I can't..."

They can't go into the mines.

Abby closed her eyes. A wave of frustration rushed through her. But not frustration at any of them; at *herself.* Hope's abduction had overwhelmed her so thoroughly that she'd stopped caring about the people she treasured. She'd stopped asking herself what was best for them, what they needed, what they wanted. She'd hurt so badly, she hadn't seen the wounds she was inflicting on everyone around her.

"I'm sorry," Riya whispered, and she sounded close to tears.

"No." Abby reached out and took her hand, squeezing as tightly as her own shaking fingers could. "Don't apologize. I wouldn't be here without you. Riya, you planned every step of this; you made sure we got here. Connor, you were beyond steadfast. You watched his house for hours, alone, without giving up. It's more than I could have done on my own. I never should have asked any of you to come into the mines with me."

Riya's breathing was fast and uneven. Tears pooled in the corners of her eyes. "I'm sorry," she said again.

"This is my family, and it's going to be my journey," Abby said. The words cemented it in her heart. "I'm going into the mines alone. Let's get everything into a backpack."

"Two backpacks," Rhys said.

She stared at him. His warm eyes met hers, unblinking, unwavering. Nothing in her life had ever been as dependable as him.

"I've asked too much from you too." The realization hurt. Every moment of the last few days had been spent reliving the pain of his own family's murders. It must have felt like thorns digging into him, every moment, and he still hadn't given up on her. "It's time for you to go home, Rhys."

"Don't." His voice was steel.

"Rhys—"

"Don't ever leave me again." He caught himself, his breathing ragged. "We'll go into the mines. Together."

Abby's throat ached so badly that she couldn't speak. Instead, she took his hand and nodded.

Together.

"The Stitcher kills technology," Riya said. "So you'll each have as many backups as we can manage, but you still can't expect to rely on any of them."

Her hands shook as she divided their purchases into two backpacks: one for Abby, and one for Rhys. She wished she'd had time to get more. To *do* more. But the sun was growing low; shadows stretched out like impossibly long arms across the street.

There was so little she could still give them. This had to be enough.

A headlamp went over Abby and Rhys's heads, held in place by elastic straps. Flashlights went into their pockets, and spare flashlights and packs of batteries into their backpacks. Then, as a final resort, two candles each and a box of matches.

"Food and water," she continued, dividing plastic bottles and protein bars between them. "Spare jackets and thermal blankets. Chalk to mark the walls so you know which way you've come."

Connor swore softly under his breath as Riya continued passing out their supplies. He must have been distracted when she was grabbing items from the general store; he hadn't realized how much she was getting, and she still wasn't done.

"Weapons," Riya said, and hoped the others wouldn't hear the way her voice wavered. "I hope you won't need to use any of them. But you'll have multiple, just in case."

A kitchen knife, its blade shielded by a cardboard cover, went into each backpack. A second, smaller pocketknife was passed to each of her friends to carry. Finally, two long, thick screwdrivers. In case a blunt-force jab turned out to be more effective than a slicing blade.

Rhys still carried his baseball bat, tucked into his backpack. A part of Riya felt as though the weapons were too much, but it was easy to silence that voice. Never in her life had she regretted overpreparing for a situation with high stakes. And these were the highest she'd ever encountered.

She gave Abby the first aid kit. The store had only had one, but it included the necessities of antiseptic, tourniquets, and painkillers.

"Maps," she said, and gave them four sets of photocopies she'd made at the library the previous day. "One for each backpack, and the one for each of you to keep in your pockets. In case they get wet or you get separated. This is the one way we can improve your odds compared to any of the Stitcher's other victims. You'll have a way to know where you are. I hope."

Abby and Rhys took the markers she passed to them along with the pages. They'd been unshakable, hanging off her every word. No one had ever listened to her as intently before.

"The maps are historical records produced by the original mining company," Riya said. "We know the official mine entrances are all sealed, so you'll either have to come back out through Vickers's house or find an undocumented exit. And, remember, the passageways may no longer be accurate. Look for unique features, when you can, and try to mark your progress. I've already circled the area where Vickers's house is likely to connect, but even that's guesswork."

"Thank you, Ri," Abby said, folding her second set of maps and pushing them into her pocket. She zipped up her backpack and hefted it. It looked too heavy. At the same time, Riya still felt like she hadn't given them enough. "We'll have our phones with us. Being under-ground will kill any reception, but we'll text you as soon as we can get back to the surface."

As though on cue, Riya's phone pinged. She pulled it out and frowned at the message. "It's from Jen. Vickers has left the main street. It looks like he's coming home."

Abby met Rhys's gaze. They seemed to share an unspoken thought, because they turned back to her and Connor in tandem, their expres-sions set. "Get us into that house."

"Right," Connor said, his voice wavering.

He led them down the cul-de-sac. Decaying gifts rattled as a cold breeze picked up. Even though they knew no one was home, they all reflexively softened their footfalls as they entered Vickers's yard and approached his door.

"I was watching when he left his house," Connor said, and bent down beside the planter next to the front door. A small shrub struggled to survive there, and Connor fidgeted around the dirt beneath it before triumphantly raising a hand. A small, silver key glittered in his grip. "Aha!"

"This is a joke," Riya said, incredulous. "He locks his place up like a fortress…and then leaves his key in the box beside his door?"

"It's hard to find unless you know where to look," Connor said. "And no one else lives in the street to see him hide it."

"He probably thought the key was safer here than on his person, in case he was pickpocketed or attacked while in town," Abby added. Her smile looked crooked. "Either way, I'm not going to complain."

Riya grabbed the key and unlocked the door, her teeth gritting as she begged it to open. The handle turned smoothly and the door glided inward.

She hadn't seen inside the house before. Traces of Abby and Rhys's experience in there remained, though. There was a bare hook in the wall where the broken mirror must have once hung. The wall opposite looked shiny, as though it had been washed, and she thought she could still see faint traces of blood.

The house was dark and smelled of dust and decay. Just being there made her skin itch.

Nicholas's words echoed in her mind. *In the center of the hallway, less than a dozen feet from the front door, was a hole.*

Abby pressed into the hallway. Her gaze was fixed on one location: a rug, not far past the door. It was a plain rug, designed to blend into the hall and go unnoticed, but it was thick. Abby crouched next to it and swept it back.

Until that moment, Riya hadn't known how much belief to put into Nicholas Rigney's story. It had seemed fantastical. She prided herself on being strongly grounded in logic and realism, and resurrections and monsters were a step too far for her.

Now, she stared down at the concealed trapdoor and felt her doubt in the story crumble. The square was only a couple of feet across and made of the same wood as the rest of the hall. It would have been nearly invisible except for the metal handle tucked into an indent.

Abby didn't even hesitate. She hauled on the handle. The wood groaned painfully as it rose out of the floor. A small cascade of dust spiraled in the fading light. The hatch tipped over, thudding into the rug.

They all craned forward. Beneath the wood was a rough-hewn hole. Riya saw layers—wood beams, concrete foundation, then dirt, then stone. Everything beyond that vanished into darkness.

Rhys reached for his headlight and switched it on. The beam reflected down the endless depths before it, too, faded out.

Metal rungs had been affixed to one side of the hole to form a rusted, tight ladder. The space was barely large enough for an adult man. They would have to climb down single file.

Abby took a short, sharp breath, then turned back to Riya. "Can I ask one last favor?"

If she could have, she would have given her friend the world. "Anything."

"I'm going to come back. But…if I don't…make sure Momma's not forgotten about. There's money in the drawer of my nightstand. It's not a lot. But it should be enough to do *something*. Your mother's always been kind to Momma. She might be able to help."

"She will," Riya said. Her mother had always tried to look after Mrs. Ward in small ways: dropping off food and giving them medicine when sickness set in. She'd help now too. "Of course. And Rhys, I'll look out for Alma too."

"Thank you," he murmured.

"We're coming back," Abby repeated. "But…just in case."

"Yeah."

"One final thing…" Abby fixed both Riya and Connor with a sharp gaze. "If you don't hear from us again, I want you to do what Bridgette said. I want you to forget about us. Live as though we never existed. Stick to your plans; get out of Doubtful. And don't ever, ever regret anything that happened today. Because I won't."

Riya couldn't speak. She pulled both Abby and Rhys into a hug, and a second later Connor joined in, his arms wrapping around all of them.

"Be careful," Connor whispered.

They let go. Abby hitched her backpack higher on her shoulders, then she and Rhys crouched at the edge of the hole.

"I'll go first," Rhys said, but Abby had already swung her legs over the edge. She shimmied down until her feet found purchase on one of the metal rungs, then sent one final look toward the outside world, and began her descent.

Rhys waited until she was far enough that he wouldn't step on her hands, then lowered himself into the hole, as well. He was larger than Abby, and with the added bulk of the backpack it became a tight fit, but he pressed his body close to the rungs as he climbed.

"Good luck," Riya called, and Connor echoed her words, his hands clenched together so tightly that the joints looked like they were threatening to pop.

They stayed there as long as they dared until Abby and Rhys's headlights became distant and dim. And then Riya, her hands shaking, pulled on the trapdoor to swing it closed again.

Vickers couldn't be far away. And it was important he had no idea that the friends had made it into the tunnels. Once the trapdoor slammed closed, Riya carefully arranged the rug over top, exactly the way it had been when they arrived.

"Let's go," Riya said, and the two of them slipped out the front door. They locked it behind themselves, then Connor returned the key to the garden planter.

Riya's phone chimed as they were closing the driveway gate behind them. Riya sucked in a sharp breath as she checked it. About to turn down Stokes Lane.

"Hurry," she hissed, grabbing Connor's arm and running with him toward the nearest house, the one they'd used for their vigil. They barely made it behind the crowded trees before Vickers appeared at the end of the street. His shadow cut through the fading sunlight like a knife, pointed directly at his home. Riya, crouched and one hand pressed over her mouth to muffle her breathing, watched him walk the street languidly, and slowly climb the steps to the front porch.

He bent to pick the key out of the planter, then hesitated. His body language shifted from placid to tense as he straightened and turned to face the street.

"Did we put the key back exactly the way it was?" Riya whispered.

Connor, pressed tight against her side, didn't make a sound. He just sent her a tense, helpless glance.

Vickers stared along the road, his gaze passing across each house in turn. The placid expression had vanished. Now, the parts of his face that had always seemed rounded and soft had turned hard. His glasses reflected blank light as he moved, slowly, back to the door and unlocked it. Stepped through. Shut it behind himself.

They were too far away to hear the locks being fastened, but Riya could see the door shiver as the bolts were turned. After a moment, lights began to turn on. One room at a time, the glow gradually spread through the building. Riya had the distinct impression that Vickers was searching the house.

"Hey," a soft voice called. "Found you."

Jen came toward them from the abandoned house's backyard. She looked impeccably calm; more like someone who was out for an afternoon stroll than someone who'd been trailing a potential serial killer.

Riya could only imagine what a frazzled mess she must seem in comparison. She hadn't showered in days, let along gotten a full night's sleep. Jen didn't look at her as though she was weird or repulsive, though. If anything, there was a trace of admiration in her dark eyes. "Did the other two get in?" she asked.

"Yeah." Riya nodded toward the house. "Just in time too. Thank you."

"Not a problem. I hope they find what they need down there, monster or no." Jen leaned her back against the house's side. They watched through the cover of trees as still more house lights turned on. Vickers's silhouette passed in front of windows, his sloped shoulders unmistakable.

"Hey, I wanted to ask something," Jen said. Her head tilted a fraction as she watched for Riya's reaction. "Earlier, at the retired officer's house, he said something about there being three bodies at the funeral Rhys attended. What's the story there?"

"The story…" Riya glanced at Connor, who sent her a tight-lipped smile and a nod in return. "Rhys would be okay with you knowing, I guess. Especially considering everything that's happened today. When he tells the story of the day his family was taken, he only talks about his parents. But there were four people in the car that day."

"Yeah?" Jen prompted.

"His parents, Angie and Hugh Weekes. And his younger brother, Asher, age six." Riya took a quick breath, and it hurt on the way down. "When his mother, Angie, got out of the car, she told Rhys to look after his brother until she came back. But Asher didn't want to be apart from her. He cried and squirmed and eventually opened the door to run after his parents. He was never seen again."

"Damn," Jen said.

"Rhys tells the story of how his parents were taken, when he has to, but he can't talk about Asher without choking. It hurts too much, I guess. It's easy to look at it from the outside and say he couldn't have done anything. If he'd tried to chase after his brother, none of them would have lived. But…"

"He still feels guilty," Connor finished.

"Yeah." Riya was reminded of how many younger siblings Connor had. He had to feel that same pressure—to look out for them, to protect them.

Three bodies were found in the woods on the day Rhys's family was returned. Three bodies, sewn together in a horrifying patchwork.

He almost never talked about it. But sometimes, Riya wondered if Rhys ever wished he'd been sewn up with them, as well.

"Two people who have lost everything to the Stitcher." Jen stared toward the house. The lights were starting to switch off again. "Two people with nothing left." She said it as an observation, not a question, but Riya still nodded.

"I feel like having nothing left is the only way you could go down there."

"Mm." Jen sighed, then pushed away from the house's wall. "What're your plans now? Are you going to keep watching him?"

"No." There was nothing else she could do to help Abby and Rhys. They'd either get themselves back out, or they wouldn't. She blinked, her eyes burning. "For now, I'm going to pass by Mrs. Ward's house and make sure she has something to eat. And then… And then I'm going to go home to my parents. They haven't seen me in days. So I'll go home and eat dinner with them, and pretend it's a normal night, and try to be grateful for what I have, and I'm going to try very hard not to cry."

Connor chuckled, his arms folded around his chest as he blinked at the ground. "Same."

The three of them turned, sticking to the shadows and the hidden areas as they left Charles Vickers's house behind.

TWENTY-EIGHT

〰〰〰

METAL RUNGS GROANED UNDER ABBY'S HANDS.

She moved lithely and quickly. When she tilted her head up, she could see Rhys's shoes and the tunnel's hard stone walls. When she looked down, she could only see those same walls, spreading out endlessly until her headlight's beam was swallowed by the darkness.

Their breathing echoed around them. Rhys hadn't said a word since they'd entered the tunnel, but he matched her relentless pace.

She'd been fighting to get here for so long that, now that it was happening, she didn't know how she felt. Full of quivering anticipation. Relief. Dread. Fear. All wrapped up beneath a numbing layer of single-minded purpose.

To find Hope.

Her sister had been missing for nearly forty-eight hours. That was two days in the mines, with nothing but her nightclothes for warmth. No water. No food. No light.

Nearly forty-eight hours of hell.

Wait for me. Wait just a little longer.

Something soft grazed Abby's hand. A spiderweb, she assumed, as she tried to brush through it. The web didn't break, though; it caught around two fingers, pinching painfully.

She directed her headlight toward it.

A red thread had been looped around the ladder's rung. It speared off in both directions, vanishing into the hard stone walls on either side, through pinprick holes Abby could barely see.

She untangled her hand and called to Rhys, "Careful. There are threads here."

He made a soft noise of acknowledgment. They kept climbing.

The tunnel echoed sounds, magnifying each breath and each thud of their shoes. Abby had lost all context for how deep they were. She only knew they were well, well past the town's roots.

Then, finally, her light caught on solid floor below. She moved faster, almost racing, flakes of rust peeling off the metal rungs. And then she stepped off the final piece of the metal ladder and into the mines proper.

As Abby touched down, her headlight flickered. She hesitated, waiting, but the beam became steady again. Even so, she tapped her pocket where the first backup flashlight was kept, just to remind herself of where it was.

The passageway was narrow, barely wide enough for two people to stand side by side, and only inches above the top of her head. She turned, sending her light down each direction, but the tunnels curved slightly and stole her view within twenty paces.

She moved aside as Rhys came down beside her. He pulled the maps out of his pocket and shook them open. There were multiple pages, and Abby couldn't see how they fit together. They were crisscrossed with thin lines marking tunnels, and larger rounder sections for open caverns.

One page had an area circled. That was Riya's best guess for the section of tunnels directly beneath Vickers's house. There were three passageways threading through it that could match the one they were in. They'd have to keep moving until they found a more notable landmark. She met Rhys's eyes, confirming he didn't have any preference, then turned left.

More threads crossed their path. Sometimes they snagged over rocks, running across the tunnel's walls like wiring. Sometimes they crisscrossed the path, and Abby had to duck to get under them. Sometimes they disappeared into the solid stone walls, as though someone had used a needle to pierce the rocks.

Her headlight fluttered again. She kept moving, even when it faded entirely, and pulled her flashlight out of her pocket. It turned on and stayed on.

The path narrowed, squeezing them in at the sides, then abruptly opened.

They'd found a natural cavern. When Abby tilted her head back, she could barely see glistening rocks high above them. Pools of water had gathered on the ground in natural indents formed by thousands of years of dripping erosion.

Bridgette talked about finding water to drink. It looked inky black under her light. *She said it tasted...bad.*

"This could be one of two caverns." Rhys used his chalk to draw a large arrow on the stone wall of the tunnel they'd come from, pointing toward the exit, then used the pen to make marks on their maps. It narrowed down their location, at least. "Do you want to cross it? Or go back?"

The cavern's opposite side was hard to see, but shadowed alcoves suggested the form of multiple other tunnels, both natural and man-made.

"Across," she decided.

Something rattled far down the path behind them. They swung, their dual lights aimed down the tunnel they'd emerged from, but there was nothing to see.

A loose rock falling, Abby thought. *Maybe.*

She kept leading them forward.

Riya sat neatly, wearing clean clothes and her hair washed, as she ate dinner with her parents.

She answered questions about the study-sleepover she hadn't attended and the quiz she hadn't prepared for and what she thought of their odds at the lacrosse match she didn't want to go to.

She pretended to be excited when her mother announced that she'd prepared rabri for dessert, as a reward for her studious daughter.

She nodded when her father suggested a board game after dinner.

They were happy. And she tried her best not to let them see how much she felt like death on the inside.

"I'm home," Connor called as he unlocked his front door and entered his house.

Video game noises came from upstairs. The dishwasher was running. So was the tumble dryer, based on the distant rattle. Someone was watching television in the living room and frequently changing the channel to try to find one that wasn't jittery.

He'd gotten two texts from his parents over the last two days. One asking him to pick up his brother from soccer practice. One, at the previous dinner, asking where he was. They'd accepted his poorly constructed lie about helping a friend with homework, which, honestly, they should have seen through instantly. People knew better than to ask Connor for help with studying.

He told himself that it was fine, that he'd much rather have this free-range approach compared to the smothering number of messages Riya had gotten from her parents. Riya's lies were waterproof and included multiple alibis, and even so, she was terrified of being uncovered.

Still. He'd be lying if it didn't sting a bit that no one came to give him a hug as he walked through the door.

"Just spent the last couple of days stalking the Stitcher," he yelled into a house that wasn't listening. "Turns out you were right, Mom, and he's a monster after all. Sorry."

The TV channel changed. The tumble dryer rattled. Someone yelled for Connor to keep it down, they were trying to focus.

Connor sighed.

It could be worse, he told himself as he dropped his bag by the door and went upstairs to enjoy the privileges of a shower and a toilet that actually flushed. Two text messages were more than either Abby or Rhys would get from their families, even if they were missing for weeks.

Jen's father had gotten pizza for dinner again, which meant the empty fridge situation still hadn't been rectified.

They tried to talk over dinner, but the conversation kept stalling out, no matter how much they both tried to make it work.

She thought they might be suffering from the same problem: a mind full of things that were growing increasingly hard to comprehend. A thousand pieces of new information. A thousand instances of doubt.

A whole lot of new experiences, and no way to put any of them into words. Not even with the person they cared for most in the world.

Rhys's headlight went out within an hour. Not long after that, Abby's first flashlight failed, as well. They picked their path using only Rhys's flashlight, to conserve their final backup lights.

They were fairly sure they'd figured out which route they were on. Abby tracked the path in marker on their map. At each intersection, Rhys marked the way back with lines of white chalk at shoulder-height.

It truly was a labyrinth.

Man-made tunnels intersected natural passageways. Sometimes it was hard to tell them apart until the holes began to narrow and squeeze so tightly that Abby couldn't fit.

They tried to stay to the largest pathways. Their theory was that Hope would be more likely to find and follow what seemed like main routes instead of the smaller, natural holes. At least, that was what they hoped.

Something brittle crunched underfoot. Abby pulled her shoe back while Rhys shone his light down. There was a bone lying in the pathway. It looked like a femur, and was long enough to belong to a human.

Abby's stomach squirmed. The bone had shattered like old pottery. She tried not to think about how long it might have been lost down here, or what happened to the rest of the skeleton.

"Look," Rhys said, and she followed his light toward the walls.

Pale white lines ran along the darker stone. There were four of them, running parallel along the passage for at least ten feet.

As though someone had scraped enormous nails across the rock wall.

Abby lifted her own hand and held it just an inch above the scrapes. Even when she spread her fingers as wide as possible, she still couldn't cover the same surface area as the marks. Her fingers shook as she drew them back into a fist at her side.

She half turned back to Rhys. "Are you still sure you want to do this? It's probably not too late for you to get out."

"I'm here as long as you are," he answered.

She nodded.

The ground became uneven. Puddles of water formed in the indents, and Abby's shoes flicked little drops onto her heel with every step. She was surrounded by the damp, moist, decaying smell that she'd associated with Charles Vickers and his home. He'd be constantly surrounded by it, with a vent opening into his own front hallway.

The echoes had become so persistent that it took Abby too long to notice another sound had joined them. She halted, her breath held, as she strained to listen.

Sounds came from far, far deeper in the tunnels. Noises she couldn't quite place.

Noises that seemed to be growing nearer.

Rhys stopped so close that she could feel his warmth even through her layers. Ahead, five more lines of red threads spread across the passageway.

"Bridgette Holm mentioned something." Rhys kept his voice low, but it still reverberated through the tunnels and formed increasingly distorted echoes. "*Stay away from the threads.*"

"The denser they are, the closer you're getting to its lair," Abby finished. Bridgette had given the advice as a warning. But, now, Abby found herself moving toward the crisscrossing lines. "That's where the Stitcher would take Hope."

Rhys's arm snaked out and grabbed Abby's wrist. He nodded down, toward the ground.

More bones were scattered there. They were old and discolored and dry. Some looked animal; others may have come from a human. It was hard to be sure.

Rhys dropped his backpack over one shoulder so that he could pull his baseball bat out. Abby reached for the pocketknife instead; it was small enough to fit inside her palm, but the blade was fresh and sharp.

They stepped over, under, and through the threads. Each one quivered as they passed it, and Abby had a horrible sense that they shouldn't be disturbing the threads, as though maybe the Stitcher could hear it or *feel* it, but the gaps were too small to pass through without at least brushing them.

The paths twisted as they led down, and the man-made passages transformed into something far less regimented. They lost all context of where they were on the maps. Rhys finished his first stick of chalk and brought out another.

Then, Abby froze, one hand raised as she asked for silence.

They'd been hearing sounds behind them for hours. Quiet tapping, almost like a rock tumbling down a slope, only the sound repeated and repeated as though it was on a loop.

Now, though, there was a different sound. Something coming from ahead of them.

Something that sounded like humming.

"Hope!" she yelled.

Rhys grabbed her arm. One finger pressed against his lips. His eyes were aimed at the space behind them. The tapping sounds had gone silent.

But the humming continued.

"It's her," Abby whispered, her voice catching. Hope hadn't answered her call, but that didn't matter, because she could still hear her. "She's alive. She's *here*."

"We'll find her," he murmured back. "We just have to do it quickly and quietly, before *it* finds *us*."

He was right. Drawing the Stitcher nearer wouldn't help anyone, least of all Hope. She swallowed and tried to focus on the tune. She recognized it. The humming was a schoolyard song, one of the ones Hope and her friends liked to sing when they were younger, only its tune was slower than Abby had ever heard it. Melancholic.

It bounced around the twining passages. Abby closed her eyes and turned her head slowly, trying to find where it was strongest. Ahead, and to the right, she thought. She followed the wavering trail.

Rhys's flashlight seemed to be growing dim; the halls around them felt increasingly tight, and Abby could barely see three feet ahead of them. Lines of red thread rose out of the gloom. Abby, desperate, tried to push through them. They caught across her chest and arms, as tight and unyielding as wires.

She couldn't afford to creep around them any longer. She flicked the blade out of her pocketknife and sawed it through the threads. It was possible to hear as they snapped: tiny little pops that echoed through the space.

Forward and forward she moved, cutting through any threads that blocked the route. They reached an intersection and she followed the song left. Then a turn to the right. And then Abby was forced to slow as the paths branched again.

The song was coming from a small hole in the wall. Abby crouched and Rhys moved in behind her to shine his light into it.

No more than three feet wide and two feet high, it looked like a terrifyingly tight squeeze. Ten feet ahead, it seemed to narrow further and turn, making it impossible to see what was on the other side.

But, as Abby leaned close to the gap, there was no doubt. The tune was coming from somewhere on the other side of it.

She wouldn't be able to fit with the bag on her back. But maybe…

"You can wait here, if you need to," she said, and dropped the backpack off her shoulders. She replaced the batteries in her headlamp and was rewarded as it fluttered weakly to life. Then she pushed her bag into the hole ahead of herself as she began to squirm down it.

The hole was too low to crawl; she had to drop onto her stomach and reach her hands forward to drag herself down the passageway. Loose shale scraped over her forearms, chest, and legs. Every time she lifted herself, even just an inch, she felt the ceiling press into her back.

The humming song continued to lead her forward. It seemed to be growing slower and lower, the notes no longer hitting the highs of the schoolyard rendition, but instead groaning out like a funeral dirge.

As though the singer was dying.

Please, hold on. Wait for me just a little more.

She pushed her backpack ahead of herself, then reached forward. Pressed her open palms into the rough floor. Raised herself, just enough to squirm, and dragged herself forward. The walls were drawing in tighter, and each time she repeated that series of movements, she gained less distance. Three inches. Then two. Then one at a time.

And then she hit the bend.

She pushed her backpack around it first. That was the only way she could bring her supplies with her, but the backpack filled nearly the entire tunnel and made it impossible to see what was ahead.

Sounds came from behind her. A scrape, a scuffle.

"Rhys?" she called.

His voice was low and tense. "I'm following."

Abby was struggling to fit. She didn't know how he would. "I'll come back for you."

Another scrape. "That's not a chance I can take."

She swallowed, then used her fingertips to nudge the backpack slightly further forward. Palms onto the floor. Press down. Drag forward. Her shoulder blades scraped the rough rock above. She paused just to breathe, and each time her lungs expanded, she felt stones bite into her sides.

She'd made it around the bend, at least, but the natural passage didn't end.

Forward again. Push the backpack. Press her palms. Drag forward. Breathe. Push. Press. Drag. Breathe.

Push—

Her backpack vanished.

A muffled thump echoed around the tunnel. Abby's headlamp barely clung to life. She could see the narrow walls to either side, but her fingertips faded into the gloom ahead. The backpack was no longer within reach, though.

Which meant it had fallen over a ledge.

She could only hope it was a shallow one, and one she could fit down, otherwise they'd lost half of their supplies.

Palms pressed flat. Lift. Drag. Breathe. Reach forward. Repeat.

Her fingers found the tunnel's end first and curled around the rough border. This time, she didn't even pause to breathe as she pulled herself forward.

Forward, and into a cavern filled with trinkets.

TWENTY-NINE

〤〤〤〤

ABBY DROPPED TO HER HANDS AND KNEES OUTSIDE THE NARROW tunnel. Her headlamp was almost gone again. The backpack lay on the ground beside her, and Abby raced to pull it open and find the second flashlight Riya had given her. When it came on, its circle of light caught over a thousand red threads and a thousand unfamiliar shapes.

The cavern wasn't as large as the first one they'd found. Shaped more like an underground train station, the cavern arched overhead and continued down ahead of them until even the flashlight couldn't find its end.

Objects had been fastened to the walls with red thread. Still more were suspended from the ceiling; they twisted languidly, held up by a single line.

Abby's light landed on the nearest shape. It was a sneaker. The off-white laces hung loose and the sole was peeling. Old stains discolored what had probably been white and gray fabric. *Bloodstains*, Abby's mind whispered. The shoe was soaked in them.

She moved her flashlight to the left. A metal wristwatch glittered. Its dial was cracked. She hadn't seen someone wear a watch like that in decades. She wondered if that was how long it had been down here.

She shifted her light again. This time, it landed on an umbrella. It was held up by a thread looped around the handle. Old metal spokes were rusted. The fabric covering was shredded.

A sound coming from behind made her flinch. She turned. Rhys was still following through the tight passage; she could barely see the backpack he was pushing ahead of himself.

"Sorry," Abby whispered. She put her light on the ground and reached into the tunnel to pull the backpack through. Then she found Rhys's dirt-caked hands, fastened her own around them, and said, "Exhale."

He did. Abby pulled. She could feel the rocks catching on his clothes and skin. It had to be hurting him, but he didn't make a sound.

Abby wedged her shoes against the wall to get better leverage, and pulled harder. Rhys's head and shoulders emerged from the hole, and then the rest of him fell free.

They sat together on the ground, breathing heavily. A thin streak of blood marred Rhys's jawline, and they were both covered in dust. But at least they were through.

Rhys nodded to the space around them. "What is this?"

"I think…" She took her light up again and pointed it at the objects around them. A jacket. A wig, dusty and matted with dried blood. Purses and satchels and wallets and shopping bags. "I think these are the things people had with them when they were taken."

It was as though they'd been put on display. A museum to death.

The humming tune had gone silent when Abby crawled out of the passage. Abby craned her neck, straining to see through the rows of mementos. She wet her lips and whispered, "Hope?"

There was a beat of silence. Abby counted the passing seconds; *two, three, four, five—*

A humming note answered her. It sounded very, very close. Abby shoved off the floor and half ran toward it as the song began again.

Her light shimmered off cell phones, house keys, winter jackets, and hats. Through them, she hunted for a flash of human skin. A glimpse of dyed hair. She couldn't find it, and abruptly, the tune was coming from behind her, instead of ahead.

"Where…" Her flashlight flickered as she turned.

Rhys had come to a halt, facing the wall. The energy seemed to drain from him. "Abby."

She crossed to him in three long paces.

A children's music box stood crookedly on a jagged rock. A tiny, painted horse circled it as it relayed its tune. It looked old, its paint all flaking off and its mirrored surface dull. And it was playing the slow, haunting melody she'd been chasing.

No. Abby's eyes burned as she stared at it. Even as she watched, it ground to a halt, then began rewinding, playing backward.

Any batteries must have died years before, but it still called its mournful song into the darkness. It had the jitters. Just like any kind of technology that came too close to the Stitcher.

The mirrored surface was blurred with years of beading moisture and rock dust. Abby appeared in it as a shadow, crooked and faded. Next to her was a near-identical shape: Rhys.

And behind them...

A shape shifted across the reflection.

Abby swung, her light raised. It flashed across the opposite wall and its collection of trinkets, then fixed on the passageway they'd come through.

She was just in time to see an enormous, pallid hand retract back into the darkness.

"Oh," came out as something between a gasp and a moan.

Rhys grabbed her arm and dragged her back, away from the opening. She staggered with him. Trinkets bounced off their backs and then swung like pendulums, obscuring their view of the room.

Abby felt frozen. She knew what she'd seen. That didn't make it any easier to absorb. The image was seared into her mind, horrifyingly clear.

Five fingers, larger and longer than any she'd seen on any human. The skin was as gray and weathered as a tombstone. It had been criss-crossed with lines where the flesh had been separated, and then pulled back together with stitches of red thread.

Bridgette Holm and Nicholas Rigney had been telling the truth.

Doubtful was haunted by a monster.

Rhys kept moving, dragging Abby with him. He held his baseball bat in his other hand, and Abby momentarily wondered where his light had gone before she realized it had died. Her own was barely holding on. It stuttered across the shapes around them, pulling them out of the gloom like waking nightmares. Shoes. Scarves. A pager. A Halloween mask, its painted lips pulled back in a leering smile.

"Stay close to me," Rhys said, and his hold on her was fierce. "It doesn't like us being together."

The victims are only ever taken one at a time. Even Rhys's family had left the car separately. Abby's breathing was shallow as they raced, but her mind was moving even faster than her feet. *Something's stopping it from taking us when we're together.*

One of their rules had been *don't walk alone*. Even back before they knew the Stitcher was a monster, they'd treated it as more of a common precaution. Now, Abby was starting to think that rule might be more vital than they'd ever imagined.

But, if the arm reaching through the tunnel to pluck at them was any indicator, the Stitcher was prepared and willing to separate them by force.

They were nearly at the opposite end of the cavern. Abby could see a tunnel there, wider than the one they'd come through. Rhys aimed for it.

A jacket was strapped to the wall by lines of thread. Abby staggered to a halt, transfixed by it. The fabric was old and tattered and dusty. Except for one thing, it would have been no different from any other remnant in the space: a final reminder of the person who had been lost to the Stitcher.

Abby pulled free from Rhys's hold. She stepped toward the jacket, her eyes burning and unblinking, as she stared at the patch sewn into its sleeve.

Her mother had mended that sleeve when Abby was still a small child. She'd seen it every morning as her father had slung his jacket over his shoulder and every afternoon as he'd hung it on the hook by the door.

The last time she'd seen it was on the night when he'd left to confront Charles Vickers.

"At least I know, now," she managed.

"Oh," Rhys said, realizing what they were looking at.

Abby swallowed and felt the lump in her throat ache. Her father had been gone for years. Hope, for just two days. She could grieve for her father later, once she had her sister back.

They felt no closer to finding her. But they knew there was one other living thing down in the mines, and it was just barely out of sight.

Abby adjusted her grip on the flashlight and held the pocketknife in her spare hand. Then she stepped into the new tunnel, and left the hall of mementos behind.

Jen gasped.

Her blankets were strangling her. Her brain felt fevered from bad dreams. Images of animals screaming, of faceless people sobbing, and of black inky clouds rolling across the landscape infested her mind, but as quickly as she tried to piece together what the dreams had been about, they were gone again.

Moonlight poured in through the window, but judging by her dry mouth and full bladder, it was closer to dawn than midnight. Jen rose out of bed, grimacing as she rolled her shoulders and felt how tight they were, and left for the bathroom.

She cradled a glass of water as she returned, and pressed it against her hot forehead. It had been a long time since she'd had dreams that bad. She knew from experience it would be hard to fall asleep again, so she stood at her window, staring out at the sparse forest where strings of abandoned police tape fluttered in the wind.

Two glinting eyes stared up at her.

Jen rocked back, her breathing shallow. It was a deer, almost perfectly disguised by the dappled moonlight at the trees' edge. It gazed up toward her room, but there was something wrong with its neck. Something bulging out to one side.

She knew what it was even before the deer turned. The tumorous growths grew like bunches of swollen grapes along its jaw and flanks. They were leaking dark liquid.

It was a different deer than the first one she'd seen—this one had no antlers and still had its eyes intact—but it was suffering no less. Its footfalls were unsteady as it staggered toward the trees.

Jen didn't like to believe in fate, or destiny, or anything that bordered too close to superstition.

She was still fairly sure the retired officer they'd spoken to the previous afternoon was the nexus of some massive, town-wide delusion. It was the most plausible explanation, at least.

But...

Sometimes things happened too close together for her to believe there wasn't a connection. And the deer, right outside her window, right when she woke up, right while her two not-quite-friends-but-slightly-more-than-acquaintances-it's-complicated companions were traveling somewhere deep underground… That was too much to chalk up to chance.

The deer disappeared between the trees, but it was moving slowly. She thought she might be able to catch up to it if she was fast enough.

Don't leave your house after dark. She worked her mouth. *That's their rule. I guess tonight's a good night to make some rules of my own.*

She moved fast as she pulled clothes on over her pajamas. Her phone went into one pocket; a small knife she'd begun to keep on her bedside table went into the other. Then she slipped through the house and out through the groaning door, grimacing and desperately hoping her father wouldn't hear. Her house stayed quiet and dark as she crossed the yard to reach the woods.

The deer wasn't hard to track. Its hooves crackled through dried leaves, and every few seconds it exhaled heavily, as though it was struggling to breathe.

She pushed through a mesh of leaves and stumbled to a halt. The animal was directly ahead. Her phone's beam shimmered over the dappled fur and the swollen, oozing tumors. It faced away from her but didn't try to turn, even though Jen was nearly close enough to touch. Its body shuddered.

And then…

It tilted its head back. The skin stretched further and further, the neck bending horrifically, until its head was completely inverted and its dark eyes faced Jen down the length of its back.

She staggered back and hit a tree. Jen pressed herself against it, unable to breathe, as the deer's gaze pierced her.

Its neck had to have twisted far enough to break, but it still stood upright. Its legs began moving again, carrying it forward, even as its head bobbed upside down on the end of its contorted neck.

Something sleek and dark shifted to Jen's right. She flinched back as another deer emerged from the woods. Its eyes were gone to the tumors. She wanted to believe it was the deer she'd first seem, just after moving into her home, but then another animal shuffled through the forest to her left, so close that it nearly grazed her side, and she didn't know *what* to think any longer.

She could turn around. Go back inside, pretend she'd never seen anything, and hope the deer's twisted form didn't invade her multiplying nightmares.

Her feet dragged across the leaves as she took a step forward. She'd made a choice to get involved, for better or worse.

And the deer seemed to be drawn toward something. They all moved in the same direction, as though they were being led.

She had to know what was calling them.

Abby tried not to think about how far they were into the caverns. She knew they were deep. The passageways all seemed to lead downward, and already daylight and fresh air were starting to feel like distant memories.

Her shoes were wet and her feet sore from the uneven surface. A hundred small bruises pocked her from where she'd misjudged her distance from a wall. It was impossible to tell how long they'd been down there already, but she knew it had to be hours. Somewhere between six and ten, by her best estimate.

But they didn't dare stop moving. The Stitcher was still following. They could hear the slow, low rattle echoing along the tunnels.

Just like she'd lost all context of distance traveled and time, she couldn't tell how far away Silas might be. Only that he seemed to know *exactly* where *they* were.

They ate food and drank from their water bottles without stopping. Rhys had burned through most of his chalk as he marked their path. They'd given up trying to pinpoint their location on the maps; it wasn't going to help them when they didn't know where they needed to go. They could find a path out if and when they found Hope.

"Here," Rhys whispered, passing her an opened bottle of water. "Drink before you get dehydrated."

Abby gratefully took the bottle. The caves were damp and cool, but rock dust lingered in the air and dried out her throat. She swallowed just enough to clear the bad taste from her mouth and then passed the bottle back. Rhys took his turn, then tucked the bottle into his bag.

"Wait…" Abby hesitated, her lips held apart as she inhaled. "Do you smell that?"

Rhys came to a halt and tilted his head back, frowning. "You have a better nose than I do."

The mines were full of scents. Dry, cold rock. The slightly unsettling odor of water that had festered for decades. And something else, something older and sicker and more rotten. The same scent that filled Charles Vickers's house. The smell of the Stitcher, she was almost certain.

Now, though, a different scent wove between the others.

Metallic. Queasy. Cloying.

Abby knew it instantly. Blood.

"I think..." she swallowed again, and drew in quick, shallow breaths. "I think the Stitcher must have a place where he does his cutting. And I think it has to be nearby."

Irregular drips came from somewhere ahead. And, behind, the distant *scrape, scrape, tap* of Silas creeping ever closer.

Rhys didn't question her. He just nodded. And so Abby moved forward, trying to trace the tang of metal and rot through the passages.

Silas had a room for the trinkets he took from his victims. Most of them were bloodied, but none of it had dripped onto the floor. They were all added to the room after their owners were dead.

Which means Silas has a separate room for carving and stitching.

And that's where he'd bring everyone, at first. It was where he would bring Hope.

Her spine ached as shivers traveled down it. She didn't want to think about her sister in the cutting room, or what might have happened there.

Bridgette made it out. She was able to escape from whatever space the Stitcher had dragged her to. Which means Hope could have escaped, as well.

But, if she was right, finding the Stitcher's central lair would at least show them where Hope had *been*. It would give them a place to start. And maybe, just maybe, there would be clues about which direction they needed to go.

Following the scent wasn't easy. Abby had to backtrack again and again, weaving slightly closer with each pass, until she finally found a tall but narrow gap in the walls. When she leaned close, the tang was strong enough to make her recoil.

"Here," she said, and slung her backpack off her shoulders again.

This time, there was no crawling on her stomach, but she had to turn her body sideways to fit between the narrow walls. There was barely a finger of spare space, and rocks scraped every piece of exposed skin as she inched her way through the pass.

The tightness made her body itch and her lungs burn, but, if they were lucky, the pass might be too narrow for the Stitcher to follow them through. She hoped.

There was no doubting the smell anymore, though. Even Rhys was gasping under its strength. Abby's eyes burned, but she shuffled her feet faster and faster, gritting her teeth as stones grazed along her chest and cheek, and then suddenly she was out the other side.

Abby gasped and lurched back to press herself into the stones. Her shaking flashlight flickered over ground that was pocked with holes. Some were only as large as a finger. Some were big enough for a leg to drop through them. Some could swallow an entire person.

"Careful," she whispered as Rhys edged out of the narrow squeeze.

Abby raised her light. It was hard to tell how large the space might be. The area was bisected with dozens of pillars of natural stone, and their surfaces looked like dripping candles. She reached up to touch the nearest one. It even *felt* waxy.

Stalactites and stalagmites. Formed from dripping water over hundreds of thousands of years. Grown millimeter by millimeter before finally connecting in the center to create a pillar.

Some of the columns were wide enough that an entire person could hide behind them. They must have been ancient.

Rhys switched on his own light. Their two beams highlighted more of the pillars and crystalline walls.

"Formations like this would be a tourist attraction anywhere else," he said.

He was right. Under any other situation, it would have been spectacular. People bought tickets to visit limestone caves just like this one.

And theirs had remained a secret. Not just from the tourists, but even from the miners who had excavated the coal deposits nearby.

It wasn't untouched, though.

Threads crisscrossed every surface. There were more of them here than anywhere else they'd found in the mines. Some wrapped the structures in tight loops; others were draped from the ceiling like cobwebs. They looked damp; beads of liquid had formed at their lowest point, waiting for any small disturbance to shake free.

The red thread was so pervasive that it helped mask the other traces of red in the room.

As Abby's light trailed down the pillars, it highlighted dark stains in the pale, near-translucent stone. They were covered in what looked like streaks of long-dried blood.

It wasn't just on the pillars. It was *everywhere*, creating a gradient from natural, waxy stone near the ceiling into rust red closer to the ground.

Her light came to rest on one shape in particular. A handprint, pressed high into the wall, stark and clear and likely very old.

She turned her light lower toward the pockmarked floor. Scraps of rags were discarded in piles. They were clothes, Abby realized. Torn into scraps and thrown away as their owners were reassembled.

Some of them hung into the holes that marked the floors. The openings didn't seem as natural as the pillars around them. In fact, most of them looked as though they'd been carved. And Abby abruptly understood what they were intended to be.

Drainage holes.

This was it. The Stitcher's cutting room.

Abby pressed the back of her hand over her mouth and nose as she stepped deeper into the space, careful to avoid the holes. She pointed her light into some of them, but she couldn't see their end.

The smell of old blood and rot was overwhelming. The ground was slimy from generations of death.

Driven by single-minded focus, Abby had found it possible to push past nearly anything. The discovery that the Stitcher was not a man but a monster; breaking into Vickers's house; the claustrophobically tight tunnels. She'd been able to endure each new barrier with nothing but a pure, raw need to reach her sister.

But, as she crossed that room, she found herself shaking uncontrollably.

Doubtful was a town built on and enveloped by death. But she had never been as surrounded by it as she was right then.

She could no longer hear the scuttling, tapping sounds of the Stitcher behind them. She didn't know if that was better or worse.

"Hope?" she whispered.

Her light flashed from a bloodied pillar to a heap of red-soaked rags to the damp, dripping threads above them. She tried focusing on the fabric, looking for any that might be fresh or might match the pink nightclothes Hope had been wearing when she was taken. Pink was a difficult color to find in a cavern painted in crimson. Her movements became increasingly erratic as she shone her flashlight over scraps of indistinct, soaked material.

A drop of liquid landed on her forearm. It was tinted red. She shook it away.

Then she rounded a curtain of limestone walls and came to an abrupt halt. Objects had been suspended there, sheltered from sight until that moment. They were hung out like a gory display. A prized collection. Something to be admired.

Abby opened her mouth, but she couldn't tell if the scream made it out.

THIRTY

BODY PARTS HAD BEEN HUNG BEHIND THE LIMESTONE CURTAIN. Like a butchery display, they trailed at the end of looping red threads, suspended there for when they might be needed.

Stretches of skin. A foot. A hanging chain of teeth, intricately lashed together with thread.

"No," Abby whispered. "No, no, no."

At the arrangement's center was an arm.

It was pale, thin, and horribly familiar. The fingers were curled slightly, as though the owner was resting. Two of the fingernails were chipped. The palm held the remnants of lines of ink. The patterns Hope had drawn on herself at the fireside, faded by washing but not entirely gone.

There was no body attached to the arm.

Abby collapsed to the ground. She felt as though her breath had been sucked out of her. The arm twisted on its thread, the slightly curled fingers seeming to beckon to her.

Rhys crouched down next to her.

"I'm sorry," he whispered, and his voice was so hoarse that Abby knew it was hurting him to speak. "I'm so, so sorry."

She didn't know what to say. Her mind was overloading:

Maybe she's still okay—maybe this is a hallucination—maybe we've made a mistake—if we can just work harder, run faster, search more—

Rhys made a sharp noise. His eyes had gone wide. His hand tightened over Abby's shoulder. She looked down.

The enormous, pallid hand snaked out of one of the largest holes in the floor. And it was wrapped around Rhys's ankle.

We didn't hear it following us. Because it didn't need us to hear it anymore. We were going exactly where it wanted us to.

The thoughts came too late. Abby lunged for the hand, the pocket-knife aimed for the gray flesh.

It moved so suddenly that Abby barely had time to react. The limb snaked back down into the hole in a flurry of motion, pulling Rhys with it. Abby's knife stabbed into the stones just inches from his leg.

He gasped as he hit the floor and threw out his hands, clawing for purchase. His fingers slid through the oily grime coating the stones, leaving lines in the rust red coating. He came to a halt with only his torso hanging outside of the hole.

Abby grabbed at Rhys, clutching around his shoulders as she tried to drag him back out. He locked eyes with her. With what sounded like last of his breath, he whispered, "Get out."

The gray hand pulled again. Abby clung to him, burying her fingers in his clothes as she tried to hold on to him. The Stitcher was stronger.

Rhys was dragged through the hole in the floor.

Bridgette stroked her fingers through her cat's long, corpse-white fur. Its milky eyes, drowning in cataracts, stared into the far distance as its claws rhythmically curled and relaxed. They would be leaving tiny scratches in her thighs, but she didn't try to stop it. She barely had any feeling in what remained of her legs.

A soft growl came from the room's corner.

It was a dull morning, with heavy clouds hanging low on the sky, and the curtains stopped much natural light from getting in at all. Bridgette couldn't tell which dog has sounded the alarm, but within seconds, all of the animals were reacting. The cat she'd been stroking went stiff, its claws all extended and its tail bushing. The tabby in the corner hunched up, its pupils contracting. The three dogs behind Bridgette sent up rumbling, throaty growls as they paced.

She knew where they would go, if she only opened the door for them. There was a reason her home stayed locked.

The floorboards creaked in the hall behind. Vivian was almost invisible through the gloom. She stood silently, watching as every animal shuddered and salivated and cowered.

"It's happening, isn't it?" she asked.

"Yes." Bridgette didn't need the animals to alert her. She felt it through her body, crackling and prickling, as though every bone was being splintered. "Someone is being taken."

Abby's hands were empty. They were stretched out toward the space where Rhys had been just a second before. A space that was now nothing but an empty hole in the floor.

Her mouth was open but she couldn't make a sound. Inside her mind, she was screaming.

His last words had been to tell her to get out of the mines.

She couldn't do that. Not when the two most precious people in her life were still down there.

Abby clutched her backpack to her chest, hoping to shield the contents, as she dropped her legs into the hole that had claimed Rhys.

She didn't know how deep it was or what waited at the bottom. She just closed her eyes and let herself drop through.

The fall sent her heart into her throat. Her legs kicked at empty air. And then, before she was ready for it, she plunged into freezing cold water.

She hung suspended in the liquid. It felt colder than any water she'd been in before; thicker, heavier. The kind of water that holds a person down and never lets them go. Then her outstretched legs touched a solid floor, and she kicked against it to drive herself up.

Abby breached the surface and sucked in air. Liquid dripped into her mouth. It tasted like sour pennies and rotted mushrooms and poison.

Her light had died. Nothing was visible; her entire world was a blanket of inky darkness. But, as her ears cleared, she thought she heard distant noises. Not quite splashing, but soft, swift sluicing sounds, like practiced limbs brushing through water. They were moving away from her.

She spat the foul water out as she swam, backpack held in one arm while the other helped pull her toward the distant noises. The pool had already begun to sap warmth from her, and the harder she swam, the more it stole.

The sluicing sounds vanished. They were replaced with a low, heavy scraping noise. The Stitcher had reached some kind of shore.

Abby swam harder. Her heart felt as though it was about to burst. One hand ahead, scooping her forward. Legs behind, kicking rhythmically. Her clothes were weighing her down and she could barely keep her head above water, but she couldn't afford to lose time shedding clothing. Hand forward. Scoop. Kick. Hand forward—

Her fingers hit stone, and she felt her nails splinter. There was no time to nurse them. She threw the backpack ahead of herself and then clutched at the stone rise as she pulled herself out.

Liquid poured from her clothes as she crouched on the rocks. The darkness felt as heavy and cold and smothering as the pool had been. She fumbled with the backpack, desperately hunting for the zipper to get at the flashlight inside, praying it might still somehow work.

Slow, scraping noises echoed ahead of her. She'd thought they were moving away. As her fingers fixed around the zip and began to pull, the quiet, horrific realization hit her that the sounds were growing closer.

And her world was no longer dark. Two lights shimmered through the gloom. Enormous, they towered over her, fixing on her, dousing her. And Abby felt every last shred of resistance fade.

THIRTY-ONE

RIYA SAT ON THE EDGE OF HER BED. SHE CRADLED HER PHONE IN her hands. It had stayed on the pillow next to her all night, its ringer turned up to maximum so that she'd have no chance to sleep through it.

It hadn't rung.

It was now eight in the morning. Fourteen hours had passed since Abby and Rhys had vanished down the hole in Charles Vickers's house.

She scuffed her shoes together. She'd done the right thing by staying behind. The mines were close to being a death sentence, and she owed it to the people who loved her—her parents, her friends, herself—to stay alive if she possibly could.

And yet…

And yet…

It turned out a person could make the correct choice, and still feel strangled by regret.

She turned the phone over. It felt dangerously heavy in her hands, as though it carried the ability to destroy her or save her. Realistically, she knew her answers probably wouldn't come from her phone. Realistically, she'd have to let go of her hope a piece at a time, relinquishing slightly more with each day that passed, until it was impossible to keep it alive any longer.

And that was what hurt the most. If she thought Abby and Rhys had died overnight, she could begin to mourn. But the Stitcher didn't always kill quickly. There were odds that her friends were both still alive at that moment. And that they might continue to be, for days.

Riya ground her teeth as she fought to stop the pain and frustration from coming out as sounds. Her parents were downstairs. And she didn't want them to know anything was wrong.

Then her phone chimed, and Riya felt as though her heart had stopped. She nearly dropped the phone in her eagerness to read the message.

It wasn't from her missing friends. It was from Cool Girl. And Riya had to read the words three times to fully believe them.

I think I've found a way into the mines.

Abby shuddered as she pulled air into her lungs.

She lay on her side on a cold stone floor. When she tried to move her arms, she couldn't. Thin threads cut into her skin. She pulled against them, harder and harder, until they pinched her skin so tightly that pins and needles ricocheted down her limbs.

"Don't fight them," a voice whispered. "They'll only hurt you."

Abby strained toward the speaker. "Rhys!"

Pale light fluttered. A figure lay just feet away from her, barely out of reach. Abby blinked and blinked again, struggling to see.

Rhys's headlight, despite the ordeal it had been through, was still fighting for life. It winked on and then faded again, before flickering erratically.

It wasn't strong enough to see far. Just herself, and Rhys, and the patch of bare rock between them.

And the threads.

They wove across and around them like a spider's webs. They were what had made it impossible to move. Even then, with the help of the light, Abby couldn't lift her arm more than an inch before the loops cinched tight.

"Are you hurt?" she asked Rhys, but he was no longer watching her. He'd tilted his head as far as he could, and as loose stones rattled across the floor, Abby realized why.

Something enormous moved at the edge of their light.

Massive hands, the size of Abby's torso, touched down on the ground, the fingers spreading for purchase. The arms were a patchwork of skin in all shades. The pieces were held together with red thread. In some places, they stretched tightly against bone as the limbs strained; in other places, folds of flesh hung loose.

Above those arms, she could see the faintest outline of its shoulders, enormous but bone-thin, and a hairless head.

The Stitcher moved slowly and languidly as it paced past them on all fours. Even crouched like that, it towered, its back close to brushing the ceiling.

Its elongated limbs trailed past Abby. She couldn't hold still any longer; she strained against the threads again, fighting to slip even just one hand out of the loops.

The Stitcher turned toward her.

"Don't look into its eyes," Rhys whispered.

The warning came too late. Abby was already staring up toward it.

Its head was barely human any longer. Lines of red thread bisected it at every angle, piecing a loose mask of a face into place. The nose was flattened with no cartilage underneath. The lips were wide and made from pieces from many different mouths.

Sewn threads looped around the eyes in perfect circles. They held the folds of skin clear of the dark pits behind.

Dark pits, filled with light.

Two glowing disks shone from inside its head. They fixed on Abby, and she felt every muscle in her body seize before going limp.

Conscious thought drained out of her. So did her emotions. The fear, and the anger, and the desperation all faded into an easy numbness.

She felt as though she was asleep and lost in foggy dreams. Faintly, she was aware of Rhys calling to her, but she couldn't understand the words. They barely seemed to matter as the Stitcher turned away and resumed moving through the room, his lamp-like eyes shimmering across the stone walls.

"Abby," Rhys called. "Abby, come back."

She didn't want to. For the first time in days, she was comfortable, and happy, and safe. The threads cradled her. The cold clothes and painful floor were forgotten under simple contentment.

"Abby," he begged again, and a sizzle of awareness flashed through her mind.

People were near the abduction sites. The Stitcher moved behind her. One long, cold hand grazed over her head, as though to caress her hair. *No one ever heard the victims being taken.*

No screams. No cries for help. No sounds at all.

This is why.

The Stitcher moved past. She drew in a ragged breath. The numbness was lifting.

"That's right," Rhys said. "Fight it. You can break out of it if you just fight it."

Pain sizzled through her as forgotten cuts made themselves felt. She embraced them, letting them pull her back into the present.

The Stitcher circled close to Rhys. Long hands wrapped around his shoulder and his chest. Rhys squeezed his eyes closed and turned his head aside.

Another sound came from somewhere behind them. Loose stones rattling. Flesh scraping across the cold walls. Abby's heart froze. *No... Is there another one? Did it somehow build a another creation like itself?*

The Stitcher's monstrous mouth opened. The threads pulled taut, and a sound came out unlike anything Abby had ever heard before. Like gale-force winds rushing through a tunnel as every rock trembled under its force. Abby grit her teeth, her head aching and her lungs burning.

As the echoes faded, the Stitcher swung its lamp-like gaze toward her. Abby closed her eyes as tightly as she could, scrunching her whole face as she tried to avoid the glow.

Don't look don't look don't look—

A heavy moaning noise came from the monster. She cracked one eyelid up just enough to see it had turned away again. In the weakly fluttering headlamp, she saw its hands reach for Rhys's leg.

The fingers were long, and not entirely flesh and bone, she saw. They tapered at their ends, and the tips seemed unusually sharp. Almost like massive claws.

"Abby," Rhys whispered. He still had his eyes closed and his head turned away. The threads around him strained as he tried to pull free, but there were too many of them to break through.

Her knife was in her pocket, but impossible to reach from the way she was tied. She squirmed. When she threw her shoulder forward, she was able to stretch one hand out. The threads snapped taut, painfully tight, as she tried to reach toward Rhys and the pack he still wore over his shoulders. There were weapons in there. Better lights. Matches. All things that could save them.

But he was fixed to the ground in a way where he could never reach his own bag, and Abby was still separated from him by at least eight inches.

Something rattled in the hallways behind them, growing nearer. The Stitcher's sharpened fingertips dipped into the jeans Rhys wore. The sound of ripping fabric crackled through the air. It drew its finger down the length, from the knee to the ankle, tearing the material open as neatly and easily as a pair of fabric scissors.

"Abby," Rhys said, and he'd stopped struggling against the threads.

"Hold on," she whispered, hoping Silas was too far gone to understand words. She strained to gain even another inch, and felt skin shear off her wrist. "We can find a way out. Just give me a minute—I just need to get closer—"

"Abby," he said again, and his voice was rough and frightened and raw. "Abby, turn away."

The sharpened fingertip dipped into Rhys's skin just above the ankle, and fresh blood flowed.

Jen stood at the entrance to a cave.

Cave might have been generous, but *hole* didn't feel right either. She was facing a stony slope pockmarked with prickly weeds and dead leaves from the trees that grew around. And in the slope was an opening. A deep, dark, uninviting one.

She'd stretched her phone as far into it as her arm could reach, and still couldn't see if it ended.

But she didn't think it was natural. The walls weren't old and worn. They were raw and fresh and jagged, as though they'd been torn open by iron hands.

And inside were loops of the same red thread she'd found in the forest before.

She'd been staring into the hole for nearly a full hour. In that time, the sun had risen. And three deer had vanished into the depths.

Footsteps alerted her to her arriving company. She half turned her body to see them without fully losing sight of the gaping pit. Riya was dressed in her lacrosse uniform, a gym bag and stick slung across her back. Connor, looking bone weary, trailed behind her.

"I called Connor," Riya said. "I hope that's okay."

"Yeah, of course." Jen raised a hand to greet the gangly boy who followed in Riya's wake. "Didn't have your number or I would have texted you too."

"Was it a rough night for everyone else?" Connor asked, his shoulders sloped and his curling hair a messy mop. "I couldn't fall asleep."

"Sucks to be you. I slept like a rock." Jen threw them a lopsided smile. They didn't need to know about the string of increasingly horrific nightmares. "You can thank my bladder for this find."

"Thanks, bladder," Connor said.

"And the deer, I guess. I saw one from the window and followed it here. Look."

She extended her light into the narrow cavern. At first, the floor was just scratched earth and matted, dirty thread. But as she reached her light further down, bones became visible. Animal bones. Mostly deer, she guessed, but plenty of smaller animals had been drawn into the space as well.

Riya swore under her breath as she crouched at the opening. "I wasn't sure if I could believe you when I got your text, but..."

"Yeah," Connor said. He sounded shaken.

"This is real. This... This is a way into the mines."

For a moment, none of them spoke. Then Riya drew a hiccupping breath. "What should we do?"

Connor took half a step back. "We made our choices yesterday. I can't go into there. You know I can't."

"I know." Riya bit her lip. "But it's just…to find it here, now, right when we need it, can we really walk away without at least…"

Her voice faded. A sound rose from the cave.

It was distant and distorted by echoes, but terrifyingly recognizable.

Screaming.

Horrible, horrible screams.

They stretched out longer, and longer, until every nerve in Jen's body was keyed tight with a primal, urgent need to flee.

And then they faded.

All three of them were breathing hard. Riya was still crouched on the ground, closest to the opening, and her fingers had dug grooves in the soft dirt. Connor stood back, half behind a tree, clutching at the bark to keep himself steady.

Jen swallowed. She felt sick and clammy. "Was that the deer?" she tried.

"No." Riya's voice trembled. "That was human."

Connor muttered something she couldn't understand. Jen ran her hand over her face and felt prickly, cold perspiration coat her palm.

"We can help," Riya said.

Connor choked on his own words. "Ri—"

"No, we can help. *Without going into the mines.*" There was a sudden surge of energy in Riya's voice. Her eyes were enormous and bright with both terror and hope as she turned toward them. "If we can hear *them*, then they can hear *us*. And we can call to them. We can *guide them out*."

"What do you need from me?" Jen asked before she could even consider whether that was a question she should put into the world.

Yes, she decided. *Yes. I want to do this. I* need *to do this.*

"Tell me what to do," she repeated.

"Weapons." Riya was already casting around the ground around them, but the trees were spindly and sick and the largest branch wouldn't even be enough to leave a welt. "We need weapons in case… *something else* hears us. Your home is close, isn't it?"

"If I run, ten minutes," Jen said. She was already turning to the trees. "And you better believe I'm going to run."

Rhys didn't even make a noise as the Stitcher cut into him. He turned his face toward the floor, his teeth gritted, perspiration beading across his skin.

Abby screamed instead. She screamed loud enough for the both of them.

The Stitcher didn't seem to hear. It was wholly focused on its work, the knifelike claw gently carving through skin.

Behind it, something moved. Loose stones rattled. A dark shadow rose across the rear wall, barely illuminated by the flickering headlamp. There was a crackle, then light bloomed across the cavern.

Everything happened too fast to see.

The Stitcher's head snapped backward and sparking cinders flew from it. A heavy, cracking *thud* echoed through the room.

Abby's voice broke. She could only lurch forward, strangling herself in the threads as she fought to make out shapes through the darkness.

A figure stood behind the Stitcher. It was soaked in dripping crimson. A wooden stick swung from its right hand as it advanced into the room. A cloth had been tied around the stick's end and flames licked across the fabric.

"Don't look it in the eyes," Hope yelled.

She raised her weapon and swung again.

"Thompson!" Jen yelled as she barreled into their home.

There was no answer. He'd probably been called into the station, even though it was a Sunday and that was supposed to be his day off.

Barely breaking step, she passed through the kitchen. The knife block was full of large, sharp blades. She'd take some of them on her way out, but they weren't what she was really aiming for. Playing devil's advocate and assuming the stories were true, knives weren't going to do much against a monster.

She turned into their barely used garage.

Her father had added a handful of items when they moved in, in an effort to make the space feel less empty, but the shelves were still almost entirely bare.

The largest addition, by far, was the generator. It sat next to the back wall, the instruction manual unfolded on top of it and only partially read. Three jugs of fuel stood beside it.

Jen hefted two of them and turned around. Her heart hitched.

Ahead, Thompson blocked the doorway, his arms folded as he stared down at her incredulously. "What's this?"

"It's not important," she said, and hoped he'd believe her.

"I don't know, you stealing our fuel seems important to me."

She worked her jaw. He was blocking the door, and no matter how desperate she was to get back to Riya and Connor in the forest, she didn't want to force her way past him.

Thompson's eyes moved from the fuel and back to Jen. They stared at one another for a long beat before he asked, "This is about the bodies being found, isn't it?"

"Yes."

"Jen, no. Whatever's going on, it's not our fight." He took a step toward her. "I'm getting that transfer out of here. But we're not even going to wait for it to go through. Let's leave. Right now. We'll fill our bags with whatever we can and drive until this town's a distant memory and put our savings to good use for a few weeks at a motel."

"My friends are out there." A horrible ache had set up in her chest, burning like coals against her lungs. "I can't leave them."

"Jen—"

"You're right, this isn't our fight," Jen said. Her mouth was dry. "But you always, always taught me to do what was right, and to help the people who needed helping. And that's what I'm going to do right now."

A choked laugh broke out of Thompson. "No, I thought I was very clear on this. If you're in a bad situation, I expect you to cut and run and live another day. It was your mother who instilled this horrible noble streak." He pulled his glasses off and stared at the reflections in them. Jen wasn't sure what he saw in those depths, but after a second, he took a deep breath. "Okay. What do we need to do?"

"*We?*"

"I'm not going to step aside." He adjusted his glasses. His eyes suddenly seemed a lot harder, and a lot clearer. "But I'll walk with you. Tell me what you need."

She considered that for a second. "You know Charles Vickers."

"This town has made it impossible not to."

"I need you to keep him occupied for a while. Tell him you need to ask some questions, or find some reason to bring him down to the station, or...*something*. Bring another officer, if you can convince one to go. We can't afford to have him loose right now."

Thompson's eyebrows rose. "Are you going to explain what's happening?"

"Later." Jen stepped up to the door, and Thompson moved out of the way for her. "But I'm already out of time."

"You'll stay in contact with me through your phone, won't you?"

"I'll do my best, but something about this town is messing with it."

Thompson muttered something under his breath, then crossed to his office. When he came back, he held out one of his police radios.

"I've already set the frequency," he said. "It won't be picked up by anyone else on the force, but it will let us talk in case your mobile goes bad."

Jen felt her throat tighten as she took it. She clipped it onto a loop in her jeans. "Thanks. Keep Vickers busy until I give you the all clear. I'll see you soon."

THIRTY-TWO

〰〰〰

"DON'T LOOK AT IT," HOPE SAID. "*DO NOT LOOK AT ITS FACE.*"

She had her eyes squinted half closed. The stick was stretched ahead of her. The cloth wrapped around its end was burning up fast; charred remnants scattered across the floor.

The Stitcher lurched away from Rhys. Its lamp-like eyes fixed on Hope.

The fire had hurt it. Smoldering threads curled up from the side of its face and its neck. The patchwork skin began to peel back as their connections were lost.

The Stitcher's mouth stretched wide and the horrendous, inhuman howling filled the cavern, shaking the stones and burning in Abby's bones.

Hope refused to shift. She stood, her eyes closed and legs planted, the makeshift torch extended like a sword.

The Stitcher's glowing eyes bored into her for a final heartbeat, then it crept backward, its enormous hands dexterously sliding across the stones as it vanished into the darkness licking at the edges of the cavern.

The fire burnt out. Hope lowered the stick, slumping.

"Hope," Abby managed.

Her sister looked almost unrecognizable. She'd been saturated in red-tinted liquid that had dried in rough streaks. Her clothes and her hair's colors had vanished under it. The only part of her skin that wasn't colored were the lines under her eyes where tears had washed it away.

She took a step closer, and the flickering headlamp showed the space where her left arm belonged. It ended not far below the shoulder in a line of red threads.

Hope dropped her stick. She wore a vest that didn't belong to her and looked four sizes two big, and reached her right hand into one of the pockets. She brought out a lighter. "Hold still," she whispered to Abby, and clicked the flame to life before holding it beneath the threads. "I found these in one of the passageways. The original owner didn't need them as much as I did, I guess."

The threads shriveled, blackened, and snapped in just seconds. Hope moved quickly, burning through the lines that held Abby immobile.

"You're alive." Abby couldn't tear her gaze off her sister's face. It looked pinched and drawn and older somehow. But then a tentative smile grew, and it was so quintessentially Hope that Abby thought she was going to cry.

"You came for me," Hope said.

"I wasn't going to leave you. Never."

"Maybe it would have been better if you had." Hope's smile quivered.

A bunched tangle of threads snapped as the flame cut through them, and Abby's arms were freed. She lurched up and pulled Hope into a hug. She clung to her for just a second, savoring it, before pulling back and wrestling the pocketknife out from her jacket.

"I can take care of this," she said, indicating to the threads still around her chest and legs. "Start on Rhys."

He still hadn't made a sound. She could barely hear his breathing, but it was there, low and ragged.

Abby sawed through the threads furiously. She thought she could still hear the Stitcher at the edge of the cavern. Cold, dead flesh scraped over the rocks as it crept through the ring of darkness.

Don't look.

The temptation was almost overwhelming. Just a glance, thrown over her shoulder, to make sure the elongated hands weren't reaching for the back of her throat.

But she remembered the way she'd felt under the floodlight eyes. The way everything had faded into numbness.

She thought she understood why the Stitcher only took victims when they were alone. Its eyes could freeze its prey like deer in headlights, but it could only focus its gaze on one person at a time. A second party might be able to scream, or attack it, or run. And the Stitcher had long ago learned to avoid that.

Though Abby doubted any of those complications would keep it at bay for long here, in the depths of its labyrinthine maze.

The final clump of threads snapped as she jerked her knife across them. She scrambled forward to reach Rhys. He was pale. Perspiration beaded on his forehead and dripped toward the floor.

Abby turned to his leg. It wasn't gone. But a deep cut had been made in it, and blood flowed freely.

"I'm sorry," she said, and used her knife to slice off the sleeve of her jacket. "This is going to hurt."

"Do it," he said.

She wrapped the fabric around the ankle, tied a knot, and cinched it as hard as she could. Rhys grunted. His other leg twitched. He pushed himself up to sit, but the movement seemed to cost him.

The headlamp fluttered one final time, then blinked out.

The depth of the darkness was overwhelming. She could feel Rhys's body under her hands, and Hope's shallow breathing at her side, but except for that she could have believed the world no longer existed.

She could no longer hear the Stitcher. She didn't know if he'd slunk away to repair his wounds, or whether he might still be at the back of the cavern somewhere, watching.

"Hold still," Abby said. She felt around Rhys to get the backpack off him.

It was drenched from going through the subterranean pool. Abby, blind, fumbled to get the zipper open and sifted through the contents. She found one of the candles and placed it on the floor ahead of herself, then continued searching for the matches.

Her fingers closed around a small plastic bag. Riya had had the forethought to waterproof them, and Abby's fingers shook as she took out a match and struck it.

Two drawn faces were briefly visible on either side of her before she lowered the match to light the candle. The wick was damp and took two more matches before it caught. Even then, the light didn't reach far. Just enough to give them a moment of relief from the oppressive dark.

Abby found herself staring at her sister again. Hope stared back, her eyes huge and intense. She'd been formidable when she'd stood between Abby and the Stitcher, but now, Abby couldn't overlook just how fragile she was. Her face was pinched. Her hand, braced on the floor, trembled. Her breathing was labored in a way that frightened Abby badly. She didn't know how much blood Hope might have lost, but she knew it had to be substantial.

Then she glanced down at Rhys's leg. The fabric she'd tied around his ankle was already drenched. Abby swallowed. He was losing too much, too fast. She reached into the bag for the first aid kit, but Riya had only been able to get one, and it had been in Abby's backpack. A backpack that was now irretrievably lost.

Abby swallowed, then fumbled for a water bottle instead.

"Yes," Hope gasped when she saw it. She grabbed it, and her other shoulder twitched. She was trying to use her lost arm to open the cap.

"Here," Abby said, reaching for it, but Hope just shook her head. She clamped the bottle between her knees and used her right hand to unscrew the top, then tipped the bottle back and drank deeply.

"There's puddles of water here," she said as she surfaced, breathing heavily. "But they taste so foul, you have no idea."

Abby managed a smile. She remembered tasting the pool she'd plunged into. "I can imagine."

Hope drank again, and trickles of water trailed down her jaw, washing tracks through the red staining. Abby's heart ached.

"What happened?" she asked. "After he took you."

Hope lowered the bottle. Her breathing seemed rougher as she slumped. "He just…let me free. He didn't try to tie me up, like he did with you. I guess because he didn't need to. He found me pretty easily when he wanted my arm."

Abby repressed a shudder.

Hope's smile twitched, then vanished again. "I think he uses the threads to tell where you are. He can feel when you bump into them. And they're everywhere… I got tangled in some, once. I thought they were going to kill me before I got free. How long have I been down here?"

"Two days."

"It feels longer."

That was what Bridgette Holm had said about her time in the tunnels too. The lack of light had to distort time.

"I've been walking this whole time," Hope said, and lifted her head again. Her jaw trembled. "I got lucky and tripped over the remains of some other poor person. This is their jacket and their lighter. And I just burnt up their shirt."

Abby glanced behind them, to the remains of Hope's weapon. She'd thought the fabric had been wrapped around a stick. Now, she saw, the cloth had been wrapped around a human femur.

"You bought us some time," she said. It was hard to be sure when the cavern was so dark, but she was fairly sure the three of them were alone. "It burnt some of the threads holding the Stitcher together. I get the feeling he's retreated to repair himself."

"Possibly back to the cutting room," Rhys agreed.

She didn't know how long that would buy them, but it would probably be less than they wanted.

"I can walk," Rhys said, as though guessing her thoughts. "Hope, are you okay to keep moving?"

"It's better than staying here," she said. Her eyebrows furrowed. "But I don't know how to get out of here. I've been walking for so long, but it never seems to end."

"We have maps." Abby tipped the backpack onto its side to sift through its items. She found their paper printouts, folded and completely soaked, and began picking them apart. "They won't cover the natural caves or the tunnels the Stitcher made, but if we can find the mines, we should be able to figure out where we are."

And then they only had to find their way back to the tunnels leading into Vickers's house. If they could get close enough to the surface for their phones to get service, they could call Riya, who would call the police, who would get them out.

Hope passed the empty water bottle back to Abby. "Let's go, then."

Abby zipped up the backpack, then slung it over her shoulders. Rhys began to rise. A small pool of blood had spread around his leg, and movement seemed to make it worse. Abby reached out to help him up. "Lean on me," she said, and draped his arm around her shoulder.

Hope took up the candle. She stretched it out, searching the shadows, then sent one final glance back to Abby. The whites of her eyes shone uncannily in the flickering light. "Hold on to my jacket. Just in case."

Just in case the light goes out. Just in case the Stitcher tries to tear us apart. Just in case we're not able to find one another in this labyrinth a second time.

Abby hooked her spare hand into the grimy jacket and held on tight as Hope led them out of the chamber.

THIRTY-THREE

"ABBY! RHYS! *ABBY!*"

Riya sagged, dropping into a crouch. Years of lacrosse had kept her fit, but she'd still underestimated the sheer toll that yelling at the top of her voice would take.

They'd been at it for nearly twenty minutes. Jen hadn't returned. Both Riya and Connor's phones were jittering too badly to send any messages. And their calls into the mine had gotten no answer yet.

"Hello!" Connor yelled at her side. He leaned close to the hole, his hands cupped around his mouth as he tried to direct as much noise into the cavern as possible. "Abs! Rhys! Whoever!"

He dropped his hands and carefully lowered himself to the ground. Like Riya, he was winded.

"I dunno," he said through gasping breaths. "I don't think this is going to work. Maybe we could go, get some stuff like an amp or a drum or anything that would be more effective than just hollering, and try again later."

That was the sensible route, she knew. If they hadn't been heard by twenty minutes, odds were her and Connor's voices just weren't traveling far enough. Maybe it was time to call it, to reassess and reconvene later.

But she still couldn't get herself to leave.

She'd heard someone in there. Someone who was screaming.

It felt...*wrong* to just leave them.

She met Connor's gaze. His hair was tangled and frizzy. His freckles stood out against his pale skin. He looked bone tired.

"I know," he said, answering her unspoken thoughts. "I want them back too."

Leaves crackled behind them. Riya, her nerves keyed tight, swung. Jen emerged from between the trunks, her arms full.

"I didn't mean to take so long," she said, sliding down the slope to reach the clearing. "But I didn't want to cut corners either."

Riya stared at the two cartons and bulging duffel bag Jen dropped beside them. "Is that...fuel?"

Jen didn't get a chance to answer. Connor lunged forward, one hand stretched toward them and waving frantically. "Shh," he hissed. "Shh, *shh, listen.*"

For a few precious heartbeats, Riya couldn't hear anything. Then a sound drifted up from the depths of the tunnel, faint and wavering and indistinct. It sounded like a faraway voice.

Her fingernails curled into the dirt. "Abby! Rhys! Hope! We're here!"

They crowded closer, each of them pressing up against the opening. Jen raised her phone and turned its flashlight on. The beam cut down the long passage of bare earth. They couldn't see an end. It flickered, then faded into nothing.

The voice repeated. It was so far away that it felt like it could have been an echo from a dream.

"Hurt…" A pained gasp interrupted the words. *"Huuuurt…"*

Riya felt like she was suffocating. She cupped her hands around her mouth and yelled as loudly as she could manage: "Follow our voices! There's a way out! Just follow our voices!"

Her words hung in the air as echoes, but they weren't being answered. Painful seconds stretched out, becoming minutes as the three friends crouched there, suspended, waiting.

"I…" Riya blinked rapidly, her eyes burning. "I… I have to…"

A hand fixed around her arm. Connor's lips were pale and his eyes huge. "We don't know who that is."

"Connor's right," Jen said. "I don't know your friends as well as you do, but that didn't sound like them to me."

Riya shook her head. She knew she was panicking and turning reckless, and she couldn't stop it. "Whatever called to us, it was human. It might not by Abby or Rhys, but it's *someone*, and they're in pain. I can't… I can't just *leave* them."

"We had a plan," Connor said, speaking fast. "We were going to stay on the surface. We all agreed."

"This is different." Her choice was solidifying, even as it terrified her. Riya grabbed for the sports bag she'd arrived with. "It's an open entrance. And whoever's down there is within hearing range. I'm not going to be running through the tunnels blindly; I just need to go in far enough to get whoever that is, and then I'm coming straight back out. Jen, did you bring any weapons?"

Jen deftly unzipped her duffel bag. "As requested. And you're going to need light too."

"Yes." Riya's mind raced as she took the two alarmingly long kitchen knives from Jen. She'd have her lacrosse stick; that would serve as a ranged weapon. "My phone won't work, so—"

"Yeah, and flashlights are going to be unreliable, right?" Jen's gaze was cool and sharp. "Call it intuition, but I had a horrible sense someone was going to try to go into the cave. I have wooden stakes. Cotton T-shirts. Gas. And matches. Everything you need for a torch."

Riya choked on a laugh. For once, she wasn't the overprepared one. "Okay," she said, and stared into the depths of the dark, twisting chasm ahead of her. "Okay. Five minutes. Ten, at the most. I'll be back as quickly as I can."

Connor made a faint choking noise, like something between a sob and a laugh. "I'm coming," he said.

"Con, no—"

"Don't walk alone." He flexed his hands and the tendons made faint popping noises. "I want them back, too, Ri."

She found his arm and gave it a tense squeeze, then turned to Jen. "Will you stay here, at the opening? Just in case? I'm not going far enough to get lost, but it would help if there was someone outside I could hear too."

"Yeah, I can do that."

"Then let's make our torches."

Abby, Hope, and Rhys staggered through the dark. Hope led, with only the candle to guide them. Its flame was low and fighting for survival. It was all they had left; none of their lights or phones would work any longer.

They were moving through a pockmarked maze of natural caverns. It was slow and hazardous; the floor was constantly shifting, forcing them to climb and stagger for every foot of gained ground.

Rhys's breathing was rough in Abby's ear. She couldn't hear or see any sign of the Stitcher. She hoped he'd retreated entirely. Maybe the injury had been enough to make him wary.

She didn't like thinking about the alternative: that he was still following, just far enough behind that they couldn't hear him. That he was in no hurry, because he knew there was no escape.

Abby kept them close together; one arm was around Rhys, holding him up, and the other gripped Hope's vest. Remaining in a tight group was one of the few defenses they had left.

After all of their years of building rules to keep themselves safe from the Stitcher, Abby was finally understanding the reasons behind them.

Victims were taken when they were alone, because the Stitcher's paralyzing lights could only be directed at one person at a time. No one heard them scream, because the moment they looked on the unblinking eyes they lost their ability to make noise. It operated mostly at night, because its targets were more likely to look at the only bright objects in a dark world.

They were all of the answers Abby had wanted. And they were coming right at the moment when they might be too late.

They moved as fast as they could. Neither of Abby's companions were in good shape. They couldn't stop Rhys's bleeding, and he left a trail of bright crimson droplets in their wake. And Hope, for all the fight that still existed in her, was crumbling from two days of constant exhaustion and dehydration and blood loss and prolonged terror.

Sometimes she would glance back at Abby, and there were depths in her eyes that Abby had never seen before. It was like she'd aged a decade while in the abandoned mines.

"I'm sorry," Hope said abruptly.

Abby didn't break stride. "What?"

"I'm sorry for telling you I didn't want to be forgotten." Her voice dropped. "I know it's why you came looking for me. I shouldn't have said it."

A lump built in Abby's throat, and she nearly choked on it. "I'm here because you're my sister," she said, emphatically. "That night at the lakeside had nothing to do with it."

Hope didn't answer, but her jaw quivered.

Abby hesitated, then added, "I never forgot Dad either. Just so you know. I didn't talk about him, but he was always there in the background. Always."

"He was for me too," Hope whispered.

Rhys drew a ragged breath. He tugged on Abby, pulling her to a stop. "Look," he said.

Natural openings pockmarked the walls around them. Rhys was

focused on one in particular, though. Hope turned toward it, holding her candle out as far as she could.

Two lines of metal ran along the floor. The metal was old, and rusted, and twisted, but unmistakably intended to carry a cart.

They'd found one of the mining tunnels.

The darkness closed over Riya as she descended into the tunnel. The passage was so steeply sloped that she had to dig her heels in to keep from skidding. Connor followed so close behind that he bumped her shoulder with each staggering step.

Flames licked at the end of her torch and sent leaping shadows clawing across the walls.

The fuel soaking the tightly wrapped shirt would last for at least twenty minutes, but she still couldn't afford to press her luck. She and Connor had agreed that if they couldn't find the source of the voice within ten, they'd return to the surface to regroup.

She just hoped it wouldn't come to that. There were a lot of ugly choices to be made in Doubtful, but abandoning a Stitcher victim seemed like one that would hang over her for the rest of her life.

"Hello!" Riya called. Her voice echoed along the tunnel. She didn't get an answer. If Connor and Jen hadn't heard the voice as well, she would have been tempted to believe she'd imagined it.

She glanced over her shoulder. Far above was an oval of light. A distant shape blocked part of it: Jen, crouched and watching them intently.

Something brittle cracked under her sneakers. Jen lowered her torch and felt her stomach flip.

"Is that…" Connor's words faded.

"Bones." Thousands of them. All animal, she thought. Most of them were small enough to belong to birds or mice, but some of the larger ones could have come from cats, dogs, and deer. They'd gathered at the base of the entrance, like a snowdrift heaped against the slope.

The Stitcher's sustenance, called to him by some unseen force. The same force, she thought, that made it so difficult for people to leave the town. Like a magnetic pull that became harder to resist the longer someone was exposed. *Focus. Ten minutes. Ten minutes, and then you're out again.*

Riya tried not to look at any of the bones too closely, but lengthened her steps as she waded through them. Every movement brought a cacophony of crackles and snaps as the old, dry remains fractured under pressure. She could hear Connor grinding his teeth as he followed.

Then the bones thinned into scattered fragments, and the dirt floor became visible again under the wavering flame. Riya increased the pace, knowing that she didn't have many seconds to waste. The tunnel seemed to carry her on forever, but she still couldn't see the source of the voice.

"Hello!" Riya called again. "If you can hear me, I need you to answer me!"

She heard the crack of dirt and bone under their feet. The soft rush of the flames. Not much else.

Then a long, slow, pained moan dragged out of the gloom.

Riya frowned and turned. The narrow tunnel stretched out straight ahead, but the voice had come from the right. She craned as she searched the rough-hewn walls until she found it: a narrow gap between boulder shards, leading into a second passageway to the right. They'd need to crouch to get through.

The voice floated out of the earth, thin and babbling and delirious. *"Took my legs... he took... he took my legs..."*

Riya's whole body turned cold, like ice water had been poured over her. The voice didn't belong to Abby, Rhys, or Hope, but it was saturated with misery. She wet her dry lips. "I can hear you! Keep talking to me, we're going to get you out!"

Riya stretched her torch into the opening, and squeezed her body in afterward.

Abby had the map out and was fighting to read it under their candlelight.

The paper was saturated and stained red. She'd had to peel the sheets apart gingerly and struggled to make out the lines, which had been overlapping and convoluted to begin with.

They were trying to pinpoint their location, using a combination of the turns in the path, the intersections, and any significant formations.

It was a nightmare task. A lot of the system had been altered since the maps were made. Rockfall-blocked passages that should have been open; new tunnels had been carved by the Stitcher. Abby's map was covered in a mess of circles and *X*s as the three of them tried to find a way back to the passages beneath Vickers's house.

They chose passages that led upward every chance they had, and kept to the man-made tunnels. Otherwise, they could be ten minutes from the surface, or half a day.

The Stitcher hadn't returned for them yet. That was a small miracle, and one Abby knew she couldn't rely on indefinitely.

More pressing, though, were her companions. Neither Hope nor Rhys had said anything yet, but she knew it was only a matter of time before one or both of them were no longer able to keep walking.

And that was a terrifying prospect.

Abby made one final mark on the map, then folded it again. She reached her arm around Rhys to take his weight. His clothes were damp from clammy sweat. Without a word, Hope raised the candle again and turned down the intersection they'd chosen.

The threads were growing denser again. They hung in loops from the ceiling and ran like veins across the floor. Strands crisscrossed the path, and Abby used her pocketknife to slash through them. They were supposed to be a bad omen, but the alternative involved turning back and retracing path they'd already covered.

And as Abby listened to Hope's shallow breathing and the unsteady, dogged scrape of Rhys's shoes across the floor, she knew they had precious little time left to waste.

Then Hope stopped in her tracks. As she turned, the candle's light threw harsh shadows across her face, distorting it until it looked like a melted, broken skull.

Her voice wavered from exhaustion and dread and some third emotion Abby couldn't read. "Did you hear that?"

"Hello!" Rocks jammed into Riya's shoulder as she forced her way through the narrow gap. Cold, slimy red threads brushed across her skin like spiderwebs. She was pushing past the ten-minute time limit, but the voice had sounded close. Too close to give up on now. "Keep talking! Let me know where you are!"

"Where…" he coughed, and it sounded bad, like parts of his lungs were missing. "Where… Where he can't find you…"

"Slow down," Connor called from behind. "I can't go as fast as you!"

Riya clenched her jaw. She was running on fear-fueled adrenaline. Every second she spent inside the tunnels felt like a gamble she could never justify the odds on. But the voice was coming from just around the corner. She reached her torch out as she clambered over a fallen slab of stone, only to be confronted by another stretch of empty, ragged caves.

"Where are you?" She dropped down into the new area and swung the lacrosse stick ahead of herself. Lines of red thread crowded the space, like a mimicry of the police tape crisscrossing the town above. Shadows leapt as she moved her torch in a broad arc, searching the space. "Say something!"

A new voice rose out of the gloom. It was younger and muddy with tears. "I'm so cold. I'm so cold and so tired…"

"What the hell," Connor whispered. "The *hell*."

He dropped down beside Riya, breathing hard. She backed up to put herself right next to him. Something wasn't right.

The first voice returned. "Legs are all gone. He just took them… All gone… All gone… All gone… All gone…"

The voices were further away again. They sounded like they were coming from deeper in the passageway. Just out of reach.

Always just out of reach.

Riya's heart skipped a beat. "We have to get out," she hissed.

"But—"

"This was a mistake. Run!"

Connor didn't hesitate. He scrambled for the opening they'd just come through. Riya guarded his back as he crawled through, her light aimed at the gloom where the strange, distorted voices had echoed from.

They never answered her questions. But they kept calling unmatched phrases from just out of sight, drawing her deeper into the maze like a lure she couldn't turn away from.

As if on cue, a third voice called out: "Somebody help me! *Help meeee, help meeee.*"

It was like listening to a bad recording of a voice. A memory of the way words had sounded. A re-creation of the phrases the Stitcher had heard screamed again and again through the tunnels.

Something shifted at the edge of Riya's vision. Something enormous and bowed. Something that scraped the tunnel's ceiling as it dragged impossibly long limbs toward her.

Connor had cleared the gap. Riya knew she needed to follow. But it had become impossible to move, let alone breathe.

Twin lights shone out of the darkness. The enormous shape crept toward her, its hands extending one at a time to press into the rubble. The unblinking eyes shone at her like headlights, and they burrowed into her, devouring her thoughts, her fear, her desperation. The torch hit the ground with a rough clatter. It was followed by the lacrosse stick. She hadn't even felt her hands move.

The Stitcher was close enough to see its details. The crisscrossing lines of red wrapping across its body strained with every movement. The jaw hung slack and open. The throat vibrated as stolen vocal cords were jangled to life.

There were no words in this rendition: just crying. A dozen recordings of the sound, from a dozen mouths, all merged together into one sobbing, howling shriek of pain and despair.

The lights loomed high overhead as the Stitcher towered over Riya. She felt herself slump to the ground, but any sensations that came from it faded into nothing. The Stitcher reached out one enormous, clawed hand, and the last thing she saw was the loop of red thread hanging from its fingers, drifting toward her.

THIRTY-FOUR

ⱲⱮⱮⱮ

THAT'S RIYA.

Abby's body ached as she ran. Rhys's fingers dug into her shoulder as he clung to her, his injured leg skimming the ground, his jaw clenched against the pain as they raced time.

It had only been a single word—*run*—but the voice had been unmistakable. It belonged to Riya.

She was in the tunnels.

And she was not alone.

Their friend had gone silent, but a new sound had risen to fill the silence. The Stitcher. Horrendous, jarring, howling cries reverberated through the passageways.

And then they abruptly cut out.

We thought the Stitcher was hiding somewhere, repairing itself. We thought the fire might have been enough to actually make it fear us.

We were wrong.

It left because it knew it could come back for us at any time.

It left because it heard fresh prey approaching its lair.

They rounded a corner and, suddenly, Hope's near-dead candle was no longer the only source of light.

Abby found herself frozen as she stared at the scene.

Red thread tangled across the path, obscuring the view but not able to hide it. Riya was slumped in the center of the tunnel. Her arms were slack, her head angled upward, her eyes blank. A flaming torch lay, useless, at her side.

The Stitcher towered over her. One of its enormous hands reached toward her head, the sharp tips highlighted by the licking shadows.

Abby had a mental image of the Stitcher wrapping its hand around Riya's head, as easily as someone might palm an apple, and dragging her away down the tunnel.

The monster was faster than Abby or either of her companions. If it took Riya away now, she doubted they would ever see their friend again.

She didn't know what else to do. She screamed at Riya: "Don't look at its eyes!"

Riya's eyelashes fluttered, but there was no other response.

The Stitcher heard her, though. Its head swung, rotating on a neck that was too long. The glowing eyes washed across Abby. She and Rhys both threw hands across their faces, while Hope turned aside.

"Don't look at it!" Abby yelled again, hoping that something small might be able to break through the fog Riya was trapped in. "Don't look into its eyes!"

She kept her own gaze on the ground and let her peripheral vision blur.

When she did that, she could just make out the Stitcher staring at her with a furious, ravenous intensity. Its clawed hand twitched over Riya's face, and Abby had the impression of red blood blooming under one of the talons.

Then a voice rose. It wasn't a word, but simply a scream: full of anger and horror and fear and finality.

Connor appeared from seemingly nowhere. He had a torch. He held it straight ahead, like he was brandishing a sword, as he charged toward the monster.

The Stitcher swiveled back toward him, but Connor had his whole face scrunched up to keep his eyes closed.

The torch smacked into the creature's chest. Sparks flew and flames licked over the desiccated skin. Red threads blackened and curled as they broke.

The Stitcher threw one of its long arms out. It swiped Connor aside as though he were a rag doll. He tumbled onto the ground with an aching grunt.

"Quick," Rhys hissed, and Abby launched forward again.

The threads snagged around them, pulling taut and snapping. Abby sliced her knife through any that wouldn't break.

On the ground, Riya was stirring. She drooped to one side, blood seeping from a narrow incision on her forehead, and she shook her head as though trying to clear it.

"Ri, don't look in its eyes," Abby yelled.

Hope dropped the candle, which was burnt down to a stub. She ducked to pick up a rock from the ground and hurled it toward the Stitcher.

It bounced off the creature's hide, but it was enough to draw the monster's attention away from Connor. It turned back toward them, each vertebrae rotating one at a time with a sickening *click*.

Abby followed her sister and snatched a stone off the ground. This one hit the Stitcher's forehead. She forced herself to look away before its eyes could sear into her.

On the monster's other side, Connor staggered back to his feet. He had a hand pressed to his shoulder. He staggered toward the torch, but seemed unsteady.

And then Riya rose from the floor. She moved suddenly, sweeping her dropped lacrosse stick up toward the figure towering over her.

The sound it created when it connected with the Stitcher's jaws made Abby flinch. There was a deafening crack, mixed with the smaller pops of breaking threads. The Stitcher jerked backward, sinking into the shadows that rose across the stone walls, its red-threaded hands pressed across its own face.

Abby's knife sliced through the final threads keeping her from her friends. Riya stood on unsteady feet, her eyes still slightly glazed, her mouth hanging open as she panted. She clasped her lacrosse stick in both hands, but it had broken at the two-thirds mark, and the end hung from a splinter of wood.

Connor stumbled close up beside them. His expressive face washed through a spectrum of emotions in the span of a second: fear, then relief, and then back to dread.

The Stitcher was lowering its hands. Abby could barely see it in the gloom, but she had the nightmarish impression of broken threads hanging loose from the jaw like nerves from pulled teeth.

Abby picked up the torch Riya had dropped. The five friends bunched together, backing away as the Stitcher loomed above them.

"Connor," Abby whispered.

"Yeah?"

"Do you know the way out?"

He glanced behind them, then swallowed thickly. "Yeah."

"You'll have to be the leader. On the count of three, we run."

It had been longer than ten minutes.

A *lot* longer.

Jen crouched near the cave's opening, waiting. Her skin crawled. She'd heard sounds she couldn't put any kind of name to. The kinds of sounds that made her want to back away, to get out of the clearing, to jog home and not look back.

But she was still there, and still waiting, the muscles in her legs cramping and ants creeping over her clothes, as every nerve in her body stayed keyed as high as it could go.

A distant noise seemed to come from the tunnel. Jen's breath caught. She turned her head to angle an ear at it, trying to hear it better.

Drying leaves trailed around her as a gust of wind wove through the trees.

Then the sound came again, slightly louder and slightly clearer. Riya, calling Jen's name.

The relief felt like a breaking dam. Jen cupped her hands around her mouth and called back. "I'm here!"

Riya yelled something else, but this time the words became muddied by echoes. Jen felt her smile fade. There wasn't any kind of relief or elation in Riya's voice. Just pure, aching terror.

"Fire!" Riya called again.

Then Abby's voice rose from the tunnel, distorted by distance. "The Stitcher's coming! Fire can hurt it!"

Stitcher. Fire. Jen's eyes trailed toward the cartons of fuel.

She moved fast, wrenching the cap off the first container and racing with it to the tunnel's opening. It wasn't hard to guess what her new friends were asking for. She poured the fuel out just inside the cave's entrance, creating a line from one wall to the other and letting it pool in the compacted dirt and rocks.

She needed to get her friends out.

And she couldn't let the Stitcher follow.

Riya's head swam. She had one arm around Hope and was half carrying, half dragging her toward the surface.

They were so close. Light flooded across them through the opening above. They just had to *reach* it.

Bones tangled underfoot, threatening to trip her. She held an arm out for balance as she skidded on the slope, mandibles and tibiae and ribs spinning away under her feet.

Abby and Connor were behind her, supporting Rhys. He looked close to collapsing. One leg was dragging behind him, and she didn't like its angle.

But they couldn't stop moving. They'd bought a few desperate seconds to get to the surface, but it wasn't enough. The Stitcher was closing the gap, and any second they would feel the desiccated, threaded hands snagging at their feet.

But they were so close. And Riya could smell the tang of gas, and knew Jen had understood what needed to be done.

Bones slipped under them. The angle was impossibly steep, more of a mountain than a slope. Riya had to use her spare hand to claw at the uneven floor, using her numb fingers to pull them higher.

Jen was in the opening, her lips pressed tight as she stretched a hand toward them. Riya passed Hope out first, and Jen leaned back as she hauled her out. Then Abby was at Riya's side, dragging Rhys and Connor with her, and Riya helped pushed them both through the opening.

Something cold and fleshy and thread riddled grazed along her leg. Riya bit down on a scream as she kicked, then threw herself through the exit and into the light.

Riya didn't stop scrambling until she was at least ten paces from the tunnel, then rolled onto her side to stare back at it.

Something enormous and humanlike emerged from the gloom.

She hadn't been able to see it clearly in the depths of the tunnel. Now, as it emerged piece by piece into the light, pure dread poured through Riya's limbs.

It was skeletally thin. Long, dexterous hands grazed the ground. Its patchwork skin didn't cover its body correctly; it bulged in some areas, and hung loose in others, and stretched taut in more places.

The Stitcher had grown enormously in the century it had spent dismantling and rebuilding itself in the dark. By the way it had put itself together, it was clear it barely remembered what it was supposed to look like any longer.

Some patches of its skin seemed fresh, and Riya's terrified mind asked her if any of those pieces might belong to January Spalling. Other patches were growing old and shriveling, the seams pulling increasingly large holes in it and exposing dark, raw flesh beneath.

Very likely, Hope had been intended to replace them.

The worst part was its face. Flat and unemotive and a mess of overlapping threads. Only one part still seemed to hold life. The round, lamp-like eyes.

Riya twisted her head aside to avoid its gaze. And she found herself staring at two open plastic jugs laying on the ground just outside the cave.

You never know how you'll act under pressure until you're forced to find out.

Thompson had told her that once. The words hung in her mind as Jen faced the enormous creature coming out of the cave entrance.

She held a third and final torch, made hastily. Her friends were scattered on the ground. They were closer than she'd wanted, but she was out of time to move them.

And the creature was lurching free from the darkness. An enormous hand swung free and knocked over one of the open fuel containers. Gas began to pour free, and Jen knew this was the only chance she'd have.

She threw the torch. Her aim was good. The licking flames made contact with the fumes, and Jen barely had time to cover her face before the explosion rocked them all.

Plumes of flames billowed upward. The fire wrapped around the Stitcher, swallowing it, and an earsplitting shriek burst from its mangled throat.

Rocks cracked from the pressure. The cave entrance vanished in a rain of smoke and sparks. The monstrous creature burst out of the explosion. Its arms were thrown wide, its head bent backward as it bellowed at the sky. Fire crackled on every part of its body, consuming it.

The Stitcher lurched forward, broad hands slapping the ground as it raced toward Jen.

Jen threw herself to the side, and one of its burning hands slammed into the grass where she'd just been laying. Then it passed her, racing into the trees, its flaming body leaving a wake of smoke and sparks in its path.

Bridgette Holm lurched forward, gripping the armrests of her chair with enough force to pop tendons. She couldn't find even enough breath to scream.

Some of the Stitcher's threads had been left inside her during her days in the mines. Those threads now squirmed like live things, like parasites, fighting to burst through her skin and spill out of her legs.

Around her, cats wailed. Dogs snarled, their fur rising into ridges along their backs. They all felt it. The whole *town* felt it.

It was happening.

Two mothers watched their children play.

The park was otherwise empty. Not many people wanted to be out when things were this bad, but their children had begged, and the mothers had relented.

They watched their children like hawks, though. And it took them less than a second to be on their feet when the youngest boy tripped.

The mothers and the other children formed a circle around him, staring down at what had caught his foot. A loop of red thread rose out of the ground. Nervous glances were exchanged. The thread hadn't been here when they'd arrived, had it?

A girl shrieked. More thread was rising up. Endless yards of it, bursting out of the wood chips, tangling, as though some immense force was extruding it from the earth.

The mothers snatched their children up and held them to their chests as they ran.

The woman gagged. Something was in her throat. Something that choked her. She hunched forward and retched. Again and again.

It was right there, at the back of her mouth. She reached dirty fingers in and scrabbled them across her tongue. A cracked fingernail caught on the edge of the foreign object. She pulled.

Red thread slid out of her. Slimy and old and matted. She pulled and pulled, but it just kept coming, suffocating her. Tears stung her eyes. Her lungs burned, her throat ached. And then, finally, the largest knot slid free and the tangled mess landed on the ground ahead of her.

She stared at the threads, and at her wet hands, and at the holes surrounding her, and then finally up toward the sun.

Sarah Ward felt as though she could breathe properly for the first time in years.

Abby rolled onto her hands and knees.

Black smoke rose from the now-collapsed cave entrance. Flames still flickered between the debris.

More flames crackled on fallen leaves and tree branches, marking the path the Stitcher had taken through the forest.

She had a horrible idea of where it was headed.

"Stay here," she said, placing one hand each on Hope and Rhys, who were both collapsed on the ground.

Rhys's hand snaked out to grab at her. "Where—"

"I have to end this." Her mouth tasted of ash and blood and pain. "If I can."

She got to her feet. The explosion had scorched her top and one arm, and blisters were already forming. She barely felt them, though, as she began to run through the trees.

Footsteps followed her. Riya on one side. Jen on the other. They'd both had exactly the same thought as she had. Jen had dropped everything except for what looked like a police radio, and she held it up to her mouth as she ran. "Get out, Thompson. Get out, now!"

It wasn't hard to follow the Stitcher's path. Scorched wood and tiny spot fires marked its trail. It had burnt as brightly as the bonfires they'd built down by the lake's edge; its skin was old and drying, and had caught easily.

It can't survive this, Abby promised herself as the three of them tore through the smoking trees. *It can't, it can't, please, let it not be able to survive this.*

They burst out of the woods and faced the backyards of two abandoned buildings. Abby recognized them instantly, and felt her heart sink as her suspicions were confirmed.

They were at Stokes Lane.

In its pain and its fear, the Stitcher had returned to the one place it had always considered home. The one place where, no matter what, there was always an open entrance into the mines.

She ignored her burnt arm as she vaulted through a half-collapsed fence. The Stitcher had grazed the building; its cracking, dry wood smoldered. More flames burnt in the long, dead grass. They were in danger of spreading if no one stopped them.

Abby raced between the two empty homes and onto the street, with Jen and Riya right beside her. A man already stood there, next to his police cruiser: Jen's father, Officer Thompson, held his glasses in one hand, his face slack and stunned. He didn't acknowledge them as they came to a halt at his side.

Together, they faced the house at the end. A voice, panicked, yelled. "No! *No!*"

Charles Vickers's house was already catching on fire.

The front door was missing; it lay in the yard, apparently wrenched off its hinges. The Stitcher forced itself through the front doorway and toward the tunnel. Charles Vickers pressed himself against the wall, his face contorted in horror as he watched his ancestor burn.

If it gets back into the mines—if we let it get away—

Abby ran, her lungs burning and her heart pumping out of control. She was already too late to stop it, though. The creature, wild with pain and terror, tore the trapdoor off the tunnel with a deafening crack. Then it raised its head.

The Stitcher's lamp-like eyes were dead, scorched out by the fire. One arm hung loose, only connected to the rest of its body by a strip of skin. It was falling apart as the flames devoured it. Its nostrils flared. Small flames crackled across its back and stomach, and the gaps between the patchwork skin were glowing hot embers.

It staggered, then turned.

Abby realized what was about to happen and flinched backward.

The Stitcher might not be dead, but it was very close to it. It was desperate for material to patch its crumbling form. The blind eyes fixed on its handler, who was pressed tightly against his hallway wall where the mirror had once been.

"No," Charles Vickers said one more time.

The Stitcher's hand snaked out lightning fast and fixed around his torso. Vickers screamed. His glasses clattered to the floor and his face contorted in terror. He beat his fists at the scorched flesh holding him as his cardigan began to smoke, but the Stitcher neither felt the blows nor cared. It turned and vanished headfirst into the mine entrance, dragging Vickers with it.

His screams lasted all the way down the tunnel.

Abby felt numb as she climbed the porch to Vickers's home. Small fires smoldered on the dry wood and discarded rug. She stopped at the edge of the hole, staring down into its bleak, dark depths.

Charles Vickers was gone. And she didn't think anyone would be trying to get him back.

Jen and Riya stopped on either side of Abby and stared into the pit. After a moment, the creak of old floorboards told them a fourth participant had arrived.

"That was it, wasn't it?" Officer Thompson asked.

"Yeah," Jen said simply.

He took a slow, deep breath, then said, "I have a third carton of fuel at home. We'd better finish the job."

Minutes later, they stood at the end of the street and watched as Charles Vickers's house crumbled under the force of the flames. The roof caved in first, followed by walls that fell like dominos. Toxic black smoke billowed upward.

"Good thing the houses around are all empty," Riya said. "We should probably still call the fire department, though, to stop the flames from spreading too far."

"Yeah," Abby said, and tilted her head back as she felt the cooling afternoon air brush over her skin. "We'll do that. Later. I want to be with Rhys and my sister, first."

THIRTY-FIVE

‿‿‿‿‿

COOL AIR RUSHED ACROSS ABBY'S SKIN AS SHE BIKED through town.

There was still time before night fell, but the earliest traces of a sunset were beginning to spread across the horizon. Houses lit up around her.

She still knew when night fell, down to the minute. Just like she still locked her window at night, and just like how she still preferred bikes to get around town. They were some of a thousand little habits that would likely follow her for the remainder of her life.

It was five months since they'd emerged from the tunnel. And five months since anyone had been taken.

At first, the Jackrabbits had been intensely cautious. They'd watched for flickering lightbulbs. They'd traveled everywhere in pairs. They'd compared nightmares and watched the animals and flinched when they saw headlights in the distance.

Riya had been the first to notice it. "The town's changing," she'd said one day. "Can't you feel it?"

And Abby realized she could.

It was like something heavy and poisonous had been drained out of the air. Like the town had been carrying a weight for its whole life and had finally shrugged free of it.

Abby let her bike coast around a corner, and put out one foot as she came to a halt at the head of Vickers's street.

She always stopped there when she passed it.

The house was nothing but a charred, crumbled wreck. Police tape circled it, just like it did for every one of the locations where the Stitcher's victims had been found. She suspected the town planned to leave it that way. Forgotten, as much as it was possible to forget the Stitcher's home.

No one except a select number of people knew what had happened in the mines. Chief Hewitt had interviewed all of them, but her questions had been gentle and easy. She'd nudged the right people to rule the house fire as accidental. Vickers was marked as a missing person, and a token handful of posters bearing his face had been placed on bulletin boards, where he too would turn sun bleached and creased.

Most of Doubtful's population would never know what had caused the change to their town. And the Jackrabbits had all agreed that was the way they wanted it.

Abby leaned on the pedals again to pick up speed. A shape moved toward her from a side street, and a second later, Rhys came up alongside her, biking to perfectly match her speed.

They didn't need to travel in pairs any longer. But he still always waited to ride with her.

As they neared the forest, Abby caught the sounds of children playing a ball game in one of the cul-de-sacs. Cars drove by, their headlights bright as dusk descended.

The town was changing slowly. And so was Abby's family.

When she'd left home, Hope had been in her room, recording a video. She was still full of the same bubbly joy she'd always had, but she'd seemed older since her time in the mining tunnels. More thoughtful, more observant. The missing arm would be a permanent reminder of what she'd endured.

And Abby's mother…

She hadn't come back entirely. But she remembered her own name now. And, more than that, she remembered Abby and Hope. She smiled at them. She kissed them. Sometimes she would hum lullabies as she stroked their hair. And she seemed to become a sliver stronger and a sliver more herself with each day.

Rhys and Abby pulled up outside the forest. They left their bikes leaning against the trees and stepped between the trunks. As the darkness wrapped around them, Rhys's hand lightly brushed Abby's. She reached back for him, and let their fingers twine together. They held on to one another like that as they followed the familiar path to the lakeshore.

The trees parted. Ahead was the sandy shoreline, and in the distance, a bonfire. Three figures were already gathered around it for the Jackrabbits' meeting. Connor was attempting to balance a soft drink bottle on his nose while Riya, exasperated, tried to snatch it away from him. Jen sat beside them, covering her mouth to muffle her laughter.

"Looks like they've already started the party," Abby said.

Rhys chuckled. It was a precious sound. He still rarely laughed and rarely smiled, but every passing week brought slightly more of each.

Once, she'd thought their only chances of being happy depended on escaping from Doubtful. That was changing. She wasn't sure if Doubtful would ever feel like a normal town, or if she would ever be capable of living an average life. The burns over her throat and arm would be permanent scars. Just like the town would not easily forget its trauma.

But there was goodness in Doubtful, now. For the first time in her life, she saw a future there.

She gazed up at Rhys. He glanced down at her, then leaned closer. Abby rose onto her toes to meet his kiss.

As they broke apart, Abby leaned against Rhys's shoulder. He rested his head on top of hers. Together, they followed the sandy shore toward their places at the bonfire.

An old friend's words returned to her. Only, this time, they sounded slightly different.

Do you want to see something good?

ACKNOWLEDGMENTS

A huge amount of gratitude goes to my amazing editor, Mary Altman, who was a guiding hand and champion of *Where He Can't Find You* from its first inception to its final draft.

I also want to thank the team that helped turn this story into a reality: Gretchen Stelter and Heather Hall, who polished this book into its final form. Katie Klimowicz, who not only created the cover but hand-stitched the title. And Liz Dresner, who managed every detail of the design.

Extra thanks to Mandy Chahal, Rebecca Atkinson, Sean Murray, and the marketing team, as well as Steph Rocha, Brittany Vibbert, Tara Jaggers, Jessica Thelander, Thea Voutiritsas, Theodore Turner, Susan Barnett, and the rest of the Sourcebooks Fire team.

ABOUT THE AUTHOR

Darcy Coates is the *USA Today* bestselling author of *Hunted*, *The Haunting of Ashburn House*, *Craven Manor*, and more than a dozen other horror and suspense titles. She lives on the Central Coast of Australia with her family, cats, and a garden full of herbs and vegetables. Darcy loves forests, especially old-growth forests, where the trees dwarf anyone who steps between them. Wherever she lives, she tries to have a mountain range close by.

FIREreads

ⓢ #getbooklit

Your hub for the hottest young adult books!

Visit us online and sign up for our
newsletter at FIREreads.com

 @sourcebooksfire

 sourcebooksfire

 firereads.tumblr.com